Jane H___ ___ the aut... ... The D___

awards including the 2015 Victorian P___
Unpublished Manuscript, the 2017 In___
the 2017 Australian Book Industry Awards ~~Book of the Year~~___
and the CWA Gold Dagger Award 2017. Rights have been sold in
twenty-seven territories worldwide, and film rights optioned to Reese
Witherspoon and Bruna Papandrea. Jane worked as a print journalist
for thirteen years both in Australia and the UK and lives in Melbourne.

'Jane Harper, the new Queen of Crime'   *Sunday Times*

'Harper has produced another humdinger of a thriller'
                                                         Sunday Express

'Harper creates an atmosphere of stifling claustrophobia as the novel
inexorably telescopes in ... This is that rare thing, a whodunnit
where the writing is as satisfying as the thrills'   *Metro*

'This follow-up novel shows Harper is a crime-writing force to be
reckoned with'   *Sunday Mirror*

'A three-day team-building hike in the Australian bush ends in
disaster when the unpleasant Alice Russell disappears. Throw in a
serial killer, industrial espionage, and several unreliable narrators and
you have a tense thriller that made me feel good about my decision
never to go camping'   *Red*

'Harper has a fine gift for making her readers comfortable in
inhospitable territory – psychological as well as physical'
                                                       Daily Telegraph

'*Lord of the Flies* in the Australian outback, with grown women in
place of school boys. I loved every chilling moment of it. A blistering
follow-up to *The Dry* from one of the best new voices in crime fiction'
      Sarah Hilary, author of the bestselling DI Marnie Rome series

'*Force of Nature* bristles with wit; it crackles with suspense; it radiates
atmosphere. An astonishing book from an astonishing writer'
      A. J. Finn, bestselling author of *The Woman in the Window*

Also by Jane Harper

The Dry

JANE HARPER

FORCE OF NATURE

ABACUS

First published in Australia in 2017 by Macmillan
First published in Great Britain in 2018 by Little, Brown
This paperback edition published in 2018 by Abacus

1 3 5 7 9 10 8 6 4 2

A CIP catalogue record for this book
is available from the British Library.

ISBN 978-0-349-14212-8

Printed and bound in Great Britain by
Clays Ltd, St Ives plc

Papers used by Abacus are from well-managed forests
and other responsible sources.

Abacus
An imprint of
Little, Brown Book Group
Carmelite House
50 Victoria Embankment
London EC4Y 0DZ

An Hachette UK Company
www.hachette.co.uk

www.littlebrown.co.uk

For Pete and Charlotte, with love

Prologue

Later, the four remaining women could fully agree on only two things. One: No-one saw the bushland swallow up Alice Russell. And two: Alice had a mean streak so sharp it could cut you.

The women were late to the rendezvous point.

The men's group – clocking in at the beacon a respectable thirty-five minutes ahead of the midday target – slapped each other on the shoulders as they emerged from the tree line. A job well done. The retreat leader was waiting for the five of them, looking warm and welcoming in his official red fleece. The men threw their high-tech sleeping bags into the back of the minivan, breathing with relief as they climbed in. The van was stocked with trail mix and thermos coffee. The men leaned past the food, reaching instead for the bag containing their surrendered mobile phones. Reunited.

It was cold outside. No change there. The pale winter sun had fully emerged only once in the past four days. At least the van was dry. The men sat back. One of them cracked a joke about women's map-reading skills and all of them laughed. They drank coffee and waited for their colleagues to appear. It had been three days since they'd seen them; they could wait a few more minutes.

It was an hour before smugness gave way to irritation. One by one the five men prised themselves from the soft seats and trudged up and down the dirt road. They thrust their phones towards the sky as though the extra arm's length would capture the elusive signal. They tapped out impatient text messages that wouldn't send to their better halves in the city. *Running late. We've been held up.* It had been a long few days and hot showers and cold beers were waiting. And work, tomorrow.

The retreat leader stared at the trees. Finally, he unclipped his radio.

A handful of reinforcements arrived. The park rangers' voices light as they pulled on high-vis vests. *We'll pluck 'em out of there in no time.* They knew where people went wrong and there were hours of daylight left. A few, anyway. Enough. It wouldn't take long. They plunged into the bush at a professional pace. The men's group bundled themselves back into the van.

The trail mix was gone and the coffee dregs were cold and bitter by the time the searchers re-emerged. The shapes of the gum trees were silhouetted against the darkening sky. Faces were set. The banter had disappeared with the light.

Inside the van, the men sat silent. If this were a boardroom crisis, they'd know what to do. A drop in the dollar, an unwanted clause in a contract, no worries at all. Out here, the bushland seemed to blur the answers. They cradled their lifeless phones like broken toys in their laps.

More words were muttered into radios. Vehicle headlights bored into the dense wall of trees and breath formed clouds in the frigid night air. The searchers were called back in for a briefing. The men in the van couldn't hear the details of the discussion, but they didn't need to. The tone said it all. There were limits to what could be done after dark.

At last, the search group broke apart. A high-vis vest clambered into the front of the minivan. He'd drive the men to the park lodge. They'd have to stay the night, no-one could be spared to make the three-hour trip back to Melbourne now. The men were still letting the words sink in when they heard the first cry.

High-pitched and birdlike, it was an unusual sound in the night and every head turned as four figures crested the hill. Two seemed to be supporting a third, while a fourth tripped along unsteadily beside them. The blood on her forehead looked black from a distance.

Help us! One of them was screaming. More than one. *We're here. We need help, she needs a doctor. Please help. Thank God, thank God we found you.*

The searchers were running; the men, phones abandoned on the minibus seats, panting several paces behind them.

3

We were lost, someone was saying. Someone else: *We lost her.*

It was hard to make the distinction. The women were calling, crying, their voices tumbling over one another.

Is Alice here? Did she make it? Is she safe?

In the chaos, in the night, it was impossible to say which of the four had asked after Alice's welfare.

Later, when everything got worse, each would insist it had been them.

Chapter 1

'Don't panic.'

Federal Agent Aaron Falk, who until that moment had had no plans to do so, closed the book he'd been reading. He swapped his mobile phone to his good hand and sat up straighter in bed.

'Okay.'

'Alice Russell is missing.' The woman on the other end said the name quietly. 'Apparently.'

'Missing how?' Falk put his book aside.

'Legitimately. Not just ignoring our calls this time.'

Falk heard his partner sigh down the line. Carmen Cooper sounded more stressed than he'd heard her in the three months they'd been working together, and that was saying a lot.

'She's lost in the Giralang Ranges somewhere,' Carmen went on.

'Giralang?'

'Yeah, out in the east?'

'No, I know where it is,' he said. 'I was thinking more of the reputation.'

'The Martin Kovac stuff? It doesn't sound anything like that, thank God.'

'You'd hope not. That'd have to be twenty years ago now anyway, wouldn't it?'

'Going on for twenty-five, I think.'

Some things would always linger, though. Falk had been barely a teenager when the Giralang Ranges had dominated the evening news for the first time. Then three more times over the next two years. Each time, images of search teams tramping through overgrown bushland with sniffer dogs straining at their leads had been projected into living rooms around the state. They'd found most of the bodies, eventually.

'What was she doing all the way out there?' he said.

'Corporate retreat.'

'Are you joking?'

'Unfortunately not,' Carmen said. 'Turn on the TV, it's on the news. They've called out a search crew.'

'Hang on.' Falk climbed out of bed and pulled on a t-shirt above his boxers. The night air was chilly. He padded through to his living room and turned to a twenty-four-hour news channel. The anchor was talking about the day in parliament.

'It's nothing. Just work. Go back to sleep,' Falk heard Carmen murmur in his ear, and realised she was talking to someone at the other end. He'd automatically pictured her in their shared office, squeezed behind the desk that

6

had been shoehorned in next to his twelve weeks earlier. They'd been working closely since, quite literally. When Carmen stretched, her feet knocked his chair legs. Falk checked the clock. It was after 10 pm on a Sunday night; of course she would be at home.

'See it yet?' Carmen said to him, whispering now for the benefit of whoever she was with. Her fiancé, Falk assumed.

'Not yet.' Falk didn't need to lower his own voice. 'Wait −' The ticker tape scrolled across the screen. 'Here it is.'

SEARCH TO RESUME AT DAWN IN GIRALANG RANGES FOR LOST MELBOURNE HIKER ALICE RUSSELL, 45.

'Melbourne *hiker*?' Falk said.

'I know.'

'Since when has Alice −' He stopped. He was picturing Alice's shoes. High. Pointy.

'I know. The bulletin said it was some sort of team-building exercise. She was part of a group sent out for a few days and −'

'A few days? How long has she actually been missing?'

'I'm not sure. I think since last night.'

'She called me,' Falk said.

There was a silence at the other end of the line. Then, 'Who did? Alice?'

'Yes.'

'When?'

'Last night.' Falk pulled his mobile away and scrolled through his missed calls. He put it back to his ear. 'You still

7

there? Early this morning, actually, around four-thirty. I didn't hear it. Only saw the voicemail when I woke up.'

Another silence. 'What did she say?'

'Nothing.'

'At all?'

'There was no-one there. I thought it was a pocket dial.'

The TV bulletin put up a recent picture of Alice Russell. It looked like it had been taken at a party. Her blonde hair had been pinned in a complicated style and she was wearing a silvery dress that showed off the hours she spent in the gym. She looked a good five years younger than her true age, maybe more. And she was smiling at the camera in a way she never had for Falk and Carmen.

'I tried to call her back when I woke up; probably around six-thirty,' Falk said, still watching the screen. 'It rang out.'

The TV cut to an aerial shot of the Giralang Ranges. Hills and valleys rolled out to the horizon, a rippling green ocean under the weak winter light.

SEARCH TO RESUME AT DAWN . . .

Carmen was quiet. Falk could hear her breathing. On screen, the ranges looked big. Enormous, in fact. The thick carpet of treetops appeared completely impenetrable from the camera's vantage point.

'Let me listen to the message again,' he said. 'I'll call you back.'

'Okay.' The line went dead.

Falk sat on his couch in the semi-dark, the blue light of the TV screen flickering. He hadn't drawn his curtains, and beyond the small balcony he could see the glow of the Melbourne skyline. The warning light on top of the Eureka Tower flashed, regular and red.

SEARCH TO RESUME AT DAWN IN GIRALANG ...

He turned down the TV and dialled his voicemail. Call received at 4.26 am from Alice Russell's mobile.

At first Falk could hear nothing and he pressed his phone harder against his ear. Muffled static for five seconds. Ten. He kept listening, right to the end this time. The white noise lurched in waves, it sounded like being underwater. There was a muted hum that might have been someone talking. Then, out of nowhere, a voice broke through. Falk jerked the phone away from his ear and stared at it. The voice had been so faint he wondered if he'd imagined it.

Slowly, he tapped the screen. He closed his eyes in his quiet flat and played the message one more time. Nothing, nothing, and then, in the darkness, a faraway voice spoke two words in his ear.

' ... *hurt her* ... '

Chapter 2

Dawn hadn't yet broken when Carmen pulled up outside Falk's flat. He was already waiting on the pavement, his backpack on the ground. His hiking boots felt stiff from lack of use.

'Let's hear the message,' she said as he climbed in. She had the driver's seat pushed back. Carmen was one of the few women Falk had met who was tall enough to look him in the eye when they stood face to face.

Falk put his phone on loudspeaker and pressed a button. Static filled the car. Five, ten seconds of nothing, then the two words emerged, tinny and thin. A few more muffled seconds, and the call cut out.

Carmen frowned. 'Once more.'

She closed her eyes and Falk watched her face as she listened. At thirty-eight, Carmen outranked him by only six months both in age and experience, but it was the first time their paths in the Federal Police had crossed. She was new to the financial investigation unit in Melbourne, having moved down from Sydney. Falk couldn't work out if she regretted it. Carmen opened her eyes. Under the orange glow of the streetlight, her skin and hair both looked a shade darker than usual.

'"Hurt her,"' she said.

'That's what it sounds like to me.'

'Could you hear something else right at the end?'

Falk turned up the volume to the maximum and hit replay. He found himself holding his breath as he strained to hear.

'There,' Carmen said. 'Is that someone saying "Alice"?'

They listened once more and this time Falk caught the faint inflection in the muffled noise, a sibilant hiss.

'I don't know,' he said. 'It might be static.'

Carmen started the engine. It roared loud in the pre-dawn. She pulled away and onto the road before she spoke again.

'How confident do you feel that that's Alice's voice?'

Falk tried to recall the timbre of Alice Russell's tone. Her voice was fairly distinctive. It was often clipped. Always decisive. 'There's nothing to say that it's *not* her. But it's hard to hear.'

'Very hard. I'm not sure I could even swear that was a woman.'

'No.'

In the side mirror, the Melbourne skyline was growing smaller. Ahead, in the east, the sky was turning from black to navy.

'I know Alice is a pain in the arse,' he said, 'but I really hope we haven't landed her in the shit.'

11

'Me too.' Carmen's engagement ring caught the light as she turned the wheel to join the highway. 'What did the state cop have to say? What was his name?'

'King.'

Falk had hung up from Alice Russell's voicemail the previous night and immediately dialled the state police. It had been half an hour before the senior sergeant leading the search had called back.

'Sorry.' Senior Sergeant King had sounded tired. 'Had to get myself to a landline. The weather's stuffing up the reception worse than usual. Tell me about this voicemail.'

He'd listened patiently while Falk spoke.

'Right,' King said, when he'd finished. 'Look, we've run a check on her phone records.'

'Okay.'

'What did you say your relationship was with her?'

'Professional,' Falk said. 'Confidential. She was helping me and my partner with something.'

'And what's his name?'

'Her. Carmen Cooper.'

Falk could hear the rustle of paper as the man wrote it down.

'Were either of you expecting her to call?'

Falk hesitated. 'Not specifically.'

'Are you particularly skilled at bushcraft?'

Falk had looked down at his left hand. The skin was still pink and strangely smooth in patches where the burns hadn't healed quite as well. 'No.'

'Is your partner?'

'I don't think so.' Falk realised he didn't really know.

There was a pause. 'According to the phone company, early this morning Alice Russell attempted to get through to two numbers,' King said. 'Triple zero and you. Can you think of a reason why that would be?'

It was Falk's turn to pause. He could hear the sergeant breathing down the phone.

Hurt her.

'I think we'd better come up there,' Falk said. 'Speak in person.'

'I think that'd be a wise move, mate. Bring your phone.'

Day 4: Sunday Morning

The woman could see her own fear reflected in the three faces staring back at her. Her heartbeat thumped and she could hear the others' rapid breathing. Overhead, the pocket of sky carved out by the trees was a dull grey. The wind shook the branches, sending a shower of water down on the group below. No-one flinched. Behind them, the rotten wood of the cabin groaned and settled.

'We have to get out of here. Now,' the woman said.

The pair on her left nodded immediately, united for once by their panic, their eyes wide and dark. On her right, the briefest hesitation, then a third nod.

'What about –'

'What about what?'

'. . . What about Alice?'

An awful hush. The only sound was the creak and rustle as the trees watched down over their tight circle of four.

'Alice brought this on herself.'

Chapter 3

When Falk and Carmen stopped after a couple of hours, the sky was fully light and the city lay far behind them. They stood by the side of the road and stretched as the clouds threw shifting shadows across the paddocks. The houses and buildings were few and far between. A truck carrying farming supplies roared past, the first vehicle they had seen for thirty kilometres. The noise startled a flock of galahs, sending them scattering from a nearby tree, flapping and screaming.

'Let's keep moving,' Falk said. He took the keys from Carmen and climbed behind the wheel of her battered maroon sedan. He started the engine. It felt instantly familiar. 'I used to have a car like this.'

'But you had the sense to get rid of it?' Carmen settled into the passenger's seat.

'Not by choice. It got damaged earlier this year, back in my hometown. A welcome-home gesture from a couple of the locals.'

She glanced over, a tiny smile. 'Oh, yeah. I heard about that. Damaged is one way to put it, I suppose.'

Falk ran his hand over the steering wheel with a pang of regret. His new car was okay, but it wasn't the same.

'This is Jamie's car anyway,' Carmen said as he pulled away. 'Better for longer distances than mine.'

'Right. How is Jamie?'

'Fine. Same as usual.'

Falk didn't really know what the usual was. He had met Carmen's fiancé only once. A muscular guy in jeans and a t-shirt, Jamie worked in marketing for a sports nutrition drink company. He'd shaken Falk's hand and given him a bottle of something blue and fizzy that promised to enhance his performance. The man's smile seemed genuine, but there was a touch of something else in it as he took in Falk's tall thin frame, his pale skin, his white-blond hair and his burned hand. If Falk had had to guess, he'd have said it was mild relief.

Falk's mobile beeped from the centre console. He took his eyes off the empty road to glance at the screen and handed it to Carmen. 'That sergeant's sent an email through.'

Carmen opened the message. 'All right, he says there were two groups on the retreat. One men's group, one women's, both doing separate routes. He's sent the names of the women in Alice Russell's party.'

'Both groups from BaileyTennants?'

'Looks like it.' Carmen took out her own phone and opened the BaileyTennants website. Falk could see the boutique accountancy firm's black and silver lettering on the screen out of the corner of his eye.

16

'Okay. Breanna McKenzie and Bethany McKenzie,' she read out loud from his phone. 'Breanna is Alice's assistant, isn't she?' Carmen tapped her screen. 'Yep, here she is. God, she looks like she could advertise vitamins.'

She held out her phone and Falk glanced at the beaming staff headshot of a girl in her mid-twenties. He could see what Carmen meant. Even in unflattering office light, Breanna McKenzie had the healthy glow of someone who jogged each morning, practised yoga with intent and deep-conditioned her glossy black ponytail religiously every Sunday.

Carmen took her phone back and tapped. 'Nothing's coming up about the other one. Bethany. Sisters, do you think?'

'Possibly.' Perhaps twins even, Falk thought. Breanna and Bethany. Bree 'n' Beth. He rolled the sounds over his tongue. They sounded like a pair.

'We can find out what the deal is with her,' Carmen said. 'Next is Lauren Shaw.'

'We've come across her, haven't we?' Falk said. 'Middle management something?'

'Yeah, she's – Christ, that's right, strategic head of forward planning.' Carmen held out her phone again. 'Whatever that means.'

Whatever it was, Lauren's thin face gave nothing away. It was hard to estimate her age but Falk guessed mid-to-late forties. Her hair was a medium shade of brown and her light-grey eyes gazed straight into the camera, expression as neutral as a passport photo.

Carmen turned back to the list of names. 'Huh.'

'What?'

'It says Jill Bailey was out there with them.'

'Really?' Falk kept his eyes on the road but the bead of worry that had been lodged in his chest since the previous night pulsed and grew.

Carmen didn't bother pulling up Jill's photo. They were both familiar with the chairwoman's heavyset features. She was turning fifty that year and, despite her expensive clothes and haircuts, looked every day of it.

'Jill Bailey,' Carmen said, scrolling further through the sergeant's message. Her thumb stilled. 'Shit. And her brother was in the men's group.'

'Are you sure?'

'Yep, Daniel Bailey, chief executive. It's here in black and white.'

'I don't like that at all,' he said.

'No. I don't like any of it.'

Carmen clicked her fingernails lightly on the phone as she thought. 'All right. We don't know enough to form any conclusions,' she said eventually. 'That voicemail is completely without context. In every sense – realistically, statistically – it's most likely that Alice Russell has come off a trail by mistake and got lost.'

'Yeah, that is most likely,' Falk said. He thought neither of them sounded convinced.

They drove on, the radio stations dwindling to nothing as the scenery whipped by. Carmen fiddled with the knob until she found a crackly AM wavelength. The news on the hour faded in and out. The Melbourne hiker was still

18

missing. The road gently swung to the north and suddenly Falk could see the hills of the Giralang Ranges on the horizon.

'Have you ever been out here?' he said, and Carmen shook her head.

'No. You?'

'No.' He hadn't but he had grown up in a place not unlike it. Isolated terrain, where trees grew thick and dense on land that was reluctant to let anything escape.

'The history around here puts me off,' Carmen went on. 'I know it's silly, but . . . ' She shrugged.

'Whatever happened to Martin Kovac in the end?' Falk said. 'Is he still locked up?'

'I'm not sure.' Carmen tapped at her phone screen again. 'No. He's dead. Died in jail three years ago, aged sixty-two. Actually, that rings a bell, now I think about it. He got into a fight with an inmate, hit his head on the ground and didn't wake up again, it says here. It's hard to feel too sorry about that.'

Falk agreed. The first body had been that of a twenty-something trainee teacher from Melbourne, enjoying a weekend of fresh air in the ranges. A group of campers had found her, days too late. The zipper on her shorts had been wrenched apart, and her pack with hiking supplies was missing. She was barefoot, and her shoelaces were tight around her neck.

It had taken two more women's bodies, and another reported missing, over the next three years before transient labourer Martin Kovac's name was first mentioned in connection with the murders. By then the damage was well and truly done. A long and lasting shadow had been cast over the tranquil Giralang Ranges, and Falk was part of a whole generation that had grown up feeling a shiver when they heard the name.

'Kovac died without confessing to attacking those three women, apparently,' Carmen said, reading from her phone. 'Or that fourth one who was never found. Sarah Sondenberg. That was a sad one. She was only eighteen. Do you remember her parents doing those appeals on TV?'

Falk did. Two decades on and he could still picture the desperation in her parents' eyes.

Carmen tried scrolling down, then gave a sigh. 'Sorry, it's freezing up. The signal's going.'

Falk wasn't surprised. The trees along the side of the road cast shadows that blocked the morning light. 'I guess we're heading out of range.'

They didn't speak again until they left the main road. Carmen pulled out the map and navigated as the track narrowed and the hills loomed large in the windscreen. They passed a short row of shops selling postcards and hiking equipment. It was bookended by a small supermarket and a lonely service station.

Falk checked the fuel gauge and put on the indicator. They both got out while he filled up, yawning, the early start beginning to catch up with them. It felt colder here and the air had a bite. He left Carmen stretching her back with a groan and went in to pay.

The man behind the counter was wearing a beanie and

week-old stubble. He stood up a little straighter as Falk approached.

'Headed into the park?' He spoke with the haste of a bloke starved of conversation.

'We are.'

'Looking for that missing woman?'

Falk blinked. 'Yes, actually.'

'Had heaps of people come through for her. They called in the searchers. Must've had twenty people fill up yesterday. Rush hour all day. No better today.' He shook his head in disbelief.

Falk discreetly glanced around. Their car was the only one on the forecourt. There were no other customers in the shop.

'Hopefully they'll pick her up quickly,' the man went on. 'Bad business, that, when someone goes missing. Bad *for* business as well. Scares people off. Too much of a reminder, I reckon.' He didn't elaborate. There was no need to mention Kovac, Falk supposed, not around there.

'Have you heard any update?' Falk said.

'Nah. Don't think they've had any luck, though, because I haven't seen them come out. And I get them both ways. In and out. Nearest servo's over fifty kilometres away. Further if you go north. Everyone fills up here. Just in case, you know? Something about being in there makes them want to be on the safe side.' He shrugged. 'Silver lining for us, I suppose.'

'You lived out here long?'

'Long enough.'

As Falk handed over his credit card, he noticed the small red light of a security camera behind the counter.

'Are there cameras on the pumps?' Falk said, and the guy followed his gaze outside. Carmen was leaning against the car, her eyes closed and her face tilted upwards.

'Yeah, course.' The guy's eyes lingered a beat longer than necessary before he dragged them back. 'No choice. I'm on me own here most of the time. Can't risk the drive-offs.'

'Did the missing woman come through with her group on their way in?' Falk said.

'Yep. On Thursday. The cops already took a copy of the recording.'

Falk pulled out his ID. 'Any chance of another one?'

The guy looked at it, then shrugged. 'Give me a minute.'

He disappeared into a back office. Falk looked out through the glass front doors while he waited. Beyond the forecourt, he could see nothing but a wall of green. The hills hid the sky. He suddenly felt very surrounded. He jumped as the man re-emerged with a memory stick in his hand.

'Past seven days,' the guy said, handing it over.

'Thanks, mate. That's appreciated.'

'No worries, hope it helps. You wouldn't want to be lost out there for too long. It's the panic that gets you. Everything starts to look the same after a few days, makes it hard to trust what you're seeing.' He glanced outside. 'Drives 'em wild.'

Day 1: Thursday Afternoon

The windscreen was lightly spotting with rain as the minivan drew to a halt. The driver killed the engine and swivelled around in his seat.

'This is it, guys.'

Nine heads turned to the windows.

'I'm only getting out if we go left, not right,' a male voice called from the back seat, and the others laughed.

To the left, a guest lodge sat snug and warm, its wooden walls standing strong against the chill. Light spilled out of the windows and beyond, a neat row of accommodation cabins beckoned.

To the right lay a muddy track, marked with a weather-beaten sign. Gum trees knitted overhead to form a rough archway and the path meandered drunkenly before careering sharply into the bushland and disappearing.

'Sorry, mate, it's a right turn for everyone today.' The driver swung open the minivan door, sending in an icy blast. One by one, the passengers began to move.

Bree McKenzie undid her seatbelt and climbed out, dodging a large puddle at the last second. She turned with a warning, but Alice was already stepping down. The woman's blonde hair blew across her face, blinding her as one expensive boot plunged into the water.

'Shit.' Alice swept her hair behind her ears and looked down. 'Good start.'

'Sorry,' Bree said automatically. 'Has it soaked through?'

Alice examined her boot. 'No. I think I got away with it.' A beat, then she smiled and moved on. Bree gave a silent sigh of relief.

She shivered, zipping her jacket right up to her neck. The air was crisp with the scent of damp eucalyptus, and as she looked around she could see the gravel carpark was mostly empty. Off season, she guessed. She walked to the back of the van where the backpacks were being unloaded. They looked heavier than she remembered.

Lauren Shaw was already there, her tall thin frame hunched over, easing her bag out from the bottom of the pile.

'Do you need a hand?' Bree didn't know Lauren as well as she knew some of the other senior staff, but she knew how to make herself useful.

'No, it's fine –'

'I don't mind –' Bree reached for the bag as Lauren dragged it free. There was an awkward tussle as they both pulled in a different direction.

'I think I've got it. Thank you.' Lauren's eyes were the same cool grey as the sky, but she gave Bree a small smile. 'Do you need help –?'

'God, no.' Bree waved a hand. 'I'm good. Thanks.' She glanced up. The clouds seemed to be growing heavier. 'Hopefully the weather holds out for us.'

'The forecast says it won't.'

'Oh. Well, still. I suppose you never know.'

'No.' Lauren seemed almost amused by Bree's optimism. 'No. I suppose you never do.' She seemed about to say something more when Alice called her name. Lauren looked over and hoisted her pack onto her shoulders. 'Excuse me.'

She crunched away over the gravel towards Alice, leaving Bree alone with the bags. Bree dragged her backpack free and tried to lift it, staggering a little under the unfamiliar weight.

'You'll get used to it.'

Bree looked up to find the driver grinning at her. He'd introduced himself when they'd climbed into the van in Melbourne, but she hadn't bothered remembering his name. Now she looked properly, he was younger than she'd first thought, probably around her age or a few years older. No more than thirty, anyway, with the knotted hands and knuckles of a climber. He was thin but looked strong with it. His red fleece had *Executive Adventures* embroidered on the breast, but no name tag. She couldn't decide if he was attractive or not.

'Make sure it's fitted properly.' The man took the pack from her and helped her lace her arms through the straps. 'That'll help a lot.'

His long fingers adjusted the clips and buckles until

suddenly the pack felt not light exactly, but lighter. Bree opened her mouth to thank him when the tang of cigarette smoke cut through the damp air. They both turned towards it. Bree already knew what she would see.

Bethany McKenzie stood some way from the group, her shoulders hunched. One hand shielded a cigarette from the wind, the other was shoved in the pocket of her coat. She had dozed in the van on the drive up, head lolling against the window, and had woken looking embarrassed.

The driver cleared his throat. 'There's no smoking here.'

Beth paused mid-drag. 'We're outside.'

'We're within the lodge grounds. It's a smoke-free zone all around here.'

Beth looked mutinous for a minute, then, seeing all eyes turned her way, shrugged and stubbed the cigarette out with her boot. She wrapped her coat around herself. It was an old one, Bree knew, and it didn't quite fit anymore.

The driver turned his attention back to Bree with a conspiratorial smile. 'You worked with her long?'

'Six months,' Bree said. 'But I've known her forever. She's my sister.'

The man looked from Bree to Beth and back again in surprise, as she'd known he would. 'You two?'

Bree tilted her head a little and ran a hand along her dark ponytail. 'Twins actually. Identical,' she added, because she thought she'd enjoy the look on his face. He didn't disappoint. He opened his mouth when there was a distant crack of thunder. Everyone looked up.

'Sorry.' The driver grinned. 'I'd better get a move on

so you can set off. Give you enough time to reach the site before dark. The only thing worse than a wet campsite is a rushed wet campsite.'

He hauled out the last of the backpacks and turned to Jill Bailey, who was struggling to thread her thick arm through the shoulder strap of her pack. Bree stepped forward to help, taking the weight of the pack while she scrabbled.

'Do you want to make a start?' the driver said to Jill. 'I can get you ladies on your way. Or would you rather wait until everyone's arrived?'

With an effort, Jill thrust her arm through and breathed out sharply, her face red with exertion. She glanced down the approach road. It was empty. She frowned.

'With a car like Daniel's, he should have beaten us here,' one of the men said to polite laughter.

Jill gave her thin corporate smile but didn't say anything. Daniel Bailey was her brother, but he was still the chief executive. Bree supposed he was allowed to be late.

Bree had watched Jill take the call ten minutes before the minibus was scheduled to depart from BaileyTennants' Melbourne headquarters. Jill had wandered out of earshot and had stood, legs planted and hand on hip as she listened.

As always, Bree had tried to decipher the chairwoman's expression. Annoyance? Possibly. Possibly something else. She often found Jill hard to read. Either way, by the time Jill had hung up and returned to the group, the look was gone.

27

Daniel had been held up, Jill had said simply. Business, as usual. They would go ahead without him. He would follow in his car.

Now, as they milled about the lodge carpark, Bree saw the woman's mouth tighten at the corners. The clouds were definitely heavier and Bree felt the odd spatter of rain hit her jacket. The approach road still lay empty.

'There's really no point in us all waiting.' Jill turned to the four men standing by the van with their packs. 'Daniel shouldn't be far behind.'

She didn't apologise for her brother and Bree was glad. It was one of the things she admired most about Jill. She didn't make excuses.

The men smiled and shrugged. It was fine. Of course it was, Bree thought. Daniel Bailey was the boss. What else could they say?

'All right.' The driver clapped his hands. 'Let's get you ladies on the road. This way.'

The five women glanced at each other, then followed him across the carpark, his red fleece bright against the muted green and brown of the bushland. The gravel crunched under their boots before giving way to muddy grass. The driver stopped at the mouth of the trail and leaned on the old wooden sign. Below a carved arrow were two words: *Mirror Falls*.

'Got all your bits and pieces?' the driver asked.

Bree felt the group turn to look at her and she checked the pocket of her jacket. The map was folded crisp and tight and she could feel the unfamiliar plastic edge of the compass. She had been sent on a half-day course to learn how to navigate. Suddenly it didn't seem like much.

'Don't worry,' the driver was saying. 'You'll barely need them for this bit. Follow your noses and you'll find the first campsite clearing. You can't miss it. There are a few more twists and turns after that, but keep your eyes peeled and you'll be right. I'll see you at the other end on Sunday. Someone wearing a watch? Good. Noon deadline. Penalty for every fifteen minutes you're late.'

'What if we finish early? Can we drive back to Melbourne sooner?'

The driver looked at Alice.

'Good to hear you're feeling confident.'

She shrugged. 'I need to be back for something on Sunday night.'

'Right. Well, yeah. I suppose so. If both teams reach the meeting point early –' The driver glanced over at the men in the distance, chatting and leaning against the van, still one team member short. 'But look, don't break your necks. The traffic's never too bad on a Sunday. As long as you're at the meeting point by twelve, I'll get you back to the city by late afternoon.'

Alice didn't argue, but pressed her lips tight together. Bree recognised the look. It was one she generally tried to avoid generating.

'Any other questions?' The driver looked at each of the five faces. 'Good. Now, let's take a quick group snap for your newsletter.'

Bree saw Jill hesitate. The company newsletter was

questionable both in its regularity and newsworthiness, and Jill gave her pocket a half-hearted pat.

'I haven't got –' She glanced at the van, where their mobile phones lay in a ziplocked bag by the driver's seat.

'It's all right, I'll take it,' the driver said, pulling out his own phone from his fleece pocket. 'Bunch up. A bit closer. There you go. Put your arms around each other, ladies. Pretend you like each other.'

Bree felt Jill slip her arm around her waist, and she smiled.

'Great. Got it.' The driver checked the screen. 'All right, that's everything. Off you go. Good luck. And try to have fun, yeah?'

He turned away with a wave and the five women were alone. They stood frozen in their pose until Jill moved, then each untangled their arms from the others.

Bree looked at Jill and found Jill looking straight back at her.

'How far is the first campsite?'

'Oh. I'll just –' Bree unfolded the map, fumbling as the wind caught the edges. Their start point had been circled and the route marked in red. She could hear packs being shifted as she traced a finger along the line, trying to find the first site. Where was it? Spots of rain bled into the paper and one corner blew back over itself, forming a crease. She smoothed it out as best she could, exhaling silently as she spotted the site next to her thumbnail.

'Okay, it's not far,' she said, trying to decipher the scale on the map legend. 'Not too bad.'

'I suspect your definition of not bad might be different from mine,' Jill said.

'About ten kilometres?' Bree accidentally made it sound like a question. 'No more than ten.'

'All right.' Jill hoisted her pack a little higher on her shoulders. She already looked uncomfortable. 'Lead the way.'

Bree set off. The path grew darker within a matter of steps as the branches curved over the trail, blocking the sky. She could hear water dripping from leaves and, from somewhere well hidden, the sound of a bellbird cry. She looked over her shoulder at the four faces behind her, shadowy under their jacket hoods. Alice was nearest, wisps of blonde hair catching in the wind.

'Good job,' she mouthed. Bree decided she probably meant it, and smiled.

Lauren was following, her eyes trained on the uneven ground, while Jill's round cheeks were already flushed a little pink. Bree could see her sister bringing up the rear. Beth, half a step behind in her borrowed boots and too-tight coat. The sisters' eyes met. Bree didn't slow her pace.

The path narrowed and turned a corner, and the last visible light from the lodge blinked and disappeared as the trees closed in behind them.

Chapter 4

The lodge carpark was full. Search volunteers' trucks were squeezed tight alongside news vans and police vehicles.

Falk double-parked outside the lodge and left Carmen sitting in the car with the keys. He stamped his boots on the verandah, a wave of warmth hitting him as he opened the door. A group of searchers huddled in a corner of a wood-panelled reception area, poring over a map. To one side, a doorway opened to a communal kitchen. On the other, Falk could see a lounge with worn couches and a shelf full of battered books and board games. An ancient computer lurked in the corner under a handwritten sign that said: *For guest use only.* Falk wasn't sure if it was an offer or a threat.

The ranger behind the desk barely glanced up as he approached.

'Sorry, mate, we're completely full,' the ranger said. 'You've come at a bad time.'

'Sergeant King around?' Falk said. 'He's expecting us.'

The ranger looked at him this time. 'Oh. Sorry. I saw you pull up and thought you were –' He didn't finish. *Another city wanker.* 'He's out at the search HQ. You know where that is?'

'No.'

The ranger spread a park map over the desk. The paper was a green sprawling mass of bushland, shot through with crooked lines indicating routes or roads. The ranger picked up a pen and explained what he was marking. The driving route followed a small rural road, slicing through green mass to the west until it hit a crossroads, then turned abruptly north. The ranger finished his instructions and circled the finish point. It appeared to be in the middle of nowhere.

'It's about twenty minutes in the car from here. Don't worry.' The guy handed the map to Falk. 'I promise you'll know it when you get there.'

'Thanks.'

Back outside, the cold was like a slap. He opened the car door and climbed into the driver's seat, rubbing his hands. Carmen was leaning forward, staring through the windscreen. She shushed him as he began to speak, and pointed. Falk followed her gaze. Across the carpark, a man in his late forties wearing jeans and a ski jacket was reaching into the boot of a black BMW.

'Look. Daniel Bailey,' Carmen said. 'Isn't it?'

Falk's first thought was that the BaileyTennants chief executive looked different out of a suit. He hadn't seen

Bailey in person before; the man moved with an athleticism that wasn't captured in photos. He was a little shorter than Falk had expected but was broad around the shoulders and back. His thick hair was a rich brown, with no signs of grey. If the colour wasn't natural, it was an expensive and convincing imitation. Bailey didn't know them – shouldn't know them, at least – but nevertheless Falk found himself sitting a little lower in his seat.

'I wonder if he's actually helping with the search,' Carmen said.

'Whatever he's doing, he hasn't been sitting around.' Fresh mud caked Bailey's boots.

They watched the man rummage through the boot of his BMW. The car sat like a sleek exotic animal amid the well-worn trucks and vans. Finally, he stood, shoving something dark into his jacket pocket.

'What was that?' Carmen said.

'Pair of gloves, it looked like.'

Bailey tapped the boot and it glided shut in luxurious silence. He stood for a moment longer, staring out at the bushland, then walked towards the accommodation cabins, his head bowed against the wind.

'Both him and Jill being up here could make things tricky,' Carmen said, as they watched his retreating form.

'Yeah.' It was an understatement, and they both knew it. Falk started the engine, and passed Carmen the map. 'Anyway. In the meantime, here's where we're headed.'

She looked at the circle on the mass of green.

'What's there?'

'It's where they found the other four.'

The sedan's suspension was struggling. They bumped along the unpaved road, feeling every jolt as the peeling eucalyptus trunks stood guard on both sides. Over the hum of the engine, Falk could hear a faint but shrill whistling.

'Jesus, is that the wind?' Carmen squinted through the windscreen.

'I think so.' Falk kept his eyes on the road as the bushland grew thicker around them. His burned hand gripped the steering wheel. It was starting to ache.

At least the ranger had been right. They couldn't have missed it. Falk rounded a bend and the lonely road ahead transformed into a hive of activity. Vehicles were parked nose to tail along the side of the road, and a reporter spoke earnestly into a camera and gestured at the search teams behind her. Someone had set up a trestle table with a coffee thermos and water bottles. Leaves fluttered from the trees as a police air wing chopper hovered overhead.

Falk pulled in at the very end of the line of cars. It was approaching midday, but the sun was barely a weak glow in the sky. Carmen asked a passing ranger for Senior Sergeant King and they were pointed in the direction of a tall man in his fifties. He was lean with an alert gaze that was darting from map to bushland, and he looked up with interest as Falk and Carmen walked over.

'Thanks for coming.' He shook their hands as they introduced themselves, and glanced over his shoulder at the TV camera. 'Let's move away from the chaos.'

They walked a short way up the road, ducking in beside a large truck that offered a partial windbreak.

'No luck then?' Falk said.

'Not yet.'

'How many of these searches have you done?'

'Lots. I've been up here nearly twenty years. People wander off the track all the time.'

'And how quickly do you normally find them?'

'It really depends. How long is a piece of string? Occasionally we get lucky straight away, but often it can take a bit longer.' King blew out his thin cheeks. 'She's been on her own for at least thirty-odd hours, so ideally we want to pick her up today. It sounds like they had the sense to collect rainwater, which is something, but she probably hasn't got any food. You've got the hypothermia risk as well. That can set in pretty fast when you're damp. But a lot depends on how she's handling it. She might be in luck; apparently she did a fair bit of camping when she was younger. Often they walk out on their own.' He paused. 'Sometimes they don't.'

'But you always manage to find them?' Carmen said. 'Eventually, I mean.'

'Almost always. Even in the Kovac years they found them, you know, in the end. Except for that one girl. Since then I can only think of the odd one or two who never turned up. We had an old bloke about fifteen years ago. He wasn't well, dodgy heart. Shouldn't have been hiking on his own really. Probably sat down for a rest in a quiet spot and had a heart attack. And there was a Kiwi couple about ten years ago. That was a bit of a strange one. Early thirties, fit, fairly experienced. It came out quite a lot later that they'd run up some heavy debts back in New Zealand.'

'So, what, you think they disappeared on purpose?' Falk said.

'Not for me to say, mate. But it wouldn't have been the worst thing in the world for them to fall off the radar.'

Falk and Carmen exchanged a glance.

'So what's happened this time?' Carmen said.

'Alice Russell was in a group of five women dropped off at the start of the Mirror Falls trail on Thursday arvo – someone can show you that later if you want – armed with your basic supplies. A map, tents, compass, some food. They were supposed to head pretty much due west, complete some of those bloody teambuilding obstacles during the day, camp for three nights.'

'Is it a park scheme?' Carmen said.

'No. It's organised by a private company but they've been operating here for a few years. Executive Adventures? They're not bad, tend to know what they're doing. There was a group of five blokes from BaileyTennants doing it as well. Different route, but both groups were due at the meeting point here by noon yesterday.'

'But the women didn't arrive.'

'No. Well, four of them did in the end. But six hours late, and in a bad way. There were some injuries. Various

37

cuts and bruises all round. A knock to the head. One got herself a snakebite.'

'Jesus, which one?' Falk said. 'Is she okay?'

'Yeah. Mostly. Breanna McKenzie. I think she's essentially a glorified assistant, from what I can gather. They've all got these bloody fancy job titles. Anyway, it was probably just a carpet python, not that they knew that at the time. Scared them shitless. Thought it was a tiger snake and she was about to drop dead. It wasn't, definitely non-venomous, but the bite's infected so she's landed herself in the medical centre for a couple of days.'

'Back in Melbourne?' Carmen said, and King shook his head.

'Community hospital in town,' he said. 'Best place for her. You overdose on ice in a city squat, you want the doctors in a city hospital. You get nipped by a snake, you want to be around doctors who know their wildlife, believe me. Her sister's with her at the hospital.' He pulled a small notebook from his pocket and glanced down. 'Bethany McKenzie. She was on the trek too but came out relatively unscathed.'

King glanced over his shoulder at the searchers. A group was preparing to go in, their orange overalls bright against the mass of trees. Falk could see a break in the tree line, where a path delved in. It was marked by a lone wooden beacon.

'We know they went off track sometime on the second day because they didn't make the campsite that night,' King went on. 'There's a fairly large kangaroo trail leading

38

off the main route. We think that's where they went wrong. It only took them a few hours to realise it, but that's plenty of time to land yourself in trouble.'

He looked again at his notebook and turned a page.

'The details get a bit hazier from there on in. My officers managed to get what they could from them last night and this morning. A few holes that still need filling, though. When they realised they'd gone wrong it seems they floundered around, tried to work their way back. Easy way to make things worse. They were supposed to pick up food and water supplies at the second night's campsite, so when they didn't make it, the panic started to set in.'

Falk was reminded of what the attendant in the service station had said. *It's the panic that gets you. Makes it hard to trust what you're seeing.*

'They were all supposed to leave their phones behind, but Alice had taken hers, as you know.' King nodded at Falk. 'Signal's crap out there, though. Sometimes you get lucky, but not usually. Anyway, they wandered around until the Saturday when they stumbled on a disused cabin.'

He paused. He seemed about to say something else, then changed his mind.

'At this point, we're not sure where exactly that cabin is located. But they holed up in there for the night. When they woke up yesterday morning, the missing woman was gone. Or so say the other four.'

Falk frowned. 'What did they think had happened to her?'

'That she'd cracked the shits. Gone off on her own.

39

There'd been some back and forth between them about the best thing to do. Apparently this Alice had been making noises about bush-bashing north to find a road. The others weren't keen, and she wasn't too happy.'

'And what do you think?'

'Could be right. Her backpack and the phone were gone along with her. She'd taken the group's only working torch.' King's mouth formed a hard line. 'And judging by the injuries and the amount of stress they'd have been under, between you and me, it sounds like there'd been a bit of aggro at some point.'

'You think they fought? Physically?' Carmen said. 'About what?'

'Like I said, there's still a fair bit to be ironed out. We're moving as fast as we can, under the circumstances. Minutes count out there. The search has to take priority.'

Falk nodded. 'How did the other four find their way back?'

'They struck a course due north until they finally hit a road, then followed it round. It's a rough technique, doesn't always work, but they probably didn't have much choice. What with the snakebite and everything else. Took them hours but paid off in the end.' He sighed. 'We're focusing on trying to find the cabin. Best case scenario, she's found her way back and bunkered down there.'

Falk didn't ask what the worst case was. Alone and lost among the perils of the bush, he could think of a string of possibilities off the top of his head.

'So that's where we are,' King said. 'Your turn.'

Falk got out his phone. He had saved the voicemail from Alice Russell as a recording and was now glad that he had. His screen showed no signal at all. He passed the handset to King, who pressed it hard against his ear.

'This bloody wind.' King covered his other ear with his hand and closed his eyes, straining to hear. He listened twice more before handing the phone back, his face set.

'You able to tell me what you were talking to her about?' he said.

The helicopter flew low again, shaking the trees into a frenzy. Falk looked over at Carmen, who gave a tiny nod.

'We saw Daniel Bailey in the carpark back at the lodge,' Falk said. 'The chief exec of the company they all work for. His name was on that participant list you sent us.'

'The boss? Yeah, I know who he is. He was on the blokes' team.'

'Did the men's group have contact with the women's group while they were out there?'

'Officially, no. Unofficially?' King said. 'Yeah, I'm told there was some. Why?'

'That's what we've been talking to Alice Russell about,' Falk said. 'Daniel Bailey.'

Day 1: Thursday Afternoon

Jill Bailey could see the back of Alice's head grow further away with every step.

They had been walking for only twenty minutes and already the left heel of Jill's boots was rubbing ominously, despite the three-figure premium she'd paid for something described as 'quick-wick comfort technology'. It was cold, but her t-shirt clung under her arms and a bead of sweat trickled down and pooled in her bra. Her forehead felt damp and shiny and she wiped it subtly with her sleeve.

The only person she thought might be doing it tougher was Beth. Jill could hear the rasp of smoker's lungs behind her. She knew she should turn and offer a few words of encouragement, but at that moment, she could think of nothing to say. Nothing convincing, at least.

Instead, she focused on keeping her own rhythm steady, trying not to let the discomfort show. The gentle drip of water from branches reminded her of the meditation tracks they piped through at spas. That was more her idea of a good weekend away; the outdoor pursuits had always been Daniel's thing. *Bloody Daniel*. She wondered if he'd arrived at the lodge yet.

She sensed a change in the movement ahead and looked up from the path to see the others slowing. The trail had widened as trees started to thin around them and she now realised what she'd thought was the wind was actually the rush of water. She caught up to the others at the edge of the tree line, and blinked as bushland abruptly parted to reveal a tumbling wall of white.

'Oh my God. Unbelievable,' Jill breathed. 'It looks like we've found the falls.'

Stunning was the word that came to mind. A lively river drove its way past the trees, bubbling and frothy as it raced beneath a wooden bridge before freefalling over a rocky edge. It plunged like a heavy curtain with a deafening white roar into a dark pool below.

The five women clattered onto the bridge and leaned against the railing, staring down into the chasm as the water tumbled and churned. The air was so crisp Jill felt she could almost touch it, and the freshwater spray cooled her cheeks. It was a hypnotic sight, and as she drank it in she almost felt the weight of her pack lift a little from her shoulders. She thought she could stand there forever.

'We should go.'

The voice came from the far side of the bridge. Jill dragged her eyes away. Alice was already surveying the trail ahead. 'We'll probably lose light early up here,' she said. 'We should keep moving.'

Immediately, the blister forming on Jill's heel flared up and her shirt began to chafe against her skin. She glanced at the heavy sky, then looked back once more at the view. She sighed.

'All right. Let's go.'

She prised herself away from the safety railing in time to catch Bree staring at the map and frowning.

'All good?' she asked, and Bree flashed her straight white teeth.

'Yes. It's this way.' She refolded the map, pushed her dark ponytail over her shoulder and pointed to the single track ahead. Jill nodded, saying nothing. One track, one choice. She hoped Bree felt as confident when there was a decision to be made.

The path was muddy, and Jill feared she might slip with every step. An ache had started to inch its way along her spine. She wasn't sure if it was from the weight of the pack, or from constantly bending her neck to watch where she put her feet.

They hadn't gone far when the hum and trill of the bushland was broken by a shout up ahead. Bree had stopped and was pointing up at something off the path.

'Look. It's the first flag. Isn't it?'

A crisp white square of cloth flapped bright against the stringy bark of the gum trees. Bree dropped her pack and tramped through the undergrowth to look.

'It is. It's got the Executive Adventures logo on it.'

Jill squinted. She couldn't make out detail from that distance. Bree stretched up, fingertips reaching. She jumped and fell short.

'I need something to stand on.' Bree looked around, her hair blowing across her face.

'Oh, let's just leave it.' Alice was looking at the sky. 'It's not worth breaking your neck for. What do we get if we find all six? A hundred dollars or something?'

'Two hundred and forty each.'

Jill turned at Beth's voice. It was the first time she'd heard her speak since they'd set off.

Beth put her pack down. 'I'll give you a boost.'

Jill watched the enthusiasm fade from Bree's face.

'No, it's all right. Let's leave it.'

But it was too late, her sister was already heading over. 'Two hundred and forty bucks, Bree. I'll get it myself if you're not going to.'

Jill stood beside Alice and Lauren, their arms folded across their chests against the cold, and watched. Beth knelt in front of her sister, threading her fingers to create a makeshift step and waiting until Bree reluctantly placed a muddy boot in her clasped palms.

'This is a waste of time,' Alice said, then glanced sideways at Jill. 'Sorry. Not the whole thing. Just this.'

'Oh, let them have a go.' Lauren watched as the twins wobbled against the tree trunk. 'They're not doing any harm. A couple of hundred is worth a lot in your twenties.'

Jill looked at Alice. 'What's your hurry anyway?'

'Just that we'll be putting these tents up in the dark as well as the wet at this rate.'

Jill suspected that Alice was right. The sky had grown dimmer and she realised she could no longer hear birdcall. 'We'll move on in a minute. I was actually talking about you wanting to get back to Melbourne early on Sunday. Didn't you say you had something on?'

'Oh.' There was an awkward pause, then Alice waved a hand. 'It's nothing.'

'It's prize night at Endeavour Ladies' College,' Lauren said, and Alice shot her a look Jill didn't quite catch.

'Is it? Well, we'll get you back in time for that,' Jill said. 'What's Margot receiving?'

Every time Jill met Alice's daughter, she'd always come away with the strange feeling of having been somehow *appraised*. Not that the opinion of one sixteen-year-old held any value in Jill's world – her need for that kind of approval was thirty-five years behind her – but there was something about Margot Russell's cool gaze that was strangely unnerving.

'She's getting the dance award,' Alice said.

'That's nice.'

'Hmm,' said Alice, who Jill knew held a master's degree in business and commerce.

Jill glanced at Lauren. She'd never met Lauren's daughter, but knew she was also an Endeavour girl. She'd overheard the woman complaining about the fees more than once. Jill dug deep, but could not dredge up the girl's name.

'Do you need to get back too?' she said, finally.

A pause. 'No. Not this year.'

At that moment there was a small cheer, and Jill turned with a flutter of relief to see the sisters brandishing the flag.

'Well done, ladies,' Jill said, and Bree beamed. Even Beth was smiling. It changed her face, Jill thought. She should do it more.

'At last,' Alice said, not quite far enough under her breath. She hoisted her pack onto her shoulders. 'Sorry, but we're really not going to make it before nightfall if we don't move.'

'Yes, thanks, Alice. You've said.' Jill turned to the sisters. 'Nice teamwork, girls.'

As Alice walked away, Bree's smile held bright and firm. The single twitch at the corner of her mouth was so slight that if Jill hadn't known better, she might have thought she'd imagined it.

Alice had been right. The campsite was pitch black by the time they arrived. The last kilometre of the hike had been done at a snail's pace, picking their way along the path by torchlight and stopping every hundred metres to check the map.

Jill had expected to feel relief when they reached the clearing, but she felt only exhaustion. Her legs ached and her eyes felt strained from peering into the gloom. It was difficult to tell in the dark, but the site seemed larger than she'd expected. It was surrounded on all sides by swaying gums, their branches black fingers against the night sky. She could see no stars.

Jill set her pack down, glad to be free from the weight. As she stepped back, her heel caught on something and she stumbled, landing hard on her tailbone with a cry.

'What was that?' A light flashed in Jill's eyes, blinding her. There was a tiny laugh of surprise, bitten off before it began. Alice. 'God, Jill. You startled me. Are you all right?'

Jill felt someone grasp her arm.

'I think you found the fire pit.' Bree. Of course. 'Let me help you.'

Jill felt Bree buckle a little under her weight as she clambered to her feet.

'I'm fine. Thanks.' Her palm felt grazed and raw, and she thought it might be bleeding. She reached for her torch but found her jacket pocket empty.

'Damn.'

'Are you hurt?' Bree was still hovering.

'I think I dropped my torch.' Jill looked where she'd fallen, but it was too dark to see.

'I'll get mine.' And Bree was gone. Jill could hear the sound of rummaging through a bag.

'Here.' The voice came out of nowhere, close to her ear, and Jill jumped. Beth. 'Take this.'

Jill felt something placed into her hands. It was an industrial metal torch, long and heavy.

'Thank you.' Jill fumbled until she found the switch. A powerful beam sliced through the night, boring straight

48

into Alice. The woman flinched and raised a hand to shield her eyes, her features harsh and exposed.

'Jesus, it's a bit bright.'

Jill took half a beat longer than necessary to drop the beam from Alice's face to her feet. 'It looks like it does the job. We might be glad of it later.'

'I suppose.' Alice stood with her feet captured in the circle of light, then took a single step to the side and disappeared.

Jill swung the beam slowly across the site. The white light stripped out most colours, washing everything with monochrome shades. The path they'd walked along looked thin and uneven, and the fire pit at her feet was black at the centre. A silent circle of trees grew all around, their trunks luminous under the beam. Beyond, the bushland was black. A shadow caught Jill's eye as she swept the light along and she stopped. She moved the beam back, more slowly this time.

A slender figure stood motionless at the very edge of the clearing and Jill jumped, nearly stumbling again and sending the light bouncing in a crazy pattern. She caught herself, steadying her hand. The light shook very gently as she focused the beam.

Jill breathed out. It was only Lauren. Her tall, thin frame was almost absorbed by the vertical lines of the trees and the dark space beneath them.

'Lauren, my God, you gave me a fright,' Jill called. Her pulse still felt a little fast. 'What are you doing?'

Lauren stood frozen, back to the group, staring into the darkness.

'Lau–'

She put up her hand. 'Shh.'

They all heard it at once. A crack. Jill held her breath, her ears ringing in the void. Nothing. Then another crack. This time the broken rhythm of debris snapping underfoot was unmistakable.

Jill took a fast step backwards. Lauren turned, her face grey in the stark light.

'There's someone out there.'

Chapter 5

'Daniel Bailey?' King said, looking from Falk to Carmen. 'Why are you looking at him?'

The wind threw clouds of dust and leaves into the air and on the far side of the road, Falk could see the group of searchers disappear into the bushland. Melbourne felt a long way away.

'This is strictly confidential,' Falk said, and waited until King nodded.

'Of course.'

'It's around money laundering. Allegedly.'

'At BaileyTennants?'

'We believe so.' Among others. The boutique accounting firm was one of a number under simultaneous investigation by the AFP.

'I thought they're supposed to be a respectable firm? Family-owned for generations and all that.'

'Yeah. We think Daniel and Jill Bailey's father was involved before them.'

'Really?' King raised his eyebrows. 'So he's, what, passed on the family trade?'

'Something like that.'

'How bad are we talking?' King said. 'A bit of fiddling the books or –?'

'The allegations are serious,' Carmen said. 'Organised. High level. Ongoing.'

In truth, Falk knew he and Carmen weren't sure how far the full investigation had spread. They had been assigned to investigate BaileyTennants specifically, and told only what was directly relevant. The firm was a cog in a larger network, that much they knew. How far that network reached, and how deep it ran, had not been shared with them. They guessed nationally, suspected internationally.

King frowned. 'So Alice came to you to dob in –?'

'We approached her,' Falk said. She possibly hadn't been the right choice; he could admit that now. But on paper she had ticked all the boxes. High enough up the ladder to have access to what they needed, deep enough in the shit to give them sufficient leverage. And she was not a Bailey.

'So it's both Daniel and Jill Bailey you're after?'

'Yes,' Carmen said. 'And Leo. Their father.'

'He must be well into retirement, isn't he?'

'He's still active. Allegedly.'

King nodded, but Falk could see a look settle in his eyes. It was one he knew well. Falk was aware that in the grand scheme of things, most people ranked money laundering somewhere between shoplifting and fare evasion. It shouldn't happen, of course, but a handful of rich people determined to avoid their fair share of tax was hardly worth stretching police resources for.

It was about more than that, Falk would sometimes try to explain. If the time was right and the other person's eyes weren't too glazed. If serious money was being hidden, it was for a reason. Those pristine white collars only got grubbier the further down the trail, until by the end they were downright dirty. Falk hated it. He hated everything about it. He hated the way men in plush offices were able to wash their hands at arm's length and tell themselves it was simply a bit of creative accounting. The way they could spend their bonuses and buy their mansions and polish their cars, all the while pretending that they couldn't begin to guess what was rotting at the far end. Drugs. Illegal firearms. Child exploitation. It varied, but it was all paid for in the common currency of human misery.

'Do the Baileys know they're being investigated?' King said and Falk glanced at Carmen. It was the question they had been asking themselves.

'We haven't got any reason to think so,' he said finally.

'Except that your contact called you the night she disappeared.'

'Except that.'

King rubbed his chin, stared out towards the bush.

'What does all this mean for them?' he said at last. 'Alice Russell gives you what you need, and then what? The Baileys lose their firm?'

'No, ideally then the Baileys go to prison,' Falk said. 'The firm will close, though.'

'So all the other employees lose their jobs?'

'Yes.'

'Including those other women out there with her?'

'Yes.'

King didn't look impressed. 'How did Alice Russell feel about that?'

'To be fair,' Carmen said, 'she didn't have much choice. If she hadn't helped us, she'd be taking her chances along-side the Baileys.'

'Right.' King thought for a minute. 'And this has been going on for some time, yeah?'

'We've been working with her directly on and off for three months,' Falk said.

'So why would she need to call you yesterday?' King said. 'Why the urgency?'

Carmen sighed. 'The data Alice has given us so far was due to be passed along to the broader investigative team,' she said. 'Today.'

'Today?'

'Yeah. There are still some key documents we need, but what we had was ready to be turned over for examination.'

'So have you done that? Turned it over?'

'No,' Carmen said. 'Once that happens, it's out of our hands. And Alice's. We wanted to get an idea of the situation up here first.'

'Was she trying to back out, do you think?' King said.

'We don't know. It's possible. But it's the eleventh hour

54

for her to pull a stunt like that. She's facing prosecution if she does. She'd need to have a bloody good reason.' Carmen hesitated. 'Or no choice, I suppose.'

All three looked at the dark landscape that had so far refused to release Alice Russell.

'So what is it you're still waiting on from her?' King said.

'There's a series of commercial documents,' Falk said. 'Historic ones.' BT-51X to BT-54X were the official names, although he and Carmen mainly referred to them as *the contracts*. 'We need them to tie in Daniel and Jill's father.'

What had unfolded in the past was crucial, Falk and Carmen had been told. It was Leo Bailey who'd set up the business in its current form, and it was he who'd built the connections with a number of key players under investigation. It might be in the past, but the cord connecting with the present was pulsing and vital.

King went quiet. In the distance they could hear the thrum of the helicopter. It sounded further away.

'Right,' he said eventually. 'Look, at this point, my first and only priority is Alice Russell. Finding her, and bringing her out of there safely. Most likely scenario when someone goes AWOL out there is that they've wandered off trail and lost their bearings, so that's the plan I'm sticking with for now. But if there's a chance that her talking to you has caused problems with that group, then that's good to know. So, thanks for being frank.'

The sergeant was fidgeting now, keen to get back. A strange expression had settled on his face. Something almost like relief. Falk watched him for a moment more, then spoke.

'What else?'

'What else, what?'

'What else are you hoping hasn't happened?' Falk said. 'Neither of those scenarios sounds good to me.'

'No.' King didn't meet his eye.

'So what's worse than either of those?'

The sergeant stopped fidgeting, then he glanced along the road. The searchers had been swallowed up by the woods, their orange suits lost to sight. The media were hovering at a safe distance. Still, he leaned in a little and sighed.

'Kovac. Kovac is worse.'

They stared at him.

'Kovac is dead,' Carmen said.

'Martin Kovac is dead.' King ran his tongue across his teeth. 'We're just not too sure about his son.'

Day 1: Thursday Night

Lauren felt like screaming.

It was only the men. She had watched with her heart racing and a sour taste in her throat as the group of five had emerged from the trees. Their white grins glowing as they brandished bottles of wine. Leading the way was Daniel Bailey.

'So you made it eventually?' Lauren snapped, the adrenaline making her bold. Daniel slowed his step.

'Yes –'

His eyes creased and Lauren thought at first that he was angry, then realised he was simply trying to summon her name. He was rescued as his sister appeared through the gloom.

'Daniel. What are you doing here?' If Jill was surprised, or annoyed, she didn't show it. But then she rarely gave much away, Lauren knew from experience.

'We thought we'd come and say hello. See how you're

settling in.' He looked at his sister's face. 'Sorry. Did we scare you?'

Perhaps Daniel could read his sister better than most, Lauren thought. Jill said nothing, simply waited.

'Is everyone doing okay?' Daniel went on. 'Our camp's only a kilometre away. We brought drinks.' He looked to the other four men, who held up their bottles obediently. 'One of you help the girls get their fire going.'

'We can do it,' Lauren said, but Daniel waved his hand.

'It's fine. They don't mind.'

He turned to his sister and Lauren watched them walk away. She went over to the fire pit, where a skinny man from marketing was attempting to ignite a firelighter on a pile of damp leaves.

'Not like that.' Lauren took the matches from him. He watched as she picked around a fallen tree at the edge of the clearing, collecting sticks that had been protected from the weather. Across the clearing, Lauren could hear Alice instructing the twins on how to put up the tents. It sounded like the sisters were doing most of the work.

She crouched at the fire pit, trying to remember how this went. She arranged the sticks in a teepee over some kindling and examined her work. That looked right. Lauren lit a match and held her breath as the flame caught, then rose, bathing the surrounds in an orange glow.

'Where did you learn that?' The man from marketing was staring.

'School camp.'

A rustle in the dark and Alice stepped into the glow.

'Hey. The tents are up. Bree and Beth are in one, so you and I are sharing. Jill's got the one-man to herself.' She nodded at the fire, her features twisted by the light of the flames. 'Nice. Let's put the food on.'

'Should we check with Jill?' The clearing was wide and it took Lauren a moment to spot the woman, standing at the edge with her brother, deep in conversation. Jill said something and Daniel shook his head.

'They're busy,' Alice said. 'Let's get started. You and I will have to do it anyway, she won't know how to cook over flame.'

That was probably true, Lauren thought, as Alice started pulling out pots and rice and boil-in-the-bag beef stew.

'I remember promising myself at camp that I'd never do this again, but it's like riding a bike, isn't it?' Alice said a few minutes later as they watched the water begin to bubble. 'I feel like we should be back in school uniform.'

With the smell of eucalyptus and burned firewood in her nostrils and with Alice by her side, Lauren felt the dust breathe and lift on a thirty-year-old memory. McAllaster Camp.

Endeavour Ladies' College's bushland campus still featured heavily in the school's glossy prospectus. An opportunity – a compulsory opportunity – for Endeavour's Year Nine ladies to spend a full academic year in the remote setting. The program was designed to develop character, resilience and a healthy respect for Australia's natural environment. And – subtly spelled out between the carefully written lines – designed to keep teenage girls away from everything teenage girls were drawn to at that age.

At fifteen, Lauren had been homesick from day one and raw from blisters and mosquito bites from day two. She was unfit and well past the age where it could still be called puppy fat. Just one long week in, and she had found herself blindfolded as well. *What was the point in a trust challenge when she didn't trust any of her classmates?*

She knew she had been led away from the main camp and into the bushland, that was obvious from the crunch of leaves under her feet, but beyond that she was lost. She could have been on the cusp of a cliff edge or set to plunge into a river. She could hear movement around her. Footsteps. A giggle. She had stretched a hand out, grasping at the blackness in front. Her fingers closed around nothing but thin air. An unsteady step forward almost sent her stumbling as her toe caught the uneven ground. Suddenly, a hand had gripped her arm, firm and steady. She'd felt warm breath on her cheek and heard a voice in her ear.

'I've got you. This way.' Alice Russell.

It was the first time Lauren could remember Alice speaking to her properly, but she'd recognised her voice immediately. Lauren, then fat and friendless, could still recall that mingling rush of confusion and relief as Alice took her arm. Now, nearly three decades on, Lauren looked across the campfire at the other woman, and wondered if she was remembering that day too.

Lauren took a breath, but was cut short by movement

behind her. Daniel appeared at her shoulder, his face bathed in orange.

'They got the fire started then? Good.' His pupils looked black in the half-light of the flames and he pushed a bottle of red into Lauren's hand. 'Here, enjoy a drink. Alice, I need a quick word, please.'

'Now?' Alice didn't move.

'Yes. Please.' Daniel put his palm very lightly on her upper back. After the briefest pause, Alice let him steer her away from the group. Lauren watched as they almost disappeared to the edge of the clearing, absorbed by the shadows. She heard the low, indistinct hum of Daniel's voice before it was drowned out by the surrounding chatter.

Lauren turned back to the fire and poked the boil-in-the-bag meals. They were ready. She opened them up. Added exactly the same amount of rice to each.

'Dinner's ready,' she said to no-one in particular.

Bree came over, clutching the flag she'd found earlier and trailing two men in her wake.

'I saw it right there in the tree next to the path,' she was saying to them. 'Maybe you missed yours.'

Her cheeks were flushed and she was sipping from a plastic cup in her hand. She picked up a meal bag.

'Thank you. Lovely.' She poked inside with her fork and her face fell a little.

'You don't like beef?' Lauren said.

'Yes, I do. It's great. It's not that, I just –' Bree stopped. 'It looks delicious, thank you.'

Lauren watched as Bree took a small mouthful. All meat, no rice. Lauren recognised someone avoiding carbs at night when she saw it. She felt the itch to say something but kept her mouth shut. This was none of her business.

'If your dinner tastes anything like ours did, you'll need something to wash it down,' one of the men said, leaning in towards Bree. He'd refilled her cup with wine before she could answer.

Lauren kept half an eye on them as she got her own food and sat on a log by the fire to eat. She opened the bag. The beef and rice stared back at her. She should eat, she thought, then looked around. No-one was watching. No-one here cared either way. She put her fork down.

A shadow fell across Lauren's lap and she looked up.

'Can I have one of those?' Beth was pointing at the food.

'Of course.'

'Thanks. I'm starving.' Beth nodded at the log. 'Okay if I sit here?'

Lauren moved up and felt the log creak and dip under Beth's weight. Beth ate fast, watching as her sister held court amid the men. Bree tilted back her long white neck and took a sip from her cup. It was immediately refilled.

'She doesn't like to drink much usually,' Beth said, her mouth not quite empty. 'It goes to her head when she does.'

Lauren remembered the bottle of red Daniel had thrust on her and held it out, but Beth shook her head.

'No thanks, I'm right.'

'You don't like it either?'

'I like it too much.'

'Oh.' Lauren couldn't tell if Beth was joking or not. The woman wasn't smiling.

'Do you mind if I smoke?' Beth crumpled her empty boil-in-the-bag and pulled out a packet of cigarettes.

Lauren did mind a bit, but shook her head. They were outside; let the woman light up. They watched the flames. The laughter and chatter around grew louder as more bottles were emptied. One of the men prised himself away from Bree to wander over.

'Can I borrow a cigarette?' He grinned down. Beth hesitated, then held out her pack.

'Thanks.' He took two, putting one in his mouth and the other in his pocket. He had turned his back on her before he took his first drag. Lauren saw Beth's eyes follow him, as he wandered back to her sister.

'How are you liking BaileyTennants?'

Beth shrugged. 'It's okay. It's good.'

She tried to sound enthusiastic, but fell a notch short. Lauren didn't blame her. Data archiving was notoriously poorly paid, even for an entry-level role, and the team was housed in the basement level. Anytime she had to go down there, Lauren emerged craving natural light.

'Are you enjoying working with your sister?'

'Yeah, definitely.' The enthusiasm sounded genuine this time. 'It's thanks to her I even got the job. She put in a good word.'

'Where were you before?'

Beth shot her a glance and Lauren wondered if she'd somehow put her foot in it.

'Between jobs.'

'Oh.'

Beth took a drag, and sighed out a cloud of smoke. 'Sorry. I'm grateful to have the work. It's just all this.' She gestured around the clearing. 'It's not really my thing.'

'I'm not sure it's really anyone's thing. Except maybe Daniel's.'

Lauren suddenly remembered Alice and looked up. The corner where she'd been standing with Daniel was empty, and across the clearing Lauren could see him now. He and his sister were standing a little apart from the group, watching. No Alice in sight.

There was a distant crack of thunder and the conversation dimmed as faces turned to the sky. Lauren felt a drop on her forehead.

'I'm going to check that my pack's in my tent,' she said and Beth nodded.

She crossed the clearing and picked her way over the taut guy ropes. The sisters had done a good job putting up the tents, she thought as she knelt down and unzipped the door.

'Alice!'

Alice jumped. She was sitting cross-legged in the centre of the tent, her head down, an eerie blue wash across her face. In her lap, she held a mobile phone.

'Shit.' Alice clutched the phone to her chest. 'You scared me.'

'Sorry. Are you okay? The food's ready if you want it.'

'I'm fine.'

'Are you sure? What are you doing?'

'Nothing. Really, I'm fine. Thanks.' Alice pressed a button and the phone screen went dark, her features disappeared with the light. Her voice sounded strange. Lauren wondered for a moment if she might have been crying.

'What did Daniel want?' Lauren said.

'Nothing. Something about the agenda for the AGM.'

'That couldn't wait?'

'Of course it could've. You know Daniel.'

'Oh.' Lauren's knees were aching from being crouched in the doorway. She could hear the rain hit the canvas near her head.

'Is that your mobile? I thought you handed it in.'

'That was my work one. Hey, do you have yours?'

'No, we weren't supposed to bring them.'

A short hard laugh. 'So of course you didn't. It doesn't matter. I can't get a signal anyway.'

'Who are you trying to call?'

'No-one.' A pause. 'Margot.'

'Is everything okay?'

'Yes.' Alice cleared her throat. 'Yes, everything's good. She's good.'

She pressed a button and the screen lit up again. Her eyes definitely looked a little watery.

'Still no signal?'

No answer.

'Are you sure everything's okay?'

'Yes. I just –' There was the thump of a phone being tossed on a sleeping bag. 'I need to get through.'

'Margot's sixteen, Alice. She's okay on her own for a couple of days. You'll see her on Sunday anyway. At prize night.' Lauren could hear the bitter note creep into her tone. Alice didn't seem to notice.

'I just want to make sure she's all right.'

'Of course she is. Margot will be fine. Margot's always fine.' Lauren forced herself to take a deep breath. Alice was clearly upset. 'Look, I know what it's like. I worry about Rebecca too.' That was an understatement. Lauren sometimes felt she hadn't slept a full night through in the sixteen years since the day her daughter was born.

No answer. The sound of fumbling, then the blue screen light appeared again.

'Alice?'

'I heard you.' Alice sounded distracted. Her features were hard as she stared down into her lap.

'At least Margot seems to be doing well for herself. With the dance award, and everything.' The bitterness was back.

'Maybe. I just –' Lauren heard Alice sigh. 'I was hoping for better for her.'

'Right. Well. I know how you feel.' Lauren thought of her own daughter at home. It was dinner time. She tried to imagine what she might be doing now and the familiar sinking feeling blossomed in her stomach.

Alice rubbed her eyes with the heel of her hand. Suddenly her head shot up. 'Why is it so quiet out there?'

'It's raining. The party's over.'

'Daniel's leaving?'

'I think they all are.'

Alice pushed past her, clambering out of the tent, catching Lauren's finger with the heel of her boot. Lauren followed, rubbing her hand. Outside, the campsite had cleared. The twins were nowhere to be seen, but torch-light shone through the canvas of their tent. Jill stood alone in the circle, with her jacket zipped tight and the hood up. She was picking at a meal with her fork, staring into the dying fire as drops of rain hissed and sizzled. She looked up when she heard them.

'There you are.' Jill's eyes flicked over them. 'Please tell me you're not breaking the rules, Alice.'

Silence. 'Sorry?'

Jill nodded at Alice's hand. 'Phones aren't allowed.'

Lauren heard the woman breathe out. 'I know. I'm sorry. I didn't realise it was in my bag.'

'Don't let Bree and Beth see it. The rules are the same for everyone.'

'I know. I won't.'

'Is there any signal out here?'

'No.'

'Oh well.' The last remnants of fire sputtered and died. 'Then it's no help to you anyway.'

Chapter 6

Falk and Carmen stared at King. The chopper swooped overhead, the *wap* of its blades beating down.

'I didn't know Kovac had a son,' said Falk finally.

'No, well, it wasn't exactly your ideal family set-up. The kid would be nearly thirty now, product of an on-off thing Kovac had with a barmaid at his local. They ended up with this boy, Samuel – Sam – and it seems Kovac surprised everyone by taking to fatherhood more than you'd expect from your average lunatic.' King sighed. 'But he was already locked up by the time the kid was four or five. The mum had alcohol problems, so Sam ended up bouncing through foster care. He resurfaced in his late teens, started visiting his dad in prison – pretty much the only person who did, by all accounts – then dropped off the radar again about five years ago. Missing, presumed dead.'

'Presumed, but not confirmed?' Carmen said.

'No.' King glanced over as a group of searchers emerged

from the trailhead, their faces showing no good news. 'But he was a small-time crook with ideas above his station. Dabbled in drug dealing, hung around the fringes of the bikie gangs. It was only a matter of time before he followed his old man into prison for something or other, or ended up pissing off the wrong person and paying for it. We've got some people in Melbourne trying to firm it up.' He gave a grim smile. 'Would've been better if it had been done at the time. But no-one's too upset when a bloke like Sam Kovac goes AWOL. Only person who gave much of a shit was his dad.'

'What makes you think he has anything to do with Alice Russell?' Falk said.

'Look, I don't. Not really. But there was always this theory that Martin Kovac had a base somewhere in the bushland. Some place where he could lie low. At the time, they thought it was probably near to where the victims were taken, but if it existed, it was never found.' He frowned. 'From the descriptions the women gave, there's a remote chance this cabin they found could be connected to him.'

Falk and Carmen looked at each other.

'How did the women respond to that?' Carmen said.

'We haven't told them. Decided there was no point worrying them until we were sure there was something to worry about.'

'And you've no idea where this cabin is?'

'They think they were in the north somewhere, but "north" is a bloody huge area in here. There are hundreds of hectares we don't know well.'

'Can you narrow it down from Alice's phone signal?' Falk asked, but King shook his head.

'If they'd been on high ground, then maybe. But it sounds like that wasn't the case. There are pockets where you get lucky but there's no real rhyme or reason. Sometimes they're only a few metres square, or the signal will come and go.'

From the trail, a searcher called King's name and the officer waved an acknowledgement.

'Sorry, I'd better get on. We'll talk again later.'

'Are the rest of the BaileyTennants group still up here? We might need to speak to them,' Carmen said as they followed him back across the road.

'I've asked the women to stick around for now. All the men have gone back except for Daniel Bailey. You can tell them you're assisting me, if it helps. As long as you share, of course.'

'Yeah. Understood.'

'Come on, I'll introduce you to Ian Chase.' King raised a hand and a young man in a red fleece extracted himself from a group of searchers and headed over. 'He runs the Executive Adventures program out here.' He almost smiled. 'Let him tell you in person how bloody foolproof this is all supposed to be.'

'It's really easy if you follow the routes properly,' Ian Chase was saying. He was a wiry, dark-haired bloke with eyes that kept flicking to the bushland as though he expected Alice Russell to emerge at any time.

70

They had driven back to the lodge, Falk and Carmen following Chase's minibus along the isolated rural route. Now, Chase leaned one hand on a wooden sign marking a trailhead. Carved letters worn smooth by the seasons read: *Mirror Falls*. At their feet, a dirt track meandered into the bush before disappearing from sight.

'This is where the women's group started,' Chase said. 'The Mirror Falls trail isn't even our hardest route. We might have fifteen groups a year go along here and we haven't had any problems.'

'Ever?' Falk said, and Chase shifted his weight.

'Once in a while, maybe. You get groups that are late sometimes. But usually they're slow rather than lost. If you follow the route backwards, you find them dragging their heels near the final campsite. Sick of carrying their bags.'

'Not this time, though,' Carmen said.

'No.' Chase shook his head. 'Not this time. We leave food and water in lock boxes at the second and third nights' campsites so the groups don't have to carry everything the whole way. When the girls didn't come out at the end, a couple of the rangers went in. They know the short cuts, you know? Checked the lock box at the third site. No sign they'd ever been there. Same at the second. That's when we called in the state officers.'

He pulled a map from his pocket and pointed to a thick red line curving in a gentle northward arc before finishing in the west.

'This is the route they were following. They probably went wrong somewhere around here.' He stabbed the paper between crosses marking the first and second camp-sites. 'We're pretty sure they took the kangaroo track. The problem is where they ended up after that, when they tried to double back.'

Falk examined the route. It looked easy enough on paper, but he knew how the bushland could distort things.

'Where did the men's group walk?'

'They started from a point about ten minutes' drive from here.' Chase pointed to another line, marked in black this time. It stayed almost parallel to the women's trail for the first day, then curved south before finishing at the same spot in the west. 'The blokes were about an hour late setting off but still had plenty of time to get to their first site. Enough time to make it over to the girls' camp for a couple of drinks, apparently.'

Carmen raised her eyebrows. 'Is that usual?'

'It's not encouraged, but it happens. It's not a difficult walk between the two but you always take a risk going off track. When it goes wrong, it can really go wrong.'

'Why were the men late?' Falk said. 'I thought you all drove up together?'

'Except Daniel Bailey,' Chase said. 'He missed the bus.'

'Oh, yeah? He say why?'

Chase shook his head. 'Not to me. He apologised to the other fellas. Said he got held up with business.'

'Right.' Falk looked again at the map. 'Do they all get given this on the day, or –?'

Chase shook his head. 'We send them out a couple of weeks beforehand. But they only get the one per team and are told not to copy it. We can't stop them, of course, but it's part of the process. Makes them appreciate scarcity out here, that things can't always be replaced. Same with not taking the phones. We like them to rely on them-selves rather than technology. Plus the phones don't work well anyway.'

'And how did the group seem when they set off?' Falk said. 'In your opinion?'

'They were fine,' Chase answered straight away. 'A bit nervous maybe, but nothing out of the ordinary. I wouldn't have sent them off if I'd had any concerns. But they were happy enough. Look, you can see for yourself.'

He fished his phone out of his pocket and tapped the screen before holding it out so Falk could see. It was a photo.

'I took that before they set off.'

The five women were smiling, their arms around each other. Jill Bailey stood in the centre of the group. Her right arm was around Alice's waist, who in turn had her arm around a woman Falk recognised as Lauren Shaw. On Jill's other side were two younger women who looked a little, but definitely not a lot, alike.

Falk stared at Alice, her blonde head cocked a little to the side. She was wearing a red jacket and black pants, and her arm rested lightly across Jill's shoulders. And Ian Chase was right. In that snapped single moment, they did all look happy enough.

Falk handed the phone back to him.

'We're getting copies printed for the searchers,' Chase

said. 'Come on. I'll show you the start of the trail.' He looked Falk and Carmen up and down, taking in their little-used boots. His gaze lingered briefly on Falk's burned hand. 'It's a bit of a walk to the falls, but you should be right.'

They plunged into the trees and almost immediately Falk's hand started to prickle with pins and needles. He ignored it, focusing instead on his surroundings. The path was well defined and Falk could see scuffs and indents, old footprints possibly, that had been blurred by rainfall. Above, tall eucalyptus trees swayed. They were walking in constant shadow and Falk saw Carmen shiver under her jacket. He thought about Alice Russell. He wondered what had been going through her mind as she'd entered the bushland, walking towards something that would stop her from leaving.

'How does the Executive Adventures program work?' Falk's voice sounded unnaturally loud against the rustle of the bushland.

'We organise tailor-made activities for staff training and teambuilding,' Chase said. 'Most of our clients are based in Melbourne, but we offer activities all over the state. Ropes courses, one-day retreats, you name it.'

'So you run the program here on your own?'

'Mostly. There's another guy running a survival course a couple of hours away. We each cover when the other's on leave, but most of the time it's just me.'

'And you live up here?' Falk said. 'Do you have accommodation in the park?'

'No. I've got a little place in town. Near the service station.'

Falk, who had spent his formative years firmly in the back end of nowhere, thought even he would be hard-pressed to describe the handful of shops they'd passed as a town.

'It sounds a bit lonely,' he said, and Chase shrugged.

'It's not too bad.' He was navigating the uneven path with the ease of someone who had walked it many times before. 'I like being outdoors and the rangers are okay. I used to come camping up here when I was younger so I know the terrain. I've never wanted an office job. I signed up with Executive Adventures three years ago, been up here for the past two. It's the first time this kind of thing has happened on my watch, though.'

In the distance, Falk could make out the distinct sound of rushing water. They had been walking slowly but surely uphill since they had set off.

'How long do you reckon they have to find Alice?' Falk asked. 'Best case scenario.'

The corners of Chase's mouth turned down. 'It's hard to say. I mean, we're not talking winter conditions to rival Alaska, but it gets bloody cold up here. Especially at night, and especially with no shelter. Stuck outside, a bit of wind, bit of rain, it can be game over quite soon.' He sighed. 'But you know, if she's smart, stays as warm and dry as she can, keeps hydrated, then you never know. People can be tougher than you think.'

Chase had to raise his voice as they rounded a bend and

came face to face with a curtain of white water. A river tumbled over a cliff edge and into the pool far beneath them. The falls roared as they walked out onto the bridge.

'Mirror Falls,' Chase said.

'This is amazing.' Carmen leaned against the railing, her hair whipping across her face. The fine spray seemed almost suspended in the crisp air. 'How high is it?'

'She's only a baby, about fifteen metres tall,' Chase said. 'But the pool at the bottom is at least as deep again and the water pressure is crazy so you wouldn't want to go over. The drop itself isn't too bad, it's more the shock and the cold that'll kill you. But you're lucky, this is the best time of year to see her, she's not as impressive in the summer. This year we were down to a trickle. Had the drought, you know?'

Falk clenched his hand with its slick new skin inside his pocket. Yes. He knew.

'But it's been good since the weather broke,' Chase went on. 'Great winter rainfall, so you can see why it gets the name.'

Falk could. At the foot of the crashing falls, most of the churning water was swept along by the river. But a deviation in the landscape had created a natural dip off to the side, an overflow into a pool that lay large and calm. It rippled gently, as its surface reflected the magnificent surroundings. An identical image, a few shades darker. Falk stood entranced, gazing down at the thundering white noise. Chase's radio beeped on his belt, breaking the spell.

'I'd better be getting back,' he said. 'If you're ready.'

'No worries.'

As Falk turned to follow Chase, his eye caught a splash of colour in the distance. On the far side of the falls, where the trail disappeared into deep bush, a tiny lone figure stared out over the water. A woman, Falk thought, her purple hat contrasting with the greens and browns of the surroundings.

'There's someone there,' Falk said to Carmen.

'Oh, yeah.' She looked to where he was pointing. 'Do you recognise her?'

'Not from this distance.'

'Me neither. Not Alice, though.'

'No.' The build was too thin, the hair poking out beneath the hat too dark. 'Unfortunately.'

The woman couldn't possibly have heard over the distance and the roar of the falls, but she turned her head sharply in their direction. Falk raised a hand, but the tiny figure didn't move. As they followed Chase to the trail, he glanced back once or twice. The woman continued to watch until the trees closed in behind them, and Falk could see her no more.

Day 2: Friday Morning

Beth unzipped the tent door from the inside, wincing as the noise vibrated across the canvas. She looked back. Her sister was still sleeping soundly, curled on her side, her eyelashes long against her cheeks and her hair casting a dark halo around her head.

She had always slept like that as a child. They both had, almost nose to nose, their hair entwined on the pillow, and their breath shared. Beth used to open her eyes each morning and see an image of herself looking back. That hadn't happened for a long time. And Beth didn't sleep curled up anymore. Beth's sleep these days was broken and uneasy.

She crawled out into the cold air and zipped the tent shut behind her, cringing as she slipped her boots on. They had got damp yesterday and stayed damp today. The sky was as grey and heavy as the day before. There was no movement from the other tents. She was alone.

She had an urge to wake her sister, so they could be alone together for the first time in . . . Beth wasn't sure how long. She wouldn't though. She'd seen Bree's look of disappointment when Alice had tossed the sisters' backpacks together in front of the same tent. Bree would rather share with her boss than her own sister.

Beth lit a cigarette, savouring the first drag and stretching her sore muscles. She wandered to the fire pit, where last night's embers lay black and cold. Discarded boil-in-the-bag wrappers had been stacked under a stone, their contents oozing gently. Old stew was smeared and crusted on the ground – an animal must have found it in the night – but there was still a lot left over. What a waste, Beth thought as her stomach rumbled. She had quite enjoyed hers.

A kookaburra perched nearby, watching her with its black eyes. She picked up a strip of beef from one of the abandoned packets and tossed it towards the bird, who scooped it up with the tip of her beak. Beth smoked as the bird jerked her head, whipping the meat back and forth. Satisfied at last that it was dead, the kookaburra swallowed it in one gulp and flew away, leaving Beth alone once more. She bent to stub out her cigarette and her boot caught a half-empty wine bottle. It toppled over, spilling its contents like a bloodstain on the ground.

'Shit.'

She felt the hot prickle of annoyance. Alice was a cheeky bitch. Beth had kept her mouth shut while Alice barked orders about the tents, but when she'd told her to fetch the booze, Beth had stared at her in confusion. Amused, Alice had opened Beth's bag herself and, rummaging around at the bottom, pulled out three bottles of wine. Beth had never seen them before.

'They're not mine.'

Alice had laughed. 'I know. They're for everyone.'

'So why were they in my bag?'

'Because they're for everyone.' She spoke slowly, as if to a child. 'We all have to help carry the supplies.'

'I'm already carrying my share. Those weigh a tonne. And . . .' She'd stopped.

'And what?'

'I'm not supposed to –'

'Supposed to what? Help?'

'No.' Beth had glanced at her sister but Bree was glaring back, her cheeks pink with embarrassment. *Stop kicking up a bloody fuss.* Beth sighed. 'I'm not supposed to be in possession of alcohol.'

'Well.' Alice tapped the bottles. 'Now you're not. Problem solved.'

'Does Jill know?'

Alice had stopped at that. The smile was still on her face, but the amusement was gone.

'What?'

'Does Jill know you put those in my bag?'

'It's a couple of bottles, Beth. Lodge a complaint if you feel that grievously injured.' Alice had waited, the silence stretching on until Beth had shaken her head. She'd seen Alice roll her eyes as she turned away.

Later, when Lauren had held out a bottle by the campfire, Beth had been more tempted than she'd been in a long time.

The bush seemed like the kind of place that kept secrets well. And Bree seemed too distracted to police her. The scent of the wine had been as warm and familiar as an embrace, and Beth had made herself say no before she accidentally said yes.

She wished Daniel Bailey hadn't brought the men over. That they hadn't brought the extra booze. She found it harder to resist in a group setting. It felt too much like a party, albeit a crap one.

It was the first time Beth had seen the chief executive in person. He didn't slum it down in the bowels of the data archives, and she had certainly never been invited up to the twelfth floor. But from the way people spoke about him, she'd somehow expected more. Around the campfire he'd just been one more bloke with a hundred-dollar haircut and a smile he'd obviously once been told was charming. Maybe he was different in the office.

Beth had been watching Daniel and considering this when she'd seen him take Alice aside and disappear with her into the dark. Was there something between them? Beth wondered. Something about his manner made her think not, but what did she know? It had been years since anyone had wanted to disappear into the dark with her.

She'd caught a snatch of their conversation as she'd wandered around the site, looking for someone to talk to. No. She'd been right the first time. Definitely not a prelude to pillow talk.

'The boss is a bit full of himself, isn't he?' Beth had whispered to her sister later, when they were zipped into their sleeping bags.

'He pays your salary, Beth. He's allowed to be.'

With that, Bree had rolled over, leaving Beth to stare at the canvas and long for a cigarette or, preferably, something stronger.

She stretched now, as the sky grew lighter, and was no longer able to ignore the ache in her bladder. She looked for the tree they'd earmarked in the dark as their makeshift toilet area. There it was. A short way from the clearing, behind the tents. The one with the broken branch.

Beth tramped over, careful where she put her feet. She didn't know much about the local wildlife, other than there were probably a heap of things out here that she wasn't keen to step on. Behind her, there was movement in the campsite. The rustle of a tent zipper, followed by low voices. Someone else was up.

At the tree she stopped. Was this it? It looked different in the daylight, but she thought it was right. There was that broken branch at head height. And if she concentrated, she thought she could detect the faint whiff of urine.

As she stood there, she heard voices float over from the campsite. They were speaking softly but she could still recognise them. Jill and Alice.

'You did have a bit to drink last night. Not just you, all of us –'

'No, Jill, it's not the booze. I just don't feel well. I need to go back.'

'We'd all have to go back with you.'

'I can find my way alone –'

'I can't let you walk back by yourself. No, listen to

me – there's a duty of care, for one thing. We'd all have to go.'

Alice didn't reply.

'And the company still has to pay so we'd forfeit the cost of the course for all five of us. Which obviously isn't important if you're unwell.' Jill let the disclaimer hang in the air. 'But we'd need a doctor's letter for the insurance so if it's a case of one too many wines –'

'Jill –'

'Or a rough first night in the tent. Believe me, I know this isn't anyone's cup of tea –'

'It's not –'

'And we can't get driven back to Melbourne until Sunday anyway, so as a senior team member it would be far better –'

'Yeah.' A sigh. 'All right.'

'You're well enough go on?'

A pause. 'I suppose so.'

'Good.'

The wind rattled the branches above Beth's head, dislodging a shower of water from the leaves. An icy drop ran down her neck and, instantly decided, she pulled down her jeans and squatted behind the tree. Her knees started to ache immediately and she could feel the cold on her thighs. She shifted her boot to miss the flow along the ground when she heard fast footfall behind her. Startled, she turned, toppling backwards with a bump. Her bare skin hit the ground, cold and warm and wet at the same time.

'Jesus Christ. Really? Right by the tents?'

Beth blinked up against the bright grey sky, her jeans around her knees, her palm in something warm. Alice stared back down. Her face was pale and tight. Maybe she really was ill, Beth thought vaguely.

'If you're too bloody lazy to walk out to where we agreed, at least have the manners to do it near your tent and not mine.'

'I thought –' Beth clambered to her feet, hauling up her jeans. Tight and twisted, they betrayed her with every tug. 'Sorry, I thought –' She was standing now, thank God, a single warm trickle damp against her inner thigh. 'I thought this was the right tree.'

'This one? It's barely a couple of metres from the tents.'

Beth risked a glance. It was more than a couple of metres, wasn't it? It had seemed more in the dark but it looked at least five.

'And it's not even downhill.'

'Okay. I said I was sorry.'

Beth longed to shush Alice, but it was already too late. A rustle of canvas and three heads popped up over the tents. Beth saw her sister's eyes harden. Bree didn't need to know exactly what she was seeing to know enough. *Beth's done it again.*

'Problem?' Jill called.

'No. It's under control.' Alice straightened. 'That's the right tree.' She pointed at a spot in the distance. Not a broken branch in sight.

Beth turned to the three faces at the tents. 'Sorry. I thought – I'm sorry.'

'You see the one I mean?' Alice said, still pointing.

'Yeah, I can see it. Look, I'm sor–'

'It's all right, Beth,' Jill called, cutting her off. 'And thank you, Alice. I think we're all familiar with the tree now.'

Alice kept her eyes on Beth, then slowly lowered her arm. Beth didn't look at any of the others as she trudged back to the clearing, her face hot. Her sister stood at their tent entrance, not speaking, the whites of her eyes bloodshot. She was hungover, Beth could tell, and Breanna didn't do hungover well.

Beth ducked inside, zipping the door shut. She could smell the urine on her only pair of jeans and felt a tight ball burning behind her eyes. She squeezed them closed and made herself stay completely still, like they had taught her in the rehab centre. Deep breaths and positive thoughts until the urge passed. *In and out.*

As she counted her breaths, focusing her mind, she imagined inviting the other women to stand with her in a circle. The image was clear and Beth could picture herself extending a hand to Alice. *In and out.* Beth imagined herself reaching up, stretching out her fingers and winding them through Alice's blonde highlights. *In and out.* Tightening her grip and pulling the woman's expensive face towards the ground. Grinding it into the dirt until she thrashed and squealed. *In and out.* When she reached one hundred, Beth breathed out a final time and smiled to herself. Her counsellor had been right. Visualising what she wanted really did make her feel a lot better.

Chapter 7

It was a relief to exit the Mirror Falls trail. Falk took a deep breath as the sky opened and the trees parted. Up ahead, light spilled from the windows of the lodge, its glow not quite reaching the dark undergrowth of the path. He and Carmen followed Chase across the carpark, feeling the gravel crunch under their boots. As they neared the lodge, Falk felt Carmen tap his arm.

'Two for one over there,' she whispered.

Daniel Bailey was standing beside his black BMW with a woman Falk instantly recognised. His sister, Jill. Even from that distance, Falk could see the stain of a bruise across her jaw, and he remembered what Sergeant King had said. *Some injuries.* Jill hadn't had that bruise in the group photo from the first day, that was for sure.

Now, she was face to face with her brother and they were arguing. The frozen-muscled, tight-lipped argument of people conditioned not to make a public scene.

Jill was leaning in as she spoke. She jerked her hand

towards the bushland then immediately away. He responded with a single shake of the head. Jill tried again, leaning in closer. Daniel Bailey looked past her, over her shoulder. Avoiding her eye. Another shake of the head. *I said no.*

Jill stared at him, her face impassive, then without another word, turned and walked up the steps and into the lodge. Bailey leaned against his car and watched until she disappeared. He shook his head and his gaze landed on Ian Chase in his red Executive Adventures fleece. He looked embarrassed for a moment at having been caught arguing but swiftly recovered.

'Hey!' Bailey raised an arm, his voice ringing across the carpark. 'Any news?'

They walked over. It was the first chance Falk had had to see Daniel Bailey up close. His mouth was set firm and there was definite tension around his eyes, but he still managed to look younger than his forty-seven years. He also looked a lot like the photos Falk had seen of his father, who was still on the board and a firm fixture in the company brochure. Daniel was less bent and wrinkled than Leo Bailey, but the resemblance was clear.

Bailey looked over at Falk and Carmen with polite interest. Falk waited, but could detect no visible spark of recognition in his eyes. He felt a small stirring of relief. That was something, at least.

'Nothing new to tell you, I'm afraid,' Chase said. 'Not yet anyway.'

Bailey shook his head. 'For Christ's sake, they said they'd have her back today.'

'*Hoped* to have her today.'

'Would more funds help? I've said we'll pay. They know that, don't they?'

'It's not the money. It's everything else.' Chase glanced at the bushland. 'You know what it's like in there.'

Before they'd left the search site, Sergeant King had unfolded a grid map and shown Falk and Carmen the areas to be combed through. It took about four hours to properly search one square kilometre, he'd said. And that was in medium-density bushland. Longer if the terrain was thick or steep or had a water crossing. Falk had started to count the number of squares. He'd given up when he'd hit twenty.

'Have they searched the north-west ridge yet?' Bailey said.

'It's inaccessible this year. And too dangerous in this weather.'

'All the more reason to check it, no? It's easy to get off track around there.'

There was something about the way Bailey was demanding answers that rang a little hollow.

Falk cleared his throat. 'This must be very difficult for you and your staff. Do you know the missing woman well?'

Bailey looked at him properly for the first time, both a frown and a question in his eyes. 'Are you –?'

'They're police,' Chase said. 'Helping out with the search.'

'Oh, right. Good. Thank you.' Bailey held out a hand, introduced himself. His palm was cold, and the tips of his fingers were calloused. Not the hand of a man who spent all of his time stuck behind a desk. Bailey obviously got out and about in some form or another.

'So you do know her well?' Falk repeated as they shook.

'Alice?' Bailey's frown deepened. 'Yes. Quite well. She's worked with us for four years –'

Five, actually, Falk thought.

'– so she's a valued team member. I mean, they all are, of course. But for her to drop off the radar like this –' Bailey shook his head. 'It's very worrying.' He sounded like he meant it.

'You didn't see Alice Russell before she set off with her group on Thursday, is that right?' Carmen asked.

'No. I arrived late. I'd been held up. I missed the group bus.'

'May I ask why?'

Bailey looked at her. 'It was a private family matter.'

'I guess heading up a family firm you're never really off the clock.' Carmen's voice was light.

'No, that's true.' Bailey managed a tight smile. 'I do try to keep some sort of separation though, where possible. You'd go mad otherwise. This was unavoidable, unfortunately. I apologised to the other team members. It wasn't ideal, obviously, but it only set us back about an hour. It made no real difference in the end.'

'Your team didn't have any trouble reaching the meeting spot on time?' Falk said.

'No. It's challenging terrain, but the routes themselves aren't overly difficult. Or they're not supposed to be, anyway.' Bailey glanced at Chase, who dropped his eyes.

'It sounds like you know the area?' Falk said.

'A bit. I've done a couple of hiking weekends here. And we've run winter corporate retreats here with Executive Adventures for the last three years,' Bailey said. 'It's a great spot. Usually. But not the kind of place where you want to stay lost for long.'

'And you've always come on the retreats?'

'It's the best excuse I have to get out of the office.' Bailey started to form an automatic smile, then caught himself halfway, leaving his face locked in an unfortunate grimace. 'We've always found the retreats to be very good and generally well organised. We've always been pleased, until –' He broke off. 'Well, until now.'

Chase continued to stare at the ground.

'You did see Alice Russell during the retreat, though,' Falk said.

Bailey blinked. 'On the first night, you mean?'

'Was there any other time?'

'No.' His reply was almost too quick. 'Only that first night. It was a social call between camps.'

'Whose idea was that?'

'Mine. It's good for us to connect in a different space from the office. We're all one company. All in the same boat.'

'And you spoke to Alice Russell then?' Falk watched Bailey closely.

'Briefly, at the start, but we weren't there for long. We left when it started to rain.'

'What did you talk about?'

Bailey furrowed his brow. 'Nothing, really. General office chat.'

'Even on a social visit?' Carmen said.

A tiny smile. 'Like you say, I'm never really off the clock.'

'And how did she seem to you that night?'

A beat. 'She seemed fine. But we didn't speak for long.'

'You didn't have any concerns about her?' Falk said.

'Like what?'

'Anything. Her health, her mental state? Her ability to complete the course?'

'If I had any doubts about Alice, or any of our employees,' Bailey said, 'I would do something about it.'

Somewhere, deep in the bush, a bird called, sharp and shrill. He frowned and glanced at his watch.

'I'm sorry. Look, thanks for your help with the search, but I'm going to have to make a move. I want to drive up to the site in time for the night briefing.'

Chase shifted his weight. 'I'm going up there myself. Do you want a lift?'

Bailey patted the roof of his BMW. 'I'm good, thanks.'

He fished out his keys and with another round of handshakes and a brief wave was gone, invisible behind the tinted glass as the car drove away.

Chase watched him leave, then looked somewhat forlornly at the Executive Adventures minibus hulking in the corner of the carpark.

'I'd better get up there myself. I'll let you know if there's any update,' he said, and trudged off, keys in hand. Falk and Carmen found themselves alone once more.

'I'd love to know why Bailey was late getting up here,' Carmen said. 'Do you believe it was a family issue?'

'I don't know,' Falk said. 'BaileyTennants is a family firm. That could cover pretty much anything.'

'Yeah. Although, I have to say, if I owned a car like his, I'd have missed the bus too.'

They walked over to their own sedan, parked in the far corner. Grit and leaves had collected in the crevices, and flew up in a haze as they opened the boot. Falk pulled out his battered backpack and hoisted it onto his shoulder.

'I thought you said you weren't into hiking,' Carmen said.

'I'm not.'

'You should tell your bag. It looks like it's on its last legs.'

'Oh. Yeah. It's been pretty well used. Not by me, though.' Falk said no more, but Carmen was looking at him expectantly. He sighed. 'It used to be my dad's.'

'That's nice. He gave it to you?'

'Kind of. He died. So I took it.'

'Oh. Shit. I'm sorry.'

'It's okay. He doesn't need it anymore. Come on.'

Falk turned before she could say anything further and they walked across the carpark into the lodge reception area. It was like a furnace compared with the outside, and he felt the sweat prickle on his skin. The same ranger as before was behind the welcome desk. He checked the list of rooms reserved for police and searchers and handed them each a key.

'Back out the way you came, follow the walkway round

to the left,' he said. 'You're at the end of the row, next to each other.'

'Thanks.'

They headed out and around the side of the lodge until they came to a long, sturdy, wooden hut. It had been split into individual cabins with a shared porch stretching along the front. Falk could hear the tap of rain start against the tin roof as they walked along. Their rooms were right at the end, as promised.

'Regroup in twenty minutes?' Carmen said, and disappeared through her door.

Inside, Falk's room was small but surprisingly cosy. A bed took up most of the space, with a wardrobe crammed into one corner and a door leading to a tiny ensuite. Falk shrugged off his coat and checked his mobile. No signal here either.

He propped his backpack – his dad's backpack – against the wall. It looked tatty against the clean white paintwork. Falk wasn't quite sure why he'd brought it. He had other bags he could have used. He'd found it at the very back of his wardrobe while he was digging out his hiking boots. He'd almost forgotten it was there. Almost, but not quite. Falk had pulled the bag out, then sat on the floor for a long time in his quiet flat, looking at it.

He hadn't been fully honest with Carmen. He hadn't so much taken the bag when his dad died seven years earlier as been handed it by a specialist cancer nurse at the hospice. It had been light, but not empty, containing Erik Falk's final few possessions.

93

It had taken Falk a long time to go through the bag and even longer to donate or otherwise dispose of the belongings inside. In the end, he'd been left with only the bag and three other items. Two photos and a separate large, worn envelope. The envelope was creased and tired around the edges and had never been sealed.

Now, Falk opened the top pocket of the backpack and pulled it out. The envelope was even more battered than he remembered. He spread the contents across the bed. Contours, gradients, shadings and symbols lay in front of him. Peaks and valleys and bushland and beachfront. Nature's best, all there on paper.

As Falk's fingers ran over the maps, he felt almost dizzy from the surge of familiarity. There were more than two dozen. Some were old, and some better used than others, their paper thin and well examined. His dad had corrected them, of course. He knew best. Thought he knew best, anyway. Erik Falk's handwriting looped and curved across the routes of the state's major hiking regions. Observations he'd made each time he'd tied up his boots, hoisted the bag on his back and left the city behind him with a grateful sigh.

It had been a very long time since Falk had looked at the pages. And he'd never been able to bring himself to examine them closely. He shuffled through the maps now until he found the one he was searching for: Giralang Ranges and the surrounds. It was an older one and was yellowed at the corners. The folds were fragile and fuzzy.

Falk took off his boots and lay back on the bed, letting

his head sink into the pillow, just for a minute. His eyes felt heavy. It was much warmer inside than out. He opened the map at random, squinting against the light. The grey pencil marks had faded in places over time and the words blurred at the edges. Falk pulled the map closer to his face and felt the blunted ache of well-worn irritation. His dad's handwriting had always been bloody impossible to read. He tried to focus.

Water spot. Campsite: unofficial. Blocked path.

Falk blinked again, for longer this time. The cabin was warm.

Short cut. Lookout point. Fallen tree.

Blink. The wind bayed outside, pressing itself against the glass of the window.

Not safe in winter. Take care.

An echoed warning.

Tread carefully. Danger here.

Falk closed his eyes.

Day 2: Friday Morning

It took longer than expected to pack up the campsite. The tents refused to fold quite as small as they had originally, and the zippers on their bags jammed and strained in protest.

Jill knew that her backpack could be no heavier than it had been the day before. She knew it, but as she swung it on her shoulders, she didn't believe it. They were already behind schedule, but she let the others linger in the weak morning light, fiddling with straps and water bottles. She felt reluctant to leave the campsite, and suspected she wasn't the only one. The other sites along the trail were smaller and less well established, she knew, but it wasn't just that. There was something about leaving the safety of the start point for the unknown ahead that made her feel a little edgy.

Jill had kept half an eye on Alice while packing. The woman had barely spoken and had had to be asked twice for the tent pole bag. But she wasn't ill, Jill was certain.

And she wasn't going to get permission to leave this trip early. Jill was certain of that as well.

She watched Alice gather up the empty wine bottles and bag of communal rubbish and hand them straight to Beth. No remorse about the morning's outburst, apparently. Jill was debating whether to say something, but Beth simply took the rubbish and put it her backpack without comment. Jill let it slide. She'd learned how to pick her battles.

An hour late and all excuses exhausted, they at last started to walk. Alice soon pulled out ahead, with Bree clutching the map and trailing at her heels. Jill watched the backs of their heads and shifted her pack. She could feel the straps rubbing on her shoulders. The man in the shop had told her they were made from special breathable material for added comfort. The memory of that conversation infused Jill with a sense of deep and lasting betrayal.

At least the path was flat, but its uneven surface meant she had to watch her feet. She stumbled once, then again, nearly losing her balance this time. She felt a steadying hand grasp her arm.

'Are you all right?' Lauren said.

'Yes. Thanks. I'm not used to the boots.'

'Painful?'

'A bit,' she admitted.

'Two layers of socks might help. A thin pair under a thick pair. Listen, Jill –' Lauren's voice dropped a notch lower. 'I wanted to apologise.'

'For what?' She knew. Or perhaps she didn't. When Jill

thought about it, Lauren could be feeling guilty about a number of things.

'The other week, at the briefing,' Lauren said. 'I mean, I'm sorry I wasn't *at* the briefing. But Andrew said he could make the presentation alone and –' She stopped. 'I'm sorry. I should have been there, I know. I've been under some pressure at home lately.'

Jill looked over at that. Pressure at home was one language she spoke.

'Is it anything we can offer you some support for?'

'No. Unfortunately. Thank you, though.' Lauren kept staring straight ahead. She was very thin these days, Jill noticed now, the bones in her neck and wrists sliding against her skin.

'Are you sure?'

'Yes.'

'All right. Because the briefing –'

'I really am sorry –'

'I know, but it wasn't the first time for something like that. Or even the second.'

'It won't happen again.'

'Are you sure, Lauren? Because –'

'Yes. I'm sure. Things will improve.'

Things would have to, Jill thought. Lauren had been high on the list in the latest round of cuts. Highest, in fact, until Alice had argued for a merger of part-time roles to make equivalent savings. Jill also suspected Alice had covered for Lauren at least twice in recent months, narrowly averting mistakes in the making. If Jill was aware of two instances, there were almost certainly more. She knew the two women went back a long way. What that meant for Lauren was another question.

Up ahead, they could see Alice's head, fair against the gloomy trail. Jill thought of something.

'You did a good job with the fire last night. I saw you light it.'

'Oh. Thanks. I learned it at school.'

'They taught you well.'

'You'd hope so. It was the Endeavour Ladies' College full-year special at their McAllaster Outdoor Campus. A long time to learn all sorts of things out there. Alice went as well.' Lauren looked at Jill. 'You must have gone to private school, didn't yours do something like that?'

'I was educated in Switzerland.'

'Oh. I suppose not, then.'

'Thank God.' Jill glanced sideways with a small smile. 'I'm not sure I could cope with a year of this sort of thing.'

Lauren smiled back but Jill could sense the unasked question in her eyes. If Jill was so uncomfortable, why agree to this at all? Jill had lost count of the thousand different ways the question had been framed over the past thirty years, but her answer had always been the same. BaileyTennants was a family firm. And Jill Bailey did what was best for the family.

'Anyway,' Lauren said. 'That's all I wanted to say, really. I do realise things haven't been good enough at work.'

Ahead, Jill saw Alice and Bree had stopped. The track had hit a fork, a path to the left, a smaller one to the right. Bree had pulled out the map and was sitting on a stump, examining it, her nose close to the paper. Alice stood, hands on hips, watching her. She looked up as they approached, her blue eyes alert and head tilted. Jill wondered suddenly if she'd been listening to their conversation. No. Surely she was too far away.

'And I'm really grateful for my job and the opportunities.' Lauren had lowered her voice. 'And for your patience. I want you to know I'll make it up to you.'

Jill nodded. Up ahead, Alice was still watching.

'I know you will.'

Chapter 8

When Falk awoke with a start, the window outside his cabin was darker than he remembered. He heard the rustle of paper and looked down. His dad's map was still open across his chest. He rubbed a hand over his eyes and squinted at the rain hitting the window pane. It took a moment before he realised the tapping was coming from the door.

'You took your time,' Carmen said as he opened it, a cold rush of air sweeping in with her.

'Sorry. I was asleep. Come in.' Falk looked around the room. No chairs. He pulled the dent in the bedspread straight. 'Take a seat.'

'Thanks.' Carmen cleared a space among the maps on the bedspread. 'What are all these?'

'Nothing. They used to belong to my dad.'

Carmen picked up the Giralang Ranges map lying open on the top of the pile. 'This one's all marked up.'

'Yeah. They all are. It was kind of his hobby.'

'I don't suppose there's a big black X with the words "Alice is here" on it?' Carmen said. She examined the pencil markings. 'My nanna used to do this to her recipe books, write little notes and corrections. I've still got them all. It's nice, like she's talking to me. And she was right. Half a teaspoon of juice mixed in with the zest will give you the best lemon drizzle cake you've ever tasted in your life.' She put down the map she was holding and picked up another. 'Did you visit these trails together?'

Falk shook his head. 'No.'

'What, none of them?'

Falk stacked the maps slowly. 'We didn't really see eye to eye.' His mouth felt dry and he swallowed.

'Why not?'

'It's a long story.'

'Is there a short version?'

Falk looked down at the maps. 'When I was sixteen, Dad sold our farm and moved us to Melbourne. I didn't want him to, but there'd been a lot of trouble in our home-town. Things there went south pretty fast, and I think Dad thought he was doing it for my benefit. I don't know, he felt he had to get me away, I suppose.'

As an adult, years later and with the benefit of twenty-twenty hindsight, Falk knew a part of him could now understand that. At the time, he'd simply felt sold out. It had seemed wrong, running away to the city with the scent of fear and suspicion lodged in their nostrils.

'It was supposed to be a fresh start,' he said. 'But it didn't really work out like that. Dad hated it. I wasn't much better.' He stopped. And they had never talked about it. Not about their past life, not about their new life. The unspoken words had hung between them like a veil, and it was as if a new layer had been added every year. It grew so thick that by the end, Falk felt he couldn't even see the man on the other side. He sighed. 'Anyway, every weekend he could, Dad used to pack a bag, drive out somewhere and go hiking. Use his maps.'

'You were never tempted to go along?'

'No. I don't know. He used to ask. At first, anyway. But you know, I was sixteen, seventeen. Angry.'

Carmen smiled. 'Aren't most kids at that age?'

'I suppose.' It hadn't always been the case, though. Falk could remember a time when he used to follow his dad like a shadow. Out on the paddocks on their farm, his head no higher than the low fence line as he chased his dad's long, steady paces. The heavy sun had made their shadows even taller and their blond hair glow almost white. Falk had, he remembered, wanted to be just like him. That was another thing he could see with the cold clarity of hindsight. The pedestal had been too high.

Carmen was saying something.

'Sorry?'

'I asked what your mum made of it all?'

'Oh. Nothing. She died when I was really young.'

Giving birth to him in fact, but Falk avoided specifying that where possible. It seemed to make people very uncomfortable, and prompted some – women, usually – to look at him with an appraising glint in their eye. *Were you*

103

worth it? He avoided asking himself the same question, but at times caught himself wondering what his mother's last thoughts had been. He hoped not entirely full of regret.

'Anyway. That's how I ended up with these.' He added the last of the maps to the stack, put them aside. Enough. Carmen took the hint. The wind whistled and they both looked over as the window rattled in its frame.

'So. No Alice,' Carmen said.

'Not yet.'

'What now, then? Is there any mileage in us staying up here tomorrow?'

'I don't know.' Falk sighed and leaned back against the headboard. The search was in professional hands. Even if she were found in the next hour – in any state from safe and sound to weather-beaten and bloodied – Falk knew they would have to find another way to get the contracts they needed. Alice Russell would not be returning to work immediately, if at all.

'Daniel Bailey didn't know who we were,' he said. 'Or if he did, he did a good job of hiding it.'

'No. I agree.'

'It's almost enough to make me feel this has nothing to do with us, except . . . ' He glanced at his phone, silent on the bedside table.

'I know.' Carmen nodded.

The recording. *Hurt her.*

Falk rubbed his eyes. 'Forget what was said for now. Why would Alice try to call me from out there?'

'I don't know. It sounds like she tried to call triple zero

first but couldn't get through.' Carmen thought for a moment. 'Still, honestly, you would not be the person I'd be calling if I were stuck out there.'

'Thanks. Even with all my maps?'

'Even so. But you know what I mean. It has to be something to do with us. Or you. I can only think she was backing out. Did she seem worried last time you spoke to her?'

'You were there,' Falk said. 'Last week.'

'Oh right. No other contact since then?'

It had been a forgettable meeting. Five minutes in the carpark of a large supermarket. *We need the contracts*, they had said. *The ones linking to Leo Bailey. Please prioritise them.* It had been framed as a request. The tone had made it clear it was an order. Alice had snapped that she was doing her best.

'Did we push her too hard?' Falk said. 'Make her somehow slip up?'

'We didn't push her any harder than usual.'

Falk wasn't sure that was true. They'd been feeling the pressure from above themselves and had duly passed it down the line. Shit rolling downhill, the most traditional of business models and one Falk was sure Alice would be familiar with. *Get the Leo Bailey contracts.* The Chinese whisper passed from their ears to Alice Russell's. Falk and Carmen had not been entrusted with the significance, but the secrecy surrounding the order spoke volumes. *Get the contracts.* Alice Russell may have disappeared, but the pressure from above had not. *Get the contracts.*

That was the priority. Still, Falk glanced again at his phone. *Hurt her.*

'If Alice slipped up, someone had to notice for it to cause problems,' Carmen said. 'What about speaking to Alice's assistant? Breanna McKenzie. If something's up with the boss, the assistant's usually the first to know.'

'Yeah. I suppose the question is whether she'd tell us or not.' Falk thought that might depend on how much shit Alice herself had sent rolling in her assistant's direction over time.

'All right.' Carmen squeezed her eyes shut, rubbed a hand over her face. 'We'd better let the office know. You haven't spoken to them today?'

'Not since last night.' Falk had called in after getting off the phone with Sergeant King. News of Alice Russell's disappearance had not gone down well.

'Do you want me to take the hit?'

'It's all right.' Falk smiled. 'I'll do this one.'

'Thanks.' Carmen sighed, leaned back. 'If Alice had a problem before the retreat, she would have called us before setting off. So whatever's happened, it happened in there, yes?'

'Seems that way. Ian Chase said she seemed all right when they set off. Not that he would necessarily be able to tell.'

If they knew one thing about Alice, it was that the woman was good at putting on a front. Or at least, Falk hoped she was.

'Where's that CCTV footage from the service

106

station?' Carmen said. 'The bit showing the group on its way up here.'

Falk pulled his laptop out of his bag. He found the memory stick the service station attendant had given him earlier and opened the computer screen so Carmen could see. She moved in a little closer.

The footage was in colour, but the screen was mostly a mass of grey as the camera focused on the paved forecourt around the petrol pumps. There was no sound but the image was decent quality. The recording covered the past seven days and cars zipped on and off the screen as Falk fast-forwarded through to Thursday. When the time stamp ticked around to mid-afternoon, he pressed play and they watched for a few minutes.

'There.' Carmen pointed as a minivan pulled up. 'That's it, isn't it?'

The footage held steady from its high vantage point as the driver's door opened. Chase climbed out. His lanky figure in its red fleece was entirely recognisable as he walked to the pump.

On screen, the main door of the vehicle slid open, thumping silently on its hinges. An Asian guy climbed out, followed by two dark-haired blokes and a balding man. The bald man headed towards the shop while the other three stood in a loose group, stretching and chatting. Behind them, a large woman clambered out, stepping down heavily.

'Jill,' Carmen said, and they watched as Jill Bailey pulled out her phone. She tapped at it, put it to her ear, then pulled it away, staring at the screen. Falk didn't need a clear view of her face to sense her frustration.

'Who was she trying to call?' he said. 'Daniel, maybe?'

'Maybe.'

Just then a woman stepped down onto the forecourt, her long dark ponytail swinging across her shoulder.

'Is that Breanna?' Carmen said. 'It looks like her photo.'

The dark-haired woman looked around, turning as a third woman climbed out of the van.

Carmen breathed out. 'There she is.'

Alice Russell stepped out, blonde and lithe as she stretched her arms up like a cat. She said something to the dark-haired girl, who was hovering at her elbow. They both took out their phones, their body language mirroring Jill's from a minute earlier. Check, tap, check, *nothing*. The slight shoulder slump of frustration.

The dark-haired woman put her phone away, but Alice kept hers in hand. She peered through one of the minivan windows, where a hefty shape was pressed up dark against the glass. The footage was not clear enough to make out the specifics but to Falk, everything about it suggested the relaxed vulnerability of a sleeping form.

They watched as Alice held up her phone to the window. There was a flash, then she checked the screen, showing it to the three men standing nearby. They laughed soundlessly. Alice showed the dark-haired girl who paused, then turned up her mouth in a pixelated smile. Inside the van, the shape moved, the window lightening and darkening as the form shifted. The hint of a face appeared behind the glass, features invisible but body language clear. *What's going on?*

Alice turned away, a single wave of her hand, instantly dismissive. *Nothing. It's only a joke.*

The face remained at the window until Chase came out of the shop. He was with the service station attendant. Falk recognised the guy's hat. The two men stood chatting on the forecourt while the BaileyTennants team climbed back into the van.

Alice Russell was the last one in, her porcelain features disappearing as the door slammed behind her. Chase slapped the attendant on the back and slipped into the driver's seat. The minivan shuddered as the engine started and the tyres rolled.

The attendant stood watching as the vehicle pulled away. He was the only one there.

'Lonely job,' Falk said.

'Yeah.'

After a few seconds, the attendant turned and walked off camera, leaving the forecourt a deserted slab of grey once more. Falk and Carmen watched as the footage ran on, nothing moving on the screen. Finally, Carmen sat back.

'So, no real surprises there. Alice is a bit of a bitch who rubs people up the wrong way. We knew that already.'

'She looked relaxed enough then,' Falk said. 'More than she ever is with us.' That wasn't particularly surprising either, he thought.

Carmen stifled a yawn, hand over her mouth. 'Sorry, the early start's catching up with me.'

'I know.' Outside the window, the sky had turned a deep blue. Falk could see their faces reflected in the glass. 'Let's call it a day.'

'You'll ring the office?' Carmen said as she stood to leave, and Falk nodded. 'And we'll go to the hospital tomorrow, see what Alice's assistant has to say. Who knows?' She gave a grim smile. 'Getting a snakebite on company time would be enough to piss me off. Maybe she's feeling chatty.'

A fresh blast of cold air as she opened the door, and she was gone.

Falk looked at the landline phone on the bedside table. He picked it up and dialled a familiar number, then sat on the bed as he listened to the tone, ringing a few hundred kilometres west in Melbourne. It was answered quickly.

Had the woman been found? No. Not yet. Had they got the contracts? No. Not yet. When would they get the contracts? Falk didn't know. A pause at the other end of the line. They needed to get the contracts. Yes. It was imperative. Yes, he understood. There was a time factor, others were waiting. Yes, he knew. He understood.

Falk sat and listened, letting the shit roll down the hill in his direction. The occasional word of affirmation. He understood what they were saying. But so he should, he had heard it all before.

His eyes fell on the stack of maps, and as he listened, he shuffled through, opening the Giralang Ranges cover. Ordered grid markings were filled with winding routes, showing other paths to other places. He followed the lines with a finger as he listened down the phone. Was Alice out there now, looking at those same lines by torchlight or moonlight, scanning the landscape as she tried to connect print with reality? Or, a voice whispered, was it too late for that? Falk hoped not.

He looked up at the window. It was too bright in the room; all he could see was his reflection holding the phone. He reached over and snapped off the bedside light. Darkness. As his vision adjusted, blue-black details outside came into focus. He could make out the Mirror Falls trailhead a way in the distance. The trees on either side seemed to breathe and pulse in the wind.

At the trailhead there was a sudden glimmer of light and Falk leaned forward. What was that? As he watched, a silhouette emerged from the tree line, head down, hunched over against the elements, walking as briskly as the wind would allow. Running, almost. A thin beam of torchlight bouncing at their feet.

It was dark and cold to be out for a walk. Falk stood and put his face close to the glass, the receiver still at his ear. In the dark, from that distance, the figure's features were invisible. A woman, though, he thought. Something about the way she moved. He could see no flash of reflective clothing. Whoever it was, they weren't part of the official search team.

In Falk's ear, the one-sided conversation was slowing.

Get the contracts. Yes. Get them soon. Yes. Don't let us down. No.

A click, and it was over, for now. Falk stood, the receiver dead in his hand.

Outside, the figure skirted the path, avoiding the light spilling from the lodge into the carpark. She – they? – rounded the building and disappeared from view.

Falk hung up, and looked at his mobile lying useless next to the landline. *Hurt her.* He wavered for a second, then snatched up his key and pulled open the door. Cursing the far end position of his cabin, he jogged along the walkway, the frigid air sliding under his clothing and up against his skin. He wished he'd grabbed his coat. He rounded the corner of the lodge, scanning the empty carpark, not sure what he was hoping to find.

It was deserted. He stopped and listened. Any sound of footsteps was buried by the wind. Falk jogged up the stairs and into the lodge, hearing a clink of cutlery and the faint sounds of chatter floating from the kitchen area. A different ranger sat alone behind the desk.

'Did someone come in here?'

'Other than you?'

Falk gave her a look and the ranger shook her head.

'You didn't see a woman outside?' he said.

'No-one in the last ten minutes.'

'Thanks.' He pushed back outside. It was like plunging into a swimming pool and he folded his arms across his chest. He stared out into the bushland then crunched across the gravel towards the trailhead.

All ahead was dark, the lights of the lodge brilliant behind him. Over his shoulder, he could see what he thought was his own cabin window in the middle distance, the window a blank square. Beneath his boots, the path was a mess of footprints. There was a rustle as a bat darted overheard, a jagged shape against the night sky. Other than that, the trail was deserted.

Falk turned in a slow circle, the wind biting at his skin. He was alone. Whoever had been there was gone.

Day 2: Friday Morning

Bree was sweating. Despite the cold, the moisture clung to her skin and she could smell the alcohol coming from her pores as she walked. She felt disgusting.

Her head had been aching since waking up. Packing the campsite made it worse and the whole thing had taken ages, far longer than it should have. Only Alice had seemed keen to get moving. Bree had seen her shove a tent into a bag with so much force she worried she might rip it. Bree hadn't offered to help. She was having enough trouble with her own tent.

With the zip finally closed, Bree had ducked behind a distant tree and vomited, hot and silent. How much had she had to drink last night? She couldn't remember refilling her glass, but she couldn't remember it being empty, either. It was the bloody men's fault, she thought, and felt a spike of anger. Not so much at them, but at herself. She was usually more switched on to things like that.

Bree now wiped a bead of sweat from her eye as she

stared at Alice's back. Alice had pulled out ahead soon after setting off and Bree was struggling to keep up for once. Had Alice seen her drinking too much last night? She hoped not. Alice had been safely tucked away talking to Daniel most of the time. When Bree had next seen her, her head already swimming a little, Alice had been walking towards the tents. Bree may have got away with it last night, but she knew she was paying for it now.

Twice that morning they'd hit forks in the trail, and twice Alice had stopped and looked over. Bree had checked the map, ignoring the rocks clanging in her head, and pointed out the direction. With a nod, Alice had walked on without a word.

Bree heard a low groan behind her. It could have come from any of the others. She guessed shoulders, heels and nerves were all starting to fray. The track had grown thin and they'd resorted to single file a few kilometres earlier. The uphill gradient was enough to discourage talking. Ahead, Alice stopped once more as the trail turned a gentle corner and widened, splitting into two. Bree heard another groan behind her. Definitely Jill this time.

'Hold on, up there,' Jill called. 'Let's break here for lunch.'

Bree breathed out with relief but Alice checked her watch. 'It's still quite early,' she called back.

'It's not that early. This is a good place to stop.'

It wasn't really, Bree thought as she set her backpack down. The ground was muddy and there was no view other than the trees towering over them. She shivered and sat down on her pack, her legs a little wobbly. It was colder now they'd stopped moving. Quiet too, without the sound of footfall. She could make out the chirp and squeak of invisible birds. Bree heard a rustle in the bush behind her and spun around, her thoughts plunging down a black hole and landing with a thump before the spectre of Martin Kovac.

There was nothing there, of course. Bree turned back, feeling silly. It *was* silly. She was too young to remember the stories from the time, but she had made the mistake of stumbling across them online while looking up information about the Giralang Ranges. She'd been at her office desk absorbed in the fate of the last alleged victim – Sarah Sondenberg, eighteen and never found – when the junior accounts manager had come up behind, startling her.

'You be careful out in Giralang,' he'd said with a grin and a nod at the screen. 'She looks a bit like you.'

'You be careful I don't report that kind of comment to HR.' Their mild flirtation had been ramping up over the past month. Bree thought she would probably say yes when he finally asked her out for a drink.

Once he'd gone, she'd looked back at the screen. Did Sarah Sondenberg really look like her? Maybe a little around the nose and mouth. The girl was pretty, there was no doubt about that. But in her own way. Besides, Sarah Sondenberg was blonde, blue-eyed. Bree had shut down the website, and thought no more about it, until now.

She checked once more over her shoulder. Nothing. Still, perhaps it would be best if this were a short break.

She took a gulp from her water bottle to try to ease the ache in her head, and closed her eyes.

'Could you please move away if you're going to do that?'

Bree winced at Alice's voice and prised her eyes back open. Alice wasn't talking to her, of course. Not like that. But she was looking at Beth, who was leaning against a tree, lit cigarette in hand.

Christ, all this fresh air and her sister couldn't wait to pollute it. Immediately, she heard their mum's voice in her ear. *Leave her alone, better she's addicted to the ciggies than . . .* Her mum would always trail off then. She could never bring herself to say the word.

Beth shrugged and Bree watched her trudge away, the trail of smoke mingling with the scent of eucalyptus in the air. Alice fanned her hand.

'Lunch,' a voice said.

Bree looked up to see Lauren standing over her, holding out a cheese roll wrapped in cellophane and an apple.

'Oh. Thanks.' She tried to smile, but her stomach lurched at the thought.

'You should eat.' Lauren was still standing over her. 'It'll help.'

The woman made no attempt to move until Bree had unwrapped a corner and nibbled a bit of crust. Lauren watched her swallow before moving on.

Alice shot a glance at Bree as if seeing her properly for the first time that day. 'Too much to drink last night?'

'Just tired,' Bree said. 'I didn't sleep well.'

'Join the club.'

Alice did look pale, Bree saw now, surprised she hadn't noticed before.

'Are you okay to navigate?' Alice said.

'Yes. Definitely.'

'Are you sure? It'll eat up a lot of time if we go wrong.'

'I know. We won't.'

The words came out a little louder than she'd meant and Jill looked up. She was sitting on a rock further along the path with one boot off, fiddling with her sock.

'Everything all right?'

'Good, thank you,' Bree said at the same time as Alice said: 'Bree's tired from last night.'

Jill looked from one to the other. 'Right.'

'I'm not. I'm fine.'

Jill said nothing for a minute, but something in her face made Bree think she may have seen more last night than Alice had. Bree felt her cheeks grow hot.

'Do you want someone to take over with the map for a while?' Jill's voice was light.

'No. Not at all. Thank you. I can do it.'

'All right.' Jill turned back to her sock. 'But please say if you do.'

'I don't. Thank you.'

Bree bit the tip of her tongue in irritation. She could feel Alice still watching her, and she tried to focus on the sandwich in her lap. She took a small mouthful to stop herself from speaking, but found it hard to swallow. After a moment, she rewrapped the sandwich and stuffed it into her backpack.

118

'I wasn't trying to drop you in it,' Alice said. 'But we have to get back on time on Sunday.'

Something in her voice made Bree look up. She flicked through her mental calendar. What did Alice have on? Sunday. Prize night at Margot Russell's school. Bree closed her eyes rather than roll them.

She had met Margot only once, two months earlier. Alice had asked her to pick up her daughter's formal dress from the drycleaners and drop it at her house. It was well outside Bree's job description, obviously, but perhaps as a personal favour? Of course, no problem. The dress was beautiful. Bree had worn something similar, if less couture, to her own formal. Even without the photos in Alice's office, she would have recognised Margot as soon as she opened the door. A younger version of her mother. She was with a friend, sipping kale smoothies from one of Bree's favourite health stores.

'Hey, those are great, aren't they?' Bree said. She knew that kind of drink and she knew that kind of girl, with their glossy hair and smooth skin and desirable figures and amused looks. She *was* that kind of girl at school. Still was.

Margot had said nothing for a moment, then pointed her straw at the drycleaning bag Bree was clutching.

'Is that my dress?'

'Oh. Yes. Here. I'm Bree, by the way.'

'I know. Thanks.' A rustle of plastic and the door was shut. Bree stood alone on the step, staring at the glossy paint.

'Who was that chick?' a faint voice floated through an open window.

'One of my mum's minions.'

'She's a bit needy.'

'That's what my mum says.'

Bree had stepped back. Now, she looked at Alice. Thirty years older than her daughter but with the same expression in her eyes.

Bree made herself smile. 'Don't worry. We won't be late back.'

'Good.'

Bree stood and, under the guise of doing a few stretches, wandered along the path to a tree stump. She could see her sister in the distance, still smoking, and staring out into the bush. Bree propped a leg up on the stump and bent over, feeling her hamstrings pull and her head spin. Her stomach heaved and she swallowed the hot surge in her gullet.

She unfolded the map and lay it out so she could look at it as she stretched. The paths swirled a little on the page.

'Are you feeling okay?'

Bree looked up. Her sister was standing over her, holding out a water bottle.

'I'm fine.' She didn't take the drink.

'Do you know where we're going?'

'Yes. Christ, why does everyone keep asking me that?'

'Maybe because it seems like you don't.'

'Just shut up, Beth.'

Her twin shrugged and sat on the log. It creaked under her bulk. Bree wondered how much she weighed now. They'd been able to swap clothes all through their teens. Not anymore, that was for certain.

When Beth had called six months ago, Bree had let it go through to voicemail, as always. When the message asked if she could name Bree as a referee on a job application, Bree had done precisely nothing. A week later, a second message shared the news that Beth had secured an entry-level data-processing position at BaileyTennants. Bree had assumed it was a joke. It had to be. She had been through too much to get her role and she didn't just mean her degree in commerce and two unpaid internships. And now she had to work in the same place as her sister, with her cheap haircut and size Large clothes and her *mistake* that had to be legally declared on job applications?

Their mother had confirmed it was indeed the case.

'She's inspired by you. I've told you.'

Bree thought her sister was more likely inspired by fear of her benefits being cut off. She had made a subtle inquiry to human resources. Apparently Jill Bailey herself had approved the unusual appointment. Unofficially, Bree was told, it seemed her own stellar service to the company had tipped the balance in her sister's favour. Bree had locked herself in a bathroom stall for ten minutes and blinked back tears of rage as she processed that information.

At that point, she had only seen her sister once in the past eighteen months. It had been coming up to Christmas when their mother had called, asking Bree, *begging* her, to forgive. Bree had listened stony-faced to her mum crying down the phone for fifty minutes before she caved. It was Christmas, after all. So she had returned to her childhood home, armed with presents for every family member except one.

Beth, unemployed and broke, of course, was looking surprisingly clear-eyed after her stint away. She'd given Bree a photo of the two of them as children, printed out and placed in a cheap frame that would look terrible in Bree's flat. The accompanying Christmas card simply read, *I'm sorry*. Because their mother was watching, Bree had not pulled away when her twin moved to hug her.

Back at her own home, the festivities over, Bree had removed the photo and dropped the frame off at a charity shop. An hour later, she'd returned and bought it back. Photo reinstated, the gift was last seen shoved in the back of a high cupboard behind the Christmas decorations.

On Beth's first day at BaileyTennants, their mum had called Bree and asked her to do everything she possibly could to help her sister keep this job. *Now, looking at her sister smoking and sitting on a log, Bree wished she hadn't promised.*

'Are you girls ready over there?'

A voice came up the path and Bree turned. Jill, Alice and Lauren were already on their feet, eyeing their backpacks with reluctance.

'Yes. Coming.' Bree grabbed the map and jogged back. Too fast. She felt a bit dizzy.

'Is it left or right from here?' Jill hauled her pack onto her shoulders. Where the trail split, both routes were narrow with overgrown shrubbery crawling out on to the path. The earth on the left-hand trail looked more compressed, but Bree knew that at every fork for the first part of the day they had to go right. She checked again, feeling four pairs of eyes resting on her. They were impatient to get going now they had the weight on their backs again. She ran a finger over the route, her hand shaking a little and her empty stomach swirling. Yes, they had turned twice today, this was the third time.

'If you need help, Bree . . . ' Alice shifted her feet.

'I don't.'

'Okay. So, which way . . . ?'

'Turn right.'

'Are you sure? That looks a little rough and ready.'

Bree held out the map. Pointed at the fork. The red line. 'Here. Right turn.'

'We're there already?' Alice sounded surprised. 'Yeah, okay then.'

Bree snapped the map shut along its folds.

'See, we're making good time. There's nothing to worry about.' Or bitch about, for once. Bree forced a deep breath into her lungs and a smile on her face. 'Follow me.'

Chapter 9

It was like stepping into a funhouse mirror. Two faces, each a distorted reflection of the other, looked up in unison at the knock on the hospital room door.

'Breanna McKenzie?' Falk said.

The woman in the bed had lost the healthy glow she'd had in her staff photo. Dark circles now hung under her eyes and her lips were pale and cracked. Her right arm was heavily bandaged.

'We're from the police. Did the nurse tell you we've been waiting to see you?'

'Yeah.'

Falk had been speaking to Breanna, but it was the woman sitting on a plastic chair next to the bed who answered. 'She said you had some more questions about Alice.'

'That's right. It's Bethany, is it?'

'Beth's fine.'

It was the first time Falk had seen Beth McKenzie in

person and he looked at her with interest. The likeness was a strange one, almost as though Breanna's neat features had melted in the sun, becoming slacker and fleshier. Beth's skin was ruddy with broken veins around her nose and jawline. Her hair had the harsh flatness of a poor home dye job and hung in a style that was neither long nor short. She appeared ten years older than her twenty-something twin, but when she looked at him, her gaze was firm.

A tray with the remains of lunch lay waiting to be cleared by the side of the bed. It didn't look like much had been eaten. They had found the community hospital two streets behind the service station. It seemed to be one step up from a GP clinic, designed to cater for everything from locals' ailments to tourists' injuries. The nurse behind the reception desk had firmly pointed them back towards the door and told them to return in ninety minutes when Breanna's sleeping pills should have worn off. They walked up and down the town's row of shops three times, then sat in their car for seventy-eight minutes. When they went back in, they were informed that lunch had just been served.

'No visitors during meal times. No exceptions.'

Finally, the nurse crooked a finger and beckoned them to the reception desk. They could go in. Breanna McKenzie was in the shared overnight ward at the end of the hall, the nurse told them, but she was the only patient. Winter season.

In the room at last, they dragged a couple of chairs to the bed.

'Have they found Alice yet?' Beth was watching Falk and Carmen closely. 'Is that why you're here?'

'Not yet,' Falk said. 'I'm sorry.'

'Oh. So what was it you wanted to ask?'

'It was your sister we wanted to speak to, actually,' Carmen said. 'Alone, preferably.'

'I think I should stay.'

Bree shifted against her pillow. 'For God's sake. It's fine, Beth. Go and let them get on with it.' She winced. 'Are there any painkillers?'

'It's not time yet.' Beth didn't appear to glance at the clock.

'Ask the nurse.'

'It's too early. They won't give you any more until tonight.'

'Jesus. Go and ask. Please.'

Beth hauled herself out of the chair. 'All right. I'll be out the back having a smoke. And yes —' she said as her sister opened her mouth, 'I'll ask the nurse. It's too soon, though, I'm telling you.'

They watched her leave.

'Sorry. She's upset because they don't trust her with the medication in the room,' Bree said as the door swung shut.

'Why not?' Carmen said.

'It's not a big deal, really. She had a couple of substance abuse issues in the past, but she's been fine now for more than a year. I guess the nurses feel they can't be too careful. It would probably be easier if she weren't here, but she . . . ' Bree looked down. 'Wants to stay, I guess.'

'Is anyone else coming up to be with you?' Falk said. 'Boyfriend? Your parents?'

'No.' Bree started picking at her bandage. Her nails had at some point been painted a deep bold pink. Several were now chipped or broken. 'Mum's got MS.'

'I'm sorry.'

'It's okay. Well, it's not, but it is what it is. She can't make the trip. Dad has to stay with her most of the time these days. Anyway –' She tried for a smile. 'I have Beth.'

There was a heavy pause.

'We wanted to ask you about Alice Russell, if you don't mind,' Falk said. 'How long have you worked for her?'

'Eighteen months.'

'As her assistant?'

'Administrative coordinator.'

Falk thought he saw Carmen suppress a smile. She recovered fast. 'What does that involve?'

'At first it was mainly administration duties, but then the role became more of a mentorship. I shadow Alice, learning skills to help prepare me for internal promotion.'

'Good boss?'

A fraction of a heartbeat. 'Yes. Definitely.'

They waited, but Bree said no more.

'So you feel you know her well?' Falk said.

'Yes. Very well.' There was an odd note in Bree's voice. Falk watched her, but could see no sign of recognition when she looked back. Like Daniel Bailey, if Bree knew who they were, she wasn't letting it show.

127

'So how did Alice seem to you on the retreat?' Carmen said.

Bree picked at her bandage. The edges were already growing frayed. 'Before we got lost she was her normal self, really. She can be snappy sometimes, but none of us was at our best out there. After we got lost?' Bree shook her head. 'Everyone was scared.'

'Did she mention anything she was worried about?' Carmen said. 'Other than being lost, of course?'

'Like what?'

'Anything. Work, home, any issues with colleagues?'

'No. Not to me.'

'But as someone who knew her well,' Carmen said, 'did you sense anything wrong?'

'No.'

'What about back in the office? Before the retreat. Any strange requests or appointments that caught your eye?'

'What does that have to do with what happened out there?'

'Nothing, necessarily,' Falk said. 'We're trying to get a sense of what went wrong.'

'I can tell you exactly what went wrong.' Something rippled across Bree's face. 'And it wasn't all my fault.'

'What wasn't?'

'Us getting lost. It was that stupid kangaroo trail on the second day. That's what the other officers said. They said it was an easy mistake to make.' Bree stopped, and the only sound was the gentle beep of the hospital machines. She took a breath. 'The others shouldn't have dropped me in

128

it with the navigation. I didn't know what I was doing. I got sent on a half-day course with coffee breaks every twenty minutes and I'm supposed to be an instant expert?'

She moved her injured arm and grimaced, sweat breaking out on her forehead.

'What happened when you realised you were off track?' Falk said.

'Everything went wrong after that. We never found the second campsite so we never got our supplies for that night. We were low on food. We were stupid and the tents got damaged.' A small laugh. 'It's almost funny how fast it all fell apart. But we weren't thinking straight, and we were making bad decisions. It's difficult to explain what it's like out there. You feel like the only people left in the world.'

'How did Alice react to being lost?' Falk said.

'She was quite pushy about what we should do. When she's feeling stressed that can make her seem aggressive. She'd done a lot of camping and hiking when she was at school – one of these outdoor campus years. I think she felt that gave her more of a say than the rest of us. I don't know.' Bree sighed. 'Maybe it did. But Lauren – Lauren Shaw? She was in our group too – she'd done the same course at school and she didn't think Alice was always right either. Like when we found that cabin on the third day. I mean, it was horrible. I didn't like it there, but it was the best of our bad options. The weather was getting worse and we needed the shelter. So we stayed.' Bree paused. 'Alice was the only one who didn't want to.'

'She couldn't convince you to leave?' Falk said.

'No. And she wasn't happy about it. She said she knew how to find our way out, wanted us all to keep walking. But we wouldn't. That's what got us in trouble in the first place. Walking blindly. There was a bit of an argument. Alice said she'd go alone but Jill wouldn't let her. In the morning when we woke up, Alice had taken the phone and gone.'

'Did Jill Bailey say why she didn't want to let Alice go?' Carmen said.

'Because it was dangerous, of course. And obviously, she was right.'

Bree looked from one to the other, daring them to argue.

'What did you do when you realised she wasn't there?' Falk said finally.

Bree shook her head. 'I'm not the best person to ask. I thought I was the first one awake so I went out to go to the toilet in the bushes. I was walking back when I tripped. I didn't realise what had happened at first, I thought I'd fallen onto something sharp. Broken glass maybe. Then I saw the snake disappear, and I knew.'

Bree bit her bottom lip so hard it turned white. Her gaze went straight through them.

'I thought I was going to die out there. I really believed that. We'd been told there were tiger snakes. I had no idea where we were. I thought I would never see my family again, never get to say goodbye to my mum.' She took a shaky breath. 'I remember feeling dizzy and like I couldn't breathe. The doctor here told me I was probably having a

130

panic attack, but at the time I thought it was the venom. I made it to the cabin, and I don't really remember the rest well. They put something tight around my arm. I was in pain. I'm not sure at what point I realised Alice wasn't with us.'

Bree picked at her bandage.

'When the others said we should leave – leave without her – I didn't argue. I walked where I was told. Lauren managed to get us north until we found a road. I don't really remember much about it. The doctor says I was probably in shock by then. I had this idea that Alice had gone ahead to get help and would be waiting for us at the meeting point.' Bree looked down. 'I think I even asked for her, but my head was really in a bad state. I didn't know what I was doing.'

The tears finally brimmed over and Falk handed her a tissue. They waited, listening to the hum of the machines, while she wiped her eyes.

'Alice had her phone out there,' Carmen said. 'Did she make any calls while she was with you?'

'No.' The answer came quickly. 'I mean, she tried, obviously. She called triple zero a lot, but we never got through. It was completely useless.'

'But she still took the phone when she left?'

A tiny shrug. 'It was hers, I suppose.'

She looked fragile against the pillow, with her long loose hair and bandaged arm. Her chipped nails, her story.

'You say you know Alice well,' Falk said. 'Were you surprised she left you?'

'Under normal circumstances, I would have been.' Bree's eyes were wide as they looked back into Falk's. *She knows how to lie to men.* The thought came out of nowhere.

'But like I said, it's different out there. I wish now we'd listened to her. Then maybe none of this might have happened.'

'But then all of you could be lost.'

'Maybe. But maybe anything else would have been better than the way it's turned out.'

She shifted her bandaged arm and a jolt of pain crossed her face. Falk and Carmen exchanged a glance.

'That's probably enough for now. We'll let you get some rest,' Carmen said as they stood. 'Thanks, Breanna.'

She nodded. The shadows under her eyes looked darker than when they had arrived.

'When you see my sister out there, tell her to either send in the nurse with the painkillers, or to bloody leave so they can put me on a drip. Please.'

The room was cool, but as he pulled the door closed, Falk could see that a fresh band of sweat had broken out across Bree's forehead.

Day 2: Friday Afternoon

The pale sun had moved across the narrow band of sky and the grass was as high as their ankles before someone finally said it.

'Is this right?'

Beth breathed a silent sigh of relief at Jill's words. She had wanted to ask the same question for twenty minutes but couldn't. Bree would have killed her.

Her sister stopped and looked back.

'It should be right.'

'Should be? Or is?'

'Is.' Bree didn't sound sure. She glanced down at the map. 'It has to be. We haven't turned off anywhere.'

'I realise that. But –' Jill swept a hand at their surroundings. The overgrown path, the trees closing in tighter every few dozen steps. Forget what the map said, it didn't *feel* right.

All around, hidden birds shrieked at each other in call and response. Beth couldn't shake the feeling that the bushland was talking about them.

133

'We haven't seen a marker flag all day,' Jill said. 'Not since the one in the tree yesterday. There are supposed to be six. Surely we should have seen another one by now. At least one.'

'Maybe that fork we took after lunch was wrong. Can I see?' Alice had plucked the map from Bree's fingers before she could answer. Bree froze with her empty hand extended, looking lost in every sense. Beth tried to catch her eye, but wasn't able to.

'Look.' Alice was frowning at the paper. 'I bet it was. I thought we'd got there too soon.'

'I really don't –'

'Bree.' Alice silenced her. 'It's not right.'

For a moment, there was nothing but the strange hush of the bush and Beth looked up at the gum trees. Their bark hung off in slack strips like flayed skin. They seemed very close and very tall, all around. *Boxed in*, she thought suddenly.

'So what now?' There was a subtle new note in Jill's voice that Beth couldn't quite place. Not quite fear, not quite yet. Concern, perhaps. Keen interest.

Alice held the map out so Jill could see.

'If we'd made the proper turn, we should be here.' Alice pointed. 'But if not, I don't know. We're probably somewhere more around here.' She made a small circling motion on the page.

Jill leaned close, then closer again, the lines deepening around the corners of her eyes.

She couldn't read the map, Beth realised. The print must

be too small. Jill might have been scanning the page, but that paper could be blank for all the good it was doing her. Beth had seen her grandmother pull off a similar pretence, when she didn't want to admit her reading vision was shot. As Jill did a reasonable job of pretending to examine the page, Alice was watching her with an interested look on her face. She had clocked it too, Beth thought.

'Hmm.' Jill made a noncommittal noise and handed the map to Lauren. 'What do you think?'

Lauren looked a little surprised, but took the map. She bowed her head, running her eyes over the paper. 'No, I don't think it's right either,' she said. 'Sorry, Bree.'

'So what should we do?' Jill was looking at her.

'I think we should turn around and try to retrace our steps.'

Alice groaned. 'Christ. Retracing takes absolutely ages. We'll be out here for hours.'

'Well.' Lauren shrugged. 'I'm not sure what other choice we have.'

Jill's head turned back and forth between the two as though at a tennis match. Bree was standing only a metre or two away, but she might as well have been invisible.

Alice looked back at the trail. 'Would we even be able to retrace? The path's pretty faint. We might lose it.'

Beth saw with a start that Alice was right. Behind them, the route they had forged now appeared fluid at the edges, blending seamlessly into the background. Beth automatically felt for her cigarettes. Not in her pocket. Her heart beat a little faster.

135

'I think it's still the best option,' Lauren said. 'The safest, anyway.'

'It'll add hours to the hike.' Alice looked at Jill. 'We'll be walking in the dark again before we reach the campsite, no question.'

Jill glanced down at her new boots and Beth could tell the prospect of extra kilometres was not a popular one. Jill opened her mouth. Shut it again and gave a small shake of her head.

'Well, I don't know,' she said finally. 'What's the alternative?'

Alice studied the map, then looked up, her eyes narrowed. 'Can everyone else hear a creek?'

Beth held her breath. The faint rush of water was almost drowned out by the blood pounding in her ears. God, she was unfit. The others were nodding, at least.

'If we went wrong here, that creek should be this one here.' Alice pointed at the map. 'It sounds near. We can use that to orientate ourselves. If we work out where we are we could try to cut through and rejoin the right path further along.'

Lauren had crossed her arms over her chest, Beth noticed. Her lips were pressed together in a line.

'Do you think –' Jill cleared her throat. 'Do you feel confident we can orientate ourselves from there?'

'Yes. We should be able to.'

'What do you think?' Jill turned to Lauren.

'I think we should retrace our steps.'

'For God's sake, we'll be out here all night,' Alice said. 'You know we will.'

Lauren said nothing. Jill looked from one to the other, then down at her feet once more. She gave a tight sigh.

'Let's find this creek.'

No-one bothered asking Bree what she thought.

Beth followed as the sound of water grew more distinct. It had a different quality from the roar of the falls the day before, thicker and more muted. They pushed through a bank of trees, and Beth found herself on a muddy ledge.

The clay ground fell away near her feet, dropping more than a metre to a swollen brown strip below. It was definitely more river than creek, she thought as she stared at the water. It had been engorged by rainfall and left a foamy tidemark as it lapped at the bank. Floating debris hinted at a rapid speed beneath the surface.

Alice pored over the map, while Jill and Lauren looked on. Bree drifted at the fringe, looking forlorn. Beth slipped off her pack and thrust her arm inside, feeling around for her cigarette packet. She couldn't find it and despite the cold, her palms began to sweat. She pushed in deeper. At last, her fingers closed around the familiar shape and she pulled her arm out, dragging clothing and odds and ends with it.

Beth didn't notice the shiny metal canister rolling away until it was too late. It bounced out of reach of her outstretched fingertips, turned one more revolution towards the bank and then dropped over the side.

'Shit.' She shoved the cigarette pack in her pocket and scrambled after it.

'What was that?' Alice's eyes flicked up, hard above the map.

'I don't know.' Beth peered over and breathed a half-sigh of relief. Whatever it was, it was suspended in a tangle of dead branches above the water.

'Great.' Alice was looking now. They all were. 'It's the gas canister for the stove.'

'The . . . what?' Beth watched the metal shimmer as the branches swayed.

'The canister. For the stove,' Alice repeated. 'We need that to cook our meals tonight. And tomorrow. Jesus, Beth. Why did you drop it?'

'I didn't even know I had it.'

'We split the communal stuff, you know that.'

A stray piece of wood rushed along in the water, colliding with the branches. The canister wobbled, but held.

'Can we get by without it?' Jill said.

'Not if we want to eat dinner tonight.'

Another surge in the water and the canister quivered again. Beth could feel Alice's eyes on her. She stared straight down at the swollen river, knowing what was coming. Alice stepped in close behind her and she felt an invisible hand prodding her spine.

'Fetch it.'

Chapter 10

Beth was leaning against the wall outside the hospital, one hand shoved in her coat pocket, and her eyes slitted as the cigarette smoke drifted across her face. She straightened a little as she saw Falk and Carmen come out.

'You finished in there?' she called. 'Is Bree okay?'

'She's a bit uncomfortable,' Carmen said as they walked over. 'She reminded you to ask the nurse for painkillers.'

'I did. It's too soon. She never listens to me.' Beth turned her head to blow smoke away from them, fanning the air. 'What's the latest with Alice? Still no sign?'

'Not as far as we've heard,' Falk said.

'Shit.' Beth picked a fleck of tobacco from her lower lip. She glanced at the trees encroaching on the back of the hospital lot. 'I wonder what's happened to her.'

'What do you think?'

Beth focused on her cigarette. 'After she walked off? Who knows. Anything could happen out there. We all tried to tell her.'

Falk watched her. 'What is it you do at BaileyTennants?'

'Data processing and archiving.'

'Oh, yeah? What does that involve?'

'Pretty much what it sounds like. Filing, data entry, making sure the partners can access the documents they're looking for.'

'So you have access to the company's files?'

'The unrestricted stuff. There are confidential and deep archive files the senior partners have to access themselves.'

'So did you see much of Alice Russell at work?'

'Yeah, sometimes.' Beth didn't sound happy about it. 'She was down in the data room a fair bit, getting bits and pieces.'

Falk felt Carmen shift next to him.

'Did you two chat much while she was down there?' Carmen said mildly. 'Talk about what she was looking for?'

Beth cocked her head, something flitting across her face. Calculating, almost.

'No, she didn't talk to anyone in data processing unless she had to. Anyway, it's all Greek to me down there. I don't get paid enough to think.'

'And what about out on the retreat? Did you get along any better with her out there?' Falk asked, and Beth's face hardened, her cigarette frozen halfway to her mouth.

'Is that a joke?'

'No.'

'Then no. Alice Russell and I did not get along. Not at work, not on the retreat.' Beth cast a glance at the hospital doors. 'My sister didn't mention it?'

140

'No.'

'Oh.' Beth took a final drag and ground out her cigarette butt. 'She probably thought you knew. Alice didn't like me, and she didn't bother to hide it.'

'Why was that?' Carmen asked.

'I don't know.' Beth shrugged. She pulled out her cigarette pack, offering it to Falk and Carmen. They both shook their heads. 'Actually,' she said, putting one in her own mouth. 'I do know. She didn't like me because she didn't have to like me. I didn't have anything to offer her, I wasn't interesting, I'm not Bree –' Beth waved a hand vaguely up and down herself from her sallow face to her thick thighs. 'It wasn't hard for Alice to make things difficult for me and she took her chance.'

'Even with your sister there?'

Beth gave a crooked smile. 'Especially with my sister there. I think that's what made it fun.'

She cupped her hands and lit up. The wind ruffled her hair and she pulled the coat tighter around herself.

'So Alice gave you a hard time,' Carmen said. 'Did you stand up to her? Push back at all?'

There was the briefest ripple across Beth's features. 'No.'

'Not at all? It must have been frustrating for you.'

She shrugged. 'There'll always be someone acting like a bit of a bitch. It's not worth me rocking the boat. Not while I'm on probation, anyway.'

'What are you on probation for?' Falk asked.

'Don't you know?'

'We can find out. It would be easier if you tell us.'

Beth's eyes flicked to the hospital doors. She shifted her weight from one foot to the other and took a deep drag before answering.

'What kind of cops did you say you were again?'

'AFP.' Falk held out his Federal Police identification and Beth leaned in to look.

'I'm on probation . . . ' She stopped. Sighed. 'Because of that thing with Bree.'

They waited. 'You'll have to give us more than that,' Carmen said.

'Yeah, sorry. I don't really like to talk about it. A couple of years ago I –' She seemed to inhale the rest of the cigarette in a single draw. 'I wasn't doing so well. I broke into Bree's flat and stole some of her things. Clothes, her TV. Some stuff she'd saved up for. Some jewellery our nanna had given her before she died. Bree came home to find me loading it into the back of a car. When she tried to stop me, I hit her.'

The last words tumbled out like they had a bad taste.

'Was she badly hurt?' Falk asked.

'Physically, nothing too bad,' Beth said. 'But she'd been smacked on the street by her twin trying to steal her possessions for drug money, so yeah. She was badly hurt. I badly hurt her.'

It sounded like a phrase she'd had to repeat often in front of a therapist. She finished her cigarette but took her time putting this one out.

'Look, to be honest, I don't really remember much of it. I had a drug problem for a few years, since –' She stopped

142

what she'd been about to say. Ran a hand over her arm. The movement reminded Falk of her sister, picking at her bandage in the hospital bed. 'Since my final year of uni. It was stupid. I was picked up straight away by the police trying to sell her stuff. I didn't even know I'd hit her until my lawyer told me. I had a record by then, so I got sent away. It wasn't Bree's fault. Obviously. But I mean, she didn't go to the police. She could have, no-one would have blamed her. A neighbour who saw us fighting was the one who reported it. Bree still won't talk about it. She doesn't talk to me much anyway. Most of what I know about it comes from the court documents.'

'What happened to you?' Carmen said.

'A couple of months in a correctional facility, which wasn't so good, then a bit longer in rehab treatment, which was better.'

'They helped you recover?'

'Yeah. I mean, they did their best. And I'm doing my best. Recovery is an ongoing thing, but they taught me to take responsibility for my choices. And for what I did to my sister.'

'How are things between you now?' Carmen said.

'Okay. She helped get me this data job, which was great. I was studying computer science and technology before I left uni, so the BaileyTennants work's a bit mundane, but it can be hard to find anything on probation so I'm grateful.' Beth's smile came out a little forced. 'We used to be really close, though. We dressed the same every day until we were, like, fourteen, or something ridiculous. Way too long. Like

143

we were the same person. We seriously used to think we could read each other's thoughts.' She glanced at the hospital door. 'We can't.' She sounded a little surprised by that.

'It must have been frightening for you when she got bitten,' Falk said.

Beth's mouth went tight. 'Yeah, it was. I was so scared I was going to lose her. I'd got up early to go for a pee and just dozed off again when Bree came crashing in clutching her arm. We had to get her to a doctor, but bloody Alice had gone AWOL. We ran around like headless chooks trying to find her, but there was no sign.' She ran a stubby thumbnail over her lips. 'To be honest with you, I didn't give a shit. I only cared about Bree. Alice could fend for herself, as far as I was concerned. We were just lucky Lauren knew how to navigate in a straight line, or we'd still be stuck out there. She kept us going north, got us to the road so we could follow it round. I've never been so happy to see tarmac in my life.'

'Did you actually see Alice walk off?' Falk asked, watching her closely.

'No. But I wasn't surprised. It was what she'd been threatening to do.'

'And we hear she took the phone.'

'Yeah, she did. It was pretty bloody selfish, but that's Alice for you. Anyway, it didn't really matter. It never worked.'

'Never?'

'No.' Beth looked at them like they were slow. 'Or we would have called for help.'

'Were you surprised Alice wasn't already at the meeting spot when you got back?' Falk said, and Beth seemed to consider the question.

'Yeah. I was a bit, actually. Especially as we were probably on the same track, only a few hours behind her. If we didn't pass her, and she didn't make it back before us, what happened?'

The question hung in the air. Falk could make out the sound of the police helicopter circling far off in the distance. Beth looked from one to the other.

'Listen.' She shifted her weight and her voice dropped a notch lower. 'Was Alice up to something?'

'Like what?' Falk said, keeping his face neutral.

'You tell me. You're the AFP.'

Falk and Carmen said nothing, and eventually Beth shrugged.

'I don't know. But I told you she'd been requesting a lot of information from data processing. The thing is, she'd started to come and get the stuff herself, which was a bit weird. I only noticed because she used to send Bree down to get it, but then she began coming herself. And she was accessing the restricted items more regularly. It's just now with her missing . . . ' Beth glanced past them at the hills towering in the distance and shrugged again.

'Beth,' Carmen said. 'How sure are you that Alice walked away from that cabin of her own accord?'

'Look, I am sure. Fair enough, I didn't see her do it, but only because she knew we would've stopped her. She didn't want to be stuck out there. She'd already tried to convince Jill to let her go back alone after the first night, but Jill said no. Then again at the cabin, the same thing.'

'So there was some tension between them?' Carmen said.

'Of course.'

'Because when we saw Jill Bailey briefly, it looked like she had a bruise on her face. Around her jawline.'

There was a long pause while Beth examined her cigarette. 'I'm not quite sure how she got that. I know she tripped a couple of times on the hike.'

Falk let the silence string out, but Beth didn't look up.

'Okay,' he said. 'So things weren't great between Jill and Alice.'

'Yeah, but that wasn't totally surprising. Alice could start a fight in an empty room. And she was already pissed off, way before Jill did anything. Alice had been in a bad mood since the first night when she had her little heart-to-heart with Daniel Bailey.'

Somewhere behind the hospital doors, Falk could hear the insistent beep of an alarm.

'Daniel Bailey?' he said.

'Jill's brother? He's the chief exec. The men's group came to our camp that first night and he took Alice off for a private chat.'

'Any idea what it was about?'

'Not really. I didn't hear much. But Alice was asking how he had found out about something and Daniel said because he'd seen it with his own eyes. She kept asking, "Who else knows?" and he said, "No-one yet".' Beth

146

frowned as she remembered. 'Daniel said something like: "It's about respect, that's why I wanted to warn you".'

'Warn her?' Falk said. 'You definitely heard him say that?'

'Yeah, but I'm not sure what he was talking about. It caught my attention because Daniel Bailey's not exactly known around the office for his respect for women.'

'Aggressive?' Carmen said.

'More dismissive, apparently.'

'Right,' Falk said. 'What was his tone like that night? Did he seem angry?'

'No, he was calm. But he wasn't happy. It didn't sound like a conversation he wanted to have.'

'And how did Alice sound?'

'Honestly?' Beth thought for a moment. 'I thought Alice sounded scared.'

Day 2: Friday Afternoon

'Get down there, Beth.' Alice pointed at the swollen river. 'Quick. Before we lose it.'

Lauren peered over the bank. The small metal stove canister hung in its cradle of broken branches, quivering as the murky water rushed underneath.

Beth hovered at the edge of the bank. She mumbled something.

'What's that?' Alice snapped. 'What are you waiting for?'

'I said, can't we just light a fire tonight?'

'They're only legal at the first campsite,' Alice said. 'We're going to need the canister to cook. Just climb down there and grab it.'

Beth's eyes flicked to the river and back. 'But how?'

It was a good question, Lauren thought. The bank was steep and muddy, plunging straight into the water. Surface debris collected around the broken branches like a filthy coat.

'I'll fall in.' Beth was still frozen by the edge. 'I can't swim.'

Alice looked almost amused. 'Seriously? At all?'

'Not well.'

'Jesus. Better not fall in then.'

A gust of wind shook the branches. The canister shifted a notch.

'Perhaps we should leave it.' Jill seemed to find her voice for the first time. She was watching the river warily. 'I'm not sure this is safe.'

'We can't leave it. We need it. We're stuck out here for days,' Alice said.

Jill glanced at Lauren, who nodded. Alice was right. It was going to be a long time until Sunday without a working stove.

'Beth!' Alice snapped. 'Get down there. We're going to lose it.'

'No!' Beth's cheeks were flushed and her eyes were bright. 'Look, I'm not doing it, all right? I'll fall.'

'Don't be so pathetic. There'll be no dinner tonight without it.'

'I don't care! None of you even ate your bloody food last night! I'm not breaking my neck because you're a bit hungry now.'

Beth stood firm, but Lauren could see that her hands were shaking.

'You dropped it, Beth,' Alice said. 'You get it.'

'You put it in my bag without telling me.'

'So?'

'So you get it.'

The two women were face to face. Beth shoved her hands in her pockets.

'Jesus, Beth –' Alice started.

'I'll go.' Lauren had said the words before she quite realised it. Four pairs of eyes turned to her in surprise. She immediately wished she hadn't spoken, but it was done now. 'I'll climb down. You all have to help me, though.'

'Thank you.' Beth's face flushed darker with relief.

'Are you sure?' Jill edged further away from the bank. 'Maybe we really should just –'

Lauren cut her off before she changed her mind. 'No. I'll get it. We do need it.'

She looked over the edge. The bank was steep, but it had one or two rocks and tufts of weeds that could be used as hand and footholds. She took a breath, unsure how to approach the task. Finally, she sat down and twisted to lower herself over the edge. The ground was cold and gritty against her palms. She felt a couple of pairs of hands holding her forearms and jacket as she scrambled down, the toes of her boots sliding against the muddy bank.

'Good. We've got you,' Alice said.

Lauren didn't look up. She kept her sights on the canister, and the running water underneath. She stretched out her hand and her fingertips scraped air. Nearly. A gust of wind shook the branches and she saw the canister loosen in its nest.

'I need to get closer.'

She stretched again, leaning against the pull of gravity, her toes sliding in the mud. She was close. Her fingers had just brushed the smooth metallic finish when something gave. A slip of the foot and suddenly she was weightless as she plunged through the branches. A crack and she was in the water.

150

She managed a single sharp exhalation before the river closed over her head. The cold made her lungs seize as the water flooded thick and earthy into her mouth. She tried to kick but her feet were heavy in her boots. Without warning, she broke the surface, sucking at the air, blinded by water.

'Help!' The word was lost as she swallowed another mouthful of river.

'Reach up! Reach up!'

Lauren heard the muffled shout above her as someone clambered and skidded down the bank. Something was being held out to her and she grabbed it with both hands, feeling the clack of movement inside canvas as her fists tightened. It was the tent pole bag.

'Hold on, we'll pull you in.'

She forced her wrist into the handle strap and twisted it until it was tight. The silvery glint of the canister swept by her face, carried along by the current, and Lauren snatched at it.

'I can't –'

The hunk of wood came from nowhere. Solid and slimy with sodden leaves, it surfaced in the rushing water and careered into the side of her skull. The last thing she saw was the bloodied piece of wood ricochet away and disappear without a trace back into the water.

Lauren was freezing. She was shaking so hard her joints were knocking against the hard ground. She forced her eyes open. She was lying on her side. Everything seemed painfully bright, but the daylight had a different quality from before. How long had passed? She thought she could hear crying followed by a harsh whisper. The noise stopped.

'You're awake. Thank God.' Alice's voice.

'Is she all right?' Jill.

'I think so.'

I'm not, Lauren wanted to say, but couldn't find the energy. She struggled to sit up. Her head was pounding. She touched the pain. Her fingers came away bloody. She was draped in a coat that wasn't hers. Underneath, her clothes were soaked through.

Next to her, Bree sat huddled knees to chest, a camping towel around her shoulders. Her hair was sopping wet. A pool of watery vomit lay between them. Lauren wasn't sure which of them was responsible. Her own mouth tasted dank and foul.

Jill and Alice stood over her. Both were white-faced with fear. Beth hovered behind, shivering, her eyes red-rimmed. She was not wearing her coat and Lauren realised she was lying under it. She wondered vaguely if she should offer it back, but her teeth were chattering too hard to speak.

'You're okay,' Alice kept saying, a defensive note in her tone.

What happened? Lauren wanted to ask, but couldn't form the words. Her face must have said it all.

'Bree pulled you out,' Jill said. 'You were breathing, but you took a knock to the head.'

It felt like more than a knock. Lauren felt dizzy simply sitting up.

'Did we at least get the canister?'

Their faces gave her the answer.

'What about the tent pole bag?'

More bleak faces.

'Lost in the river,' Jill said. 'It's no-one's fault,' she added quickly.

Well, it's not *my* fault, Lauren thought immediately. 'What do we do now?'

Alice cleared her throat. 'There should be spare supplies at the campsite.' She was trying to sound optimistic. It came off as false.

'I'm not sure I can make it.'

'You'll have to,' Alice said. Her tone softened. 'I'm sorry. But we can't stay here without the tents. It'll get too cold.'

'So light a fire.' Every word was an effort. Lauren could see Jill shaking her head. 'Please. Jill, I know we're not allowed, but –'

'It's not that. The lighter got wet.'

Lauren wanted to cry. She felt sick again and lay back. The cold ground made her headache worse. She felt a drop of liquid run across her forehead and down her temple. She couldn't tell if it was river water or blood. With effort, she lifted her head a fraction. Alice was still standing over her.

'Phone for help,' Lauren said.

Alice didn't move.

'Call someone, Alice. On your mobile.'

Jill looked uneasy. 'She's already tried. We couldn't get through.'

Lauren let her head drop back against the ground. 'So what do we do?'

No-one spoke. Something scurried in the bush.

'Maybe we aim for higher ground,' Alice said at last. 'See if we can get a signal.'

'Will that make a difference?' Jill said.

'How would I know?'

There was an awkward pause.

'Sorry.' Alice unfolded the map and leaned over it. Finally, she looked up. 'Look, I'm pretty sure this river is this one here, in the north. There's a low peak with a path over here, to the west. It doesn't look too steep. The campsite's in that direction anyway. We can check for a signal on the peak. How does that sound?'

'Can you get us there?' Jill said.

'Yes. I think so. That way is west. Once we get on that path it should be obvious.'

'You've done this before?'

'A few times.'

'At school camp? Or recently?'

'At school. But I remember how. Nothing's changed since then.'

'And it worked back then?'

Alice gave a grim smile. 'Well, I didn't end up dead in the bush. But look, Jill, if you've got a plan you prefer . . . '

'It's not that.' Jill took the map and squinted. With a

frustrated noise she thrust it to Lauren. 'You did this camp as well. What do you think?'

Lauren's fingers were so numb she had trouble holding the paper. She tried to work out what she was looking at. She could feel Alice looking at her. There were a couple of peaks. She couldn't tell which one Alice had been referring to. The cold made it difficult to think.

'I don't know,' she said. 'I want to stay here.'

'Well, you can't.' Alice bit her lip. 'Look, we need to get some help or at the very least, get to the campsite. Come on, Lauren. You can see that.'

Lauren's head was pounding and she found she didn't have the energy to do more than nod. 'Yeah. Okay.'

'Yes? So we're agreed?' Jill sounded relieved. 'We'll go with Alice's plan?'

As Lauren got unsteadily to her feet she was reminded again of that day at McAllaster. Unsteady on her feet then as well, and blinded for the trust challenge. The overwhelming feeling of relief when Alice had taken her arm, her firm grip solid and steady. *'I've got you. This way.'* Lauren, disoriented and unsure, had felt Alice's hand warm against her skin and, one foot after the other, followed her through the unfamiliar territory.

Now, as she passed the map back to Jill, she wished she didn't once again feel quite so blinded. But at least they had a plan.

'Let's do what she says.'

You could say what you wanted about Alice, but the woman always knew exactly what she was doing.

Chapter 11

'What did Daniel say to Alice on that first night that scared her?' Carmen was staring out of the car window as the trees sped past, the hospital far behind them.

Falk didn't reply straight away. He could think of a few things, none of them good.

'Whatever it was, he obviously felt it was worth traipsing through the bush in the dark to get to her,' he said finally.

'It must have something to do with the reason why he missed the bus,' Carmen said. 'Otherwise he'd have told her – warned her, whatever – earlier.'

Falk thought back to what Bailey had said the day before in the carpark. *A private family matter.*

'Could it have been something to do with his sister?' Falk said. 'Maybe it was Jill he needed to see urgently. I don't know. Maybe we should just ask him outright.'

'Speaking of sisters,' Carmen said. 'What did you make of the twins? I know Bree's got the plush job upstairs, but

I reckon Beth's no fool. She's got her head screwed on just as tight.'

That had been playing on Falk's mind too. 'And I wouldn't be surprised if she understands those documents that pass under her nose better than she was letting on.'

'Great. That doesn't bode well for us, does it? If even the girl in the data room noticed Alice behaving strangely.'

'I don't know,' Falk said. 'I could see Alice seriously underestimating Beth. I mean, we kind of did as well. Alice might have let her guard down around her. Been sloppy.'

Or desperate, he thought. He remembered their last conversations with Alice. *Get the contracts. Get the contracts.* Pressure from above, pushing down.

'Say Beth was suspicious about Alice,' Carmen said, 'would she even care? It sounds like she needs the job, but an entry-level post hardly inspires undying company loyalty. And she's the type to be an office outsider.' She paused. 'Although outsiders often want nothing more than to be insiders.'

'Maybe Beth wouldn't care,' Falk said, 'but she might have told Bree.' Bree seemed like someone who might care a lot.

'Yeah, it's possible,' Carmen said. 'Weird dynamic between them, though.'

Falk turned the car onto the final approach to the lodge. 'I know. I couldn't tell if they love each other or hate each other's guts.'

'Both, probably,' she said. 'You haven't got any siblings, have you?'

157

'No. Have you?'

'Yeah. Loads. The love–hate relationship is very fluid. It's probably worse with twins as well.'

Falk pulled into the carpark and into the first space he saw. Something seemed out of place as he slammed the driver's door shut and he looked around, unsure, until he saw it. Or more accurately, didn't see it.

'Shit.'

'What?'

'His bloody car's gone.'

'Who? Daniel?' Carmen twisted around. No black BMW. 'Would he go back to Melbourne before Alice is found?'

'I don't know. Maybe.' Falk frowned. 'Maybe especially if he knew it was going to be a long wait.'

The rain started up again and by the time they reached the entrance of the lodge, heavy drops had already spotted their clothing. At the door of the lodge, Falk wiped his boots and ran a hand over his damp hair.

'Hey. In there,' Carmen said under her breath, nodding towards the lounge area.

Jill Bailey was sitting alone with a mug of coffee in her hand and a glazed expression on her face. Her eyes flicked over them with surprise, then faint annoyance, as they came in and sat down opposite her. Up close, the bruise on her jawline was turning a dirty yellow at the edges, and Falk could see her lip was swollen where it had been split.

'If it's about the action, you'll have to take it up with our lawyers,' she said.

'Sorry?' Falk realised too late he'd made the mistake of

158

sitting on an ancient couch so squashy he had to fight to keep his feet on the floor. He clutched discreetly at the arm to stop himself sinking further.

'Aren't you from Executive Adventures?' Her words came out a little thick and she touched her swollen lip with the tip of her tongue.

'No. Police.' Falk introduced them by name only. 'We're assisting Sergeant King.'

'Oh. Sorry. I thought I saw you yesterday with Ian Chase and assumed . . . ' She didn't finish.

Carmen looked at her. 'You're taking legal action against Executive Adventures?'

Jill swirled her mug. No steam rose from the liquid. It looked like she'd been holding it for some time.

'Not BaileyTennants, directly. But the insurance company covering the trip has sent a letter of intent. I can't say that I blame them.' She looked from one to the other. 'And that's separate from any action Alice or her family may choose to take, obviously.'

'Has Alice Russell's family come up here?' Falk asked.

'No. She has a teenage daughter who's staying with her father. He and Alice are divorced. We've offered them assistance, obviously, whatever they need. But apparently it's better for Margot – that's the girl – to be somewhere familiar than wringing her hands up here.' She looked down at her own hands. The nails on her right hand were broken, Falk noticed. Like Bree's.

'Is your brother still here?' Carmen said. 'His car's not outside.'

Jill took a deliberate sip from her coffee mug before answering. Definitely cold, Falk could tell from her expression. 'No. You've missed him, I'm afraid.'

'Where's he gone?' Falk said.

'Back to Melbourne.'

'Business demands?'

'It's a family matter.'

'It must be something urgent, to call him away with all this going on as well? Not ideal.'

Jill's face tightened with annoyance before she could help it, and Falk suspected she agreed. 'He didn't make the decision lightly.'

'You don't need to go too?'

'His immediate family. Not mine.' Jill went to take another sip, then thought better of it. 'Sorry, where did you say you were from again?'

'AFP.'

'I thought the state police were handling this? I've already spoken to them.'

'It's multi-agency,' Falk said, looking her in the eye. 'We'd be grateful if we could go over a couple of things.'

There was a tiny pause. 'Of course. Anything to help.'

Jill put the coffee mug on a side table next to her mobile. She checked the blank screen of her phone, before turning it over with a sigh.

'It's like a phantom limb, isn't it?' Carmen said.

'I think having that bloody phone with no coverage was actually one of the hardest things out there,' Jill said. 'It's pathetic, isn't it? It would have been easier having nothing, at least it wouldn't have been such a distraction.'

'Did you know Alice had taken her mobile with her?' Falk said.

'Not until the first night. I wasn't completely surprised, though. Alice is a bit like that.'

'Like what?'

Jill looked at him. 'Like someone who might bring her banned phone on a retreat.'

'Right,' Falk said. 'And do you know who she tried to call out there?'

'Triple zero, obviously.'

'No-one else?'

She frowned. 'Not that I know of. We needed to save the battery. Not that it made any difference. We never got through.'

'At all?' Falk said.

'No.' She sighed. 'God, I was so angry when she disappeared with the phone. We were relying on it, even though it was useless. But it seems ridiculous now, sitting here. I'm glad she has it. I hope it helps her.'

'Will you be staying up here while the search goes on?' Carmen said. 'Or are you heading back to Melbourne as well?'

'No. I'm staying until she's found – safe, I hope. Daniel would have stayed as well, but –' Jill ran a hand over her face, flinching a little as she touched her bruise. 'I'm sorry. This is all new territory for us. I've been with the company twenty-nine years and we've never had something like this happen. Honestly, these bloody retreats.'

'More trouble than they're worth?' Falk asked, and Jill managed a faint smile.

'Even when they go right. Personally, I'd rather people got on with the job they're being paid for, but you can't say that in this day and age. It's all about a holistic management approach now.' She shook her head. 'But, Christ, this is a nightmare.'

Behind her, the large picture window rattled and they all looked over. The rain spattering against the pane, distorting the view.

'How long have you known Alice Russell?' Falk said.

'Five years. I hired her, actually.'

'She's a good employee?' He watched Jill carefully, but the woman looked back with a clear expression.

'Yes. She is good. She works hard. Pulls her weight.'

'Was she happy to go on the retreat?'

'No more or less than anyone else. I don't think it was anyone's first choice of the way to spend a weekend.'

'We heard that Alice asked to leave after the first night, but you talked her out of it,' Carmen said.

'That's true, but honestly, I couldn't let her go, could I? I'd have to have taken the whole group back and there would have been questions to answer and costs involved and we would have all had to do it on another date anyway. I mean, in hindsight, of course I wish I'd said yes. It would have saved us all this.' Jill shook her head. 'Alice told me she felt ill and I didn't believe her. Her daughter had an event at school and I thought that was why she wanted to go back. And she'd tried to get out of the retreat the week before

162

as well, but at the time I felt she just had to put up with it, like the rest of us. None of us really wanted to be there.'

'Not even you?' Carmen said.

'Especially not me. At least Alice and Lauren had done a bit of that sort of thing at school. And Bree McKenzie is very fit. Her sister – well, I don't think she enjoyed it much either.'

There was a clatter of boots in the hallway and they all looked up through the open lounge door. A group of searchers had returned. They headed for the kitchen, their exhausted faces saying everything.

'How were the five of you selected for the trip?' Falk said.

'It's a random mix of pay grades and experience to develop cross-company teamwork.'

'And how about the real reason?'

Jill gave a small smile. 'The management team selects employees who it believes are in need of some professional or personal development through the challenge.'

'The management team being who? Yourself? Daniel?'

'Not me. Daniel, yes. The heads of department, mainly.'

'And what developmental traits was this group hoping to gain?'

'Bree McKenzie's in line for promotion, so this is part of her advancement program. Her sister –' Jill stopped. 'Have you met Beth?'

Falk and Carmen nodded.

'Well, then. I probably need say no more. She's not very ... corporate. Someone probably thought it would

163

help having her sister there, but I think they overestimated how close those two are.' Jill pursed her lips. 'Lauren – this won't go any further, will it? – she's been having performance issues. I understand she's had some problems at home, but it's been impacting her work.'

'And Alice?'

There was a silence. 'She'd had a complaint lodged against her.'

'For what?'

'Is this relevant?'

'I don't know,' Falk said. 'She's still missing. So it might be.'

Jill sighed. 'Bullying. Technically. But it's possibly just a sharp exchange of words. Alice can be blunt. And that's all highly confidential, by the way. The other women don't know.'

'Is there any merit in the complaint?' Carmen said.

'It's hard to say. It was one of the administration assistants so it could be a personality clash as much as anything but –' She stopped. 'It wasn't the first time. A similar issue was flagged two years ago. It came to nothing, but management felt Alice might benefit from some intensive teamwork. Another reason why I couldn't let her leave that first night.'

Falk considered this. 'And what about you?' he said. 'Why were you out there?'

'In our latest senior management meeting we agreed to commit to taking part in something every year. If there's a deeper reason, you'd have to ask the rest of the management committee.'

'Same for your brother Daniel?'

'Daniel actually enjoys it, believe it or not. But he's right. It's important for the company that he and I are seen to get involved.'

'Get your hands dirty,' Falk said.

Jill didn't blink. 'I suppose so.'

There was a loud bang from the hallway as the lodge door blew open. They heard the sound of feet and someone shutting it again firmly.

'I guess there are a lot of obligations that come with working for a family firm,' Carmen said. 'You can't just hide away. Your brother said something similar.'

'Did he?' Jill said. 'Well, that's certainly true. I studied English and Art History for my first degree. I wanted to be a humanities teacher.'

'What happened?'

'Nothing happened. It's a family firm, and members of the family are expected to work for the company. In that respect we're no different from a farming family, or a couple passing on their corner shop to their children. You need people you can trust. I work there, Daniel works there, our father's still involved. Daniel's son Joel will work there after university.'

'And you? Do you have children?' Falk said.

'I do. Two. Grown up now.' She paused. 'But they're an exception. They didn't have any interest in going into the business and I wouldn't make them. Dad wasn't pleased, but he got the rest of us, so I think that's a fair exchange.' Jill's expression softened a little. 'My children both got to be teachers.'

'That's nice,' Carmen said. 'You must be proud.'

'Thank you, I am.'

Falk looked at her. 'Getting back to the retreat, your brother and the men's group came to your camp on that first night. Did you know they were planning to do that?'

'No.' Jill shook her head. 'And I would have told Daniel not to if I'd known. It was . . . unnecessary. I didn't want the other women to feel like the men were checking up on us.'

'And your brother spoke to Alice Russell that night.'

'There were only ten of us. I think most people spoke to each other.'

'Apparently he spoke to her privately,' Falk said.

'That's allowed.'

'Do you know what it was about?'

'I'm not sure. You'll have to ask him.'

'We'd love to,' said Carmen. 'But he's left.'

Jill said nothing, but the very edge of her tongue flicked out again to touch the cut on her lip.

'So you didn't notice Alice seeming particularly upset or uneasy after they spoke?' Carmen said.

'Of course not. Why would she be?'

'Because she asked you to let her leave,' Carmen said. 'At least twice.'

'Well. Like I said, if I'd let everyone leave who wanted to, there would have been none of us left.'

'We understand it created some tension between the two of you.'

'Who told you that? Everyone was tense out there. It was a very difficult situation.'

Jill picked up her cold coffee cup from the table and held it. Falk couldn't quite tell if her hands were shaking.

'How did you bruise your face?' Falk said. 'It looks quite bad.'

'Oh for God's sake.' Jill set down her cup so hard it sent the liquid sloshing over the edge. 'What is that question supposed to imply?'

'Nothing. It's just a question.'

Jill looked from Falk to Carmen and back again. She sighed. 'It was an accident. It happened on the final night in the cabin when I was breaking up a stupid argument.'

'What kind of argument?' Falk said.

'A lot of fuss over nothing. I've told the state police this. Frustration and fear bubbled over and got the better of us. We're talking shoving and hair-pulling for a couple of seconds at most. Schoolyard stuff. It ended almost as soon as it began.'

'It doesn't look like it.'

'I was unlucky. I was standing in the wrong place and I took a bit of a knock. It wasn't deliberate.'

'Who was the fight between?' Falk watched her closely. 'All of you?'

'God, no.' Jill's swollen face was a picture of surprise. 'It was between Alice and Beth. We were all cold and hungry and Alice was threatening to leave, and that's when things boiled over. I blame myself, I should have seen it coming. Those two never got along.'

Day 2: Friday Afternoon

Jill's teeth chattered as she walked. She had changed into dry clothes back at the river – they all had, turning their backs on each other while they shivered and stripped – only for another sheet of rain to sweep through twenty minutes later. She would have liked to have walked a little faster to warm up, but she could see Lauren was still shaky on her feet. The plaster from the first aid kit kept peeling off her forehead, exposing a bloody gash.

Alice was out in front, map in hand. Bree had surrendered it on the river bank without a word. Beth, as usual, was bringing up the rear.

It was strange, Jill thought, how much the bushland started to look alike. Twice she'd spotted something – once a stump, the other time a fallen tree – which she was sure she remembered from earlier. It was like walking in a semi-constant sense of déjà vu. She shifted her pack on her shoulders. It was lighter without the tent poles, but their absence was weighing heavy on her mind.

'Are we still all right?' Jill said as they slowed to pick their way around a muddy ditch.

Alice took out the compass and looked at it. She turned to face the other way and looked at it again.

'All right?' Jill said again.

'Yes, we're fine. It's because the track curved back there. But this is right.'

'I thought we were supposed to be reaching higher ground.' The ground beneath their feet was overgrown, but stubbornly flat.

A voice came from behind. 'We need to check the compass more regularly, Alice.' Lauren had her hand pressed to the plaster on her forehead.

'I just did. You saw me do it.'

'But you need to do it often.'

'I know that, thanks, Lauren. You're free to step up and take over at any time, if you want.' Alice held the compass in the flat of her hand, like an offering. Lauren hesitated, then shook her head.

'Let's keep moving,' Alice said. 'We'll be starting to climb soon.'

They walked on. The ground remained flat. Jill was on the verge of asking how soon was 'soon', when she felt the telltale burn in her thighs. They were ascending. Gently, but on a definite uphill slope. She felt like crying with relief. *Thank God.* With any luck there would be a phone signal at the top. They could call someone. They could pull the pin on this whole mess.

The fear had started to crystallise back at the river bank,

169

with a quality she had felt perhaps two or three times in her life. A realisation: *This is very wrong.* That car crash when she was nineteen, when she watched the other driver's eyes grow wide and white as their vehicles slid towards each other in a macabre dance. Then again, three years later, at only her second office Christmas party. Too much to drink, too much flirtation with the wrong man and a walk home that had nearly ended badly.

And then there was that peculiar day when her father had welcomed her and Daniel into his private office – the one at home, not the one at work – and explained exactly how the BaileyTennants family business worked.

Jill had said no. She had sometimes taken comfort in that in the following years. Daniel had said yes straight away, but she had held firm for nearly eighteen months. She had enrolled in a teacher training course and sent her apologies for family gatherings.

She'd believed for a while that her decision had been accepted. Only later did she realise she was simply being given space to make the slow march towards the inevitable in her own time. But something must have happened to speed things up – she never asked what – because after eighteen months, she'd been summoned again to her father's office. Alone, this time. He'd sat her down.

'You're needed. I need you.'

'You have Daniel.'

'And he's doing his best. But . . . ' Her father, who she'd loved and trusted most in the world, had looked at her and given a small shake of his head.

'Then stop.'

'We can't.' *We*, he'd said very clearly, not *I*.

'You can.'

'Jill.' He'd taken her hand. She'd never seen him look so sad. 'We can't.'

She'd felt the tears burning in the back of her throat at that. For him, and an easy favour done a long time ago for the wrong people and the slippery chute he'd found behind that trapdoor. The greedy quick buck he had found himself still repaying decades later and a thousand times over. And for herself, and the teaching course she'd never finish, and the no that had to turn into a yes. But at least for a while, she would remind herself in the years to come, it had been a no.

Now, as Jill's lungs burned and her legs ached, she tried to focus on the immediate task ahead. Every step uphill was a step closer to where they needed to be. She watched the back of Alice's head, driving the group onward.

Five years ago, Jill had been chief financial officer and Alice was a candidate through to the third round of the interview stage. She was up against only one other applicant, a man with similar qualifications but arguably more direct experience. At the end of her interview, Alice had looked at the panel each in turn and said she could do the job, but only would for a four per cent increase in the offered starting salary. Jill had smiled to herself. Told them to hire her. Find the four per cent.

As they approached a bend in the path, Alice stopped and consulted the map. She waited until Jill caught up. The others were straggling a little way behind.

'We should be at the top soon,' Alice said. 'Do you want to take a short break?'

Jill shook her head, the memory of the previous night's stumble around a dark campsite still fresh. The day was getting on. She couldn't remember what time the sun set, but she knew it was early. 'Let's keep going while we've still got the light. Have you checked the compass?'

Alice pulled it out and glanced at it.

'All good?'

'Yes. I mean, the path's twisting a bit so it depends which way we're facing, but we're still on track.'

'Okay. If you're sure.'

Another check. 'Yeah. I am.'

They carried on.

Jill hadn't regretted her hiring decision. Certainly not the four per cent. Alice had proved herself to be worth more, over the years. She was smart, she got the lie of the land quicker than most and she understood things. Things like when to speak up and when to hold her tongue, and that was important in a firm that was more like a family. When Jill's nephew – seventeen-year-old Joel, who was so much like his dad at that age – had looked sullenly over the trestle tables at last year's company picnic and blinked at the sight of Alice's beautiful daughter, Jill and Alice had exchanged knowing looks. Jill sometimes thought that in another time and place, she and Alice might have been friends. At other times, she thought not. Being around Alice was like owning an aggressive breed of dog. Loyal when it suited, but you had to stay on your toes.

'Are we nearly there?'

Jill heard Lauren's voice behind her. The woman's plaster had peeled loose again and a single pink trail of rain and blood had dripped down her temple and cheek, settling in the corner of her mouth.

'Nearly at the top. I think.'

'Do we have any water?'

Jill took out her own bottle and passed it to Lauren, who took a deep swig as they walked. Lauren's tongue flicked to the corner of her mouth, and she grimaced as it found the blood. She cupped her hand and poured water into her palm, some escaping onto the ground, and rinsed her cheek.

'Maybe we should –' Jill started to say as Lauren went to repeat the process, but bit her words short.

'Maybe what?'

'It doesn't matter.' She had been going to say maybe they should preserve their fresh water. But there was no need. There were more supplies at the campsite. And Jill was not yet ready to admit that they might be spending the night anywhere else.

The path rose steadily steeper and Jill could hear the breathing around her grow heavy. The sloping land to their right fell away at a sharper angle until it was a hill, and then a cliff side. Jill kept her eyes straight ahead, pushing up one step after another. She had lost track of how high they'd climbed when, almost without warning, the path levelled out.

The gum trees gave way and they came face to face with

a magnificent vista of rolling hills and valleys, stretching out beneath them right to the horizon. Shadows from shifting clouds created an ocean of green that rippled like waves. They had reached the top and it was breathtaking.

Jill dropped her pack on the ground. The five women stood side by side, hands on hips, legs aching, catching their breath as they surveyed.

'This is incredible.'

Almost on cue, the clouds parted, revealing the sun hanging low in the distance. It touched the very tips of the uppermost trees, engulfing them in a blazing watery glow. Jill blinked as the welcome golden light blinded her, and she could almost imagine she could feel the heat on her face. For the first time that day, she felt a weight lift from her chest.

Alice had taken her phone from her pocket and was looking at the screen. She was frowning, but that was all right, Jill told herself. Even if they had no signal, it would be okay. They would get to the second campsite, they would get dry, they would work something out with the shelter. They would get some sleep, and everything would look better in the morning.

Jill heard a dry cough behind her.

'Sorry,' Beth said. 'But which direction are we walking in again?'

'West.' Jill looked over.

'Are you sure?'

'Yes. Towards the campsite.' Jill turned to Alice. 'That's right, isn't it? We're going west?'

'Yep. West.'

'So we've been walking west the whole time?' Beth said. 'Since we left the river?'

'Christ. Yes. I already said.' Alice didn't glance up from her phone.

'Then –' A pause. 'Sorry. It's just – if this way is west, then why is the sun setting in the south?'

Every face turned, just in time to see the sun drop another notch below the trees.

That was the other thing about Alice, Jill thought. Sometimes she could make you feel so bloody betrayed.

Chapter 12

The light was starting to go by the time Falk and Carmen left Jill Bailey in the lounge, alone with her thoughts. They headed back along the path to the cabins with the early calls of the evening chorus echoing around them.

'It gets dark so early up here.' Carmen checked her watch, the wind catching her hair. 'I suppose the trees block the light.'

They could see vans pulling up outside the lodge and weary rescue workers climbing out. Their breath formed clouds in the air. Still no good news, judging by their faces. The skies were quiet now; the chopper must have landed. Hope was fading with the day.

Falk and Carmen reached their cabin doors and stopped.

'I'm going to take a shower. Warm up a bit.' Carmen stretched and Falk heard her joints crack beneath the layers. It had been a long couple of days. 'Meet for dinner in an hour?'

With a wave she disappeared inside. Falk unlocked his own door and turned on the light.

Through the wall, he heard the sound of running water starting up.

He sat on the bed and ran over the conversation with Jill Bailey. She had an alertness about her that her brother didn't. It made Falk feel uneasy.

He rummaged through his backpack and pulled out a paper file containing his notes on Alice Russell. He thumbed through them, only half-reading. He already knew the contents well. At first, he wasn't sure what he was looking for, but as he turned the pages, it slowly became clear. He was looking for something that would ease the guilt, he realised. Some hint of reassurance that Alice Russell's disappearance was nothing to do with him. That he and Carmen hadn't trapped her in an impossible position that had forced her into making a mistake. That they hadn't made a mistake themselves. That they hadn't put Alice in danger. Hurt her.

Falk sighed, and sat back on the bed. When he got to the end of Alice's file, he went back to the start and pulled out her bank statements. She'd shared access to them voluntarily, if reluctantly, and like everything else, he'd been through them before. But he found something comforting in the way the orderly columns of figures and dates ran down page after page, documenting the everyday transactions that kept Alice Amelia Russell's world ticking over.

Falk ran his eyes down the numbers. The statements were monthly, with the first entry dated about twelve months earlier. The most recent was on Thursday, the day Alice and the others had set off for the retreat. She had spent four dollars at a motorway convenience store. It was the last time her bank card had been used.

He examined the incomings and outgoings, trying to flesh out his impression of the woman. He noted that four times a year, like clockwork, she spent several thousand dollars at the David Jones department store two weeks before the change of each season. That she paid her cleaner an amount that, depending on the hours worked, seemed suspiciously below the minimum wage.

Falk always found it interesting what people deemed valuable. He had breathed out in surprise the first time he had seen the five-figure annual sum that Alice parted with to enable her daughter to follow in her footsteps at Endeavour Ladies' College. And it seemed the cost of a top-shelf education didn't end with fees alone, he noticed now, with Alice making a significant one-off donation to the school six months earlier.

When the numbers started to blur a little, Falk rubbed his eyes and closed the file. He went to the window and looked out into the bushland, flexing his damaged hand. The start of the Mirror Falls trail was still visible in the gathering gloom. Out of the corner of his eye, he could see his dad's maps stacked on the bedside table.

He shuffled through the pile until he found the one for the Giralang Ranges, and opened it to the Mirror Falls trailhead. Falk wasn't entirely surprised to find the start of the route circled – he knew his dad had come up to the region, and this was one of the most popular trails. But as he looked at the page he still felt a jolt. When had his dad made that particular pencil mark? At their home, sitting at the kitchen table? Or perhaps standing at the trailhead, two hundred metres and ten years from where Falk stood now?

Without thinking about it, Falk pulled on his jacket and shoved the map in his pocket. He wavered, then grabbed his torch as well. Through the wall, he could still hear running water. Good. He wanted to do this without explanation. He pulled the cabin door shut and followed the path across the carpark to the trailhead. Behind him, the lodge glowed.

He stopped at the entrance to the Mirror Falls trail, taking in the surroundings. If Erik Falk had walked this path, he would have once stood on this very spot. Falk tried to imagine what his dad would have seen. The trees around him were decades old. It was possible, he thought, that their two viewpoints were close to identical.

He stepped in. At first all he could hear was his breathing, but slowly the evening sounds became more distinct. The thick line of trees gave him the vaguely claustrophobic sense of being under siege. His hand ached in his pocket, but he ignored it. It was psychosomatic, he knew. There had been rainfall, he told himself as he walked, there would be no fire here. He repeated it under his breath until he felt a little better.

Falk wondered how many times his dad had walked along this path. A couple at least, judging by the markings on the map. Far away from the city he hated. And alone, because his son refused to come with him. Although Falk suspected, honestly, that he'd probably enjoyed the solitude. That was one way, at least, in which they'd always been alike.

There was movement somewhere deep in the bushes and Falk jumped, laughing a little at the spike in his heart rate. Had his dad felt unnerved at all by the Kovac history? It was easy to feel isolated out here. And the notoriety would have been much fresher in collective memory then than it was now. Falk doubted it had troubled Erik much. His dad had always been a pretty practical bloke. And he was always more comfortable around trees and trails and outdoor spaces than he ever was around other people.

Falk felt a few spots of rain hit his face and pulled up his jacket hood. Somewhere in the distance, he could make out a low rumble, but wasn't sure if it was thunder or the falls. He should go back. He wasn't even sure what he was doing out here, alone in the dark. It was his second time on this trail but he recognised nothing. The landscape seemed to shift and alter when unobserved. He could be anywhere. He turned and started back in the direction of the lodge.

He'd taken only two steps when he stopped dead. He listened hard. Nothing; only the wind and the scurry of invisible paws. The path was empty in both directions. How far away was he from the nearest person? He hadn't walked a long way, he knew, but he felt like he could be the only one for miles. He stood completely still, looking and listening. Then he heard it again.

Footsteps. The tread was light but made the hairs on his neck stand up. He swivelled, trying to work out which direction it was coming from. He glimpsed the light through the trees a moment before it came around a bend, flashing straight into his eyes. He heard a gasp and the sound of something clattering to the ground. Blinded, Falk groped in his pocket for his torch, his fingers cold and clumsy as he felt for the switch. He turned it on, the beam casting a distorted shadow. The bushland hung on either side like a thick black curtain, and in the middle of the path, a slight figure shielded her eyes.

Falk squinted as his vision adjusted. 'Police.' He held out his ID. 'Are you all right? I didn't mean to scare you.'

The woman was half-turned away, but he recognised her from her photograph. Lauren. She was trembling as she bent to pick up her torch and when Falk stepped closer, he could see a nasty cut on her forehead. It had tentatively knitted together, but the area was swollen, the stretched skin shining in the glare of the torchlight.

'You're with the police?' Lauren peered at the ID, her voice wary.

'Yeah. Helping with the Alice Russell search. You're Lauren Shaw, aren't you? You were in the BaileyTennants group?'

'Yes. Sorry, I thought –' She took a deep breath. 'For a second there – it's stupid – when I saw someone alone on the path I thought it might be Alice.'

Falk, for a split second, had thought exactly the same thing. 'I'm sorry I scared you. Are you okay?'

'Yes –' She was still breathing heavily, her thin shoulders rising and falling underneath her jacket. 'I just got a shock.'

'What are you doing out here in the dark?' Falk said. Although she was perfectly entitled to ask him the same thing, Lauren shook her head. She must have been out there for a while. He could feel the chill coming off her clothes.

'Nothing sensible. I've been going out to the falls during the day. I meant to come back earlier, but it gets dark so quickly.'

Falk remembered the shadowy figure he'd seen leaving the trail. 'Were you out there last night as well?'

She nodded. 'I know it's probably ridiculous, but I thought Alice might find her way back to the start of the trail. We passed the waterfall on the first day and it's a really distinctive landmark. I was driving myself crazy sitting around the lodge, so I've been sitting out there instead.'

'Right.' Falk clocked her purple hat for the first time. 'We saw you out there yesterday afternoon.'

'Probably.'

There was a rumble of thunder and they both looked up.

'Come on,' he said. 'We're nearly at the lodge. I'll walk back with you.'

They moved slowly, their torch beams throwing cones of light on the uneven ground.

'How long have you been with BaileyTennants?' Falk said.

'Nearly two years. I'm strategic head of forward planning.'

'What does that involve?'

A heavy sigh. 'It involves identifying the future strategic

182

needs of our firm and putting together action plans –'
She stopped. 'Sorry. It all seems so pointless, after what's
happened to Alice.'

'It sounds like you all had a very difficult few days.'

Lauren didn't answer straight away. 'We did. It wasn't
any one thing that went wrong, it was a hundred little
things. It all kept adding up until it was too late. I just
hope Alice is okay.'

'Did you two work together a lot?' Falk asked.

'Not so much directly. But I've known her on and off
for years. We were at secondary school together and then
we ended up working in the same industry, so our paths
crossed a bit. And our girls are the same age. They both go
to our old school now. When Alice found out I'd left my
old firm she put in a good word for me at BaileyTennants,
and I've been there ever since.'

'We heard it was you who managed to lead the group
to a road,' Falk said. 'Get the others back.'

'That's probably overstating it. I'd done a bit of navigating at school, but we just walked in a straight line
and hoped for the best.' She sighed. 'Anyway, it had been
Alice's idea to take that path. When we realised she'd gone,
I thought we'd only be a couple of hours behind her. I
couldn't believe it when she wasn't at the end.'

They rounded a corner and the start of the trailhead
came into sight. They were back. Lauren shivered and
wrapped her arms around herself as they emerged. The air
seemed heavy with the threat of a storm and the lodge up
ahead looked warm and inviting.

'Shall we talk inside?' he said, but Lauren hesitated.

'Can we stay out here? Do you mind? Nothing against Jill, but I don't have the energy for her tonight.'

'Okay.' Falk could feel the cold coming through his boots and wriggled his toes inside his socks. 'Tell me about this school camp you and Alice went on.'

'McAllaster? It was out in the back end of nowhere. We did academic subjects, but the main focus was on the outdoor activities. Hiking, camping, problem-solving activities, that sort of thing. No TV, no phone calls, the only contact with home during term time was through handwritten letters. They still do it, my daughter went two years ago. Alice's daughter too. A lot of private schools run them.' Lauren paused. 'And it's not easy.'

Even in Falk's childless world, he had heard tell of the dreaded full-year camp. The odd story over the years from colleagues who had graduated from one of the more prestigious establishments. The tale was usually told in the hushed tone of someone who has survived a bear attack or walked away from a fatal plane crash. Disbelief mixed with pride. *I got through it.*

'It sounds like it helped you a bit at least,' Falk said.

'A bit, perhaps. But I keep thinking that having rusty skills might be worse than having no skills. If we hadn't gone on that camp, maybe Alice wouldn't have got the stupid idea that she could walk out alone.'

'You didn't think she was equipped to do that?'

'I didn't think any of us were. I wanted to stay put and wait for help.' She sighed. 'I don't know. Or maybe we

184

should have gone with her and at least stayed together as a group. I *knew* she might try to go alone once she'd been outvoted. She always –'

She stopped. Falk waited.

'Alice always overestimated her skills. At camp she was a group leader a lot of the time, but she wasn't chosen because she was particularly outstanding. I mean, she was good. But she wasn't as good as she thought.'

'Popularity contest?' Falk said.

'Exactly. She was voted team leader because she was popular. Everyone wanted to be her friend, wanted to be in her group. I can't blame her for buying into the hype. If everyone around you is constantly telling you you're fantastic, it's easy to believe it.'

Lauren glanced over her shoulder at the trees.

'I suppose in one way she did us a big favour, though. If we'd stayed at the cabin and waited for help, we'd still be out there waiting. Apparently they still can't find it.'

'No. That's true.'

Lauren looked at him.

'They're searching very hard, though, from what I can tell,' she said. 'That cabin is the only thing some of the officers want to talk about.'

'I suppose because that was the last place Alice was seen,' Falk said. He remembered what King had said. *We haven't told the women about Sam Kovac.* Falk wondered if that was the best move under the circumstances.

'Maybe.' Lauren was still watching him closely. 'It feels like more than that, though. The place had been empty for a while, but not forever. I told the other police. At least some-one knew about it because someone had been out there.'

'How do you know?'

'They'd buried a dog.'

There was a silence. Dead leaves blew around their feet.

'A dog.'

'At least one.' Lauren picked at her nails. Her hands were birdlike, the bones in her wrists visible under the skin. 'The police keep asking if we saw anyone else while we were out there.'

'Did you?'

'No. Not after the first night, when the men's group came to our camp. But –' Lauren's eyes darted to the bush-land and back. 'It was strange. Sometimes it did feel like we were being watched. We weren't, obviously. There's no way we could have been. You get paranoid out there though, your mind starts to play tricks.'

'And you definitely didn't see the men again?'

'No. I wish we had. But we were so off track. The only way to find us would have been to follow us.' She gave a shake of her head, dismissing the idea before it could settle. 'I can't understand what happened to Alice. I know she would have headed along that northern route. We walked that trail just a couple of hours behind her. And Alice has always been tough. Mentally, physically. If we managed to get out, she should have as well. But it was like she just vanished.' Lauren blinked. 'So now I go and sit at the falls, hoping she'll storm out, angry and pointing fingers and threatening legal action.'

Falk nodded at the dark slice across her forehead. 'That looks nasty. How did you get it?'

Lauren's fingers fluttered to the wound and she gave a bitter laugh. 'We managed to lose our stove canister and tent poles in a swollen river. I was trying to reach them and got hit in the head.'

'Not during the fight at the cabin then?' he said lightly.

Lauren stared at him for a beat before answering. 'No.'

'I only ask because Jill Bailey said that's how she got her bruise. Breaking up an argument.'

'Did she?'

Falk had to hand it to Lauren, her face gave nothing away.

'Did she not?' he said.

Lauren seemed to be weighing something up. 'Jill got her bruise during an argument. Whether or not she was breaking it up is debatable.'

'So Jill was involved?'

'Jill started it. When Alice wanted to leave. They were fighting over who would get the phone. It didn't last long, but that was what it was about. Why? What did Jill say?'

Falk shook his head. 'It doesn't matter. Maybe we mis-understood her take on it.'

'Well, whatever she told you, she was part of it.' Lauren looked down. 'I'm not proud of it, but we all were, I sup-pose. Alice as well. That's why I wasn't surprised when she left.'

A bolt of lightning cracked bright overhead, throwing the gum trees into sharp silhouette. It was followed by a rumble of thunder and all at once the clouds opened. They had no choice but to move. Pulling their hoods over their heads, they jogged towards the lodge as the rain drummed against their jackets.

'Are you coming inside?' Falk said as they reached the steps. He had to shout over the noise.

'No, I'll make a run for my room,' Lauren called as they reached the path. 'Find me if you need anything else.'

Falk waved a hand and jogged up the steps into the lodge, where the rain rattled against the porch roof. He jumped as a dark figure shifted in the shadows near the doorway.

'Hey.'

He recognised Beth's voice. She was sheltering under the porch and smoking as she stared out at the hammering rain. Falk wondered if she'd seen him talking to Lauren. He wondered if it mattered. She had a cigarette in one hand and something he couldn't see in the other. And a guilty look on her face.

'Before you say anything, I know I shouldn't,' she said.

Falk wiped his face with a damp sleeve. 'Shouldn't what?'

Beth sheepishly held up a bottle of light beer. 'Under my probation. But it's been a really hard few days. I'm sorry.' She sounded like she meant it.

Falk couldn't muster the energy to be concerned about a light beer. It had been considered barely a step above water when he was growing up.

'Just stay under the drink–drive limit.' It seemed like a reasonable compromise but Beth blinked, surprised. She smiled.

'I'm not supposed to smoke out here either,' she said. 'But for God's sake, it's outside.'

'That's true,' Falk said as they watched the downpour.

'Every time it rains it makes it harder to track someone. That's what they told me, anyway.' Beth took a sip. 'It's been raining a lot.'

'It has.'

Falk looked across at her. Even in the poor light, she seemed exhausted.

'Why didn't you mention the fight in the cabin?'

Beth glanced at her beer bottle. 'Same reason I'm not supposed to be doing this. Probation. And it really wasn't a big deal. Everyone was scared. We all overreacted.'

'But you argued with Alice?'

'Is that what you've heard?' Her eyes were hard to read in the dark. 'We all argued with Alice. Anyone who says different is lying.'

She sounded upset and Falk let the words settle.

'How is everything else?' he said eventually.

A sigh. 'All right. They might let her out tomorrow or the next day.'

Falk realised Beth was talking about her sister. 'I meant you,' he said. 'Are you going okay?'

Beth blinked. 'Oh.' She seemed unsure how to answer. 'Yeah. I suppose. Thanks.'

Through the window to the lounge, Falk could make out Carmen curled up in a battered armchair in the corner. She was reading something, and her hair fell loose and damp around her shoulders. Around the room, off-duty searchers were chatting or playing cards, or sitting with their eyes closed in front of the open fire. Carmen raised her head and nodded as she saw him.

'Don't let me keep you,' Beth said.

Falk opened his mouth to answer but was drowned out by another crash of thunder. The sky burst lightning-white, then everything fell dark. He heard a collective murmur of surprise followed by a groan from the lodge behind him. The electricity was out.

Falk blinked as his eyes adjusted. Through the glass, the low glow of the lounge room fire threw faces into black and orange shadow. The corners of the room were invisible. He heard a movement in the doorway and Carmen appeared out of the gloom. She had something under her arm. It looked like an oversized book.

'Hi.' Carmen nodded at Beth, then turned to Falk. She frowned. 'You're wet.'

'I got caught in the rain. Everything okay?'

'Fine.' She shook her head the tiniest fraction. *Don't talk here.*

Beth had tucked the beer bottle out of sight and her hands were folded primly in front of her.

'It's pretty dark out there,' Falk said to her. 'Do you want us to walk you back to the cabins?'

Beth shook her head. 'I'll stay here for a while. I don't mind the dark.'

'All right. Be careful.'

He and Carmen pulled their hoods up and stepped out from the shelter of the porch. The rain stung his face. A

190

few low-level lights glowed around the grounds, whether powered by solar or emergency generator Falk didn't know, but it was enough to help them see their way.

Another flash of lightning lit the sky and the raindrops formed a ghostly white sheet. Through them, Falk caught a glimpse of someone running across the carpark. Ian Chase, soaking wet in his red Executive Adventures fleece. It was impossible to tell where he had come from, but from the way his hair was plastered to his skull, he had been out in the storm for a while. The sky went dark again and he vanished from sight.

Falk wiped his face and focused on the path in front of him. It was slick with water and mud, and it was a relief when they rounded the corner and were under the cabin awning. They stopped outside Carmen's room. She had zipped the large book inside her jacket, against her chest. She pulled it out now and handed it to Falk while she searched her pockets for her key. It was a scrapbook with a laminated cover, he could see now. The corners were a little damp and on the front was a sticker with the words: *Property of Giralang Lodge. Do not remove from lounge.* Carmen turned in time to see him raise his eyebrows and laughed.

'Come on, I've taken it fifty metres. I'm going to return it.' Carmen opened her door and let them in, both a little breathless from the cold and the rain. 'But first, there's something you should see.'

Day 2: Friday Night

They argued about what to do until it grew too late to do anything.

Finally, as the sun set in the south, they walked a little way down the hill, looking for shelter. When the last of the day slipped away, they made camp where they stood. Made camp in the best way they could, at least.

They pooled their resources in a pile on the ground and stood in a five-point formation, torches out, silently observing their haul. Three tent canvasses, intact; less than a litre of water, split unevenly between five bottles; six muesli bars.

Beth looked at the meagre pile and felt the first stirrings of hunger pains. She was thirsty as well. Despite the cold and her damp clothes, she could feel the sweat from the uphill hike sticking under her arms. Her water bottle was one of the emptiest. She swallowed. Her tongue was thick in her mouth.

'We should try to collect some rainwater overnight,'

Lauren said. She was also staring at the mostly empty bottles with a nervous look in her eyes.

'Do you know how to do that?' Jill's voice had a pleading note.

'I can try.'

'And where are the rest of the muesli bars?' Jill said. 'I thought we had more.'

Beth felt rather than saw her sister's eyes flick towards her. She didn't look back. *Get stuffed, Bree.* Beth's conscience, for once, was clear.

'There should be at least a couple more.' Jill's face had taken on an unhealthy grey tinge in the torchlight and she kept blinking. Beth wasn't sure if it was grit in her eyes or if she simply couldn't believe her surroundings.

'If someone has eaten them, just say.'

Beth could feel the weight of their collective gaze. She dropped her eyes and stared at the ground.

'All right.' Jill shook her head and turned to Alice. 'Go and see if you can find a signal.'

Alice went, nothing to say for once. She had gone from shocked to defensive then back again, poring over the map and tapping the face of the compass. They had been walking west, she was sure of it. Her protestations had been greeted mostly with a stunned silence. It was hard to argue with the setting sun.

The group watched her walk off, her phone clutched in her hand. Jill opened her mouth like she wanted to say something else, but couldn't think what. She kicked the tent bags with the toe of her boot. 'See if you can work something out with these,' she said to Lauren, then turned and followed Alice.

Beth listened as Lauren suggested ways to use the guy ropes to stretch the tent canvasses between the trees, forming a makeshift roof. Lauren tried to demonstrate, pulling the ropes one-handed as she pressed the peeling plaster against her forehead, but eventually had to give up. She stood back, her hairline a matted, bloodied mess in the torchlight as she pointed Beth and Bree to one trunk then another. Beth's fingers grew stiff in the night air. It would have been a hard task even in daylight and she was glad for her heavy torch with the powerful beam.

At last, they were finished. The canvasses stretched between the trees, already sagging a little in the middle. It wasn't raining, yet, but Beth thought she could feel a storm in the air. That test was still to come.

At various spots along the darkened path, Beth could see Alice appear and disappear. She stood in a blue halo of artificial light and turned in circles and reached to the sky, like a desperate dance.

Beth pulled her sleeping bag out of her pack, sighing at the damp patch at the foot end. She tried to work out the most sheltered spot but it seemed pointless. All options were crap. She lay the sleeping bag out under the nearest canvas, then stood and watched her sister mess around, debating where to lay her own bag. Normally Bree would have wanted to be as close to Alice as possible. It was interesting, Beth thought to herself, how fast the wheel could turn.

Nearby, Lauren was sitting on her pack, fiddling with the compass.

'Is it broken?' Beth said.

There was no reply at first, then a sigh. 'I don't think so. But you have to use it properly for it to work. Everyone naturally veers off course over distances. I knew Alice wasn't checking it enough.'

Beth wrapped her arms around herself, bouncing up and down on her heels a little. She was shivering.

'Should we try to start a fire? My lighter has dried out.'

Lauren looked over in the dark. The fresh plaster on her forehead was already coming loose. There was only one more in the first aid kit, Beth knew.

'We're not supposed to out here.'

'Would anyone know?'

'We would know if it got out of control.'

'In this weather?'

She saw the shadow of Lauren's shoulders shrug. 'Beth, it's above my pay grade to make decisions like that. Ask Jill.'

Beth could just make out Jill in the pinprick glow of Alice's phone. They had gone a fair way searching for a signal. That didn't bode well.

She popped a cigarette in her mouth and wandered away from the shelter. The tiny flame flicked up from the lighter, destroying her night vision, but she didn't care. The familiar taste flooded her mouth as she inhaled, and for the first time in hours she felt like she could breathe properly.

Beth stood and smoked, warming her lungs, her eyes and ears slowly attuning to the night as she stared out into the bush. Beyond the grey trunks of the nearest gum trees, the darkness was absolute. She could see nothing, then felt a prickle as she realised the same would not be true the other way round. The glow from her cigarette would be obvious at the very least, and torches lit up the camp behind her. Anything out there would be able to see her as clear as day. She jumped as she heard something crack far away in the blackness. *Don't be stupid.* It was an animal. Something nocturnal. And harmless. A possum, probably.

Nevertheless, she sucked in the last of her cigarette and turned back to camp. As she did, three heads looked towards her. Jill, Alice and Lauren. She could see no sign of Bree. The trio was huddled together, holding something between them. For a minute Beth thought it was the compass, but as she walked closer she realised it was not. It was a cheese sandwich covered in plastic wrap. Jill had an apple in her hand.

'Where did you find them? Are they from lunch?' Beth said. The rumble from her stomach was audible.

'They were with the backpacks,' Jill said.

'Whose backpack?' Beth looked at the pile. The bags lay in disarray, spewing belongings from when they had pooled their resources in the growing dark. She saw their faces and realisation dawned slow and cold. 'Well, it wasn't mine.'

There was no reply.

'It wasn't. I ate my lunch. You saw me.'

'We didn't,' Alice said. 'You were up the path having a cigarette.'

Beth stared at her in the dark. 'Trying to put me in the doghouse won't get you out of it, you know.'

'Both of you, stop it,' Jill snapped. 'Beth, if you didn't eat your lunch, it is technically still your lunch. But we did say we'd all pool what we had –'

'They're not mine. Am I not speaking English?'

'Well. All right then.' It was clear Jill didn't believe her.

'I would say if they were.' Beth's eyes felt hot and tight. She waited. No response. 'They're not.'

'The food's mine.' They all turned. Bree was standing behind the group. 'Sorry. I was over there having a pee. It's mine. I didn't eat it at lunch.'

Jill frowned. 'Why didn't you say when we unloaded our bags?'

'I forgot. I'm sorry.'

When Beth was younger, she had truly believed in telepathy. She had gazed deep into Bree's eyes, placed her fingers with ritualistic precision on her twin's temples. *What are you thinking?* Bree had outgrown the game first. She'd never been very good at it, which Beth thought explained her lack of interest. When Bree had started batting away her fingers and refusing to maintain eye contact, Beth had taken to watching her from across the room, tuning in to the grace notes in her speech and the subtleties in her movements. Searching for clues. *What are you thinking, Bree?* It wasn't really telepathy, Beth realised later, more an ability to read nuances and tics.

And now, that unspoken language in which Beth had once been fluent was whispering in her ear. *Bree is lying.* Whatever reason she'd had for not sharing, it hadn't been forgetfulness.

'You don't have to cover for her, Bree.' Alice sounded disappointed.

'I'm not.' Beth could hear the wobble in her twin's voice.

'Nobody blames you. Don't lie for her.'

'I know. I'm not.'

'Really? Because this isn't like you.'

'*I know.* I'm sorry.'

Even with a confession, Bree could do no wrong. Beth almost felt like laughing. Almost, but not quite, because in the dark she could hear her sister on the verge of tears. She sighed.

'Look. Okay.' Beth tried to sound contrite. 'The food was mine.'

'I knew it.'

'Yes, Alice. You were right, well done. Sorry, Bree –'

'It wasn't –' Bree tried to interject.

'Thanks for trying to help, but it's really okay. I'm sorry, everyone.'

It was strange, she thought. She could almost feel the palpable relief. Bree was in the right and Beth was in the wrong. The natural order restored, everyone could relax. There was nothing to see here.

'All right,' Jill said finally. 'Let's split what we have and we'll let that be the end of it.'

'Fine.' Beth turned her back before she could be drawn

into a discussion about sanctions or punitive portions. 'Do whatever you want. I'm going to bed.'

She could tell they were watching as she pulled off her boots and climbed fully clothed into her sleeping bag. She burrowed down, pulling the hood over her head. It was barely warmer in than out, and the ground jabbed and prodded her through the thin material.

She could hear strains of muffled discussion as she closed her eyes. She wasn't comfortable, but sheer exhaustion pulled her towards sleep. She was on the cusp of dropping off when she felt the gentle weight of a hand on the top of her bag.

'Thank you.' The voice was a whisper.

Beth didn't respond and a moment later felt the weight disappear. She kept her eyes closed, ignoring the faint sounds of arguing, first about the food, then about a fire.

The next time she opened them, it was with a jolt. She didn't know how long she'd been asleep, but it must have rained at some point. The ground around her bag was soaked and her limbs were heavy with cold.

Beth lay shivering as she listened. Had something woken her? She blinked, but her eyes were as good as blind in the dark. She could hear nothing but the rustle of man-made material around her ears as she breathed in and out. There was something in the neck of her sleeping bag and she recoiled, then prodded it with a finger. It was a wedge of cheese sandwich and a slice of apple wrapped in damp plastic. Beth couldn't tell if it was her own fifth or her sister's quarter. She considered not eating it, but her hunger was shouting louder than her principles. Different rules applied out there, anyway.

Beth wasn't sure if the others had sensed it, but earlier she had felt the faintest stirrings in the atmosphere. Something base and elemental and almost primitive, where a bit of stale bread and cheese became a prize worth fighting for.

There was a movement outside her sleeping bag and Beth stiffened. She couldn't tell what had made it – woman or wildlife. She lay still and by the time it disappeared, the word she'd been searching for had formed on the tip of her tongue, so real she could almost taste its residue. *Feral*.

Chapter 13

Carmen's room was inky black. Falk handed her his torch and heard her swear softly as she stumbled her way to the window and opened the curtains. The emergency lights from the grounds were enough to give form to the furniture in the room.

'Grab a seat,' she said.

Like in his room, there were no chairs. Falk sat on the edge of the bed. Carmen's room was exactly the same as his, small and sparsely furnished, but the air smelled a little different. Something pleasantly light and subtle that reminded him vaguely of summer months. He wondered if Carmen always smelled like that, or if he just hadn't noticed before.

'I ran into Lauren outside the lodge,' he said.

'Oh yes?' Carmen passed him a towel and sat across from him, tucking her legs under herself. She pulled her hair across one shoulder and rubbed it dry while Falk filled her in on their conversation. About the cabin, about the argument, about Alice. Outside, the rain pounded against the window.

'I hope Lauren's underestimating Alice,' Carmen said when he'd finished. 'One of the rangers was telling me that even he would struggle out there in this weather. Assuming Alice did actually walk off of her own accord.'

Falk thought again of the voicemail. *Hurt her.* 'Are you thinking something else now?'

'I don't know.' Carmen pulled the scrapbook between them and turned the pages. They were filled with newspaper clippings, the edges wrinkled where the glue had dried. 'I was flicking through this while I was waiting for you. It's a community history for tourists.'

She found the page she wanted and turned it to face him.

'Here. They've glossed over the Kovac years – not surprising – but I guess they couldn't ignore it completely.'

Falk looked down. It was a newspaper article about Martin Kovac's sentencing. Jailed for life, according to the headline. Falk could guess why that article had been included rather than any others. It was a full stop. A line drawn under a dark period. The article was a feature piece, recapping the investigation and the trial. Near the bottom of the page, three dead women smiled out from three photographs. Eliza. Victoria. Gail. And the fourth one, Sarah Sondenberg. Fate unknown.

Falk had seen pictures of Kovac's victims before, but not recently and not all together like this. He sat opposite Carmen in the darkened cabin and shone his beam over each face. Blonde hair, neat features, slim. Definitely pretty. All at once, he saw what Carmen had seen.

Eliza, Victoria, Gail, Sarah.

Alice?

Falk met each of the dead women's eyes, then he shook his head. 'She's too old. These four were all in their teens or twenties.'

'Alice is too old *now*. But she wouldn't have been back then. How old would she have been when this was all happening? Late teens?' Carmen tilted the book to better see the photos, the newsprint skin ghostly grey in the torchlight. 'They'd all be about the same age if they'd lived.'

Falk didn't say anything. Next to the four faces was a large image of Martin Kovac taken shortly before his arrest. It was a casual shot, snapped by a friend or neighbour. It had been reproduced hundreds of times over the years, in newspapers and on TV. Kovac was standing by a barbecue. A true blue Aussie bloke in his singlet, shorts and boots. The obligatory stubbie in his hand and the grin on his face. Above that, his eyes were narrowed against the sun, and his curly hair was a mess. He looked thin but strong, and even in a photo the muscle tone was visible on his arms.

Falk knew the image, but for the first time now, he noticed something else. In the background of the shot, sliced in half by the edge of the photo, the blurred rear of a child's bicycle was visible. It wasn't much. A small bare leg, a boy's sandal on a pedal, the back of a striped t-shirt, a glimpse of dark hair. The child was impossible to identify, but as Falk stared, he felt his skin prickle. He dragged his eyes away, from the boy, from Martin Kovac, from the long-ago gazes of the four women staring up at him.

'I don't know,' Carmen said. 'It's a long shot. It just struck me.'

'Yeah. I see why.'

She looked at the bushland outside. 'I suppose whatever's happened, at least we know Alice is in there. It's a huge area, but it's finite. She has to be found eventually.'

'Sarah Sondenberg wasn't.'

'No. But Alice has got to be somewhere. She hasn't walked back to Melbourne.'

Thoughts of the city nudged something in Falk's mind. Out of the window, he could just make out the space where Daniel Bailey's car had been until today. A black BMW, spacious. Tinted windows. A large boot. A four-wheel drive was parked there now.

'We're going to need to talk to Daniel Bailey again,' Falk said. 'Follow him back to Melbourne. Find out what he said to Alice on that first night.'

Carmen nodded. 'I'll call the office, let them know.'

'Do you want me to –?'

'No, it's all right. You took it last time. I'll do it tonight. See what they have to say.'

They managed to share a smile at that. They both knew exactly what would be said. Get the contracts. It's crucial you get the contracts. Understand that it is imperative you get the contracts. The smile faded from Falk's face. He understood. He just didn't know how they were going to do it.

As the wind howled outside, he let himself ask the question that had been eating at him. If Alice was still out there because of them, was it worth it? He wished they knew more about the bigger picture of the operation, but he also knew the details didn't really matter. However it was painted, the bigger picture always showed the same thing: a handful of people at the top of the tree feeding off the vulnerable below.

He looked over at Carmen. 'Why did you join this division?'

'Finance?' She smiled in the dark. 'That's a question I usually get asked at the staff Christmas party, always by some drunk bloke with a confused look on his face.' She shifted on the bed. 'I was invited to join child protection, back when I first started. A lot of it's algorithms and pro-gramming now. I did a placement, but –' Her voice was tight. 'I couldn't handle the frontline stuff over there.'

Falk didn't ask for details. He knew some officers who worked in child protection. They all spoke in the same tight voice from time to time.

'I stuck it out for a bit longer but started to do more on the technical side,' Carmen went on. 'Chasing them down through the transactions. I was pretty good at it, and eventu-ally ended up here. This is better. I wasn't sleeping by the end, over there.' She was quiet for a moment. 'What about you?'

Falk sighed. 'It wasn't long after my dad died. I was on the drugs team for a couple of years when I started. Because, you know, you're fresh and that's where all the excitement is.'

'So they tell me at the Christmas party.'

'Anyway, we'd got a tip-off about this place in north Melbourne being used as a warehouse.'

Falk remembered pulling up outside a family bungalow on a run-down street. The paintwork was peeling and the grass out front was patchy and yellow, but at the end of the driveway sat a hand-made post box carved in the shape of a boat. Someone had cared enough about living in that house at one time to make or buy that, he had thought at the time.

One of his colleagues had banged on the door, then broken it open when there was no answer. It had gone down easily, the wood had aged over the years. Falk had caught a glimpse of himself in a dusty hall mirror, a dark shadow in his protective gear, and for a second had barely recognised himself. They'd rounded the corner into the living room, shouting, weapons raised, not sure what they'd find.

'The owner was an old bloke with dementia.' Falk could still picture him, tiny in his armchair, too confused to be frightened, his grubby clothes hanging off his frame.

'There was no food in the house. His electricity was off and his cupboards were being used to store drugs. His nephew, or a bloke who he thought was his nephew, was heading up one of the local trafficking gangs. He and his mates had free run of the place.'

The house had been stinking, with graffiti scrawled across the floral wallpaper and mouldy takeaway cartons littering the carpet. Falk had sat with the man and talked about cricket, while the rest of the team had searched the house. The man had thought Falk was his grandson. Falk, who had buried his dad three months earlier, had not corrected him.

'The thing is,' Falk said. 'They'd drained his bank accounts and his super. Taken out credit cards in his name and run up debts on things he never would have bought. He was a sick old man and they left him with nothing. Less than nothing. And it was all right there in his bank statements, waiting for someone to notice. Everything that was happening to him could have been picked up months earlier if someone had spotted the problem with the money.'

Falk had said as much in his report. Weeks later, an officer from the finance division had stopped by for a friendly chat. A few weeks after that, Falk had visited the old bloke in his care home. He'd seemed better, and they'd talked some more about cricket. When Falk had got back to the office he'd looked into the transfer requirements.

His decision had raised a few eyebrows at the time, but he knew he'd started to become disillusioned. The raids felt like a short-term fix. They were putting out one fire after another when the damage was already done. But money made the world go around for most of these people. Cut off the head and the rotten limbs withered and died.

At least, that was what he'd always thought about, every time he targeted someone in a white collar who thought their university education made them smart enough to get away with it. Like Daniel and Jill and Leo Bailey, who he knew probably believed they really weren't doing anything all that bad. But when Falk looked at people like them, he saw all the other old blokes and struggling women and sad kids, sitting scared and alone in their unwashed clothes far away at the other end of the line. And he hoped that in some way, he could stop the rot before it ever reached them.

'Don't worry.' Carmen said. 'We'll work something out. I know the Baileys think they're good at this stuff after all these years, but they're not as smart as us.'

'No?'

'No.' She smiled. Even sitting down she was as tall as him. No need to tilt her head upwards for their eyes to meet. 'For one thing, you and I know how to get away with laundering money.'

Falk couldn't help but smile back. 'How would you do it?'

'Investment properties. Easy as. You?'

Falk, who had once written an in-depth study of the topic, knew exactly how he would do it, with two decent backup plans. Investment properties was one of them.

'I don't know. Casino, maybe.'

'Bullshit. You'd have something more sophisticated.'

He grinned. 'Don't mess with the classics.'

Carmen laughed. 'Maybe you're not that smart after all. That would involve regularly kicking your heels up at the tables, and anyone who's met you would see through that in a second. I should know. My fiancé puts in the hours down there. And he's nothing like you.'

Truthfully, that was one reason why the casino wasn't even in Falk's top three. Too much legwork. But he just smiled. 'I'd play the long game. Establish a pattern of behaviour. I can be a patient man.'

Carmen gave a small laugh. 'I bet you can as well.' She shifted on the bed, stretching out her legs in the pale light. All was quiet as they looked at each other.

There was a rumble and a hum somewhere deep in the lodge and without warning the lights flickered on. Falk and Carmen blinked at each other. The confessional atmosphere evaporated with the darkness. They both moved at the same time, her leg brushing against his knee as he rose from the bed. He stood. Wavered.

'I suppose I'd better make a move before the lights go again.'

The briefest pause. 'I suppose so.'

Carmen stood and followed him to the door. He opened it, the cold air hitting him with a blast. He could feel her eyes on him as he made the short walk back to his own door.

He turned. ''Night.'

A heartbeat of a hesitation. ''Night.' Then she stepped back inside, and was gone.

Back in his room, Falk didn't turn on the light immediately. Instead he went to the window, letting the thoughts running through his head calm and settle.

The rain had finally stopped and he could make out a handful of stars through the few gaps in the clouds. There had been a time in Falk's life when he hadn't looked at the night sky for years. The lights in the city were always too harsh. Nowadays, he tried to remember to look up when he had the chance. He wondered what, if anything, Alice would see if she did the same now.

The moon hung luminous and white with silver threads of cloud suspended in the glow. Falk knew the Southern Cross must be hidden somewhere behind them. He'd seen it a lot as a kid in the country. One of his earliest memories was of his dad carrying him outside and pointing upwards. The sky bright with stars, and his dad's arm tightly around him, showing him patterns that he said were always there, somewhere in the distance. Falk had always believed him, even if he couldn't always see them.

Day 3: Saturday Morning

The icy wind blew in from the south and didn't let up. The women trudged along wordlessly, their heads down against the gale. They had found a tight path, something that was almost a path, at least, something perhaps used by animals. By mutual unspoken consent, no-one pointed out when it vanished under their feet from time to time. They simply lifted their boots higher through the undergrowth and squinted at the ground until something that was almost a path appeared again.

Bree had woken hours earlier, fractious and freezing, unsure how long she'd been asleep. Nearby, she could hear Jill snoring. The woman was a heavy sleeper. Or perhaps simply exhausted. She hadn't even woken when their makeshift canopy had blown apart in the night.

As Bree lay on the ground staring at the pale morning sky, her bones seemed to ache deep in her body and she felt thick-mouthed from thirst. She could see that the bottles Lauren had put out to collect rainwater had toppled over.

211

They'd be lucky to get a mouthful each. At least the food Bree had left tucked next to her sister's head was gone. She was both relieved and disappointed.

Bree still wasn't quite sure why she hadn't told the others about her uneaten meal. She'd opened her mouth but some long-buried lizard part of her brain had stopped the words from coming out. It scared her a little to think why. *Survive* was something she joked about doing at her desk until Friday night drinks rolled around. In any other context, the word felt alien and frightening.

She'd tried to talk to her sister that morning as they rolled up their soaked sleeping bags.

'Thank you.'

It had been Beth's turn to brush her aside. 'Forget it. But I don't know why you're so scared of them.'

'Of who?'

'All of them. Alice. Jill. Daniel, for that matter.'

'I'm not scared. I just care what they think. They're my managers, Beth. And yours, by the way.'

'So what? You're as good as any of them.' Beth had stopped packing and looked at her then. 'In fact, I wouldn't be clinging too hard to Alice's coat-tails if I were you.'

'What are you talking about?'

'It doesn't matter. But be careful around her. You might do better finding someone else's arse to lick.'

'For God's sake, it's called taking my career seriously. You should try it.'

'And you should try to get some perspective. It's only a bloody job.'

Bree didn't say anything, because she knew her sister would never understand.

It had taken twenty minutes to pack up their makeshift camp and another hour to decide what to do. Stay or go. Stay. Go.

Alice had wanted to move. Find the campsite, find a way out, do something. No, Lauren had argued, they should stay on high ground. It was safer there. But the wind was wilder there too, slapping against their faces until they were stinging and flushed. When the drizzle started again, even Jill stopped nodding patiently when Lauren spoke. They huddled under a canvas, trying to drip rainwater into a bottle while Alice walked around, waving her phone in the air for as long as they dared. When her battery hit thirty per cent, Jill ordered her to turn it off.

They should stay put, Lauren had tried again, but Alice unfolded the map. They'd crowded around, pointed at paper landmarks as the wind threatened to whip the sheet away. A ridge, a river, a gradient. None matched exactly. They couldn't agree which peak they were on.

Along one edge of the map ran a vehicle road in the north. If they could bush-bash their way to the road, they could follow it out, Alice said. Lauren had almost laughed. That was so dangerous. So was hypothermia, Alice had replied, staring at her until she'd looked away. In the end, the cold won the argument. Jill announced she couldn't stand still any longer.

'Let's find the road.' She handed the map to Alice,

hesitated, and passed the compass to Lauren. 'I know you don't agree, but we're all stuck in this together.'

They'd shared the mouthful of rainwater collected in the bottle, Bree's allocated sip only making her thirst worse. Then they had started to walk, ignoring their twisting stomachs and sore limbs.

Bree kept her eyes on the ground, putting one foot after the other. They had been going for nearly three hours when she felt something land with a gentle thump near her boot. She stopped. A tiny egg lay shattered on the ground, its core leaking out, clear and gelatinous. Bree looked up. High above, the branches were rocking in the wind and among them, a small brown bird peered down. It twitched its head. Bree couldn't tell if it understood what had happened. Would the bird miss its little lost egg, or had it forgotten it already?

Bree could hear her sister approaching from behind, her smoker's lungs giving her away.

Get some perspective. It's just a bloody job.

It wasn't, though. Bree had been twenty-one and four days away from graduating with honours when she'd realised she was pregnant. Her boyfriend of eighteen months, who she'd known had been secretly browsing rings on the Tiffany website, had said nothing for ten minutes while he paced around the kitchen of their student flat. That was one of the things she remembered most clearly. Wishing he'd sit down. Finally, he had and had placed his hand over hers.

'You've worked so hard,' he said. 'What about your

internship?' His own internship in New York was due to start four weeks later, followed by a place on a post-graduate law degree course. 'How many graduates a year does BaileyTennants take again?'

One. BaileyTennants took one graduate a year for its development program. He knew this. That year it would be Bree McKenzie.

'You're so excited.' That was true. She had been thrilled at the prospect. She still was, surely. He had added his other hand at this point, cupping her palm in both of his.

'It's mind-blowing. It is. And I love you so much. It's just –' His eyes showed true terror. 'Bad timing.'

At last, she had nodded, and by the next morning, he had helped her schedule the necessary appointment.

'Our kids will be proud, one day,' he'd said. He had definitely said 'our'. She remembered that distinctly. 'It makes so much sense to get your career under your belt first. You deserve to make the most of your opportunities.'

Yes, she had told herself later, many times. She'd done it for her career and for all those great opportunities lying in store. She had definitely not done it for him. Which was lucky, because he had never once called her again after he left for New York.

Bree looked down now at the smashed egg. Above, the mother bird had disappeared. With her boot, Bree swept some dried leaves over the broken shell. She couldn't think what else to do.

'Stop here.' Jill's voice floated forward. She was trailing the pack. 'Let's rest for a minute.'

'Here?' Alice turned and looked back. The trees were still tight, but the path had grown a little wider and no longer disappeared underfoot.

Jill dropped her pack without answering. She was red-faced, her hair sticking out in tufts. She was reaching for something in her jacket pockets when she stopped, her gaze snagging on a broken tree stump at the side of the path.

Without a word, she moved towards it. A pool of rainwater had collected in the bowl of the stump. Jill, who Bree had once seen refuse a herbal tea because the leaves had infused too long, suddenly dipped her cupped hands into the stump, lifted them to her lips and swallowed deeply. She paused to pick something black from her mouth, flicking it off her finger before dipping her hands in again.

Bree swallowed, her own tongue immediately swollen and dry, and stepped up to the stump. She plunged her hands in, the first scoop sloshing over her knuckles as her arm collided with Jill's. She went in again, lifting her palms to her lips more hastily this time. The water tasted dank and coarse, but she didn't stop, dipping in again, now jostling for space with four other pairs of hands. Someone pushed her hands out of the way, and Bree shoved back, ignoring the pain as her fingers bent backwards. She plunged in again, fighting for her share, the sound of grunts and swallows loud in her ears. She kept her head down, determined to cram as much into her mouth as possible. Before she realised it, the water was gone, and her fingernails were scraping the mossy bottom.

She stepped back quickly. Her mouth was gritty and she felt unbalanced, like she'd crossed a line she hadn't known existed. She thought she wasn't the only one; she could see her surprise and shame echoed on the faces around her. The water churned in her empty stomach and she had to bite her lip to stop herself vomiting.

One by one, they edged further away from the stump, avoiding eye contact. Bree sat down on her pack and watched as Jill pulled one boot off and peeled back her sock. Her heel looked bloodied and raw. Nearby, Lauren was checking the compass for the thousandth time. Bree hoped it was telling her something.

There was the flick of a lighter and the faint hint of cigarette smoke.

'Seriously, do you really have to do that now?' Alice said.

'Yes. That's why it's called an addiction.' Beth didn't look up, but Bree felt an uneasy ripple run through the group.

'It's disgusting, that's what it is. Put it out.'

Bree could barely smell the smoke.

'Put it out,' Alice said again.

Beth looked over this time and blew a long plume of smoke in the air. It hung there, taunting them. In one swift movement, Alice's hand darted out and grabbed the cigarette packet. She pulled her arm back and hurled it into the bush.

'Hey!' Beth was on her feet.

Alice was standing too. 'Break's over. Let's go.'

Beth ignored her and without a backward glance,

turned and waded into the long grass, disappearing through the trees.

'We're not bloody waiting for you,' Alice shouted. There was no response, just the tap of water on leaves. The rain had started again. 'For Christ's sake. Jill, let's go. She'll catch up.'

Bree felt the swell of anger, tempered only by the sight of Jill shaking her head.

'We're not leaving anyone, Alice.' Jill's voice had an edge Bree hadn't heard before. 'So you'd better find her. An apology is in order, too.'

'You're joking.'

'I'm absolutely not.'

'But –' Alice started, when there was a shout from behind the solid curtain of bushland.

'Hey!' Beth's voice was muffled. She sounded far away. 'There's something back here.'

Chapter 14

The morning sky was a dirty grey when Falk knocked on Carmen's door. She was packed and waiting. They carried their bags to the carpark, treading carefully where overnight rain had made the path slippery.

'What did the office have to say?' Falk reached across their car windscreen and fished out a handful of dead leaves that had caught beneath the wipers.

'The usual.' Carmen didn't need to spell it out. He knew it would have been a virtual repeat of his own conversation the night before. *Get the contracts. Get the contracts.* She dumped her bag in the car boot. 'Did you tell King we're off?'

Falk nodded. After leaving Carmen last night, he'd left a message for the sergeant. The officer had rung back on Falk's room landline an hour later. They'd exchanged updates – a depressingly short conversation on both sides. It sounded like the lack of progress was taking a toll.

'Have you lost hope?' Falk said.

'Not entirely,' King said. 'But it's feeling more and more like a needle in a haystack.'

'How long do you keep searching?'

'We search until there's no point anymore,' King said. He didn't spell out exactly when that would be. 'But we'll have to start scaling back if we don't find anything soon. Keep that to yourself, though.'

Now, in the morning light, Falk could see the tension on the searchers' faces as a group climbed into the waiting minivan. He dumped his own bag next to Carmen's and they headed into the lodge.

A different ranger was behind reception, leaning over the desk and issuing instructions to the woman hunched over the ancient visitors' courtesy computer.

'Try logging back in again,' the ranger said.

'I have. Twice! It won't let me.'

Lauren, Falk realised. She sounded close to tears. She looked up when she heard them slide their keys across the counter.

'You're checking out? Are you driving back to Melbourne?' She was half out of her seat already. 'Can you take me? Please, I need to get home. I've been trying to find a lift all morning.'

In the harsh morning light, her eyes were red and lined. Falk wasn't sure whether it was due to lack of sleep or if she'd been crying. Both, perhaps.

'Sergeant King's given you the all clear to leave?'

'Yes, he said I'm allowed.' She was already at the door. 'Don't go without me. Please. I'll get my bag. Five minutes.'

She disappeared before he could say anything. On the reception counter, Falk noticed a fresh stack of printed fliers. MISSING, was written in bold letters above a reproduction of Alice Russell's smiling work headshot, along with key details and a description. Below was the last group photo Ian Chase had snapped at the start of the Mirror Falls trail.

Falk looked at it. Jill Bailey stood at the centre, with Alice and Lauren to her left. Bree was on Jill's right, with Beth a half-step out from the rest of the group. It was easier to make out details on the flier than it had been on Chase's phone. Every face was smiling, but, on closer inspection, he thought every smile seemed a little forced. With a sigh, he folded up the flier and put it into his jacket pocket.

Carmen used the ranger's radio and by the time she'd confirmed what Lauren had said with Sergeant King, the woman was back. She stood in the entranceway, clutching her backpack. It was filthy, and Falk realised with a jolt that it would be the same one she'd taken on the retreat.

'Thank you so much,' she said, as she followed them across the carpark and climbed into the back seat. She pulled on her seatbelt and sat upright, her hands clutched in her lap. Desperate, Falk realised, to leave.

'Is everything all right at home?' he said, starting the engine.

'I don't know.' Lauren's face creased. 'Do either of you have kids?'

Falk and Carmen both shook their heads.

'No. Well, every time you turn your back, there's

221

bloody something,' she said, as though that explained it. Falk waited, but she said nothing more.

They passed the marker signalling the official boundary of the park and as they headed into the tiny town, Falk could see the familiar glow of the service station sign up ahead. He checked the gauge and pulled in. It was the same guy behind the counter.

'They haven't found her then,' he said when he saw Falk. It wasn't a question.

'Not yet.' Falk looked at the guy properly for the first time. The beanie cap hid his hair, but his eyebrows and stubble were dark.

'Haven't found any of her stuff? Shelter? Bag?' the man asked, and Falk shook his head. 'That's probably a good thing,' he went on. 'You find the belongings or shelter, the body's always next. Always is. You can't survive without equipment out there. I reckon there's a good chance they'll never find her now. Not if there's been no sign so far.'

'Well, let's hope you're wrong,' Falk said.

'I'm not wrong.' The guy glanced outside. Carmen and Lauren had got out of the car, their arms folded across their chests in the cool air. 'You planning on coming back this way again?'

'I don't know,' Falk said. 'If they find her, maybe.'

'In that case, hope to see you again soon, mate.'

The words had the finality of a funeral.

Falk walked back to the car and got in. The park and the town were ten kilometres behind them before he realised he was well over the speed limit. Neither Carmen nor

Lauren objected. When the horizon of the ranges was small in the rear-view mirror, Lauren shifted in the back seat.

'Apparently they think the cabin we found might have been used by Martin Kovac,' she said. 'Did you know that?'

Falk glanced in the mirror. She was staring out of the window, chewing her thumbnail.

'Who told you that?'

'Jill. A searcher told her.'

'I think it's only a suspicion at this stage. It's not confirmed.'

Lauren winced and pulled the tip of her thumb from her mouth. The nail was bleeding, a black half-moon crescent welling around the bed. She looked down at it, then started to cry.

Carmen twisted round to hand her a tissue. 'Do you want to stop? Get some air?'

Falk pulled over on the hard shoulder. The road in both directions was empty. Woodland had finally given way to farmland and he was reminded of the drive out to the ranges. Only two days earlier, but it seemed like a long time ago. It was a week tomorrow since Alice had first plunged into the bushland. *We search until there's no point anymore.*

Falk climbed out and got a bottle of water from the car boot for Lauren. The three of them stood by the side of the road as she took a sip.

'I'm sorry.' Lauren licked her lips. They were pale and dry. 'I feel bad leaving while Alice is still out there.'

'They'd let you know if there was anything you could do,' Falk said.

'I know that. And I know –' She gave a hard little smile. 'I know Alice would do exactly the same in my position. It doesn't make it easier though.' She took another sip of water, her hands a little steadier now. 'My husband called me. Our daughter's school is contacting parents. Some photos of a student have been leaked online. Explicit, apparently, whatever exactly that means.'

'Not of your daughter?' Carmen said.

'No. Not Rebecca. She wouldn't do anything like that. But – I'm sorry, thank you –' Lauren took the fresh tissue Carmen offered and wiped her eyes. 'But she had some trouble last year with this kind of thing. Not explicit stuff, thank God, but a lot of bullying. Other girls were taking pictures of her getting changed after sport, eating her lunch, stupid things. But they were sharing them on their phones and on social media. Encouraging students from the boys' school to comment. Rebecca –' Lauren paused. 'She's had a difficult time.'

'I'm sorry to hear that,' Carmen said.

'Yes, well, us too. It's unbelievable really, when I think of the amount I've paid to send her to that school. They wrote to us saying they'd disciplined a couple of the girls responsible and held an assembly about respect.' Lauren wiped her eyes a final time. 'I'm sorry. When I hear something like this, it brings it all back.'

'Girls can be real bitches at that age,' Carmen said. 'I remember. And school was hard enough even without the internet.'

'It's a whole different world, what they get up to now,'

Lauren said. 'I don't know what I'm supposed to do. Delete her accounts? Take away her phone? The way she looks at me, I may as well be asking her to cut off her hand.' She finished the water and wiped her eyes once more. She managed a watery smile. 'Sorry. I think I just really need to be at home.'

They climbed back in the car and Lauren leaned her head against the window as Falk started the engine. Eventually he could tell from her breathing that she'd fallen asleep. Curled up, she looked like a husk, he thought. Like the bushland had sucked the spirit out of her.

He and Carmen took turns driving and dozing. The rain spots on the windscreen grew lighter the further they travelled, as they left the bush and its weather in their wake. The radio crackled softly as stations came back into range one by one.

'Hallelujah,' Carmen said when her phone buzzed. 'The signal's back.'

She hunched down in the passenger seat and scrolled through her messages.

'Jamie looking forward to having you home?' Falk said, and immediately wondered why he was even asking.

'Yeah. Well, he will be. He's away on a course for a couple of days.' She unconsciously fingered her engagement ring and Falk found himself thinking of the night before. Her long legs unfolding on the bed. He cleared his throat and glanced in the mirror. Lauren was still asleep, a worried frown line still visible between her eyes.

'Sounds like she'll be glad to be back anyway,' he said.

225

'Yeah.' Carmen glanced around at the back seat. 'I know I would be after all that.'

'Have you ever had to go on one of these teambuilding things?'

'No, thank God. You?'

Falk shook his head. 'I guess it's more a private sector thing.'

'Jamie's been on a couple.'

'With the sports drinks company?'

'It's a fully integrated lifestyle brand, thanks very much.' Carmen was smiling. 'But, yes, they're really into that kind of thing.'

'Has he done anything like this?'

'I don't think so. It's mostly bonding through adventure sports. Although once he and a group had to tile a bathroom in a disused warehouse.'

'Really?' Falk laughed. 'Did they know much about tiling?'

'I don't think so. And they were pretty sure the next day's group was going to be told to tear it down. So it went about as well as you'd imagine. To this day, he still doesn't speak to one of the other blokes.'

Falk smiled. Kept his eyes on the road. 'You all set for the wedding?'

'Pretty much. It's come around fast though. Still, we've got a celebrant, and Jamie knows where and when to show up, so we'll get there.' She looked over. 'Hey, you should come.'

'What? No. I wasn't fishing.' He really hadn't been.

226

He couldn't remember the last time he'd been to a wedding.

'I know. But you should. It'll be good. It'll be good for you, anyway. I've got a few single friends.'

'It's in Sydney.'

'It's an hour's plane ride.'

'And it's in three weeks. Isn't it a bit late for seating plans and all that?'

'You've met my fiancé. I literally had to put "no denim" on the invitations for his side of the family. Does that sound like the kind of event with a concrete seating plan?' She stifled a yawn. 'Anyway, I'll give you the details. Think about it.'

There was movement in the back seat and Falk looked in the mirror. Lauren had woken and was looking around with the wide-eyed surprise of someone who had forgotten where they were. She seemed bewildered by the passing traffic. Falk didn't blame her. After only a few days in the bushland, he felt a little bewildered himself. He and Carmen swapped seats, and they each sat lost in their own thoughts as the city grew nearer, the radio playing in the background. The news came on at the top of the hour. Falk turned up the volume, then immediately regretted it.

It was the lead story. Police were investigating a potential link between the notorious Martin Kovac and a cabin where missing Melbourne hiker Alice Russell was last seen, the newsreader informed them.

Falk wasn't surprised that detail had been leaked. With the number of searchers involved, it had only been a matter of time. He twisted around and Lauren met his eyes. She looked scared.

'Do you want me to switch it off?'

She shook her head and they listened as the newsreader recapped details that had hit the airwaves two decades earlier. Three female victims, with a fourth never recovered. Then Sergeant King's voice filled the car, stressing the historic nature of the Kovac crimes. An assurance that full efforts were being made, a fresh plea for information from anyone who had been in the area and, at last, the bulletin moved on.

Falk glanced over at Carmen. There had been no mention of Kovac's son. It looked like King had managed to keep that quiet so far.

Lauren directed them to a home in one of the leafier suburbs, the kind that estate agents liked to call aspirational. Carmen pulled up outside a house that was obviously cared for, but carried the faint whiff of recent neglect. The patch of lawn at the front was overgrown and no-one had bothered removing a scribble of graffiti on the fence.

'Thank you again.' Lauren unbuckled her seatbelt, relief visible on her face. 'Someone will let me know straight away if there's any news, won't they? About Alice?'

'Of course,' Falk said. 'I hope everything's okay with your daughter.'

'Me too.' Her expression hardened. She didn't sound at all sure. They watched as Lauren took her bag and disappeared into the house.

Carmen turned to Falk. 'So, what now? Should we warn Daniel Bailey we're on our way, or surprise him?'

Falk considered. 'Let's warn him. He'll want to be seen helping the search effort and it'll keep him on side.'

Carmen pulled out her phone and put in a call to BaileyTennants. She was frowning by the time she hung up. 'He's not in the office.'

'Really?'

'His secretary was insistent. He's on leave for a few days, apparently. Personal reasons.'

'While an employee's missing?'

'I suppose Jill did say he'd come back for a family issue.'

'I know, I just didn't believe her,' Falk said. 'We could try his house?'

Carmen started the engine then paused with a thoughtful look on her face. 'You know, it's not too far to Alice's place from here. Maybe we'll get lucky and find a helpful neighbour with a spare key.'

He looked over. 'And crisp copies of the documents we need printed out and left on Alice's kitchen counter?'

'That would be ideal, yes.'

Get the contracts. Get the contracts. Falk's smile faded. 'All right. Let's see what we can see.'

Twenty minutes later, Carmen rounded a corner into a leafy street and slowed the car. They had never visited Alice Russell at home and Falk looked around with interest. The neighbourhood was a picture of expensive serenity. The pavement and fences were spotless and the very few vehicles parked on the road gleamed in the light. Falk guessed most were safely tucked away under protective covers in locked garages. The neat trees lining the nature strip looked like plastic models compared with the primal lushness that had lurked over them for the past three days.

Carmen crawled along, squinting at the shining letter-boxes. 'Christ, why don't these people put clear numbers on their houses?'

'I don't know. Keep the riff-raff away?' A movement up ahead caught Falk's eye. 'Hey. Look.'

He pointed to a large cream-coloured home at the far end of the road. Carmen followed his gaze and her eyes widened in surprise as a figure strode out of the drive-way, head down. A flick of the wrist and the black BMW parked on the road gave a subtle beep as it unlocked. Daniel Bailey.

'You're kidding,' Carmen said. He was wearing jeans and an untucked shirt, and he ran a harried hand through his dark hair as he opened the driver's door. He climbed in and fired up the engine, pulling away from the kerb. The BMW had turned a corner out of sight by the time they reached the house. Carmen followed far enough to see it swallowed up and swept away along a main artery.

'I don't feel comfortable chasing,' she said, and Falk shook his head.

'No, don't. I don't know what he was doing but it doesn't look like he was running.'

Carmen did a U-turn and stopped outside the cream-coloured home. 'I guess we found Alice's house, anyway.'

She turned off the engine and they climbed out. Falk noticed that the city air now seemed to have a fine film on it that gently coated his lungs with each breath. He stood on the pavement, the concrete oddly hard underneath his hiking boots, and surveyed the two-storey home. The lawn was large and neatly mowed, and the front door shone in a glossy shade of navy. A thick mat at its foot declared visitors welcome.

Falk could smell the decay of winter roses in the air and hear the distant rush of traffic. And on the second floor of Alice Russell's home, through a streak-free window overlooking the road, he could see a five-pointed white star of fingertips pressed against the windowpane, a flash of blonde hair and the open-mouthed circle of a face looking out.

Day 3: Saturday Afternoon

'There's something back here.'

Beth's voice was muffled. A moment later, there was a rustle and a crack and she re-emerged, forcing her way through the shrubbery growing high and wild on either side of the track.

'That way. There's a shelter.'

Jill looked in the direction Beth was pointing, but the bushland was thick and complete. She could see nothing but trees.

'What kind of shelter?' Jill craned her neck and took a step forward, her raw left heel screaming in protest.

'A little hut or something. Come and see.'

Beth was gone again. All around, the tap of rain was growing more insistent. Without warning Bree stepped into the long grass and disappeared after her twin.

'Wait –' Jill started, but it was too late. They were out of sight. She turned to Alice and Lauren. 'Come on. I don't want us getting separated.'

Jill stepped off the trail and into the bushland before anyone could argue. Branches clawed at her clothes and she had to lift her feet high. She could make out splashes of colour as the twins' jackets bobbed in and out of view. Finally, they stopped moving. Jill caught up, breathing heavily.

The cabin lay small and squat in a tiny clearing, its hard lines at odds with the twisted curves of the bushland. Two vacant black windows gaped out of rotting wooden frames, and the door sagged open on its hinges. Jill looked up. The walls might be bowed, but it appeared to have a roof.

Beth walked up to the cabin and put her face to the window, the back of her head slick and shining with rain.

'It's empty,' she called over her shoulder. 'I'm going inside.'

She pulled open the sagging door and was swallowed up by the black interior. Before Jill could say anything, Bree had followed her sister inside.

Jill was alone, her own breath loud in her ears. Suddenly Beth's face appeared in a window.

'It's dry in here,' she called. 'Come and see.'

Jill tramped through the long grass towards the cabin. At the door, she felt a prickle of unease. She had the sharp urge to turn and walk away, but there was nowhere else to walk to. Bushland and more bushland. She took a breath and stepped inside.

The interior was dim and it took Jill's eyes a minute to adjust. She could hear a tinny rattle overhead. The roof was doing its job, at least. She took another step in, feeling the floorboards creak and sag under her feet. Lauren appeared in the doorway, shaking the rain from her jacket. Alice hovered behind, watching and saying nothing.

Jill surveyed the room. It was oddly shaped and bare except for a rickety table shoved against one wall. Spider webs hung thick and white in the corners and something had built a nest of twigs and leaves in a small hole in the floorboards. A single metal cup sat alone on the table. She picked it up experimentally, noticing the perfect ring it left in the dust and dirt.

Some cheap plywood boards had been nailed together at some point to create the sense of a second room. The twins were already in there, staring silently at something. Jill followed them and immediately wished she hadn't.

A mattress was propped against one wall. Its fabric was speckled green with mould, except in the very centre. There, the floral pattern was entirely obscured by a large dark smear. It was impossible to tell what colour the mark had originally been.

'I don't like this,' Alice said from behind Jill, making her jump. She was staring past her at the mattress. 'We should keep moving.'

The twins turned, their faces hard to read. Jill could see that they were shivering, and realised she was as well. Once she noticed, she couldn't stop.

'Hang on.' Beth wrapped her arms around herself. 'We should at least think about this. It's dry in here, and a bit warmer. And it's got to be safer than wandering around out there all night.'

'Has it?' Alice looked pointedly at the mattress.

'Of course. People die of exposure, Alice,' Beth snapped. 'We've got no tents, no food. We need shelter. Don't write off this place because it was me who found it.'

'I'm writing it off because it's horrible.'

They both turned to Jill, who felt a wave of exhaustion crash over her.

'Jill, come on,' Alice said. 'We don't know anything about this place. Anyone could be using it as a base, we have no idea who knows about it —'

Jill felt the dust between her fingertips.

'It doesn't seem well used,' she said. She deliberately avoided looking at the mattress.

'But no-one knows we're here,' Alice said. 'We need to get back —'

'How?'

'Find the road! Walk north, like we agreed. We can't stay here indefinitely.'

'It's not indefinitely. Just until —'

'Until when? It could be weeks before we'd be found here. We have to at least try to get back.'

Jill's shoulders stung where her pack had rubbed two angry stripes, and every layer of clothing on her body was damp. Her heel was crippling. She listened to the rattle of rain against the roof, and knew she simply could not bear to step out into it again. 'Beth's right. We should stay.'

'Seriously?' Alice was agape.

Beth didn't attempt to hide the triumph on her face. 'You heard her.'

'No-one is bloody asking you.' Alice turned to Lauren. 'Back me up. You know we can walk out from here.'

Lauren touched her forehead. The dirty plaster was coming unstuck again. 'I think we should stay too. At least for tonight.'

Alice turned wordlessly to Bree, who hesitated, then nodded, her eyes firmly cast down.

Alice gave a small noise of disbelief.

'Christ.' She shook her head. 'All right, I'll stay.'

'Good.' Jill dropped her pack.

'But only until the rain stops. Then I'm walking out.'

'For God's sake!' Despite the cold, Jill felt a hot surge of anger flare from her aching shoulders to her raw heel. 'Why do you have to be so difficult? We've already been through this. No-one is going off alone. You'll stay until we agree to leave, Alice. As a group.'

Alice glanced at the cabin door as it swung open on its sunken hinges, throwing a rectangle of wintry light across her face. She drew a breath to say something then stopped, and closed her mouth gently, the tip of her pink tongue visible between her white front teeth.

'Okay?' Jill said. Her skull was pounding with the start of a headache.

Alice gave a tiny shrug. She didn't say anything, but she didn't need to. The meaning was clear. *You can't stop me.*

Jill looked at Alice, and at the open door and the bushland outside, and wondered if that were true.

Chapter 15

Falk banged on Alice Russell's navy blue front door and listened as the sound echoed deep within the house. They waited. There was a stillness, but not the hollow emptiness of a vacant property. He realised he was holding his breath.

The face had disappeared from the upper window as soon as he'd seen it. He'd nudged Carmen, but by the time she looked up it was a blank square. There'd been a face, he'd explained. A woman.

They knocked again and Carmen cocked her head.

'Did you hear that?' she whispered. 'I think you're right, there's someone there. I'll stay here, you see if you can get around the back.'

'Okay.'

Falk walked to the side of the house and tried a tall gate. It was locked, so he dragged a nearby wheelie bin closer and, glad he was in his hiking clothes, climbed up and over. He could hear Carmen knocking as he followed a paved path into a large back garden. It was complete with decking area and a spa pool filled with water in a shade of blue unseen in nature, while ivy climbing the wall gave the space a secluded feel.

The back of the house was made up almost entirely of windows looking into a spacious kitchen. The polished panes of glass were so highly reflective, he almost didn't see the blonde woman inside. She was standing in the doorway to the hall, perfectly still, with her back to him. Falk heard Carmen knock again and the woman jumped at the sound. At the same time, she must have sensed his movement outside because she spun around, crying out as she saw him in the garden, her familiar face wide open in shock.

Alice.

For a split second, Falk felt the giddy euphoria of relief rush through him. The adrenaline pulsed once, hard, then with a pain that was almost physical, drained as fast as it arrived. He blinked as his mind caught up with what he was seeing.

The woman's face was familiar, but it wasn't one he recognised. And woman wasn't even the right word, he thought, a groan forming low and deep in his throat. She was just a girl, staring out at him from the kitchen with fear in her eyes. Not Alice. Nearly, but not quite.

Falk pulled his ID out before Alice's daughter could scream again. He held it towards her at arm's length.

'Police. Don't be scared,' he called through the window. He tried to remember the girl's name. 'Margot? We're helping with the search for your mum.'

Margot Russell took half a step towards the glass. Her eyes looked bruised from crying as she peered at the badge.

'What do you want?' Her voice was shaky, but strangely unsettling. Falk realised it sounded a lot like her mother's.

'Can we talk to you?' Falk said. 'My colleague at the front door is a woman, why don't you let her in first?'

Margot hesitated and glanced once more at the badge, then nodded and disappeared. Falk waited. When she returned, Carmen was following. Margot unlocked the back door and let him in. As Falk stepped inside, he was able to see her properly for the first time. Like Alice, she was almost beautiful, he thought, but with the same sharpness in her features that made her something else. Striking, perhaps. She was sixteen, he knew, but with her jeans and socked feet and bare face, she looked very young.

'I thought you were supposed to be staying with your dad?' he said.

Margot gave a tiny shrug, her eyes down. 'I wanted to come home.' She held a mobile phone and was turning it over in her hands like a worry bead.

'How long have you been here?'

'Since this morning.'

'You can't be here alone,' Falk said. 'Does your dad know?'

'He's at work.' Tears welled in her eyes but didn't spill over. 'Have you found my mum?'

239

'Not yet. But they're looking hard.'

'Look harder.' Her voice wobbled and Carmen led her to a kitchen stool.

'Sit down. Where do you keep your glasses? I'll get you some water.'

Margot pointed at a cupboard, still fiddling with her phone.

Falk pulled up a stool and sat opposite her. 'Margot, do you know that man who was here before?' he said. 'The one knocking on the door?'

'Daniel? Yeah, of course.' There was an uneasy note in her tone. 'He's Joel's dad.'

'Who's Joel?'

'My ex-boyfriend.' A definite inflection on the *ex*.

'Did you speak to Daniel Bailey just then? Did he say why he was here?'

'No. I don't want anything to do with him. I know what he wanted.'

'And what's that?'

'He's looking for Joel.'

'Are you sure?' Falk said. 'It wasn't anything to do with your mum?'

'My mum?' Margot looked at him as though he was an idiot. 'My mum's not here. She's missing.'

'I know. But how can you be sure why Daniel came here?'

'How can I be sure?' Margot gave a strange strangled laugh. 'Because of what Joel's done. He's been really busy online.' She gripped her phone so hard the skin on her

240

hands turned white. Then she took a breath and held it out so Falk could see. 'I suppose you may as well see. Everyone else has.'

The Margot on the screen looked older. Her makeup was done and her hair was loose and shining. And the jeans were gone. The photos were surprisingly clear for such low lighting. The school had been right, Falk thought. They were definitely explicit.

Margot stared down at the screen, her face blotchy and her eyes red.

'How long have these been online?' Falk said.

'I think since yesterday lunchtime. There are two videos as well.' She blinked hard. 'They've already had more than a thousand views since then.'

Carmen put a glass of water in front of Margot. 'And you think Joel Bailey posted them?'

'He's the only one who had them. Or he was, at least.'

'And that's him with you in the photos?'

'He thinks they're funny. But he promised me he'd deleted them. I made him show me his phone to prove it. I don't know, he must have saved them.' She was rambling now, the words falling over each other. 'We took them last year, before we broke up. Just for –' a humourless twitch of the mouth, 'for fun. It was supposed to be fun anyway. When we broke up, I didn't hear from him for a long time, but then he messaged me last week. He wanted me to send him some more.'

'Did you tell anyone? Your mum?' Carmen said.

'No.' Margot's eyes were incredulous. 'As if I would.

I told Joel to get lost. But he kept messaging. He said I should send him new ones, or he'd show his friends the old ones. I told him he was full of shit.' She shook her head. 'He'd *promised* me he'd deleted them.'

She put a hand to her face and finally the tears spilled over, sliding down her face as her shoulders heaved. She couldn't speak for a long while.

'But he lied.' It was hard to hear her. 'And now they're out there and *everyone* has seen them.'

She covered her face and cried as Carmen put a hand out and rubbed her back. Falk made a note of the website on Margot's screen and emailed the details to a colleague in the cyber division.

Uploaded without consent, he wrote. *Age 16. Do your best re: removal.*

He didn't hold out much hope. They could probably get the images taken down from the original site, but that didn't help if they'd already been shared. He was reminded of an old proverb. Something about trying to catch feathers scattered in the wind.

After a long while, Margot blew her nose and wiped her eyes.

'I really want to talk to my mum,' she said in a tiny voice.

'I know,' Falk said. 'And they're searching for her, right now. But Margot, you can't stay here alone. We need to call your dad and get him to take you home.'

Margot shook her head. 'No. Please. Please don't call my dad.'

'We have to –'

'Please. I don't want to see him. I can't stay with him tonight.'

'Margot –'

'No.'

'Why not?'

The girl reached out and to Falk's surprise gripped his wrist, her fingers vicelike. She looked him in the eye and spoke through bared teeth.

'Listen to me. I cannot go to my dad's because *I cannot face him*. Do you understand?'

The only sound was the tick of the kitchen clock. *Everyone has seen them.* He nodded. 'I understand.'

They had to promise they'd find somewhere else for Margot to stay before she would agree to pack an overnight bag.

'Where can I go?' she'd asked. It was a good question. She'd shaken her head when they'd asked her for the name of another relative or friend she was willing to stay with. 'I don't want to see anyone.'

'We could probably line up some sort of emergency foster care,' Falk said in a low voice. They were standing in the hallway. Margot had finally agreed to gather a few things and the sound of her crying floated from her bedroom and down the stairs. 'I don't feel good about handballing her over to a stranger, though, not in the state she's in.'

Carmen held her phone in her hand. She'd been trying to get through to Margot's dad. 'What about Lauren's place?' she said finally. 'Just a thought. It's only for one night. At least she's aware of the photo situation.'

'Yeah, maybe,' Falk said.

'Okay.' Carmen glanced up the stairs. 'You try to call Lauren. I'm going to have a chat with Margot about where her mother might keep confidential documents.'

'Now?'

'Yes now. It might be the only chance we get.'

Get the contracts. Get the contracts.

'Yeah. Okay.'

Carmen disappeared up the stairs and Falk took out his phone, wandering back into the kitchen as he dialled the number. Outside the large windows, the afternoon was already growing dark. The cloud patterns were reflected in the smooth surface of the pool.

He leaned against the kitchen counter and stared at a cork noticeboard on the wall as he put the phone to his ear. A number of a handyman had been pinned to the board, alongside a recipe for something called quinoa power balls written in Alice's handwriting. There was an invitation to the Endeavour Ladies' College awards night which had come and gone last Sunday, the same day Alice was reported missing. A receipt for a pair of shoes. An Executive Adventures leaflet with the weekend's dates scribbled across the top.

Falk leaned in a little closer. On the cover of the leaflet, he could make out Ian Chase in the back row of a group staff shot. Chase was turned a little away from the camera, partially obscured by the colleague to his right.

The phone line was still ringing in his ear and his eyes wandered to a number of framed photo collages lining the kitchen walls. The pictures were all of Alice and her daughter, separately or together. Many of the shots mirrored each other – Alice and Margot as babies, on their first days of school, at dances, lying by pools in bikinis.

In Falk's ear, the ringing stopped and went through to Lauren's voicemail. He swore silently and left a message asking her to call him as soon as possible.

As he hung up he leaned in to look more closely at the nearest collage. A partly faded image had caught his eye. It was an outdoor shot in a setting that reminded him a little of the Giralang Ranges. Alice was wearing a t-shirt and shorts bearing the Endeavour Ladies' College logo, and was standing beside a raging river, head up, kayak paddle in her hand and a smile on her face. Behind her, a group of damp-haired, rosy-cheeked girls were crouched by the vessel. Falk's gaze snagged on the girl at the end, and he made a small noise of surprise. Lauren, he realised. The pinched look she wore now was buried beneath a layer of puppy fat, but like Alice, she was still entirely recognisable, especially around the eyes. That photo must be thirty years old, he thought. It was interesting how little they'd both changed.

His mobile trilled loudly in his hand, and he jumped. He looked at the screen – Lauren – and forced himself back to the present.

'Is something wrong?' she asked as soon as he answered. 'Have they found her?'

'No, shit, I'm sorry. It's not about Alice,' Falk said, kicking himself. He should have made that clear in his message. 'We've got a problem with her daughter. She needs somewhere to stay for tonight.' He explained about the online images.

There was such a long silence, Falk wondered if they'd been disconnected. Playground politics were something of a mystery to him, but as he listened to the dead air, he wondered just how fast the school mums would move to distance their offspring from Margot.

'She's not handling it too well,' he said finally. 'Especially with everything with her mum.'

Another silence, shorter this time.

'You'd better bring her around.' Lauren sighed. 'Jesus. These girls. I swear, they will eat themselves alive.'

'Thank you.' Falk hung up and headed down the hall. Opposite the stairs, a door opened onto a study. Carmen was sitting behind a desk staring at the home computer. She looked up as Falk entered.

'Margot gave me the password.' Her voice was low and he shut the door behind him.

'Anything?'

Carmen shook her head. 'Not that I can find. I'm searching blind, though. Even if Alice did save anything useful on here, she could have called the files anything, put them in any directory. We'll need to get the permits in place to take this away. Get it searched properly.' She sighed and looked up. 'What did Lauren say?'

'She said yes. Eventually. She wasn't too keen though.'

246

'Why, because of the photos?'

'I don't know. Maybe partly. Maybe not though, it sounded before like she has enough trouble with her own kid.'

'Yeah, that's true. She won't be the first or last to judge Margot over this though, you watch.' Carmen glanced at the closed door and lowered her voice. 'Please do not tell Margot I said that.'

Falk shook his head. 'I'll go and let her know the plan.'

Margot's bedroom door was open and he could see the girl sitting on her hot pink carpet. She had a small suitcase open in front of her. It was completely empty. She was staring down into her lap at her phone and she jumped as Falk knocked on the doorframe.

'We've arranged for you to stay at Lauren Shaw's tonight,' Falk said, and Margot looked up in surprise.

'Really?'

'Just for tonight. She knows what's going on.'

'Will Rebecca be there?'

'Her daughter? Probably. Is that okay?'

Margot picked at the corner of her suitcase. 'Just that I haven't seen them in a while. Does Rebecca know what's happened?'

'I imagine her mum will tell her.'

Margot looked like she wanted to say something, but shook her head. 'That's fair enough, I suppose.'

There was something about the way she said it. Daughter's mouth, mother's voice. Falk blinked, again feeling strangely unnerved.

'Okay. Well. It's only for one night.' He gestured at the empty case. 'Pack a couple of things and we'll drive you over.'

Distracted, Margot reached out and grabbed two garish lace bras from a pile on the floor. She held them in her hand, then looked up, watching him watching her. Something flickered across her face. A test.

He kept his eyes firmly on hers, his expression completely blank.

'We'll wait for you in the kitchen,' he said, feeling a wave of relief as he shut the door on the cloying pink room. When had teenage girls become so sexualised? Had they been like that at his age? Probably, he thought, except back then he had been all in favour of it. At that age, a lot of things seemed like harmless fun.

Day 3: Saturday Afternoon

For once, Beth was sorry when the rain stopped.

While it had been drumming down on the cabin roof, it had been difficult to talk. The five women had spread themselves out around the larger of the two rooms and stayed that way as the late afternoon wind blew in through the missing windows. It wasn't actually a lot warmer inside than out, Beth admitted privately, but at least it was mostly dry. She was glad they had stayed. When the rain eventually petered out, the silence draped itself thick and heavy around the cabin.

Beth shifted, feeling a little claustrophobic. She could see one edge of the mattress in the other room. 'I'm going to take a look around outside.'

'I'll come,' Bree said. 'I need the loo.'

Lauren stirred herself. 'Me too.'

Outside, the air was crisp and damp. As Beth pulled the cabin door shut behind her, she heard Alice mutter something inaudible to Jill. Whatever she'd said, Jill didn't reply.

Bree was pointing across the small clearing. 'Oh my God, is that literally an outhouse?'

The tiny shack stood some distance away, its roof rotted and one side open to the elements.

'Don't get your hopes up,' Lauren said. 'It'll be a hole in the ground.'

Beth watched her sister pick her way through the overgrowth to the ramshackle structure. Bree peered inside and recoiled with a squeal. The sisters caught each other's eye and laughed for what felt to Beth like the first time in days. Years even.

'Oh, God. Just, no,' Bree called.

'Shitty?'

'Spidery. Don't do it to yourself. Some things can't be unseen. I'll take my chances in the bush.'

She turned and disappeared among the trees. Lauren managed a smile and tramped off in the opposite direction, leaving Beth alone. The light was already fading, the sky turning a deeper grey.

They had been lucky to find the cabin at all, Beth realised now the rain had cleared. There were two or three gaps in the trees that might once have been trails, but nothing that encouraged visitors to discover the clearing. Beth felt suddenly edgy and glanced around for the others. They were nowhere to be seen. Birds cried to each other above her head, high-pitched and urgent, but when she looked up they were all hidden from sight.

Beth reached into her pocket for her cigarettes. She'd found the pack submerged in a puddle after Alice had thrown it. It had been ruined, soaked through by the dirty water, but she hadn't wanted to give Alice the satisfaction of admitting it.

Her fingers wrapped around the edge of the box, the sharp corners now soggy, and she felt the clamouring call of nicotine. She opened the pack and checked yet again that the cigarettes were beyond saving. The damp smell of tobacco sparked something in her and all at once it was unbearable to have them so near and yet so far. She felt like crying. Of course she didn't want to be an addict. Not to the cigarettes, or to anything else.

Beth hadn't even known she was pregnant when she'd miscarried. She'd sat in the sterile room in the university's medical clinic while the doctor explained that it was not uncommon within the first twelve weeks. She probably hadn't been very far along. And there was very little she could have done to avoid it. Sometimes these things happened.

Beth had nodded. The thing was, she'd explained in a small voice, she'd been out drinking. Most weekends. Some weekdays. She had been one of the only girls doing her computer science degree at the time and the guys on the course were good fun. They were young and smart and they all planned to invent the next big dot com thing, become millionaires and retire by thirty. But until that happened, they liked to drink and dance and take soft drugs and stay out late and flirt with the girl who, at age twenty, still looked a lot like her eye-catching twin sister. And Beth had enjoyed those things too. Maybe, in hind-sight, a little too much.

She had confessed to all her vices that day under the bright lights of the sterile clinic room. The doctor had shaken his head. It had probably made no difference. Probably? Almost certainly. But not definitely? It had almost certainly made no difference, he had said and handed her an information pamphlet.

It was for the best anyway, she'd thought on the way out of the clinic, clutching her pamphlet. She had dropped it in the first rubbish bin she passed. She wouldn't give it another thought. And there was no point telling anyone. Not now. Bree wouldn't understand anyway. It was fine. It wasn't like she could miss something she hadn't even known she'd had.

She had planned to go straight home, but the thought of her student flat seemed a bit lonely. So she'd got off the bus and gone to the bar, met the boys. For one drink, then a few more, because it wasn't like she had a reason to avoid alcohol or the odd narcotic, was it? It was a bit late for that now, wasn't it? And when she'd woken up the next morning, and her head was aching and her mouth was dry, she hadn't really minded. That was the one good thing about a decent hangover. It didn't leave much room to feel anything else.

Now, Beth looked out at the surrounding bushland and squeezed the damp cigarette packet in her hand. She knew the group was in the shit. They *all* knew they were in the shit. But as long as Beth had been able to smoke, it had felt like a thread linking her with civilisation. And now Alice had ruined even that. With a rush of anger, Beth closed her eyes and hurled the cigarette packet into the undergrowth. When she opened her eyes, it was gone. She couldn't see where it had landed.

A gust of wind blew across the clearing and Beth shivered. The sticks and leaves around her feet were damp. No easy firewood there. She thought back to that first night, when Lauren had checked around for dry kindling. Beth scratched her palm, empty without its cigarette packet, and looked back at the cabin. It had a lean to it, with the tin roof jutting out at one side more than the other. It probably wasn't enough to keep the ground dry beneath, but it was the best chance she could see.

As Beth made her way back towards the cabin, she could hear voices coming from inside.

'I've already said, the answer's no.' Stress clipped Jill's words short.

'I'm not asking your permission.'

'Hey, you need to remember your place, lady.'

'No, Jill. You need to open your eyes and take a good look around. We're not at work now.'

A pause. 'I am always at work.'

Beth took a step closer and all of a sudden felt herself stumbling as the ground disappeared beneath her boot. She landed heavily on her palms, her ankle twisting under her. She looked down, the groan in her chest rising to a shriek when she saw what she had landed on.

The sound cut through the air, silencing the birdcall. There was a shocked stillness from the cabin, then two faces appeared in the window. Beth heard footsteps running up behind her as she scrambled away, her twisted ankle throbbing in protest as it bumped along the ground.

'Are you okay?' Lauren was first to reach her, with Bree close behind. The faces vanished from the window and a moment later, Jill and Alice were outside. Beth hauled herself to her feet. Her fall had scattered a pile of dead leaves and forest debris, exposing a shallow but distinct dip in the ground.

'There's something in there.' Beth heard her voice crack.

'What?' Alice said.

'I don't know.'

With an impatient noise, Alice stepped forward and skimmed her boot across the dip, sweeping the leaves aside. Collectively, the women leaned forward, then almost instantly back. Only Alice remained in place, staring down. Small and yellow and partly covered by mud, even to an untrained eye they were unmistakable. Bones.

'What is that?' Bree whispered. 'Please tell me it's not a child.'

Beth reached out and took her twin's hand. It felt surprisingly unfamiliar. She was relieved when Bree didn't pull away.

Alice swept her foot across the hole again, clearing more leaves from the space. She was more hesitant this time, Beth noticed. Alice's toe caught something hard, sending it skittering a short way through the leaves. Her shoulders visibly tensed, then slowly she bent and picked it up. Her face froze, then she made a small noise of relief.

'Jesus,' she said. 'It's okay. It's only a dog.'

She held up a small rotten cross, clumsily fashioned from two uneven pieces of wood nailed together. Across the centre, in letters so old they were barely legible, someone had carved: *Butch*.

'How can you be sure it's a dog?' Beth's voice didn't quite sound like her own.

'Would you call your child Butch?' Alice glanced at Beth. 'Or maybe you would. Either way, this doesn't look exactly human.' She pointed her toe at what appeared to be a partly exposed skull. Beth looked. It did look a bit like a dog. She supposed. She wondered how it died but didn't ask the question out loud.

'Why isn't it properly buried?' she said instead.

Alice crouched next to the hole. 'The soil probably eroded away. It looks shallow.'

Beth itched for a cigarette. Her eyes darted across the tree line. It all looked exactly the same as it had minutes ago. Still, her skin prickled with the unsettling sensation of being observed. She dragged her eyes away from the trees and tried to focus on something else. On the movement of the blowing leaves, on the cabin, on the clearing –

'What is that?'

Beth pointed beyond the shallow hole containing the lonely dog. The others followed her gaze and Alice slowly stood up.

The depression sank into the earth beside the cabin wall in an apologetic curve. The hollow was so gentle, it was almost like it wasn't there at all. The grass covering it was damp and windswept and a shade different from the growth on the other side. The difference was just enough, Beth felt instantly sure, to suggest that the earth had once been disturbed. There was no cross this time.

'It's bigger.' Bree sounded ready to cry. 'Why is it bigger?'

'It's not bigger. It's nothing.' Beth's thoughts were scrambling to backtrack. It was nothing but a natural dip, probably erosion or soil shift, or something to do with some sort of science. What did she know about grass regrowth? Absolutely bugger-all.

Alice was still holding the wooden cross. She had a strange look on her face.

'I'm not trying to cause trouble,' she said, her voice oddly subdued, 'but what was the name of Martin Kovac's dog?'

Beth sucked in a breath. 'Don't bloody joke —'

'I'm not — no, Beth, *shut up*, I'm not — everyone try to think. Do you remember? Years ago when it was all happening. He had that dog that he used to lure hikers and —'

'Shut up! That's enough!' Jill's voice was shrill.

'But —' Alice turned to Lauren. 'You remember, don't you? On the news? When we were at school. What was the dog's name? Was it Butch?'

Lauren was looking at Alice like she'd never seen her before. 'I don't remember. He might have had a dog. Lots of people have dogs. I don't remember.' Her face was white.

Beth, still holding her sister's hand, felt a warm tear fall onto her wrist. She turned to Alice and felt a wave of emotion. Fury, not fear, she told herself.

'You are such a manipulative bitch. How dare you? Scaring everyone to death because you didn't get your own way for once in your bloody life! You should be ashamed!'

'I'm not! I –'

'You are!'

The words rang out through the bushland.

'He had a dog.' Alice's voice was quiet. 'We shouldn't stay here.'

Beth took a breath, her chest rattling with anger, then made herself take another before she spoke.

'Bullshit. That was all twenty years ago. And it'll be night in half an hour. Jill? You already agreed. Stumbling around in the dark is going to get one of us killed.'

'Beth's right –' Lauren started, but Alice turned on her.

'No-one asked you, Lauren! You could be helping get us out of here but you're too scared to try. So stay out of it.'

'Alice! Stop.' Jill looked from the dog bones to the trees and back again. Beth could tell she was torn. 'Okay,' she said at last. 'Look, I'm not keen on staying either, but ghost stories can't do us harm. Exposure actually might.'

Alice shook her head. 'Really? You're really going to stay here?'

'Yes.' Jill's face had darkened with an ugly flush. Her damp hair was plastered to her head, exposing a badger stripe of grey down the parting. 'And I know you've got a problem with that, Alice, but for once keep it to your bloody self. I'm sick of hearing from you.'

The two women stood face to face, blue-lipped, bodies

tense. Something invisible shifted in the undergrowth and they both jumped. Jill stepped back.

'That's enough. Decision made. Someone get a fire going, for God's sake.'

The gum trees shivered and watched as they searched for firewood, jumping at every little noise, until it was too dark to see anymore. Alice did not help.

Chapter 16

Margot Russell didn't speak much in the car.

She sat in the back seat, staring down at her mobile as Falk and Carmen drove to Lauren's house for the second time that day. She watched the videos obsessively, the screen close to her face and the tinny sound of teenage sex floating through to the front seat. Falk and Carmen exchanged a glance. After the second time through, Carmen gently suggested focusing on something else. Margot simply turned off the sound and continued to watch.

'We'll make sure the officers running the search know where you're staying tonight, in case there's any news,' Carmen said.

'Thank you.' Her voice was small.

'And I suppose the school might want to talk to you, but I guess they'll have Lauren's contact details. Maybe her daughter can collect anything you need from your locker if you don't want to go in.'

'But –' Margot looked up at that. She sounded surprised. 'Rebecca doesn't go to school anymore.'

'Doesn't she?' Falk glanced at her in the rear-view mirror.

'No. She stopped coming to classes about six months ago.'

'Stopped completely?'

'Yeah. Of course,' Margot said. 'Have you *seen* her?'

'No.'

'Oh. Well, no, she hasn't been for a while. She was getting teased a bit. Nothing serious, just some stupid pictures. But I guess she felt –' She broke off. Looked down again at her screen, her mouth tight. She didn't finish her thought out loud.

Lauren was waiting for them with the front door open as they pulled up outside her house.

'Come in,' she said as they trooped up the driveway. At the sight of Margot's tear-swollen face, Lauren reached out as though to touch her cheek. She stopped herself at the last moment.

'I'm sorry, I'd forgotten how much –' She stopped. Falk knew what she'd been about to say. *How much you look like your mother.* Lauren cleared her throat. 'How are you coping, Margot? I'm so sorry this has happened to you.'

'Thank you.' Margot stared at the long gash on Lauren's forehead until the woman's hand fluttered to it.

'Come on, give me your bag and I'll show you to your room.' Lauren looked at Falk and Carmen. 'The living room's at the end of the hall. I'll be through in a minute.'

260

'Is Rebecca home?' Falk heard Margot ask as Lauren led her away.

'I think she's taking a nap.'

The hallway led into a living room that was surprisingly untidy. Half-drunk cups of coffee languished forgotten on the side table and beside the couch, while magazines lay open, abandoned. There was a deep shaggy rug on the floor and framed pictures on every surface. At a glance, Falk could see they were mostly of Lauren and a girl who was obviously her young daughter. At some point, there had been what looked like a small family wedding and a man appeared in the shots. New husband and stepdad, he guessed.

He was surprised to see Lauren's puppy fat from school come and go over the years, her body swelling and deflating almost with the turn of the seasons. The tension around the eyes was constant, though. She was smiling in every photo, looked truly happy in none.

There were no pictures of the daughter beyond her early teens. The latest one seemed to be a photo of the girl in her school uniform, captioned *Year Nine*. She was pretty in an understated way, with a shy smile, smooth round cheeks and shiny brown hair.

'I wish Mum would take that down.' The voice came from behind them. Falk turned and had to force himself not to react. He now understood what Margot had meant in the car. *Have you seen her?*

The girl's eyes were huge and had sunk deep into her skull. The only colour on her face came from the purple rings under her sockets and a fine web of blue veins that glowed beneath papery skin. Even from a distance, Falk could make out the bones in her face and neck. It was a shocking sight.

Cancer, Falk thought immediately. His own father had had the same blow-away look before he succumbed. But he dismissed the idea as soon as it arrived. This was something else. This had the sharp edge of something self-inflicted.

'Hello. Rebecca?' he said. 'We're from the police.'

'Have you found Margot's mum?'

'Not yet.'

'Oh.' The girl was so delicate she seemed to almost hover. 'That's shit. I got lost in the bush once. It wasn't fun.'

'Was that at McAllaster?' Carmen said, and Rebecca looked surprised.

'Yeah. You've heard about that place? It was different from what's happened to Margot's mum, though. I lost my group for, like, two hours.' A pause. 'Or technically, they lost me. They came back when they got bored.'

She was fiddling with something in her hands, her fingers constantly moving. She glanced back at the empty hall. 'How come Margot wanted to stay here?'

'We suggested it,' Carmen said. 'She was a little reluctant to go to her dad's place.'

'Oh. I thought maybe it was because of the photos. I had some problems with that too. Not sex,' she added quickly. 'Food and stuff.'

She made it sound so shameful. Her fingers worked

262

faster. Falk could see she was making something. Braiding silver and red threads together.

Rebecca glanced at the door. 'Have you seen Margot's photos?' she asked, her voice low.

'Margot chose to show us a couple,' Carmen said. 'Have you?'

'Everyone's seen them.' She didn't sound gloating, simply matter-of-fact. Her fingers continued to work away.

'What are you making?' Falk said.

'Oh.' Rebecca gave an embarrassed laugh. 'It's nothing. It's stupid.' She held out a colourful woven bracelet, the red and silver threads creating an intricate pattern.

'Friendship bracelet?' Carmen said.

Rebecca made a face. 'I suppose. Not that I give them to anyone. It's supposed to be a mindfulness thing. My therapist makes me do it. Every time I feel anxious or like engaging in self-destructive behaviour, I'm supposed to focus on this instead.'

'This is actually really good,' Carmen said, leaning in to examine it.

Rebecca tied off the loose threads and handed it to her. 'Keep it. I've got loads.'

She gestured to a box on the coffee table. Inside, Falk could see a chaotic nest of silver and red. He couldn't begin to count how many bracelets were in there. Dozens. It was disturbing to imagine how much time must have been dedicated to that pile, Rebecca's thin fingers working away to distract her from the dark thoughts brewing in her mind.

'Thanks,' Carmen said, putting it in her pocket. 'I like what you've done with the pattern.'

Rebecca looked pleased, her hollow cheeks sinking further into her face as she managed a shy smile. 'I designed that one myself.'

'It's really beautiful.'

'What's beautiful?' Lauren appeared in the doorway. In comparison with her skeletal daughter, her own small frame immediately looked huge.

'We were talking about that new design. Mum has one in that pattern too.'

Rebecca glanced at Lauren's wrists. She wore a watch on her left one, but the right one was bare. Instead, a thin red mark circled the skin. Rebecca's face hardened.

Lauren looked down, horrified. 'Love. I'm so sorry. I lost it on the retreat. I meant to tell you.'

'It's okay.'

'No. It's not. I really loved it –'

'It's fine.'

'I'm sorry.'

'Mum,' Rebecca snapped. 'Forget it. It's fine. It's not like I don't have a thousand others.'

Lauren glanced at the open box on the table and Falk knew with certainty that she loathed the contents inside. Lauren looked up almost with relief as Margot appeared in the doorway, her eyes red-rimmed but dry for now.

'Hi, Margot.' Rebecca looked a little embarrassed. She reached out and snapped closed the box of bracelets.

There was a strange pause.

'So have you seen the pictures?' Margot didn't seem quite able to meet the other girl's eye, her gaze flitting around the edges of the room.

Rebecca hesitated. 'No.'

Margot gave a tiny, hard laugh. 'Yeah. Right. Then you'd be the only one.'

Lauren clapped her hands.

'Okay. Girls, go into the kitchen and decide what you want for dinner – both of you, Rebecca, please –'

'I'm not hungry.'

'I'm not arguing. No, I mean it, not tonight –'

'But –'

'Rebecca, for God's sake!' Lauren's voice seemed to come out louder than intended and she bit the words short. She took a breath. 'I'm sorry. Please, just go.'

With a mutinous glance, Rebecca turned and left the room, followed by Margot. Lauren waited until she heard their footsteps disappear down the hall.

'I'll make sure Margot's settled in. Keep her offline if I can.'

'Thank you for this,' Carmen said as they walked to the front door. 'A liaison officer's spoken to Margot's dad. He'll pick her up tomorrow when she's calmed down.'

'It's fine. It's the least I can do for Alice.' Lauren followed them out into the driveway. She glanced back at the house. There was no noise or chatter coming from the kitchen. 'It hasn't been easy around here lately, but at least I got to come home.'

Day 3: Saturday Evening

The fire was something, at least.

It glowed in the small clearing outside the cabin door. The flames were too weak to give off any real warmth, but as Lauren stood beside it she felt a little better than she had in the past two days. Not good, not by a long way, but better.

It had taken more than an hour of solid coaxing to light it. Lauren had turned her back to the wind, her hands numb as she held Beth's lighter to a pile of damp kindling. After twenty minutes, Alice had unfolded her arms from across her chest and come over to help. She was obviously more cold than she was angry, Lauren thought. Jill and the twins had retreated into the cabin. Eventually Alice had cleared her throat.

'I'm sorry about before.' Her voice had been hard to hear. Alice's apologies, when they came at all, always managed to sound begrudging.

'It's okay. We're all tired.' Lauren had braced herself for

266

another argument, but Alice had continued fiddling with the fire. She'd seemed distracted, putting sticks into small piles, then breaking them down to rebuild them.

'Lauren, how's Rebecca?'

The question had come out of nowhere and Lauren had blinked in surprise.

'Sorry?'

'I was just wondering how she's coping after that photo thing last year.'

That photo thing. It made it sound like nothing. 'She's all right,' Lauren said, finally.

'Is she?' Alice sounded genuinely curious. 'Is she going back to school?'

'No.' Lauren picked up the lighter. 'I don't know.' She concentrated on the task in front of her. She didn't want to talk about her child with Alice, sitting there with her healthy daughter and her prize nights and her prospects.

Lauren could still remember the first time she'd seen Margot Russell, sixteen years ago at the maternal health centre's vaccination clinic. It was only the second time Lauren had crossed paths with Alice since school, but she recognised her straight away. She'd watched as Alice wheeled a pink bundle in an expensive pram up to the nurses' desk. Alice's hair looked like it had been washed and her jeans were not straining at the waist. Her baby was not crying. Alice was smiling at the nurse. She looked rested and proud and happy. Lauren had slipped out into the hall and hidden in the toilets, staring at the contraception advert on the back of the cubicle door while

Rebecca screamed at her. She had not wanted to compare daughters with Alice Russell then, and she certainly did not want to now.

'Why are you asking?' Lauren focused very hard on flicking the lighter.

'I should have asked ages ago.'

Yes, you really should have, Lauren thought. But she said nothing and flicked the lighter again.

'I think –' Alice started, then stopped. She was still fiddling with the kindling, her eyes downcast. 'Margot –'

'Hey, here we go!' Lauren breathed out as a spark bloomed, rich and bright. She cupped her hands to shelter it, feeding the small flame until it caught, just in time for nightfall.

Jill and the twins came out of the cabin, relief visible on their faces, and they all stood in a circle around the flames. Lauren glanced at Alice, but whatever she'd been going to say had been lost with the moment. They stared at the fire for a while and then eventually, one by one, they spread their waterproofs on the ground and sat down.

Lauren felt the damp start to lift a little from her clothes. The way the orange light danced on the others' faces reminded her of that first night, back at the first campsite with the men and the booze. And the food. It seemed very far away and long ago now. Like it had happened to someone else.

'How long do you think it will take for them to realise we're lost?' Bree's voice broke the silence.

Jill was staring glassy-eyed into the fire. 'Not long, hopefully.'

'Maybe they're already looking. They might have worked it out when we didn't make the second campsite.'

'They don't know.' Alice's voice cut through the air. She pointed upwards. 'We haven't heard a search helicopter. No-one is looking for us.'

The sound of the spitting fire was the only reply. Lauren hoped Alice was wrong, but she didn't have the energy to argue. She wanted to sit there and watch the flames until someone came out of the trees for her. Until *searchers* came out of the trees for her, she corrected herself, but it was too late. The thought had already planted a rotten seed and she glanced around.

The closest trees and shrubs glowed red, with the camp-fire giving the illusion of twitching movement. Beyond that, it was like staring into a void. She shook her head. She was being ridiculous. Still, she didn't look in the direction of the horrific dent in the ground, which really wasn't so horrific at all when you considered it was probably soil erosion. Alice was right, though, a little voice in her head whispered. There had been no helicopter.

Lauren took a few deep breaths and dragged her gaze away from the bush, instead looking up to the sky. She felt a rush of surprise as her eyes adjusted, blinking to soak in the sight. The clouds had cleared for once, and stars spilled across the inky night in a way she hadn't seen in years.

'Everyone, look up.'

The others leaned back, shielding their eyes from the low fire.

Had it been like this on the other nights? Lauren

wondered. She could remember only oppressive cloud cover, but perhaps she simply hadn't bothered to notice.

'Does anyone know any constellations?' Alice was leaning back on her elbows, staring up.

'The Southern Cross, obviously.' Bree pointed. 'And you can sometimes make out one of the main stars in Virgo at this time of year. Sagittarius is too low on the horizon to see from here.' She noticed the others staring at her and shrugged. 'Men like to show me stars. They think it's romantic. Which it is, a bit. And original, which it's not.'

Lauren felt the hint of a smile.

'It's amazing,' Jill said. 'You can see why people used to believe their futures were written in the stars.'

Alice gave a short laugh. 'Some people still do.'

'Not you, I'm guessing.'

'No. Not me. I think we all make our choices.'

'I think so too,' Jill said. 'Sometimes I wonder though. I mean, I was born into BaileyTennants. I followed Dad into the business like I was told to, I work with my brother like I'm expected to.' She sighed. 'Every day I do what I need to do for the business, and for our family legacy and everything Dad worked for. Because that's what I have to do.'

'You have a choice, though, Jill.' Alice's voice had a quality to it Lauren couldn't identify. 'We all do.'

'I know that. But sometimes my hand feels a bit –' Jill flicked something into the fire. It flared and hissed. 'Forced.'

In the dark, Lauren couldn't quite tell if there were tears

in Jill's eyes. It had never occurred to her that Jill might be unhappy with her lot at BaileyTennants. She realised she was staring and looked away.

'I know what you mean,' Lauren said, because she felt she should. 'Everyone likes to feel in control, but maybe –' She pictured Rebecca. So controlling with what she ate, but so out of control with the illness that was destroying her. Something that no number of therapy sessions or hugs or threats or mindfulness bracelets seemed able to touch. Lauren ran a finger over the woven bracelet on her wrist. 'I don't know. Maybe we can't help how we are. Maybe we're born a certain way and there's nothing you can do about it.'

'People can change, though.' Beth spoke for the first time. 'I have. For the worse and for the better.' She was hunched forward, lighting the tip of a long straw of grass in the flames. 'It's all bullshit anyway, that astrology and destiny stuff. Bree and I were born three minutes apart under the same sign. That tells you everything you need to know about your destiny being written in the stars.'

There was a soft laugh at that, from all of them. Later, Lauren would remember it as being the last time.

They fell quiet, looking up at the stars or down at the fire. Someone's stomach rumbled loudly. No-one commented. There was no point. They had managed to fill their water bottles partway with rainwater, but the food was long gone. A cold breeze rushed through, sending the flames dancing and all around, in the dark, invisible trees rattled and groaned in a collective chorus.

'What do you think will happen to us out here?' Bree's voice was small.

Lauren waited for someone to reassure her. *We'll be all right.* No-one did.

'Are we going to be okay?' Bree tried again.

'Of course we will,' Beth answered her this time. 'They'll be looking for us by tomorrow afternoon.'

'What if they can't find us?'

'They will.'

'But what if they can't?' Bree's eyes were wide. 'Seriously? What if Alice is right? Forget having choices and being in control, what if that's all bullshit? I don't feel in control at all. What if we don't have any choice in anything, and we're actually all destined to stay lost out here? Alone and scared and never found?'

No-one answered. Overhead, the stars looked down, their cold and distant light blanketing the Earth.

'Bree, staying out here is absolutely not our destiny.' Across the fire, Alice managed a small laugh. 'Not unless one of us has done something really terrible in a past life.'

It was almost funny, Lauren thought, how in the relative privacy of the flickering half-light, every face looked a little guilty.

Chapter 17

'That was uncomfortable,' Carmen said.

'Which part?'

'All of it.'

They were sitting in their car outside Lauren's house. It had grown dark while they were inside and the glow from the streetlights gave the raindrops on the windscreen an orange sheen.

'I didn't even know what to say to Margot back at her house,' Carmen said. 'I mean, she's right. What on earth is she supposed to do now those photos are out there? It's not like she can get them back. And then Rebecca. That was shocking. No wonder Lauren's so on edge.'

Falk thought of the skeletal teenage girl and her nest of mindfulness bracelets. How much worry and stress was tied up in those threads? He shook his head.

'So what now?' He checked his watch. It felt later than it was.

Carmen checked her phone. 'The office has given the okay to visit Daniel Bailey at home, assuming he's actually there, I suppose. But they say to tread carefully.'

'Great tip.' Falk started the engine. 'They say anything else?'

'The usual.' Carmen glanced sideways, with a tiny smile. Get the contracts. She sat back in her seat. 'I wonder if his son's come home yet.'

'Maybe,' Falk said, but he doubted it. He'd seen the look on Daniel Bailey's face as he'd stormed away from Alice's house. Falk didn't have to know Joel Bailey to know that he'd likely be lying very low indeed.

The Baileys' home was hidden behind an elaborate wrought-iron gate and hedges so thick it was impossible to see through them from the road.

'It's about Alice Russell,' Falk said into the intercom speaker. The red light of the security camera blinked, then the gate swung open silently to reveal a long smooth driveway. Japanese weeping cherry trees bordered the way, looking like manicured toys.

Bailey opened the door himself. He stared at Falk and Carmen in surprise, then frowned, trying to place them. 'We've met before?' It was a question, not a statement.

'At the lodge. Yesterday. With Ian Chase.'

'Yes, that's right.' Bailey's eyes were bloodshot. He looked older than he had a day earlier. 'Have they found Alice? They said someone would call if they found her.'

'They haven't found her, no,' Falk said. 'But we'd like to speak to you anyway.'

'Again? What about?'

'Why you were banging on the door of Alice Russell's house a few hours ago, for starters.'

Bailey went still. 'You went to her house?'

'She's still missing,' Carmen said. 'I thought you wanted to see no stone unturned.'

'Of course,' Bailey snapped, then stopped. He rubbed a hand over his eyes, then opened the door wider and stepped back. 'I'm sorry. Come in.'

They followed him down a spotless hallway into a large, plush sunroom. Polished wooden floors shone beneath leather couches while low flames in the fireplace warmed the room gently. It was showroom neat. Falk had to fight the urge to remove his shoes. Bailey gestured for them to take a seat.

A professional family photo hanging over the mantelpiece showed Bailey smiling broadly next to an attractive dark-haired woman. His hand rested on the shoulder of a teenage boy, all smooth skin and wholesome white teeth and sharply ironed creases in his shirt. Joel Bailey, Falk guessed. He hadn't looked quite like that on Margot Russell's phone screen.

Bailey followed his gaze to the portrait. 'I went to the Russells' place to see if my son was there. He wasn't, or at least I don't think he was, so I left.'

'Did you try to speak to Margot?' Carmen said.

'She was in there, was she? I thought she might have

275

been. No, she wouldn't answer the door.' He looked up. 'Have you spoken to her? Does she know where Joel is?'

Falk started to shake his head when there was a movement in the doorway.

'What's that about Joel? Has he been found?' a voice said.

The dark-haired woman from the family photograph stood watching them. Like her husband, worry appeared to have aged her. She was dressed carefully, with gold jewellery gleaming at her ears and neck, but her eyes were slick with unshed tears.

'My wife, Michelle,' Bailey said. 'I was just saying I went to Margot Russell's looking for Joel.'

'Why? He's hardly going to be with her.' Michelle's mouth was rigid with disbelief. 'He doesn't want anything to do with her.'

'He wasn't there anyway,' Bailey said. 'He'll be hiding at one of his friend's houses.'

'Did you at least tell Margot to leave him alone? Because if she bombards him with any more of those pictures or videos, I'm going to the police myself.'

Falk cleared his throat. 'I don't think there's any risk of Margot sending anything more. She's very upset that they've ended up online.'

'And Joel isn't? He's more upset than anyone. He's so embarrassed he can't even face us. He didn't ask to be caught up in any of this.'

'He asked for the photos, though,' Carmen said. 'Allegedly.'

'No. He didn't.' Her words were brittle and hard. 'My son would never have done that. Do you understand me?'

Bailey started to say something but his wife waved him down.

'Even if there was some sort of a mistake –' Michelle's eyes darted to the family portrait. 'Even if they'd been flirting, for example, and he said something that Margot misconstrued, why would she send him something like that? Doesn't she have any self-respect? If she didn't want those pictures to end up online, maybe she should have thought of that before acting like such a little whore.'

The words were barely out before Bailey had jumped to his feet and ushered his wife out of the room. He was gone for a few minutes. Falk could hear the muffled sounds of a firm, low voice and frantic higher-pitched replies. When he came back, he looked even more tense.

'I'm sorry about that. She's very shaken up.' He sighed. 'She was the one who discovered the photos and videos. We'd got a new tablet for the family room and Joel's mobile phone had somehow synced with it. Probably by mistake when he was downloading something, but it saved his camera roll and she saw everything. Michelle called me. I was already on my way to catch the bus to that bloody retreat – I had to turn around and come back. Joel was here with a couple of friends. I sent them home, made him delete the images, of course. Gave him a talking to.'

'That's why you were delayed getting up to the retreat?' Falk said, and Bailey nodded.

'I didn't want to go at all, but it was too late to cancel.

It's a bad look for the boss to drop out. Besides –' He hesitated. 'I thought perhaps I'd better warn Alice.'

Falk saw Carmen's eyebrows rise.

'Even though you'd already deleted the photos?' she said.

'I felt it was important.' There was a hint of martyrdom in his voice.

'And did you manage to? Warn her?'

'Yes. On that first night of the retreat, when we went to the women's campsite. I'd tried to phone her from the road but hadn't been able to get through. By the time I got to the retreat, the women's group had already started walking.'

Falk thought of their own mobile signals, dwindling to nothing as they approached the ranges.

'But why the urgency?' he said. 'You said the photos had been deleted, so why not tell her after the retreat? If at all?'

'Yeah. Look, personally I would have been happy to wipe the images and for that to be the end of it but –' He glanced at the doorway where his wife had stood earlier. 'Michelle was – is – very upset. She knows Margot Russell's phone number. While I was driving up, I started to worry that Michelle might, I don't know, feel the need to say her piece. I didn't want Alice to come out of the retreat three days later and find a string of messages from Margot complaining about my wife and Alice knowing nothing about it. She'd have legitimate grounds for a complaint in that.'

Falk and Carmen looked at him.

'So what did you tell Alice?' Falk said.

'I thought she probably wouldn't want everyone else to

278

know, so I took her aside.' A ghost of a tight smile. 'To be honest, *I* didn't want everyone else to know. I told her that Joel had some photos of Margot but they'd been deleted.'

'How did Alice react?'

'At first, she didn't believe me about the pictures. Or didn't want to believe me.' He glanced at the doorway where his red-eyed wife had stood. 'But perhaps that's to be expected. She insisted Margot wouldn't do something like that, but when I said I'd seen the photos myself, her reaction changed. She started to take it in, asking if I'd shown them to anyone else, or if I was planning to. I said no, of course not. I think she was still trying to understand. I couldn't really blame her. I was having enough trouble with it myself.' He looked down at his hands.

Falk thought of Jill Bailey, frowning. *It's a family matter.*

'Did you tell your sister what had happened?'

'On the retreat?' Bailey shook his head. 'Not all of it. I told her I was late because we'd discovered Joel with some inappropriate photos. I didn't mention Margot was involved. I thought that was a decision for Alice to make as her mother.' He sighed. 'I had to tell Jill after the retreat though, when Alice didn't make it out.'

'How did she react?'

'She was angry. She said I should have told her the whole story on that first night at the campsite. Which maybe I should have.'

Carmen sat back in her chair. 'So how did the images manage to get out? Margot said they'd been online since yesterday.'

'I honestly don't know. I drove down yesterday as soon as I heard about it from Michelle. She'd heard it from another mum.' He shook his head. 'For what it's worth, I really don't think Joel would spread them about. I spoke to him for a long time about respect and privacy and he really did seem to take it in.'

Daniel Bailey, Falk thought, sounded a lot like his wife at that moment.

'Joel had had a couple of friends with him when Michelle discovered the files,' Bailey went on. 'I think in the chaos, it's most likely one of them copied the images.' He turned his own mobile over in his hands. 'I just wish Joel would answer his bloody phone, so we could get this straightened out.'

For a moment, the only sound was the crackle from the fireplace.

'Why didn't you mention this when we spoke before?' Falk said.

'I was trying to respect the kids' privacy. Not make things worse for them.'

Falk looked at him, and for the first time, Bailey couldn't meet his eye. There was something else. Falk thought about Margot standing, childlike and alone, in her mother's kitchen.

'How old is Margot in those pictures?'

Bailey blinked and Falk knew he was right.

'If someone looks into the dates those were taken, are they going to find she was only fifteen at the time?'

Bailey shook his head. 'I don't know.'

Falk was certain that he did. 'How old is your son now?'

A long silence. 'He's eighteen, but only just. He was only seventeen when they were seeing each other, though.'

'But now he's not.' Carmen leaned in. 'Now, he's legally an adult who has allegedly distributed sexual images of a girl under the age of consent. I hope you've got a good lawyer.'

Bailey sat on his expensive couch next to his crackling fire and raised his eyes to look at his smiling son in the glossy family portrait. He nodded, but he didn't look happy.

'We do.'

Day 3: Saturday Night

Alice had been gone for a while before anyone noticed. Bree wasn't sure how long she'd been staring at the flames when she realised there were only four of them sitting there. She scanned the clearing. There was little to see. The front of the cabin glowed orange and black, its angles creating sharp shadows in the light of the fire. All around, everything else was in perfect darkness.

'Where's Alice?'

Lauren looked up. 'I think she went to the toilet.'

Across the campfire, Jill frowned. 'That was quite a bit ago, wasn't it?'

'Was it? I don't know.'

Bree didn't know either. Time seemed to flow differently out there. She watched the flames for a few more minutes, or possibly many more minutes, until Jill shifted.

'Actually, where is she? She hasn't gone so far that she

can't see her way back to the fire, has she?' Jill sat up straighter and called out, 'Alice!'

They listened. Bree heard a rustle and a crack from somewhere far behind her. *Possum*, she told herself. Other than that, all was still.

'Maybe she didn't hear,' Jill said. Then, very lightly: 'Her bag's still here, isn't it?'

Bree got up to check. Inside the cabin, she could just make out the shapes of five backpacks. She couldn't tell which one was Alice's, so she counted them again, to make sure. Five. All accounted for. As she turned to leave, a movement through the side window caught her eye and she stepped up to the hole where glass should have been. A figure was moving by the tree line. Alice.

What was she doing? It was hard to tell. Then Bree saw the telltale pinprick of light. She sighed and went back out to the fire.

'Alice is over there, around the side.' Bree pointed. 'She's checking the phone.'

'But her bag's still inside?' Jill said.

'Yeah.'

'Can you get her?' Jill squinted into the dark. 'Please. I don't want anyone to get lost in the dark.'

Bree looked around as a rustling came from somewhere in the trees. It really was just a possum, she told herself. 'Okay.'

It was darker out of view of the fire and Bree stumbled on the uneven ground, the image of the flames dancing in front of her eyes whether they were open or shut. She took a breath, and made herself stop and wait. Gradually, the distinctions started to become clear. She could see the moving figure at the tree line.

'Alice!'

Alice jumped and turned at the sound of her name. The phone glowed in her hand.

'Hey,' Bree said. 'Didn't you hear us calling?'

'No. Sorry. When?'

Alice had a strange expression on her face and, as Bree got closer, she thought the woman might have tears in her eyes.

'Just before. Are you okay?'

'Yes. I thought – I thought for a second I had a signal.'

'Oh my God, really?' Bree almost snatched for the phone. She stopped herself in time. 'Did you manage to call someone?'

'No. It disappeared straight away. I haven't been able to find it again.' Alice looked down. 'I don't know. Maybe I imagined it.'

'Can I see?' Bree reached out, but Alice stayed just far enough away.

'There's nothing there. I think maybe I saw what I wanted to see.'

On the screen, Bree caught a glimpse of a name. Margot. Last number dialled. She hesitated. It was Alice's phone, but they were all adrift in the same miserable boat. That changed the rules. Bree took a breath.

'We should only use the phone to call triple zero.'

'I know.'

'I mean, I realise it's hard. Everyone's missing home and thinking about their families, I totally understand that but –'

'Bree. I know. I couldn't get through.'

'But even trying to call uses up the battery and we don't know how long –'

'Jesus, I know all that!' Definitely a glint of tears. 'I just wanted to talk to her. That's all.'

'Okay.' Bree put a hand out and rubbed Alice's back. It felt a little awkward, and she realised they had never shared anything more than a handshake before.

'I know she's growing up.' Alice wiped her eyes with her sleeve. 'But she's still my baby. You wouldn't understand.'

No, thought Bree, picturing the broken bird's egg, she supposed she wouldn't. Her hand stilled on Alice's back.

'Don't tell the others.' Alice was looking at her now. 'Please.'

'They'll want to know about the signal.'

'There was no signal. I was wrong.'

'Still –'

'It'll only get their hopes up. They'll all want to try to call people. And you're right about the battery.'

Bree said nothing.

'Okay?'

As Bree let her hand fall from Alice's back, Alice reached out and took it, her fingers firm against Bree's knuckles. It was almost painful.

'Bree? Come on, you're smart enough to see that I'm right.'

A long pause. 'I suppose.'

'Good girl. Thank you. It's for the best.'

As Bree nodded, she felt Alice drop her hand.

Chapter 18

Daniel Bailey looked small against the front of his sprawling mansion. Falk could see him in the rear-view mirror, watching as he and Carmen drove away. The wrought-iron gate guarding the property slid open silently to allow them to exit.

'I wonder when Joel Bailey's planning to come home and face the music,' Falk said as they drove along the pristine streets.

'Probably when he needs his mum to do his washing. I bet she'll do it as well. Willingly.' Carmen's stomach rumbled loud enough to be heard over the engine. 'Do you want to grab something to eat? Jamie won't have left any food in the house before he went away.' She peered out of the window as they passed a row of upmarket shops. 'I don't really know anywhere around here though. Nowhere that costs less than a mortgage repayment, anyway.'

Falk thought for a minute, weighing up his options. Good idea, bad idea?

'You could come to mine.' The words were out before he'd fully decided. 'I'll make something.' He realised he was holding his breath. He let it out.

'Like what?'

He mentally scanned his cupboards and freezer. 'Spag bol?'

A nod in the dark. A smile, he thought.

'Spag bol at your place.' Definitely a smile, he could hear it in her voice. 'How could I say no? Let's go.'

He put the indicator on.

Thirty minutes later, they pulled up outside his St Kilda flat. The waves in the bay had been high and rough as they'd driven past, their white crests glowing in the moonlight. Falk opened the door. 'Come in.'

His flat had the chill of a home left empty for several days, and he flicked on the light. His trainers were still by the front door where he'd kicked them aside to put on his hiking boots. How many days ago was that? Not even three. It felt like more.

Carmen trooped in behind him and looked around unashamedly. Falk could feel her watching as he did a lap of the living room, switching on lamps. The heater whirred to life and almost immediately it started to feel warmer. The entire room was painted a neutral white, with the few splashes of colour coming from the packed bookshelves that lined the walls. A table in the corner and a couch facing the TV were the only other pieces of furniture. The place felt smaller with another person in it, Falk thought, but not in a cramped way. He tried to remember when he'd last had someone over. It had been a while.

Without waiting for an invitation, Carmen seated herself on a stool at the breakfast bar that separated the modest kitchen from the living space.

'These are nice,' she said, picking up one of two hand-knitted dolls lying on top of padded envelopes on the counter. 'Gifts? Or are you starting a weird collection?'

Falk laughed. 'Gifts, thanks. I meant to post them this week but didn't get to it with everything else happening. They're for the kids of a couple of friends.'

'Oh, yeah?' She picked up the envelopes. 'Not local mates, then?'

'No. One's back in Kiewarra, where I grew up.' He opened a cupboard and concentrated hard on its contents so he didn't have to look over at her. 'The other died, actually.'

'Oh. I'm sorry.'

'It's okay,' he said, trying to sound like he meant it. 'But his little girl's doing well. She's in Kiewarra as well. The toys are belated birthday presents. I had to wait to get their names stitched on.' He pointed to the letters on the dolls' dresses. Eva Raco. Charlotte Hadler. Both growing like weeds, he'd been told. He hadn't been back to check for himself and suddenly felt a bit guilty about it. 'They're okay presents, aren't they? For kids?'

'They're beautiful, Aaron. I'm sure they'll love them.' Carmen carefully returned them to the packages as Falk continued hunting through his cupboards.

'Do you want a drink?' He unearthed a single bottle of wine and subtly wiped a layer of dust off it. He was not a big drinker in company, and certainly not alone. 'Red okay? I thought I might have some white, but . . . '

'Red's perfect, thanks. Here, I'll open it,' Carmen said, reaching out for the bottle and two glasses. 'You've got a nice place here. Very neat. I have to have about two weeks' notice to have people round. Although your taste is a little on the monastic side, if I may say so.'

'You wouldn't be the first.' He poked his head into another cupboard and emerged with two large pots. Mince from the freezer went into the microwave to defrost as Carmen poured the wine into two glasses.

'I've never had the patience with all that "let it breathe" rubbish,' she said, clinking her glass against his. 'Cheers.'

'Cheers.'

He was conscious of her eyes on him as he put oil, onions and garlic in a pan then, as they sizzled, opened a tin of tomatoes. She had a half-smile on her face.

'What?' he said.

'Nothing.' She looked at him over the rim of her glass as she took a sip. 'Just with your whole bachelor pad set-up, I was expecting sauce from a jar.'

'Don't get too excited. You haven't tasted it yet.'

'No. Smells good, though. I didn't know you could cook.'

He smiled. 'That's probably a bit generous. I can make this and a few other things. It's like playing the piano, though, isn't it? You only need to know about five decent pieces you can drag out in company and people think you're good at it.'

'So this is your signature dish, as they say on the cooking shows?'

'One of them. I've got exactly four more.'

'Still, five dishes is four more than some men can make, let me tell you.' She smiled back and hopped off her stool. 'Can I turn on the news for a minute?'

Carmen picked up the remote without waiting for an answer. The sound was low but Falk could see the screen out of the corner of his eye. They didn't have to wait long for an update. The ticker scrolled along the bottom of the screen.

GRAVE FEARS FOR MISSING MELBOURNE HIKER.

A series of photos appeared: Alice Russell, alone, then again in the group shot taken at the start of the trail. Martin Kovac, old images of his four victims, an aerial shot of the Giralang Ranges, a rolling tangle of green and brown stretching to the horizon.

'Any mention of the son?' Falk called from the kitchen, and Carmen shook her head.

'Not yet. It all sounds pretty speculative.'

She turned off the TV and moved over to examine his bookshelves. 'Good collection.'

'Feel free to borrow any,' he said. He read widely, mostly fiction, spanning from the award-studded literary to the shamelessly commercial. He stirred the pan, the aromas filling the room as Carmen examined the shelves.

She was brushing her fingers along the spines, pausing once or twice to turn her head and read the titles. Halfway along, she stopped, edging something thin out from between two novels.

'Is this your dad?'

Falk froze at the stove, knowing without looking what she was talking about. He gave one of the bubbling pots a vigorous stir, before finally turning around. Carmen was holding up a photograph. She had a second one in her hand.

'Yeah, that's him.' Falk wiped his hands on a tea towel and reached across the counter for the picture she was holding. It was unframed and he held it by the edges.

'What was his name?'

'Erik.'

Falk hadn't looked at the picture properly since it had been printed by a nurse and presented to him in a card after the funeral. It showed him next to a frail-looking man in a wheelchair. His dad's face was drawn and pale. Both men were smiling, but woodenly, as though responding to an instruction from the person behind the camera.

Carmen was looking at the other photo she'd found. She held it up. 'This one's really nice. When was this taken?'

'I'm not sure. A while ago, obviously.'

Falk had a little trouble swallowing as he looked at the second image. The photo quality was less crisp and the camerawork a little shaky, but the smiles it captured were not forced this time. He would be about three years old, he guessed, and sitting on his dad's shoulders, his hands gripping the sides of Erik's face, and his chin resting on his dad's hair.

They were walking along what Falk recognised as the trail that had skirted their large back paddock, and his dad was pointing at something in the distance. Falk had tried a number of times without success to remember what had caught their eye. Whatever it had been, it had made them both laugh. Whether it was the weather, or a stuff-up in the photo development process, the scene was awash with a golden light, giving it the appearance of an endless summer.

Falk had not seen the photo for years, until he'd brought his father's backpack home from the hospice and emptied out the contents. He hadn't known his dad had even had it, let alone how long he'd kept it with him. Among all the things in his life Falk wished had gone differently, he wished his dad had shown him this photo while he was still alive.

Not knowing quite how he felt about any of it – the belongings, the funeral, his father's death – Falk had tucked the backpack with Erik's maps inside in the bottom of the wardrobe and slid the photos between two of his favourite books until he decided what to do with them. They had all remained there ever since.

'You look just like him,' Carmen was saying, her head down, nose close to the image. 'I mean, obviously not so much in this one in the hospital.'

'No, he was pretty ill by that stage. He died quite soon after. We used to look more alike.'

'Yeah, you can really tell in this one of you as a child.'

'I know.' She was right. The man in the photo could be Falk himself.

'Even if you didn't always get on, you must miss him.'

'Of course. I miss him a lot. He was my dad.'

'It's just that you haven't put the pictures up.'

'No. Well, I don't really go for home decorating much.' He tried to make a joke of it but she didn't laugh. She watched him over her glass.

'It's okay to regret it, you know.'

'What?'

'Not being closer when you had the chance.'

He said nothing.

'You wouldn't be the first kid to feel that way after losing a parent.'

'I know.'

'Especially if you feel perhaps you could have made more of an effort.'

'Carmen. Thank you. I know.' Falk put his wooden spoon down and looked at her.

'Good. I was just saying. In case you didn't.'

He couldn't help a small smile. 'Remind me, are you professionally trained in psychology, or . . . ?'

'Gifted amateur.' Her smile faded a little. 'It's a real shame you grew apart, though. It looks like you were happy together when you were younger.'

'Yeah. But he was always a bit of a difficult bloke. He kept himself to himself too much.'

Carmen looked at him. 'A bit like you, you mean?'

'No. Far worse than me. He kept people at arm's length. Even people he knew well. And he wasn't a big talker so it was hard to know what he was thinking a lot of the time.'

'Is that right?'

'Yeah. It meant he ended up quite detached –'

'Right.'

'– so he never really connected that closely with anyone.'

'My God, seriously, Aaron, are you honestly not hearing this?'

He had to smile. 'Look, I know how it sounds, but it wasn't like that. If we were that similar, we would have got along better. Especially after we moved to the city. We needed each other. It was difficult to settle here in those first years. I was missing our farm, our old life, but he never seemed to understand that.'

Carmen cocked her head. 'Or maybe he did understand how hard it was, because he was finding it difficult himself, and that's why he invited you to go hiking on the weekends.'

Falk stopped stirring the pan and stared at her.

'Don't look at me like that,' she said. 'You would know. I never even met him. I'm just saying that I think most parents do genuinely try to do right by their kids.' She shrugged. 'I mean, look at the Baileys and their dickhead kid. He can do no wrong even when it's caught on camera. And it sounds like even a lunatic like Martin Kovac spent his last couple of years upset that his son had gone AWOL.'

Falk started stirring again and tried to think what to say. Over the past few days, the brittle image he had of his father had been slowly warping into something a little different.

'I suppose so,' he said finally. 'And look, I do wish we'd done a better job of sorting things out. Of course I do. And I know I should have tried harder. I just felt like Dad never wanted to meet halfway.'

'Again, you would know. But you're the one with the last picture of your dying father sandwiched between two paperbacks. That doesn't scream halfway mark to me.' She got up and slid the photos back between the books. 'Don't scowl, I'll mind my own business from now on, promise.'

'Yeah. All right. Dinner's ready anyway.'

'Good. That should shut me up for a bit at least.' She smiled until he smiled back.

Falk loaded up two plates with pasta and the rich sauce and carried them to the small table in the corner.

'This is exactly what I needed,' Carmen said through her first mouthful. 'Thank you.' She cleared a quarter of her plate before leaning back and wiping her mouth with a napkin. 'So, do you want to talk about Alice Russell?'

'Not really,' he said. 'Do you?'

Carmen shook her head. 'Let's talk about something else.' She took another sip of wine. 'Like when did your girlfriend move out?'

Falk looked up in surprise, his fork halfway to his mouth. 'How did you know?'

Carmen gave a small laugh. 'How do I know? Aaron, I've got eyes.' She pointed to a large gap next to the couch that had once housed an armchair. 'Either this is the most

296

aggressively minimalist flat I've ever been in, or you haven't replaced her furniture.'

He shrugged. 'It'd be about four years ago that she left.'

'Four *years*!' Carmen put down her glass. 'I honestly thought you were going to say four months. God knows, I'm not overly houseproud myself, but really. Four years. What are you waiting for? Do you need a lift to Ikea?'

He had to laugh. 'No. I just never got around to replacing her stuff. I can only sit on one couch at a time.'

'Yes, I know. But the idea is that you invite people over to your home and they sit on your other bits of furniture. I mean, it's so weird. You haven't got an armchair, but you've got –' she pointed at a polished wooden contraption gathering dust in a corner, '– that. What is that, even?'

'It's a magazine rack.'

'There are no magazines on it.'

'No. I don't really read magazines.'

'So she took the armchair, but left her magazine rack.'

'Pretty much.'

'Unbelievable.' Carmen shook her head in mock disbelief. 'Well, if you ever needed a sign that you're better off without her, it's sitting right there in your corner, magazine-less. What was her name?'

'Rachel.'

'And what went wrong?'

Falk looked at his plate. It wasn't something he let himself think about too often. When he thought about her at all, the thing he remembered most was the way she used to smile. Right at the start, when things were still new.

297

He refilled their glasses. 'The usual. We just grew apart. She moved out. It was my fault.'

'Yeah, I can believe that. Cheers.' She raised her glass.

'Excuse me?' He almost laughed. 'I'm pretty sure you're not supposed to say that.'

Carmen looked at him. 'Sorry. But you're a grown-up, you can take it. I just mean that you're a decent bloke, Aaron. You listen, you seem to care, and you try to do the right thing by people. If you drove her to the point where she had to move out, it was on purpose.'

He was about to protest, then stopped. Could that be true?

'She didn't do anything wrong,' he said finally. 'She wanted things I felt I couldn't really deliver.'

'Like what?'

'She wanted me to work a bit less, talk a bit more. Take some time off. Get married perhaps, I don't know. She wanted me to try to work things out with my dad.'

'Do you miss her?'

He shook his head. 'Not anymore,' he said truthfully. 'But I sometimes think I should have listened to her.'

'Maybe it's not too late.'

'It's too late with her. She's married now.'

'It sounds like she might have done you some good if you'd stayed together,' Carmen said. She reached a hand out and lightly touched his across the table. Looked him in the eyes. 'But I wouldn't beat yourself up too much. She wasn't right for you.'

'No?'

'No. Aaron Falk, you are not the kind of man whose soul mate owns a magazine rack.'

'To be fair, she did leave it behind.'

Carmen laughed. 'And there's been no-one since?'

Falk didn't answer straight away. Six months ago, back in his hometown. A girl, woman now, from long ago. 'I had a near miss recently.'

'It didn't work out?'

'She was –' He hesitated. *Gretchen. What could he say about her?* Her blue eyes and her blonde hair. Her secrets. 'Very complicated.'

His head was so far in the past he nearly missed the sound of his mobile buzzing from the bench top. He was slow to reach for it and by the time he picked it up, it had fallen silent.

Immediately, Carmen's mobile started ringing from her bag, shrill and urgent. She rummaged around, pulling it out as Falk checked his own phone for the name of the missed caller. Their eyes met as they both looked up from their screens.

'Sergeant King?' he said.

She nodded as she pressed a button and lifted the phone to her ear. The ringtone fell silent, but Falk could almost still hear it resonating, like a remote but insistent warning bell.

Carmen listened and her eyes flicked up to meet his. She mouthed silently, 'They've found the cabin'.

Falk felt adrenaline rush through his chest. 'And Alice?'

She listened. A single sharp movement of her head.

No.

Day 3: Saturday Night

When the rain came, it set in quickly, blocking out the stars and reducing the fire to a smoking heap of ash. They retreated into the cabin, finding their bags and belongings, each marking out their own small territory. The hammering on the roof made the space feel tight and it seemed to Jill like any camaraderie around the campfire had evaporated with the smoke.

She shivered. She wasn't sure which was worse: the dark or the cold. Something snapped loudly outside and she jumped. The dark was worse, she decided immediately. She apparently wasn't alone in the thought as someone moved and a torch clicked on. It lay on the cabin floor, illuminating the disturbed dust. It flickered.

'We should save the batteries,' Alice said.

No-one moved. With a noise of frustration, Alice reached forward.

'We need to save the batteries.'

A click. Darkness.

'Is there anything at all on the phone?' Jill said.

The sound of rummaging, and a small square of light. Jill held her breath.

'No.'

'What's that battery on?'

'Fifteen per cent.'

'Turn it off.'

The light disappeared. 'Maybe there'll be something when the rain stops.'

Jill had no idea what impact the weather would have on the signal, but she clung to the idea. Maybe when the rain stopped. Yes, she would choose to believe that.

Across the cabin, another light went on. It was stronger this time, and Jill recognised Beth's industrial torch.

'Are you deaf?' Alice said. 'We need to save the torches.'

'Why?' Beth's voice floated from her shadowy corner. 'They'll be searching for us tomorrow. This is our last night.'

A laugh from Alice. 'You are kidding yourself if you think there is any chance they're going to find us tomorrow. We are so far off track they won't even begin to look here. The only way we're being found tomorrow is if we walk out and present ourselves to them.'

After a moment, the torchlight disappeared. They were in blackness once more. Beth whispered something under her breath.

'Something to say?' Alice snapped.

No answer.

Jill could feel a headache starting as she tried to think

through their options. She didn't like the cabin – at all –
but at least it was a base. She didn't want to go back out
there, where the trees jostled for space and sharp branches
scratched her, and she had to strain her eyes for a path that
kept disappearing under her feet. But out of the corner of
her eye, she could also see the mattress with its strange
black smear. She felt sick at the thought of leaving; scared
at the thought of staying. She realised she was shaking,
with hunger or cold, she wasn't sure, and she made herself
take a deep breath.

'Let's check the bags again.' Her voice sounded different
to her own ears.

'For what?' She wasn't sure who had spoken.

'Food. We're all hungry and that's not helping anything.
Everyone check your bags, pockets, whatever. Really carefully. We must have a muesli bar or packet of peanuts or
something between us.'

'We already did that.'

'Do it again.'

Jill realised she was holding her breath. She heard the
rustle of fabric and zips being undone.

'Can we use the torches for this at least, Alice?' Beth
switched hers on before waiting for an answer. For once,
Alice didn't argue and Jill sent up a silent prayer of thanks.
Please let them find something, she thought as she dug around
in her own bag. One single victory to lift spirits until
morning. She felt someone step closer to her.

'We should check Beth's bag.' Alice's voice was
in her ear.

'Hey!' The torch beam bounced off the walls. 'I can hear you, Alice. I haven't got anything in my bag.'

'That's what you said yesterday.'

Beth swung the beam across the room and shone it in Alice's face.

'What's the problem?' Alice flinched but didn't waver. 'That's what happened, wasn't it? You lied and said you didn't have food last night. When actually you did.'

The sound of breathing. 'Well, I don't tonight.'

'So you won't mind if we check.' Alice took a fast step forward and pulled Beth's bag from her hand.

'Hey!'

'Alice!' Bree cut in. 'Leave her. She doesn't have anything.'

Alice ignored them both, opening the bag and thrusting her hand in. Beth grabbed it from her, pulling so hard Alice's arm was wrenched back.

'Jesus! Watch it!' Alice rubbed her shoulder.

Beth's eyes were wide and black in the torchlight. 'You watch it. I've had it up to here with your shit.'

'You're in luck then, because I'm sick of this. All of it. I'm walking out at first light tomorrow morning. Whoever wants to come, can come. The rest of you can stay here and take your chances.'

Jill's head was pounding now. She cleared her throat. It sounded unnatural and strange.

'I've already said, we're not splitting up.'

'And as I've already said, Jill,' Alice said, turning to her, 'at this point, I don't care what you think. I'm going.'

Jill tried to take a deep breath, but her chest was tight. It felt like there was nothing in her lungs. She shook her head. She'd really hoped it wouldn't come to this.

'Not with the phone, you're not.'

Chapter 19

Falk was back behind the wheel before first light. He pulled up outside Carmen's apartment block. It had been dark when she'd left his place seven hours earlier, and it was still dark now. She was waiting on the pavement, ready to go, and she didn't say much as she climbed in. They'd said it all the night before after the call from Sergeant King.

'How did they find the cabin?' Falk had asked, when Carmen had hung up.

'A tip-off, apparently. He didn't go into detail. Says he'll know more by the time we get up there.'

When Falk had called the office, there had been a silence on the other end of the line.

Do they still think they'll find her alive? Falk didn't know. *If they find her alive, she might start talking about all kinds of things.* Yes, she might. *You'd better go up. Don't forget we still need the contracts.* No, Falk wasn't likely to forget.

He and Carmen again took turns driving. Like before,

the roads were largely deserted as they passed now-familiar paddocks but this time, Falk thought, the journey seemed a lot longer.

As they at last neared the entrance to the park, Falk saw the green glow of the service station sign and pulled in. He thought about what the guy at the till had said last time. *Once you find the belongings or shelter, body's always next.* He blinked now as he went through the service station doors. There was a woman serving behind the counter.

'Where's the other guy?' Falk said as he handed over his card.

'Steve? Called in sick.'

'When?'

'This morning.'

'What's wrong with him?'

The woman looked at him strangely. 'How would I know?' She passed back his card and turned away. Just another dickhead from the city.

Falk took his card. He could feel her eyes on him the whole way back to the car. Above the forecourt, the cyclops eye of the camera stared down with its impassive gaze.

If the lodge had been busy before, it was in overdrive now. High-vis vests and media vans were everywhere. There was nowhere to park.

Falk dropped Carmen off at the lodge entrance and she ran in while he looked for a space. Sergeant King had said he'd leave instructions at reception. Falk crept along at slow speed and at the end of the row, was forced to double-park behind a ranger's van.

He got out while he waited. It was even colder than he remembered and he zipped up his jacket. Across the carpark, away from the hive of activity, the Mirror Falls trailhead stood still and empty.

'Hey.'

Falk heard a voice and turned around. For a second he didn't recognise the woman. She looked different out of context.

'Bree. You're out of hospital.'

'Yeah, last night. Thank God. I needed to get some air.' Her dark hair was piled up under a hat and the brisk chill had made her cheeks a little flushed. She looked, Falk thought, quite beautiful.

'How's your arm?'

'It's okay, thank you. Still a bit painful.' She looked at the bandage peering out from under the sleeve of her jacket. 'I'm more worried about everything else. Beth and I are supposed to be leaving later today. I've got an appointment with a specialist in Melbourne tomorrow morning, but ...' Bree looked over at a search party climbing into a van. She brushed a strand of hair out of her eyes. Her chipped nails had been neatly filed down, Falk noticed.

'That cabin wasn't really used by Martin Kovac, was it?' She didn't bother trying to hide the fear in her voice.

'I don't know,' Falk said truthfully. 'I suppose that's what they'll try to determine.'

Bree started to chew one of her neat nails. 'What will happen now they've found it?'

'I imagine they'll concentrate their search around that area. Look for any sign of Alice.'

Bree didn't say anything for a minute. 'I know the Kovac stuff was a long time ago, but someone else knew about that cabin, didn't they? To tip off the police? One of the searchers told me that's how they found it.'

'I suppose so. I don't know much more than you right now.'

'But if someone knew about it, then someone might have known we were out there?'

'I'm not sure that's necessarily the case.'

'But you weren't there. Sometimes the trees were so thick you couldn't see anything. You don't know what it was like.'

'No,' he admitted. 'That's true.'

They watched as the search group's van drove away.

'Anyway,' Bree said after a minute. 'I really came over because I wanted to say thanks.'

'For what?'

'Being fair to Beth. She said she told you about being on probation. Some people hear that and make judgements straight away. People quite often think the worst of her.'

'That's fine. Is she okay? She seemed a bit subdued when we spoke the other day.'

Bree looked at him. 'When was that?'

'A couple of nights ago. I saw her outside the lodge. She was watching the rain.'

'Oh. She didn't mention that.' Bree frowned. 'Was she drinking?'

Falk hesitated half a beat too long and Bree's frown deepened.

'It's okay. I thought she might have been. She's under stress. I expected it.'

'I think it was just the one,' Falk said.

Bree shook her head. 'Just the one. Just the ten. She's not supposed to have any, full stop. But that's Beth for you. She always wants to be good, but somehow never quite manages it –' Bree broke off and looked past him towards the lodge. Falk turned. On the entrance steps, out of earshot, a figure was standing and watching them. Too-tight jacket, short dark hair. Beth. He wondered how long she had been there.

Falk raised a hand. After a beat, Beth raised one in return. Even from that distance, he could see she wasn't smiling.

Bree shifted. 'I'd better get back. Thanks again.'

Falk leaned against the car and watched Bree walk across the carpark. On the lodge steps, Beth stood, doing exactly the same thing. She didn't move until her sister was back by her side.

Day 3: Saturday Night

Bree could hear her own breath loud in her ears. Alice's back was against the wall.

Jill held out her hand. 'Give me the phone.'

'No.'

'Where is it? In your bag? Let me see.'

'No.'

'It's not a request.' Jill leaned over and grabbed the backpack.

'Hey!' Alice tried to snatch it back but it was pulled from her fingers.

'If you want to go so badly, Alice, you just bloody go.' Jill thrust her arm into the bag, then, with a grunt of frustration, she upended it, spilling the contents onto the floor. 'You're on your own, and it'll serve you right if you die in a ditch on the way. But you're not taking the phone.'

'Jesus.' Alice crouched, gathering up her things as

Jill pawed through them. Damp fleece, compass, water bottle. No phone.

'It's not here.'

'It'll be in her jacket.' Beth's voice came out of nowhere and Bree jumped.

Alice looked barricaded in her corner, with her possessions clutched to her chest. Jill shone the torch in her eyes. 'Is it in your jacket? Make this easy.'

Alice flinched and turned away. 'Don't you touch me.'

'Last chance.'

Alice said nothing. Then Beth lunged at her, grabbing fistfuls of her jacket with both hands.

'This is bullshit, Alice. You were happy to search my stuff when you thought I was hiding something –'

Bree tried to pull her sister back, as Alice writhed and squealed.

'Get off me!'

Beth scrabbled at her pockets and then, with a satisfied sound, pulled out her prize and held it aloft. The phone. With her other hand, she shoved Alice away.

Alice stumbled a couple of steps then lunged forward, grasping for the phone. The pair struggled, locked together, then hit the table with a crash. There was a clatter as a torch fell to the floor and the room went dark. Bree could hear the grunts of a scuffle.

'It's mine –'

'Let go –'

Bree could hear herself shouting. 'Stop it!' She wasn't sure who she was talking to. Something heavy rolled against her foot. The torch. She picked it up, and shook it and the light bounced back on, blinding her. She fumbled as she turned it towards the noise.

Alice and Beth were on the floor in a tight knot. Bree almost couldn't tell them apart in the tangle of limbs, then one of them lifted an arm. Bree started to cry out but it was too late. The beam cast a swooping dark shadow as Beth's hand came down fast and hard. The crack as it connected with Alice's cheek seemed to shake the walls.

Chapter 20

Carmen came out of the lodge holding a map marked with a large red X.

'We're going here,' she said as they climbed back into the car. 'It's a fair way, about forty minutes. The North Road is the closest access point.'

Falk looked at the map. The cross was buried deep in the bushland. A handful of kilometres to the north, a thin vehicle access road cut through the green.

Carmen put her seatbelt on. 'Sergeant King's already at the site. And Margot Russell's here as well, apparently.'

'Not by herself?' Falk said.

'No. I saw Lauren in the lodge. A liaison officer drove them both up early this morning. Margot's still refusing to see her dad. He's driving up separately.'

As they pulled out of the carpark, Falk glimpsed a figure watching them from inside the lodge entry door. One of the twins, he thought. In the shadow, he couldn't tell which one.

The wind was whistling through the treetops again as they drove along the rural routes, Carmen speaking only to give directions. The roads became smaller and tighter until at last they found themselves bumping along a badly paved track towards a swarm of officers and searchers.

The site was buzzing with a strange mixture of concern and relief. Finally, a breakthrough of sorts, if not quite the one everyone was hoping for. As they got out of the car, Falk saw a splash of red. Ian Chase in his Executive Adventures fleece stood on the fringe of a group of rangers. He was hovering, not quite in the group, not quite out. When he saw Falk and Carmen, he gave a brisk nod and headed towards them.

'Hey, is there an update? Have they found her? Is that why you're here?' His eyes kept flicking towards the bushland and back again.

Falk glanced at Carmen. 'Not as far as we know.'

'They've found the cabin, though.' Chase was still looking back and forth. 'Her body could be near.'

'Unless she's still alive.'

Chase stopped and blinked, unable to wipe the clumsy look from his face fast enough. 'Yeah, of course. Definitely. Hopefully that's the case.'

Falk couldn't really blame him. He knew the odds were low.

An officer at the lodge had radioed ahead and Sergeant King was waiting for them at the edge of the bushland. His face was grey, but when he moved it was with an undercurrent of adrenaline. He gave a wave as they approached and glanced down at their feet with a nod of approval at their hiking boots.

'Good. You'll need them. Come on.'

He led the way, plunging into the bushland with Falk and Carmen in his wake. Within a minute, the chatter and bustle behind disappeared and a thick hush enveloped them. Falk spotted a strip of police tape flapping on a tree, guiding them along the route. Beneath his feet, the trail was faint, mostly defined by flattened patches where boots had recently trampled through.

'So how did you finally find this place?' Falk said.

They were alone but King kept his voice low.

'A prisoner out at Barwon called in with a tip-off. He's ex-bikie gang, facing a long stretch for assault, and has had enough, apparently. When he heard on the news we were looking for the cabin, he recognised a bit of leverage when he saw it. He says he had some mates who used to do the odd drug deal with Sam Kovac.'

'Oh yeah?'

'He says Sam liked to show off a bit about his old man, boasting he knew stuff the police didn't, that sort of thing. Sam brought them out here twice.' King nodded at the thin trail at their feet. 'The bikie wasn't sure exactly where it was, but knew about the North Road and a couple of other landmarks – there's a gorge a bit further up – so we were able to narrow it down. He reckons he might still have a bit more to add. He's hammering out a deal with his lawyers as we speak.'

'And you believe him about Kovac?' Carmen said. 'He

315

hasn't just stumbled across this place on his own and is trying to dress it up?'

'Yeah. We believe him.' King sighed. A tiny pause. 'We've recovered some human remains.'

There was a silence. Falk looked over. 'Who?'

'It's a good question.'

'Not Alice?'

'No.' King shook his head. 'Definitely not. They're too old. Couple of other interesting things up there as well – you'll see for yourselves – but no sign of her yet.'

'Christ,' Carmen said. 'What has gone on there?'

Somewhere deep in the bush, invisible kookaburras laughed and screamed.

'Another good question.'

Day 3: Saturday Night

Beth heard the crack of her hand against Alice's cheek a beat before the smarting sensation flooded her palm. The sound seemed to reverberate around the cabin as her hand throbbed, hot and stinging.

For a single moment, it seemed to Beth like they were balancing on a knife-edge from which she – they – could still step back. Apologise. Shake hands. File a report with human resources on their return. Then, outside, the wind blew and Alice made a tight, angry noise in the back of her throat and, all together, they teetered and fell. When the shouting started, it came from every corner of the room.

Beth felt Alice grab her hair and drag her head downwards. She lost her balance and her shoulder crashed against the floor. Her lungs emptied, winded by her own weight. A pair of hands pushed her face against the ground and Beth could feel grit scraping her cheek and taste the rank dampness. Someone was pressing down on her. Alice. It had to be. In the closeness, Beth could smell the faint

317

whiff of body odour and part of her mind found the space to be surprised. Alice had never seemed the type to sweat. Beth tried to claw back, but her arms were pinned at an awkward angle and she struggled, grasping at clothes, her fingers sliding off expensive water-resistant fabrics.

She felt a tug and another pair of hands scrabbling to pull her and Alice apart. Bree.

'Get off her!' Bree was shouting.

Beth wasn't sure who she was talking to. She tried to twist free, then felt the thud and crash as Bree unbalanced and fell on them. The trio rolled heavily to one side, smashing into the table leg and sending it squealing across the floor. There was a sharp bump and someone across the room gave a cry of pain. Beth tried to sit up but was pulled back down by a hand in her hair. Her skull hit the ground hard enough to send a sickening wave from her gut to her throat. She saw white spots dancing in the dark, and under the weight of the fumbling, clawing hands, felt herself go slack.

Chapter 21

The track became only more difficult to navigate the farther they walked. After an hour, it disappeared almost completely as it crossed a stream, then re-emerged to veer erratically towards a steep drop by the side of the gorge King had mentioned. Sentry rows of identical trees started to play tricks on Falk's eyes and he felt increasingly grateful for the occasional sight of police tape. He didn't like the idea of doing this stretch alone. The rogue temptation to wander astray was ever-present.

It was a relief when Falk began to spot splashes of orange in the surrounding bush. Searchers. They must be getting close. As if in answer, the trees slowly gave way and a few steps later he found himself entering a small clearing.

In the centre, squat and bleak behind the lines of police tape and the flash of officers' high-vis jackets, lay the cabin.

It was well camouflaged against the muted tones of the bushland and it looked purposefully lonely. From its gaping vacant windows to the unwelcoming sag of the door, it reeked of desperation. He could hear Carmen breathing next to him and, all around, the trees whispered and shuddered. The wind blew through the clearing and the cabin groaned.

Falk turned in a slow circle. The bushland pushed in from every side, with the occasional orange splash of searchers barely visible among the trees. From the wrong angle, he imagined the cabin would be almost impossible to see. The women were lucky to have stumbled across it at all. Or unlucky, he thought.

A police officer stood on guard near the side of the cabin, while another did the same a short distance away. Each had plastic sheets covering something at their feet. Both sheets sagged a little in the middle, but gave no hint at what was concealed.

Falk glanced at King. 'Lauren told us they found the remains of a dog.'

'Yep, that's it there.' King pointed to the nearest plastic sheet, the smaller of the two. He sighed. 'The other one's not though. The specialists are on their way.'

As they looked, the corner of the nearest sheet lifted in the wind and flapped back on itself. The guarding officer crouched to fix it, and Falk caught a glimpse of an exposed shallow ditch. He tried to imagine what it had been like for the women out here, alone and afraid. He suspected whatever he could conjure up would not even come close.

He realised he had always harboured a nagging feeling that the four remaining women had been quick to abandon Alice once they'd discovered her missing. But now, as he stood in front of that forlorn cabin, he could almost hear an insistent whisper in his own mind. *Get away. Run.* He shook his head.

Carmen was looking at the larger plastic sheet.

'They never did find that fourth victim way back then. Sarah Sondenberg,' she said.

'No.' King shook his head. 'They never did.'

'Any early indication?' She nodded at the sheet. 'You must be thinking it.'

King looked like he wanted to say something, but didn't. 'The specialists still have to take a look. We'll know more after that.' He lifted the tape across the cabin entrance. 'Come on. I'll show you inside.'

They ducked under the tape. The door gaped like a wound as they stepped in. A faint odour of rot and decay underscored the crisp heady scent of the eucalypts. And it was dark; the windows let in only a little daylight. As he stood in the centre of the room, Falk could first make out shapes, then details. Dust that had obviously once laid thick, now showed all the signs of disturbance. A table was shoved aside at an odd angle and leaves and debris lay scattered around. In a second room, he could see a mattress branded with a dark and disturbing stain. And, near Falk's feet, soaked into the dirty floorboards under the broken window, was a black spatter of what appeared to be fresh blood.

Day 3: Saturday Night

Lauren couldn't find the torch. Her nails were scrabbling against the filthy floorboards when she heard a thump and the screech of the table sliding across the room. She registered it flying towards her a split second before the corner clipped her face.

The shock squeezed the breath from her lungs as she toppled back, landing hard on her tailbone. She grunted and lay there, dazed, beneath the broken window. The old gash on her forehead throbbed in agony and when she touched it, her fingertips came away wet. She thought she was crying, but the liquid around her eyes was too thick. The realisation made her retch.

Lauren dragged her fingers across her eyes, wiping them clear. When she could see again, she flicked her hands, the blood from her fingers spattering onto the floorboards. Through the window, she could see only clouds. Like the stars had never been there.

'Help me!' someone was screaming. She couldn't tell

who. She almost didn't care, but then there was a thud and a loud wail. A torch came skittering across the floor, its beam bouncing off the walls at crazy angles, then it hit the wall and went out.

Lauren clambered to her feet, and staggered towards the trio on the ground, forcing her bloodied hands into the vicious huddle. She had no idea who she was grabbing as she tried to drag the group apart. Next to her, someone else was trying to do the same. Jill, she realised.

Lauren's fingers found flesh and she dug her nails in, raking them back, not caring who it was as she struggled to put some cold night air between the bodies. An arm swung up from nowhere and Lauren ducked. It caught Jill on the jaw so hard she heard the woman's teeth crack. Jill gave a wet grunt and staggered backwards, her hand clamped over her mouth.

The movement unbalanced the huddle, and as Lauren gave one final pull, it broke apart. There was nothing but ragged breathing, then the sound of each scuttling to their respective corners.

Lauren slumped against the wall. Her forehead was stinging, and now she could feel her right wrist aching where it had been bent back. She wondered if it was swelling up and ran a finger under the woven bracelet Rebecca had given her. It seemed okay for now, just sore. The bracelet was a little loose anyway, she probably didn't need to take it off.

She sat up straighter, and the edge of her foot caught something. She reached down, her fingers finding the

323

smooth plastic of a torch and she found the switch and clicked it on. Nothing happened. She shook it. Still nothing. It was broken. Lauren felt anxiety bubble in her chest and suddenly she couldn't bear the dark a minute longer. She crawled to her knees, fumbling blindly around the floor until her fingers closed around a cold metal cylinder. She grasped it, feeling the weight in her hands. Beth's industrial torch.

Shaking, Lauren turned it on, and felt a sharp relief as the cone of light cut through the dusty air. She looked down and could see her own blood on her boots, red and smeared, and another spatter on the floor near the window. She turned away in disgust and moved the beam slowly around the room.

'Is everyone okay?'

The light landed on Jill, slumped near the makeshift partition. Her lips were swollen and caked with blood and she was clutching her jaw. She flinched under the glare and as Lauren moved the beam away, she heard Jill spit. Beth was lying on the floor nearby in a dazed heap, rubbing the back of her head while her sister sat bolt upright with her back against a wall and her eyes wide.

It took Lauren a moment longer to find Alice in the dark.

She was standing by the cabin door, when the faint yellow glow finally picked her out, dishevelled and flushed. And, for the first time that Lauren could remember in thirty years, Alice Russell was crying.

Chapter 22

Falk looked at the blood spatter on the floor.

'Do we know who that belongs to?'

King shook his head. 'They'll check. But it's recent.'

'And what about that?' Falk nodded at the mattress propped against the wall. A clear plastic sheet had been taped around it, but the stain on the fabric was plainly visible.

'I'm told it's probably actually advanced mould,' King said. 'So nowhere near as bad as it looks.'

'It would look bad enough if you were stuck out here,' Carmen said.

'Yeah. I can imagine that would look very bad indeed.' He sighed. 'As I was saying, so far there's no obvious indication of what's happened to Alice. The other women said she took her backpack, and, sure enough, there's no sign of it, so hopefully she did at least have that with her. But it doesn't look like she found her way back here, or if she did, she hasn't attempted to leave any kind of message that we can see.'

Falk looked around and thought of the message left on his voicemail. Hurt her. He pulled his mobile out of his pocket. The screen was blank.

'Anyone been able to get a signal in here?'

'No.' King shook his head.

Falk took a few steps around the room, listening to the cabin creak and groan. It was an unwelcoming place, there was no question, but at least it had walls and a roof. The nights had been wild enough outside the windows of the lodge. He didn't like to think about what Alice may have faced exposed to the elements.

'So what happens now?' he said.

'We're combing the surrounds, but it's an absolute bugger to search,' King said. 'You saw what it was like walking in and the bushland's the same in every direction. It could take days to cover the immediate area. Longer if the weather gets worse.'

'Which way did the women walk out?' Carmen said. 'The same way as we came in?'

'No. We came in by the most direct route from the road, but that's not the one they took. There's a north-bound trail running behind the cabin. You have to push through the trees to find it, but once you're on it, it's clear enough. They were already on that path when they stumbled across this place. If Alice did try to walk out, best guess is that it would have been along that route.'

Falk tried to focus on what King was saying. But even as he listened, he knew that a small part of him had been holding out hope that when the cabin was finally discovered, Alice Russell would be too. Hoping that she'd found her way back to it, afraid and angry maybe, but alive. But as the damp walls creaked, he thought of the tight-knit trees, the graves outside, the bloodstain on the floor, and he felt the last remaining shred of hope for Alice Russell tear and scatter.

The cabin was empty. Whatever had happened to Alice, she was out in the open, exposed. Somewhere, beneath the howl of the wind and the groan of the trees, Falk thought he could almost hear a death knell toll.

Day 3: Saturday Night

The aftermath was quiet, mostly, apart from ragged breathing. Particles of dust swirled in lazy circles in the torchlight as Jill probed her mouth with her tongue. The flesh felt swollen and tender and a tooth on the bottom right wobbled a fraction. It was a strange sensation, one she hadn't felt since childhood. She was suddenly reminded of the kids when they were small. Tooth fairies and dollar coins. Her eyes felt hot and her throat went tight. She should call her children. As soon as she got out of here, she would.

Jill moved and felt something by her foot. A torch. She bent to pick it up, wincing, and fumbled with the switch. Nothing happened.

'This torch is broken.' Her words came out muffled through thick lips.

'So is this one,' someone said. One of the sisters.

'How many have we got still working?' Jill said.

'Only one over here.' The yellow beam flashed as Lauren

passed over the torch she'd been holding. Jill felt the industrial weight in her hand. Beth's, she realised. Maybe it had been the best choice to bring camping after all.

'Any others?' No answer. She sighed. 'Shit.'

Across the room, Jill saw Alice wipe a hand over her eyes. The woman's hair was tangled and she had dirty track marks on her cheeks. She was not crying now.

Jill waited for her to say something. Demand an apology, probably. Threaten to press charges, possibly. But instead, Alice simply sat down and brought her knees up to her chest. She stayed there, near the door, hunched and very still. Somehow, Jill found that more unsettling.

'Alice?' Bree's voice came from a dark corner.

There was no answer.

'Alice,' Bree tried again. 'Listen, Beth is still on probation.'

Still no response.

'The thing is, she'll have to go back to court if you –' Bree trailed off. Waited. No response. 'Alice? Are you listening? Look, I know she hit you but she'll get in a lot of trouble if any of this is taken any further.'

'So?' Alice spoke finally. Her lips barely moved. She still didn't look up.

'So don't take it further, okay? Please.' Bree's voice had an undertone that Jill hadn't heard before. 'Our mum's not well. She took it really hard last time.'

No reply.

'Please, Alice.'

'Bree.' Alice's voice had a strange quality to it. 'There

329

is no point asking me for a favour. You will be lucky to be employed this time next month.'

'Hey!' Beth's voice rang out, hard and angry. 'Don't you threaten her. She's done nothing but work her arse off for you.'

Alice looked up at that. Her words slid out, slow and deliberate, cutting through the dark like glass. 'Shut up, you fat bitch.'

'Alice, enough!' Jill barked. 'Beth isn't the only one here on thin ice, so watch yourself or there'll be trouble when –'

'When what?' Alice sounded genuinely curious. 'When your magical rescue party appears?'

Jill had opened her mouth to respond, when, with a spike of panic, she suddenly remembered the phone. She had slipped it into her jacket pocket before the scuffle and she groped for it now. Where was it? She felt light-headed with relief when her hand closed around the sleek rectangle. She took it out and examined the screen, reassuring herself it was intact.

Alice was watching her. 'You know that belongs to me.'

Jill didn't reply, and slipped the phone back into her jacket.

'So what happens now?' Bree said.

Jill sighed silently. She felt wholly exhausted. She was damp and hungry and in pain and repulsed by her moist and grimy body. She felt invaded by the other women.

'All right. First,' she said, in as measured a voice as she could muster. 'We are all going to calm down. Then, I want everyone to get out their sleeping bags, and we're going to agree to draw a line under this. For now, at least. We are going to get some sleep and we are going to work out a plan in the morning when we're all feeling a little more clear-headed.'

No-one moved.

'Everyone do that now. Please.'

Jill bent down and opened her backpack. She pulled out her sleeping bag, breathing out in relief when she heard the others follow her lead.

'Put your sleeping bag next to mine, Alice,' Jill said.

Alice frowned but didn't argue for once. She unrolled her bag on the ground where Jill pointed and got in. Bree was the only one who bothered going outside to brush her teeth with rainwater. Jill was glad Alice didn't try to do the same. She hadn't decided if she would have to accompany her.

Jill climbed into her sleeping bag, grimacing as it clung to her like a wet plastic sack. She felt the phone in her jacket pocket and hesitated. She didn't want to take her coat off, but she knew she wouldn't sleep well in it either. The hood and zips had tangled and pinched when she'd tried the night before and it was going to be hard enough to get any rest as it was. After a moment, she slipped it off as quietly as she could, tucking it in next to her in the neck of her sleeping bag. She thought she could feel Alice watching her, but when she glanced over, the other woman was lying on her back, staring at the tin roof.

They were all overtired, Jill knew. They needed to rest, but the atmosphere in the room felt toxic. Her head throbbed against the hard floor and she could hear the creak of bodies shifting uncomfortably. There was a movement from the sleeping bag next to hers.

'Go to sleep, everyone,' she snapped. 'Alice, if you need to get up in the night, wake me.'

There was no reply.

Jill turned her head. She could see almost nothing in the dark. 'Okay?'

'It's like you don't trust me, Jill.'

Jill did not bother to reply. Instead, she put her hand on her jacket, making sure she could feel the hard edges of the phone beneath the fabric folds before she closed her eyes.

Chapter 23

Falk was glad to get out of the cabin. He and Carmen followed King into the clearing, where they all stood blinking a little in the natural light.

'The trail the women followed out runs along there.' King pointed behind the cabin, and Falk craned his neck to look. He could make out no trail, only a wall of trees with the occasional spot of orange as searchers delved in and out. They seemed to appear and vanish with every step.

'We're working through as fast as we can, but –' King didn't finish, but he didn't have to. The bushland was dense, and dense meant slow. Dense meant some things were easy to miss. It meant some things never resurfaced at all.

Falk could hear hidden voices in the trees call out for Alice, then wait for a response. Some of the pauses seemed short and perfunctory. Falk didn't blame them. It had now been four days. A searcher emerged from the trees and beckoned to King.

'Excuse me a minute,' King said, and headed away.

Alone, Falk and Carmen looked at each other. The plastic sheets lying at the officers' feet rippled in the wind.

'I really hope it's Sarah Sondenberg under there,' Carmen said, nodding at the larger sheet. 'For her parents' sake. Having to beg Kovac for information is the kind of thing that would haunt a person. At least the other families got a funeral.'

Falk hoped it was Sarah Sondenberg as well. He didn't know what to hope for if it wasn't.

He turned and surveyed the cabin. It had probably been well made when it was first built, but now it looked lucky to still be standing. It pre-dated Martin Kovac, he was sure, judging by the state of the wood. Who had built it? A long-forgotten ranger program? A nature lover who wanted a weekend bolthole, put up when legislation around parks was lax? He wondered if it had always seemed quite so lonely.

He walked over and tested the door, swinging it open and shut a few times. The hinges were so rotten they barely creaked. The wooden frame seemed to merely give way.

'Not much noise. It would probably be possible to slip out without waking anyone. Or for someone to slip in, I suppose.'

Carmen tried it for herself. 'There are no windows directly facing the back, either. So from inside, they wouldn't have been able to see her heading for that northern trail.'

Falk thought about what the women had said and tried to

334

imagine how it had played out. They said they had woken up and found Alice no longer there. If she had walked off alone, she would have crept away behind the cabin and into the dark. He thought of the timing of the voicemail message. 4.26 am. *Hurt her.* Whatever had happened to Alice Russell, it had almost certainly been under the cover of night.

He looked across the clearing. King was still busy in conversation. Somewhere behind the cabin was the northern trail. 'Take a walk?' he said to Carmen.

They waded through the long grass and into the trees. Falk looked behind him every few steps. They hadn't gone far before the cabin disappeared. He was a little concerned they might miss the trail completely, but he needn't have worried. When they found it, they knew. It was thin, but firm underfoot. A rocky bed had stopped it turning into mud in the rain.

Carmen stood in the middle of the path, looking one way and then the other.

'I guess that way is north.' She pointed, frowning a little. 'It must be. It's actually not easy to tell, though.'

Falk turned, already a little disoriented. The bushland was almost identical on both sides. He checked the direction from which they'd come and could see the searchers behind them. 'Yeah, I think you're right. That has to be north.'

They set off, the track just wide enough to allow them to walk side by side.

'What would you have done?' Falk said. 'In their position. Stayed or tried to walk out?'

'With the snakebite factor, I would have tried to walk. No choice, really. Without?' Carmen considered. 'Stay. I think. I don't know. I wouldn't have wanted to, not having seen the state of that cabin, but I think I would have. Bunkered down and trusted the search teams to do their jobs. What about you?'

Falk was asking himself the same thing. Stay, not knowing when, or even if, you'd be found? Walk, unsure what you were going towards? He opened his mouth, still not sure what his answer was, when he heard it.

A soft beep.

He stopped. 'What was that?'

Carmen, a half-pace ahead, turned. 'What?'

Falk didn't answer. He listened. He could hear nothing but the rustle of the wind through the trees. Had he imagined it?

He willed the noise to come again. It didn't, but he could recall it clearly in his mind. Short, subtle and unquestionably electronic. It took him a fraction of a moment to place it, but only a fraction. He put his hand in his pocket, knowing already that he was right. He usually heard that sound a dozen times a day. So often that, in context, he barely noticed it. Out here though, its strange and unnatural tone made him twitch.

The screen of his mobile phone was glowing. A text message. Falk didn't bother to check what it said; the tone to alert him told him all he needed to know. He had a signal.

Falk held out the phone so Carmen could see. The signal

was weak, but it was there. He took a step towards her. It disappeared. He stepped back and the signal fluttered once more to life. Falk walked a pace the other way. Gone again. There was a single sweet spot. Elusive and fragile, but perhaps enough for a broken message to get through.

Carmen turned and ran. Back down the trail towards the cabin, plunging into the tree line while Falk stayed exactly where he was. He stared at the screen as the signal flitted in and out and in again, not daring to take his eyes off it. Carmen reappeared a moment later, trailing a breathless Sergeant King. He looked at Falk's screen, got on his radio, summoned the searchers. They delved into the bushland on either side of the trail, splashes of orange disappearing deep in the gloom.

Hurt her.

It took them less than fifteen minutes to find Alice Russell's backpack.

Day 4: Sunday Morning

The clouds had cleared and the moon was bright and full.

Alice Russell's blonde hair was a silver halo as she eased the cabin door shut behind her. There was a click and only the hint of a groan from the rotting hinges. She froze, listening. Her backpack hung over one shoulder, and she had something draped over her other hand. There was no movement from inside the cabin, and Alice's chest rose and fell with a sigh of relief.

She placed her backpack silently at her feet and shook out the item draped over her arm. A waterproof jacket. Expensive, size large. Not hers. Alice ran her hands over the fabric, unzipping a pocket. She took something out, slim and rectangular, and she pressed a button. A glow, and a small smile. Alice slipped her phone into her jeans pocket. She rolled the jacket up and shoved it behind a fallen tree near the cabin door.

Alice slung her backpack over her shoulder, and with a

click, a beam of torchlight lit the ground in front of her. She set off, quiet underfoot, heading towards the thick wall of trees and the path. As she disappeared around the side of the cabin, she didn't look back.

Far behind her, on the other side of the clearing, through the papery strips of eucalyptus bark, someone watched her leave.

Chapter 24

Alice Russell's backpack lay abandoned behind a tree. It was ten metres from the track, concealed amid thick scrub, and it was unopened. Almost, Falk thought, as though its owner had placed it down, stepped away and never returned.

Sergeant King had crouched over the pack for a long while, moving around it methodically, as if performing a choreographed dance. Then with a sigh, he had stood, sealed off the area, chosen his search team and cleared the site.

Falk and Carmen hadn't argued. They found themselves heading back to the North Road the same way they had come, following the police markers and a pair of searchers who had been relieved from their shifts. They walked in silent single file, hesitating once, then again at various splits in the trail. Falk felt glad once more for the markings in the trees.

As he followed Carmen, he thought about the backpack.

Lying there, alone, undisturbed, a man-made aberration on the landscape. It hadn't looked like it had been rifled through, and he wondered what to make of that. The contents were probably of limited monetary value, but out here, where weatherproof clothing could mean the difference between life or death, worth was measured differently. Falk knew in his gut that Alice Russell would not have abandoned her backpack willingly and the realisation sent a chill through him that had nothing to do with the weather.

Find the belongings or shelter, the body's always next. The words of the service station attendant kept running through his mind. He pictured the guy, behind the counter each time they had stopped at the service station before. Not that morning, though. *The body's always next.* Falk sighed.

'What are you thinking?' Carmen said in a low voice.

'Just that it doesn't look good. Not if she had no equipment in conditions like this.'

'I know. I reckon they'll find her soon.' Carmen looked at the bushland, hanging thick and heavy on both sides. 'If she's out there to find.'

They walked until the trees grew further apart and the daylight seemed a little brighter. Another twist and turn and they emerged, back on the North Road. Searchers and officers were huddled by the roadside, talking in low voices as the news about the backpack spread fast. Falk looked around. There was no sign of Ian Chase now and the Executive Adventures minibus had disappeared. The

341

wind whistled along the open stretch of road and Falk pulled his jacket around him more tightly. He turned to one of the officers organising the returned searchers.

'Did you see Ian Chase leave?'

The officer looked up, distracted. 'No. Sorry. I didn't realise he was gone. You could try to call him if it's urgent. There's a rangers' hut with an emergency landline connection about ten minutes' drive that way.' He pointed down the road.

Falk shook his head. 'It's okay. Thanks.'

He followed Carmen to their car and she climbed behind the wheel.

'Back to the lodge?' she said.

'I suppose so.'

She pulled away, the activity at the site growing smaller in the rear-view mirror until they turned a corner and it disappeared entirely. Cathedral walls of greenery towered over them on either side as they drove. There was no hint of the frenzy underway deep within. The bushland kept its secrets well.

'That cabin was pretty well hidden, but it wasn't unknown,' Falk said, finally.

'Sorry?' Carmen was watching the road.

'I was thinking of something Bree McKenzie said earlier. That prisoner with the tip-off knew about the cabin. So that's one person at the very least. Who's to say someone else hadn't discovered it as well?'

'Who are you thinking of? Our absent Executive Adventures friend?'

'Maybe. For one. He spends a fair bit of time out there by himself.' Falk thought about the throngs of searchers and officers and park workers at the search site. 'But I suppose a lot of people do.'

They pulled into the lodge carpark and got their bags out of the boot. A ranger they'd seen before was behind the reception desk.

'All happening up there, I hear?' He looked from Falk to Carmen in hope of an update, but they just nodded. It was not their news to spread.

The door leading to the kitchen area was ajar and through the gap Falk could see Margot Russell. She was sitting at a table and crying silently, one hand over her eyes, her shoulders heaving. She was between Jill Bailey and a woman with the distinctive look of a community social worker. Lauren hovered behind them.

Falk turned away. They could speak to Margot later, now clearly wasn't the time. Through the lodge's large front window, he saw movement in the carpark. A dark head – no, two. Bree and Beth coming from the direction of the accommodation block. They were arguing. Falk couldn't hear the words, but he saw them stop long enough to let a van drive by. The lettering on the side panel was distinctive. *Executive Adventures*. Ian Chase was back, from wherever he'd been. He nudged Carmen, who turned to look.

The ranger behind the desk had finished checking them in and handed over two keys. 'Same ones as last time,' he said.

'Thanks.' Falk took them and turned to leave, distracted

as he and Carmen watched Chase climb out of his van. They were nearly out the door when the ranger behind the desk called out.

'Hey. Wait.' He was holding a phone receiver, his brow furrowed. 'You guys are police, right? Call for you.'

Falk glanced at Carmen who shrugged, surprised. They walked back to the desk where Falk took the receiver and said his name. The voice on the other end was tinny and faint, but recognisable. Sergeant King.

'Can you hear me?' King's words were rushed.

'Barely.'

'Shit. I'm still up near the site. On the rangers' hut land-line, reception's always crap –' He cut out. 'Is that better?'

'Not really.'

'Never mind. Look, I'm on my way back. Are there any state officers there with you?'

'No.' They were the only ones in the reception area and the carpark was mostly deserted. Most officers must still be up at the site. 'Just us.'

'Okay. Mate, I need –' Static. Nothing.

'Wait. I lost you there.'

'Jesus. Hear me now?'

'Yeah.'

'We've found her.'

There was a rattle of white noise. Falk breathed in and breathed out.

'You get that?' King's voice was quiet.

'Yes. I got that. Alive?' Falk knew the answer before he asked the question. Next to him, Carmen stood frozen.

344

'No.'

The word still came like a punch to the chest.

'Listen.' King's voice was fading in and out. 'We're driving back now, quick as we can, but I need a favour. Who else is there?'

Falk looked around. Carmen. The ranger behind the desk. Margot Russell and her social worker in the kitchen with Jill and Lauren. The twins in the carpark. Ian Chase locking up his van and walking away. He relayed the list to King. 'Why?'

More static. Then King's faraway voice. 'When we found her body, we found something else too.'

Day 4: Sunday Morning

The moon dipped behind a cloud, casting Alice Russell into shadow as she disappeared around the side of the cabin.

Across the clearing, the watcher stepped out from behind the wall of eucalyptus trees, fumbling with a trouser zip. The faint whiff of urine, hot against the cold ground. What time was it? Nearly 4.30 am, the wristwatch's glowing figures reported. A swift glance at the cabin showed no movement there.

'Shit.'

The watcher wavered, then ducked around the side of the cabin. The clouds parted and the long grass glowed silver and empty. The wall of trees was still. Alice was already out of sight.

Chapter 25

Two backpacks lay on the ground by the rear wheels of a rental car. The car boot was wide open, and the twins were arguing in low voices, their heads close. The wind caught and lifted their hair, mingling the dark strands. They turned their heads in unison, the argument shrivelling to nothing as Falk and Carmen approached.

'Sorry, ladies.' Carmen kept her voice neutral. 'We need you to come back inside the lodge.'

'Why?' Beth looked from one to the other, an odd expression on her face. Surprise, perhaps. Something else, maybe.

'Sergeant King wants to speak to you.'

'But why?' Beth said again.

Bree stood silently next to her sister, her wide-eyed gaze darting from face to face. She held her bandaged arm against her chest. Her other hand rested on the open car door.

'Bree's got an appointment,' Beth said. 'We were told we could leave.'

'I understand that, but you're being asked to stay. For now, at least. Come on.' Carmen turned towards the lodge. 'You can bring your bags.'

Falk watched the twins exchange a glance he couldn't read, then reluctantly pick up their backpacks. It seemed to take Bree a long time to shut the car door and walk away. They trudged over to the lodge. As they passed the kitchen window, Falk could see Jill and Lauren staring out. He avoided making eye contact.

Carmen cleared the handful of searchers from the lounge area and ushered the twins inside.

Jill and Lauren had come out into the lobby now, their faces long with curiosity. Falk shut the door on them and turned to the twins.

'Take a seat.'

He and Carmen sat down side by side on the ancient couch. Bree hesitated, then curled up in a chair opposite. She was picking at her bandage again.

Beth stayed standing. 'Are you going to tell us what's going on?'

'Sergeant King will explain when he gets here.'

'When will that be?'

'He's on his way.'

Beth glanced out of the window. In the carpark, an off-duty searcher had his two-way radio to his ear. He listened and gave a shout, calling over two others who had been loading something into a car. He pointed at the radio. Word was spreading, Falk guessed.

Beth looked at him. 'They've found her. Haven't they?'

The floorboards creaked and settled in the silence.

'Is she dead?'

Falk still said nothing and Beth threw a sideways glance at her sister. Bree's face was frozen.

'Where? Near the cabin?' Beth said. 'It has to be. There hasn't been enough time since they found it to search much further. So she was there the whole time?'

'Sergeant King will –'

'Yeah, I know. You said. But I'm asking you. Please.' Beth swallowed. 'We deserve to know.'

Falk shook his head. 'You'll have to wait, I'm sorry.'

Beth paced over to the closed door. She stopped in front of it and suddenly turned. 'Why aren't Lauren and Jill in here as well?'

'Beth. Stop.' Bree looked up at last, her fingers picking at her arm.

'Why? It's a fair question. Why is it just us in here?'

'Seriously, Beth. Shut up,' Bree said. 'Wait until the sergeant gets here.'

Falk could still hear King's voice on the phone. Wavering in and out, but clear enough where it mattered.

When we found her body, we found something else.

What?

Beth stood very still. She was staring at her sister.

'Why is it just us?' she said again.

'Stop talking.' Bree was stiff in her chair, her fingers still pulling at her bandage.

Beth blinked. 'Unless it's not?' Her eyes darted to Falk. 'Not *us*, I mean. Not both of us.'

Falk couldn't help shoot a glance at Bree, with her grey and fraying bandage and, underneath, the infected bite wound.

When we found her body, we found something else. King's voice had been hard to hear.

What?

Hiding in a dead tree right next to her. Bloody big carpet python.

At last, Bree met her twin's eye. 'Shut up, Beth. Don't talk.'

'But –' Beth's voice shook.

'Are you deaf?'

'But –' Beth faltered. 'What's going on? Did you do something?'

Bree stared at her. Her hand had stilled, the bandage forgotten for once. 'Did *I* do something?' She laughed, short and bitter. 'Just don't.'

'What do you mean?'

'You know what I mean.'

'I don't.'

'Really? Okay, then. What I mean, Beth, is don't stand there in front of the police and ask me what I did like you haven't got a clue. If you really want to do that, then let's talk about what *you* did.'

'Me? I haven't done anything.'

'Seriously? You're going to pretend –'

'Bree,' Falk started. 'I'd strongly advise you to wait –'

'Pretend you're all innocent? Like you had nothing to do with it?'

'Nothing to do with *what*?'

'Jesus, Beth! Are you really doing this? You're really pointing the finger at me? With them right here?' Bree waved towards Falk and Carmen. 'None of this would even have happened if it wasn't for you.'

'None of *what* would have happened?'

'Hey —' Falk's and Carmen's attempts to interject were drowned out. Bree was on her feet now, eye to eye with her twin.

Beth stepped back. 'Listen to what I'm saying, I have no idea what you're talking about.'

'Bullshit.'

'No. I mean it.'

'That is bullshit, Beth! I can't believe you're actually doing this.'

'Doing what?'

'Trying to wash your own hands and drop me in it! In that case, why the hell should I even try to help you? Why shouldn't I look after myself and tell the truth?'

'The truth about what?'

'That she was already dead!' Bree's eyes were wide, her dark hair swinging. 'You know that! Alice was already dead when I found her.'

Beth took another step back and looked at her twin. 'Bree, I don't —'

Bree let loose a wail of frustration and spun around, her eyes pleading as they fell on Falk and Carmen.

'It wasn't how she's making it sound. Don't listen to her.' Bree's hand shook as she pointed at her sister. 'Please. You have to make Sergeant King understand —'

'Bree –'

'Listen, Alice was already dead.' Bree's beautiful features were twisted and there were tears in her eyes. 'I found her. On the path, early on Sunday morning. And I moved her. That's when I got bitten. But that's all I did. I didn't hurt her, I swear. That's the truth.'

'Bree –' Carmen tried this time, but Bree cut her off.

'She was just *slumped* there. She wasn't breathing. I didn't know what to do. I was scared someone would come out and see her, so I grabbed her. I was only going to hide her in the bush until –'

Bree stopped. She glanced back at her sister. Beth was gripping the back of a chair so hard that her knuckles glowed white.

'Until I could speak to Beth. But then I tripped and I felt the snake near my arm.'

'But why did you hide her, Bree?' Beth had tears in her eyes.

'Jesus. You know why.'

'I don't.'

'Because –' Bree's face was flushed, two hot spots of colour on her cheeks. 'Because –' She couldn't seem to finish her thought. She reached out a hand to her sister.

'Because why?'

'Because of you. I did it for you.' She stretched, grabbing her sister's arm this time. 'You can't get sent away again. It would kill Mum. She never told you, but it was so bad last time. She got so much worse. It was horrible, watching her so sad, knowing it was my fault and –'

'No. Bree, it was my fault I got sent away last time.'

'No, it was my fault.' Bree tightened her grip. 'It wasn't my neighbour who told the police you robbed me, it was me. I called them because I was so angry with you. I didn't realise it would go that far.'

'That wasn't your fault.'

'It was.'

'No, that was my fault. But this —' Beth stepped back, slipping her arm from her sister's grasp. 'This is so bad, Bree. Why would you do this?'

'You know why.' Bree reached out again, her fingertips snatching at thin air. 'Of course you do. Because you're my sister! We're family.'

'But you don't trust me at all.' Beth took another step back. 'You honestly think I could do something like this?'

Outside, Falk saw movement as a police car pulled up on the gravel. King climbed out.

'But what else am I supposed to think? How am I supposed to trust you, after everything you've done?' Bree was crying now, her face blotchy and flushed. 'I can't believe you're standing there *lying*. Tell them! Please, Beth. For me. Tell them the truth!'

'Bree —' Beth stopped. She opened her mouth as though about to say something more, then closed it, and without another word, turned her back.

Bree reached out, her good hand scrabbling and her cries echoing around the room as Sergeant King opened the lounge door.

'You are a lying bitch! I hate you, Beth! I hate you for

353

this! Tell them the truth!' Bree was struggling to speak through her tears. '*I did this for you.*'

With their faces twisted and angry with betrayal, Falk had never seen the twins look more alike.

Day 4: Sunday Morning

A lice Russell had stopped dead.

She was just visible a short way ahead on the northbound trail, the moonlight pooling around her. The cabin was well out of sight now, tucked away behind the trees.

Alice's head was bowed, and her backpack was on the ground, leaning against a large rock. She had one hand pressed to her ear. Even from a distance, it was clear from the phone's blue-white glow that her hand was shaking.

Chapter 26

The twins were taken away in separate police cars.

Falk and Carmen watched from the entrance hall. Lauren and Jill stood in the reception area, their mouths slack with disbelief, until Sergeant King instructed them to wait in the lounge. An officer would call them into the lodge office one at a time to refresh their statements, he said. They should be prepared to come down to the station in town if it was deemed necessary. They nodded wordlessly as he drove away.

Lauren was called to the office first, her face sunken and pale as she crossed the floor. Falk and Carmen stayed in the lounge with Jill. She seemed like a shrunken version of the woman they had met a few days earlier.

'I told Alice it would serve her right if she died in a ditch,' Jill said out of nowhere. She was staring into the fire. 'I meant it. At the time.'

Through the door, they could hear Margot Russell howling. The liaison officer's voice barely cut through the sound. Jill turned her head away, a pained look on her face.

'When did you know your nephew had photos of Margot?' Carmen said.

'Not until too late.' Jill looked down at her hands. 'Daniel finally told me the whole story on Tuesday, but only because the photos were out in public by then. But he should have told me long before that. If he'd been honest on that first night when he came to our campsite, maybe none of this would have happened. I would have let Alice leave when she asked.'

'How much did Daniel tell you that night?' Falk said.

'Only that his wife had caught Joel with some photos and that's why Daniel had been late getting to the retreat. Maybe I should have put two and two together, but it honestly did not even occur to me that the photos could be of Margot.' She shook her head. 'Things were a lot different when I was at school.'

Through the door, the sound of crying was still audible. Jill sighed.

'I wish Alice had told me herself. I would have let her go back after the first night if I'd known. Of course I would have.' It sounded a little like Jill was trying to convince herself. 'And Joel is a stupid boy. He won't be able to fix this with an apology. He's a lot like Daniel was when he was young; does whatever he wants, never thinking more than an hour into the future. Kids don't understand though, do they? They just live in the moment. They don't realise what they do at that age can still haunt them years later.'

She fell silent, but her hands shook as she clasped them in her lap. There was a knock and the lounge door opened. Lauren peered in, pale and hollow-cheeked.

'It's your turn,' she said to Jill.

'What did they ask?'

'Same as before. They wanted to know what happened.'

'And what did you tell them?'

'I told them I couldn't believe Alice hadn't walked away.' Lauren looked at Jill, then down at the ground. 'I'm going to bed. I can't face this.' Without waiting for a response, she withdrew, shutting the door behind her.

Jill stared at the closed door for a long moment then, with a heavy sigh, stood. She opened the door and walked out, with the sound of Margot's cries echoing all around her.

Day 4: Sunday Morning

Alice was almost shouting into the phone. Her cheek glowed blue in the light of the screen as her words floated along the path.

'Emergency? Can you hear me –? Shit.' Her voice was high with desperation. She hung up. Head down, she checked the phone. Tried again, punching in three digits, all the same. Triple zero.

'Emergency? Help us. Is anyone there? Please. We're lost. Can you –?' She stopped, took the phone away from her ear. '*Shit.*'

Her back rose and fell as she took a deep breath. She pressed the screen again. A different number this time, no three-digit repetition. When she spoke, her voice was far quieter this time.

'Federal Agent Falk, it's Alice. Russell. I don't know if you can hear me.' There was a tremor in her voice. 'If you get this message, please, I'm begging you, please don't pass the files on tomorrow. I don't know what to do. Daniel

Bailey has some photos. Or his son does. Pictures of my daughter. I can't risk upsetting him right now, I'm sorry. I'm trying to get back to explain. If you hold off, I'll try to think of another way for you to get the contracts. I'm sorry, but she's my daughter. Please. I can't do anything that might hurt her –'

A rustle and the tread of a footstep behind her. A voice in the dark.

'Alice?'

Chapter 27

Falk and Carmen sat alone in the lounge, not saying much. The sound of Margot Russell's sobs had floated through the door for a long time, and then all of a sudden had stopped, leaving an eerie silence. Falk wondered where she'd gone.

They heard a car pull up on the gravel and Carmen went to the window. 'King's back.'

'Any sign of the twins?'

'No.'

They met King in the lobby. His face was greyer than usual.

'How did it go at the station?' Falk said.

The sergeant shook his head. 'They're getting some legal advice, but for now they're both sticking to their stories. Bree's insisting Alice was already dead when she found her, Beth reckons she knows nothing about any of it.'

'Do you believe them?'

'God knows. Either way, it's going to be a nightmare to

prove anything. A forensics team from Melbourne's up at the site now, but she's been lying out in the rain and wind for days. There's dirt and mud and bits of rubbish everywhere.'

'Was there anything of interest in her backpack?' Carmen said.

'Like a stack of BaileyTennants' financial records?' King managed a very grim smile. 'I don't think so, sorry. But here —' He rummaged through his backpack, and pulled out a USB stick. 'Photos of the scene. You see anything you need, you can ask the forensics guys to show you when they bring it all down.'

'Thanks.' Falk took it. 'They're looking at that grave beside the cabin as well?'

'Yeah. They are.' King hesitated.

'What?' Carmen was watching him. 'What is it? Have they confirmed it's Sarah?'

King shook his head. 'It's not Sarah.'

'How do they know?'

'It was the body of a man.'

They stared at him. 'Who?' Falk said.

'We got a call at the station an hour ago,' King said. 'That ex-bikie in jail has struck a deal he's happy with, and he's told his lawyer he reckons the body in that hole is Sam Kovac himself.'

Falk blinked. 'Sam Kovac?'

'Yeah. This bloke says the bikies were paid to get rid of him five years ago. Sam had been talking up his connections with his dad, attempting to get in with the group, probably. But this guy reckons Sam wasn't right in the

362

head, too unstable to be trusted. So when the bikies got a better offer, they took it. The buyers weren't interested in how it was done as long as the body was never found. They just wanted Sam to disappear.'

'Who were the buyers?' Carmen said.

King glanced out of the window. The wind had dropped and the bushland was strangely still for once. 'They went through a middleman, but apparently it was an older couple. Well-off. Prepared to pay well. But weird. Not quite right themselves.'

Falk's mind reached for possibilities, found only one.

'Not Sarah Sondenberg's parents?' he said, and King half-shrugged.

'Too early to say for sure, but I reckon that's who they'll be looking at first. Poor bastards. I suppose twenty years of grief and uncertainty can do things to a person.' King shook his head. 'Bloody Martin Kovac. He's ruined this place. He could've given those poor people some peace. Maybe avoided a bit of heartache himself. Who knows? Either of you got kids?'

Falk shook his head, picturing Sarah Sondenberg, with her newspaper-print smile. Her parents, and what the past twenty years must have been like for them.

'I've got two boys,' King said. 'I always felt for the Sondenbergs. Between you and me, if it is them, I can't throw too much blame their way.' He sighed. 'I reckon you can never underestimate how far you'd go for your child.'

Somewhere, deep in the lodge, Margot Russell's plaintive wail started up again.

Day 4: Sunday Morning

'Alice?'

Alice Russell jumped. Her fingers fumbled to end the call as she turned towards the voice, her eyes wide as she realised she was no longer alone on the path. She took half a step back.

'Who are you talking to, Alice?'

Chapter 28

Falk felt completely deflated. From the look on Carmen's face as they followed the path to the accommodation cabins, she felt the same. The wind was up again, stinging his eyes and snatching at his clothes. When they reached their rooms, they stopped and Falk turned the memory stick Sergeant King had given them over in his hands.

'Shall we look at the photos?' he said.

'I suppose we'd better.' Carmen sounded as enthusiastic as he felt. Alice Russell's bushland grave. The ranges had finally given her up, just not in the way any of them had hoped.

Falk unlocked the door and put his backpack on the floor, pulling out items until he could free his laptop. Carmen sat on the bed and watched.

'Still got your dad's maps,' she said as he put the stack on the bedspread next to her.

'Yeah. I didn't have enough time at home to unpack properly.'

'No, me neither. Still. I suppose we'll be back there soon enough. Face the music at work, now Alice has been found. They're still going to want the contracts.' Carmen sounded defeated by the prospect. 'Anyway –' She moved over to make space on the bed as Falk opened his laptop. 'Let's get this over with.'

Falk plugged in the memory stick and they sat side by side as he opened the gallery of pictures.

Alice's backpack filled the screen. Shots taken from a distance showed the bag leaning against the base of a tree, its fabric at odds against the sea of muted greens and browns. Close-ups confirmed Falk's first impression from back in the bushland. The bag had been soaked by rain but was otherwise undamaged and unopened. There was something unnerving about the way it was propped there, poised and ready for retrieval by an owner who would never return. Falk and Carmen took their time staring at images of the bag from all possible angles, but eventually the gallery moved on.

The trees had protected Alice Russell's body from the worst of the weather, but the elements had still taken a toll. She was lying flat on her back in a bed of overgrown scrub grass, her legs straight out, and her arms slack by her side. She was no more than twenty metres from the path, but from the photos it was clear she was nearly invisible from all but close range.

Her hair was a tangled mess around her head and her skin lay loose and slack against those high cheekbones. Other than that, she could almost be sleeping. Almost.

Animals and birds had discovered her body well before the police.

The bushland had washed over Alice like a wave. Leaves and twigs and bits of rubbish clung to her hair and in the creases of her clothing. A decrepit piece of plastic wrapping that looked like it had travelled a long way was wedged under one leg.

Falk was about to move on to the next photo when he stopped. What had caught his eye? He ran his eye over the image again. Something about the way Alice was lying, sprawled, scattered with debris. A thought nagged him, skittering away as he tried to reach out and grasp it.

Falk cast his mind back to the woman he and Carmen had known. Alice's corporate lipstick and defiant expression were long gone and her body looked like an empty shell against the forest floor. She looked fragile and very much alone. Falk hoped Margot Russell would never see these pictures. Even in death, the resemblance between Alice and her daughter was striking.

They scrolled on through the photo gallery until the screen went blank. They had reached the end. 'Well, that was about as bad as expected,' Carmen said in a quiet voice.

The window rattled as she sat back, her hand falling on the pile of maps on the bedspread. She picked up the top one and opened it, her eyes running over the printed lines.

'You should use these.' She sounded sad. 'At least something good should come out of all of this.'

'Yeah. I know.' Falk shuffled through the pile until he found the Giralang Ranges map.

He opened it flat, looking for the North Road. He found it cutting through an unmarked tangle of bushland. He worked out roughly the spot where he thought the cabin lay, and then where Alice Russell's body had been found.

There were no pencil markings in the whole region, no words or notes in his dad's handwriting. Falk wasn't sure quite what he had been expecting, or hoping, to find, but whatever it was, it wasn't there. His dad had never been to that area. The printed lines on the paper stared back with blank indifference.

With a sigh, he moved the page until he found the Mirror Falls trail. The pencilled notes there were clear as his dad's hard-to-read letters looped and swirled across the yellowing paper. *Summer trail. Watch for rockfall. Fresh water source. He had corrected vigorously. A lookout point had been marked as closed, then open, then scored through heavily again with the words: Recurring danger.*

Falk stared at the words for a long time, not quite sure why. Something flickered deep in his consciousness. He was about to reach for the laptop when Carmen looked up.

'He liked this area,' she said, holding up the map in her hand. 'Lots of markings on this one.'

Falk recognised the name of the region instantly. 'That's where I grew up.'

'Really? Wow. You weren't joking, it is in the middle of nowhere.' Carmen looked a little closer. 'So you two did go hiking around there together? Before you moved.'

Falk shook his head. 'Not that I remember. I'm not sure

even he went out much himself then. He was pretty busy on the farm. Probably got enough fresh air.'

'According to this it looks like you did. At least once.' Carmen passed the map over, her finger pointing to something written in Erik Falk's handwriting.

With Aaron.

The words were written next to a light summer trail. Falk had never walked the full length of it, but he knew where it went. It followed the boundaries of the paddocks where he used to run around, blowing off steam while his dad worked on the land; near the spot at the river where his dad had showed him how to fish; along the fence line where three-year-old Aaron had one summer's day been photographed laughing and riding on his dad's shoulders.

With Aaron.

'We didn't –' Falk's eyes felt heavy and hot. 'We never really walked that together. Not in one go.'

'Well, maybe he wanted to. There are some others as well.' Carmen had been looking through the pile. She passed him a couple more, pointing out the markings. Then a handful more.

On almost every map, in handwriting faded with age and becoming shakier over time, were the words: *With Aaron. With Aaron.* A chosen route for them to tackle together. His dad, stubborn in the face of flat refusal; the words a wish for something different.

Falk sat back against the bedhead. He realised Carmen was watching him and shook his head. He thought he might have trouble speaking.

She reached out and put her hand on his. 'Aaron, it's okay. I'm sure he knew.'

Falk swallowed. 'I don't think he did.'

'He did.' Carmen smiled. 'Of course he did. Parents and children are hardwired to love each other. He knew.'

Falk looked at the maps. 'He did a better job of showing it than me.'

'Well. Maybe. But you're not alone in that. I think parents often love their kids more than the other way round.'

'Maybe.' Falk thought of Sarah Sondenberg's parents and the depths they had been forced to plunge for their daughter. What had King said? *Never underestimate how far you'd go for your child.*

Something again caught at the edge of Falk's mind. He blinked. What was it? Even as he tried to grasp the idea it twisted and threatened to evaporate. The computer was still open next to Carmen, the gallery of photos still loaded.

'Let me see again.' Falk pulled the laptop over and scrolled through the photos of Alice Russell, looking more closely this time. Something in the little details nagged him, but he couldn't tell what. He looked at her sallow skin, the way her jaw hung a little slack. Her exposed face was almost relaxed and she looked, in a strange way, younger. The howl of the wind outside suddenly sounded a lot like Margot Russell's cries.

He kept looking. At Alice's broken nails, her dirty hands, her tangled hair. The debris and stray rubbish strewn all around her. That flicker again. Falk stopped on that last image and leaned in closer. An old piece of plastic was trapped under her leg. The dirty remains of a torn food wrapper lay near her hair. He zoomed in.

A single torn red and silver thread had snagged in her jacket zip.

The flicker burst into flame as he looked at that torn thread. And suddenly he wasn't thinking of Alice or Margot Russell but instead of another girl, so fragile she was barely there, fiddling constantly with something red and silver and knotted in her fingers.

A thread caught in a zip. A bare wrist. The haunted look in the girl's sunken eyes. And the guilty look in her mother's.

Day 4: Sunday Morning

'Alice.' Lauren stared at the other woman. 'Who are you talking to?'

'Oh my God.' Alice put a hand to her chest. Her face was pale in the dark. 'You scared me.'

'Is there a signal? Did you get through to someone?' Lauren reached for the phone but Alice snatched her hand away.

'It's too weak. I don't think they can hear me.'

'Call triple zero.' Lauren reached out again.

Alice stepped back. 'I did. It kept cutting out.'

'Shit. So who were you speaking to?'

'It was a voicemail. I don't think it got through.'

'But who was it?'

'It was no-one. Just something about Margot.'

Lauren stared until Alice met her eyes.

'What?' Alice snapped. 'I told you, I tried triple zero already.'

'We have almost no signal or battery left. We need to save it.'

'I know that. But this was important.'

'Believe it or not, there are some things more important than your bloody daughter.'

Alice said nothing, but held the phone closer.

'All right.' Lauren made herself take a deep breath. 'How did you get the phone without waking Jill, anyway?'

Alice almost laughed. 'That woman slept through a thunderstorm yesterday. She was hardly going to stir because her jacket's moved.'

Lauren could believe it. Jill had always seemed to sleep better than any of them. She looked down at Alice's other hand. 'And you've taken Beth's torch.'

'I need it.'

'It's the only one we've got that's working.'

'That's why I need it.' Alice wouldn't meet her eye. The light from the torch bobbed in the gloom. The rest of the path was in darkness.

Lauren could see Alice's backpack leaning against a rock. Ready to go. She took another deep breath. 'Listen, we need to get the others. They'll want to know about the signal. I won't tell them you were leaving.'

Alice said nothing. She tucked the phone into the pocket of her jeans.

'Alice. Jesus. You're not seriously still thinking of going?'

Alice bent and picked up her backpack. She slung it over one shoulder. Lauren grabbed her arm.

'Let me go.' Alice shook her arm loose.

'It's not safe on your own. And we've got a signal now. It'll help them find us.'

'It won't. It's too faint.'

'It's something! Alice, it's a better chance than we've had in days.'

'Keep your voice down, will you? Look, I can't wait around for them to find us.'

'Why not?'

No answer.

'For God's sake.' Lauren tried to calm herself. She could feel her heart pounding. 'How are you even going to do it?'

'Walk north, like we should have been doing today. You know that'll work, Lauren, but you won't admit it because then you'd have to try.'

'No. I don't want to do it because it's not safe. Especially on your own. You're walking blind, you haven't even got the compass.' Lauren could feel the plastic disc in her own pocket.

'If you're that concerned, you could give it to me.'

'No.' Lauren's palm closed around it. 'No way.'

'Thought not. Anyway, we know this track's heading north. I can work it out if I have to. I did it at McAllaster.'

Bloody McAllaster. Lauren felt her chest tighten and her blood start to pump a little faster at the mention of the name. Thirty years ago, standing in the middle of nowhere as close together as they were now. The trust challenge. Lauren, homesick, sad and blindfolded, and the feeling of sheer relief at Alice's firm hand on her arm and her confident voice in her ear.

'I've got you. This way.'

'Thank you.'

Alice leading and Lauren following. The sound of foot-steps around her. A giggle. Then Alice's voice in her ear again. A whispered warning: 'Watch out.'

The guiding hand on her arm lifted, suddenly as light as air, and disappeared to nothing. Lauren had reached out, disoriented, her foot catching on something right in front of her and she felt the sickening sensation of falling through space. The only sound was the distant sound of a muffled laugh.

She had fractured her wrist on landing. She was glad. It meant that when she lifted the blindfold to find herself completely alone, surrounded only by dense bushland in the encroaching dark, she had an excuse for the tears in her eyes. Not that it mattered. It had been four hours before the other girls came back for her. When at last they had, Alice had been laughing.

'I told you to watch out.'

Chapter 29

Falk stared at the red and silver thread caught in Alice Russell's jacket zip, then turned the screen to face Carmen. She blinked.

'Shit.' She had her hand scrabbling in her own jacket pocket and before he said a word had pulled out Rebecca's woven friendship bracelet. The silver threads glinted in the light.

'I know Lauren said she lost hers, but was she definitely wearing it out there?'

Falk grabbed his own jacket, rummaging through until he found the crumpled Missing Person flier he'd picked up from reception. He smoothed it out, ignoring Alice's smiling face and instead focusing on the last shot taken of the five women together.

They stood at the entrance to the Mirror Falls trail, Alice's arm around Lauren's waist. Alice was smiling. Lauren's arm was placed around Alice's shoulders, hovering rather than resting, Falk thought now as he leaned

376

closer. At the edge of Lauren's jacket sleeve, a clear band of woven red encircled her wrist.

Carmen was already reaching for the room phone to dial Sergeant King. She listened for a moment then shook her head. No answer. She dialled reception. Falk had his jacket on by the time she'd checked the room number and wordlessly, they went outside and walked the length of the accommodation block. The late afternoon sun had dropped behind the trees and darkness crept in from the east.

They reached Lauren's room and Falk knocked on the door. They waited. No answer. He knocked again, then tried the handle. The door swung open. The room was empty. He looked at Carmen.

'In the lodge, maybe?' she said.

Falk hesitated, then glanced past her. The start of the Mirror Falls trailhead was empty, the wooden sign barely visible in the growing dark. Carmen saw where he was looking and read his mind, alarm crossing her face.

'You go and check,' she said. 'I'll find King and follow.'

'Okay.'

Falk set off at a brisk pace, crunching across the gravel driveway, then sinking a little as he reached the muddy path. He was the only one around, but he could see boot prints underfoot. He entered the trail.

Was he right? He didn't know. Then he thought about the thin girl and the red thread and her mother's bare wrist.

Never underestimate how far you'd go for your child.

Falk's steps grew faster and faster until, with the roar of Mirror Falls growing louder in his ears, he broke into a run.

Day 4: Sunday Morning

'I'll be able to find my way out. I did it at McAllaster.'

Lauren looked at Alice. 'You did a lot of things at McAllaster.'

'Oh God, Lauren. Not again. I've apologised for what happened back then. So many times.' Alice turned. 'Look. I'm sorry, but I've got to go.'

Lauren reached out, grabbing Alice's jacket this time.

'Not with the phone.'

'Yes, with *my* phone.' Alice pushed her away and Lauren staggered back a little. The tall shadows around her seemed to waver and she felt a thrill of anger as Alice turned away.

'Don't leave.'

'For God's sake.' Alice didn't turn back this time. Lauren lunged again, feeling a little unsteady on her feet. Her hand closed around Alice's bag, jerking her back. 'Don't leave us.'

'Jesus. Don't be so pathetic.'

'Hey!' Lauren felt something bloom and burst in her chest. 'Don't speak to me like that.'

'Fine.' Alice waved a hand. 'Look, come, if you want. Or stay. Or walk out when you finally realise they're not coming for you. I don't care. But I have to go.'

She tried to pull away, but this time Lauren kept her grip.

'Don't.' Her hand ached from holding on so hard. She felt a little light-headed. 'For once, Alice, think about someone other than yourself.'

'I am! I need to get back for Margot. Look, something's happened and –'

'And God forbid anything should trouble precious Margot Russell,' Lauren cut her off. She heard herself laugh. It sounded strange in the night. 'I don't know who's more bloody self-centred, you or her.'

'Excuse me?'

'Don't pretend you don't know what I mean. She's as bad as you. You pretend you're sorry for how you were at school – how you are now – but you turn out a daughter who acts in exactly the same way. You want her to follow in your footsteps? You've certainly achieved it.'

Alice gave a cold laugh. 'Oh, really? Well, snap, Lauren. You'd know all about that.'

There was a silence. 'What –?' Lauren opened her mouth but the words evaporated.

'Forget it. Just –' Alice lowered her voice. 'Just leave Margot out of it. She hasn't done anything wrong.'

'Hasn't she?'

Alice didn't reply.

Lauren looked at her. 'You know she was involved, Alice.'

'What, with that problem with Rebecca? That's all been

dealt with, you know that. The school investigated. The girls responsible for the photos were suspended.'

'The girls they could prove were responsible were suspended. You think I don't know they were all in Margot's group? She was involved, no question about it. She was probably the bloody ringleader.'

'If that were true, the school would have said.'

'Really? Would they? How much extra did you donate to the school this year, Alice? How much did it cost to buy Margot that blind eye?'

No answer. Something rustled in the bush.

'Yeah, I thought so.' Lauren was shaking so hard she could barely draw breath.

'Hey, I have tried my best to help you, Lauren. Didn't I recommend you for this job in the first place? And haven't I covered for you – how many times lately? – when you've been distracted and stuffed up.'

'Because you feel guilty.'

'Because we're friends!'

Lauren looked at her. 'No. We're not.'

Alice said nothing for a minute. 'Okay. Look. We're both upset. It's been a really hard few days. And I do know how difficult everything is with Rebecca. For both of you.'

'You don't know. You can't imagine what it's been like.'

'Lauren. I can.' Alice's eyes were shining in the moonlight. She swallowed. 'Look, apparently there might be some photos of Margot and –'

'And what?'

'So I need to get back –'

'And you expect me to care now that it's your girl on the wrong end of a camera and not mine?'

'Oh Christ, Lauren, *please*. Your daughter was bloody miserable long before any of those stupid photos got sent around –'

'No, she wasn't –'

'She was! Of course she was!' Alice's voice was an urgent whisper. 'You want someone to blame for Rebecca's problems, why don't you take a good hard look at yourself? Seriously. You honestly can't see where she gets it from?'

Lauren could hear the blood rushing in her ears. Alice was standing close but her words were distant and faint.

'No?' Alice was staring at her. 'You need a clue? How about sixteen years of her watching you get pushed around? Letting people walk all over you. You're never happy with yourself. Bloody yo-yo dieting for years. I bet you've never taught her to stand up to anyone in her life. You wonder why you always end up with a raw deal? You asked for it at school and you still let it happen to you now. We could all be walking out of here with your help, but you're too scared to trust yourself.'

'I'm not!'

'You are. You're so bloody weak-minded –'

'I am not!'

'And if you can't see the damage you've done to that girl, you're a worse mother than I thought, and honestly, I already think you're a complete mess.'

Lauren's head was pounding so loud she could barely make out her own words.

'No, Alice. I have changed. You're the one who's still the same. You were a bitch at school and you're even worse now.'

A laugh. 'You are kidding yourself. You haven't changed. You are who you are. It's just your nature.'

'And Rebecca isn't well –' Guilt rushed up Lauren's gullet so fast she nearly choked. She swallowed it down. 'Her problems are complicated.'

'How much do you pay your therapist to make you believe that?' Alice sneered. 'It's not that complicated, it's the way of the world, isn't it? You think I don't realise that my daughter can be a scheming little bitch? And aggressive and manipulative and everything else that comes with it? I'm not blind, I can see what she is.'

Alice leaned in. Her cheeks were flushed. She was sweating despite the cold and her hair stuck to her forehead in a clump. She had tears in her eyes.

'And God knows, she does some stupid, *stupid* things. But at least I can admit it. I can hold my hand up and accept my part in it. You want to waste thousands of dollars trying to find out why your daughter is sick and starving and sad, Lauren?' Their faces were so close their cloudy breath mingled. 'Save your money and buy a mirror. You made her. You think my daughter is just like me? Your daughter is *just like you.*'

Chapter 30

The trail was slippery and damp underfoot. Falk pounded along as fast as he could, his chest heaving as overgrown branches reached out, catching and clawing at him. The thunderous sound of rushing water drew closer and he burst from the tree line, panting, the sweat already cooling and clammy against his skin.

The wall of water tumbled down. He made himself stop and look properly, his breath ragged as he squinted into the failing light. Nothing. The waterfall viewpoint was deserted. He swore under his breath. He was wrong. *Or too late*, a small voice whispered in his head.

He took a step onto the bridge, then another, and stilled.

She was perched on the jutting rock face at the top of Mirror Falls, almost invisible against the craggy backdrop. Her legs dangled over the edge and her head hung down as she stared into the churn of white water crashing into the pool below.

Lauren sat, sad and shivering, and very much alone.

Day 4: Sunday Morning

Y*our daughter is just like you.*
 The words were still echoing into the night when Lauren crashed hard into Alice. The move took even Lauren by surprise as her body rammed against the other woman's and they stumbled, their hands scrabbling and flailing. Lauren felt a scratch of pain as fingernails raked down her right wrist.

'You bitch.' Lauren's throat felt hot and tight and her voice was muffled as they twisted and fell back as one, smashing against a boulder by the side of the trail.

A smack resonated in the air and Lauren felt the breath forced out of her lungs as she smashed into the ground. She gasped and rolled over, feeling the rocky trail bite into her back and her heart pounding in her ears.

Next to her, Alice groaned softly. She had one arm over Lauren's and was lying close enough for Lauren to feel the body heat through her clothes. Her backpack had fallen by her side.

'Get off me.' Lauren pushed her away. 'You're full of shit.'

Alice didn't reply; she lay there, slack-limbed.

Lauren sat up, trying to breathe deep. The adrenaline spike had plummeted, leaving her shaky and cold. She glanced down. Alice was still on her back, staring at the sky, her eyelids fluttering and her lips slightly parted. She moaned again, lifting one hand to the back of her head. Lauren looked at the boulder by the trail.

'What? Did you hit your head?'

No answer. Alice blinked, her eyes closing and opening slowly. Hand to her head.

'Shit.' Lauren could still feel the anger, but it was more muted now, washed over with a layer of regret. Alice might have gone too far, but so had she. They were all tired and hungry and she had lashed out. 'Are you okay? Let me –'

Lauren stood up and put her hands under Alice's armpits, hauling her to a seated position. She propped her up with her back against the boulder, and her backpack by her side. Alice blinked slowly, eyes hooded and hands slack in her lap, her gaze focused on nothing. Lauren checked the back of her head. There was no blood.

'You're okay. You're not bleeding, you're probably dazed. Just take a minute.'

No reply.

Lauren placed her hand on Alice's chest, feeling for the rise and fall. Like she had when Rebecca was a baby, standing over her cot in the dark of the early hours, strangled by the tightness of their bond, trembling under the weight of responsibility. *Are you still breathing? Are you still with me?* Now, as Lauren held her own breath, she felt the shallow rise and fall of Alice's chest under her palm. Her sigh of relief was audible.

'Christ. Alice.' Lauren stood. She took a step back. Now what? She suddenly felt very alone and very scared. She was exhausted. With everything. She felt too tired to fight.

'Look. Do whatever you want, Alice. I won't wake the others. I won't tell them I saw you, if you don't tell them –' She stopped. 'I just lost my temper there for a minute.'

No reply. Alice stared at the ground ahead through half-closed lids. She blinked once, and her chest rose, then slowly fell.

'I'm going back to the cabin now. You should too. Don't disappear.'

Alice's lips moved a fraction. There was a small noise from the back of her throat. Curious, Lauren moved closer. A small noise again. It was almost like a groan, but over the rush of the wind in the trees and the blood in her skull and the ache inside her, Lauren felt sure she knew what Alice was trying to say to her.

'It's okay.' Lauren turned. 'I'm sorry too.'

She barely remembered getting back to the cabin. Inside, three bodies lay still, breathing gently. Lauren found her own sleeping bag and climbed in. She was shivering, and as she lay down against the floorboards, everything seemed to be spinning. A hard ball pressed painfully in her chest. Not just anger, Lauren thought. Not sadness. Something else.

Guilt.

The word rose up, coating her throat like bile. Lauren pushed it straight back down.

Her eyes were so heavy and she was so tired. She listened out for as long as she could, but there was no sound of Alice creeping in after her. Finally, exhausted, she had to let go. It was only on the cusp of sleep that she realised two things. One: she had forgotten to take the phone, and two: her right wrist was bare. The friendship bracelet her daughter had made for her was gone.

Chapter 31

Falk climbed over the guard rail and onto the rocky surface. It was as slippery as ice under his feet. He made the mistake of looking down and felt himself waver, as the rock swayed beneath him. He gripped the rail and tried to focus on the horizon until the sensation passed. It was hard to tell where the land met the air, as the treetops bled into the deepening sky.

'Lauren!' Falk called, as softly as he could over the roar of the water.

She flinched at the sound of her name, but didn't look up. She was wearing only the thin long-sleeved top and trousers she'd had on earlier. No jacket. Her hair was wet from the spray and stuck to her head. Even in the growing dark her face had a blue hue. Falk wondered how long she had been sitting there, freezing and damp. It could have been more than an hour. He was worried she might topple over from sheer exhaustion.

He looked back towards the trail, unsure what to do.

The path was still empty. Lauren was so close to the edge it made him feel dizzy looking at her. He took a deep breath and started to inch his way across the rocks. At least the clouds had cleared for now. In the twilight, the pale sliver of the early rising moon cast a little light.

'Lauren,' he called again.

'That's close enough.'

He stopped and risked glancing down. He could only make out the bottom from the crash of the water. He tried to remember what Chase had said on that first day. A drop of about fifteen metres to the black pool below. What else had Chase said? It wasn't the fall that killed people, it was the shock and the cold. Lauren was shivering violently already.

'Listen,' he said. 'It's freezing up here. I'm going to throw you my jacket, okay?'

She didn't react, then nodded stiffly. He took that as a good sign.

'Here.' He unzipped his coat and took it off, leaving himself in only a jumper. The spray from the falls immediately clung to the exposed layer and within moments it was damp. He tossed his jacket to Lauren. It was a good throw and landed close. She dragged her gaze away from the water but didn't move to take it.

'If you're not going to use it, chuck it back,' Falk said, his teeth already rattling. Lauren hesitated, then slipped it on. He took that as another good sign. The jacket swamped her tiny frame.

'Alice is really dead?' Her words were hard to hear over the rushing water.

389

'She is. I'm sorry.'

'In the morning, when I went back to the path and she was gone, I thought –' Lauren was still shivering violently, struggling to get the words out. 'I thought she was the one who was going to make it.'

Day 4: Sunday Morning

Bree wasn't sure what woke her. She peeled open her eyes and was greeted with the cold grey stirrings of early dawn. The light leaking through the cabin windows was faint, and most of the room still wallowed in murky darkness. She could hear the gentle sound of breathing all around her. The others weren't up yet. Good. She groaned silently and wondered if she could get back to sleep, but the floorboards were hard against her bones and her bladder was aching.

She rolled onto her side and saw the blood spatter on the floor nearby. Lauren's, she remembered. She curled her feet up in her sleeping bag in disgust. The fight of the night before came rushing back and this time her groan was out loud. She stuffed a hand over her mouth and lay still. She didn't want to face the others any sooner than she had to.

Bree slipped off her sleeping bag cocoon and pulled on her boots and jacket. She crept to the door, wincing as the floor creaked, and stepped out into the frigid morning air. As she pulled the door shut, she felt a footstep in the clearing behind her. She jumped, stifling a scream.

'Shh, don't bloody wake the others.' Beth was whispering. 'It's only me.'

'God, you scared me. I thought you were still inside.' Bree made sure the cabin door was closed and stepped away, further into the clearing. 'What are you doing up so early?'

'Same as you, I guess.' Beth nodded towards the outhouse.

'Oh. Okay.'

There was an awkward pause, the ghost of the previous evening still clinging to them like smoke.

'Listen, about last night –' Beth whispered.

'I don't want to talk about it –'

'I know, but we have to.' Beth's voice was firm. 'Look, I know I've caused a lot of trouble for you but I'll make it right –'

'No. Beth, please. Just leave it.'

'I can't. It's gone too far. Alice doesn't get to threaten you and just get away with it. Not after how hard you've worked. She can't push people around and then be surprised when they push back.'

'Beth –'

'Trust me. You've always helped me. All my life. Helping you now is the least I can do.'

Bree had heard words like these before. *Day late, dollar short*, she thought, then immediately felt mean. Her sister was trying. To her credit, she always tried. Bree swallowed.

'Okay. Well, thanks. But don't make things worse.'

Beth waved a hand towards the bushland with an odd half-smile. 'Could they get any worse?'

Bree wasn't sure who moved first, but then she felt her arms slip around her sister for the first time in years. It was a little awkward, the body that had once been as familiar as her own now felt so different. When they pulled away, Beth was smiling.

'Everything will be all right,' she said. 'I promise.'

Bree watched as her sister turned and slipped back inside the cabin. She could still feel the warmth of Beth's body against her own.

She ignored the outhouse – there was no way she was going in there – and instead walked around the side of the cabin. She stopped short as she saw that horrible dog grave. She'd almost forgotten about that. Bree turned her face away and walked straight past it to the back of the cabin, through the long grass towards the trees and the trail until the grave was well out of sight. She was about to undo her trousers when she heard something.

What was that? A bird? The sound was coming from the trail behind her. It was a tinny noise, artificial and piercing in the still of the morning. Bree held her breath, her ears almost ringing with the effort of listening. That was no bird. Bree recognised that sound. She spun towards it and broke into a run. Up the trail, almost tripping on the uneven surface.

Alice was sitting on the ground, her legs out in front of her, leaning back against a rock. Strands of blonde hair lifted gently in the breeze, and her eyes were closed. Her head was tilted back a little towards the sky as though she was enjoying a ray of non-existent sunshine. And the pocket of her jeans was ringing.

Bree fell to her knees.

'Alice, the phone. Quick! The phone's ringing!'

She could see it wedged against Alice's thigh. The screen was smashed but it was glowing. Bree grasped it, her hands shaking so violently it nearly tumbled from her fingers. It rang in her hand, shrill and insistent.

On the shattered screen, the caller's name flashed up. Two letters: A.F.

Bree didn't know and she didn't care. With thick fingers she stabbed at the answer button, nearly missing it in her haste. She pressed the phone to her ear.

'Hello? Oh my God, please. Can you hear me?'

Nothing. Not even static.

'Please.'

She took it away from her face. The screen was blank. The name had disappeared. The battery was dead.

Bree shook it, her hands slippery with sweat. Nothing. She pressed the power button, then again, and again. The screen stared back, completely blank.

'*No!*'

Her stomach lurched as hope was snatched away like a rug pulled from under her feet. She turned and vomited bile into the bush, tears stinging her eyes, the disappointment crushing her chest. Why hadn't Alice bloody answered it sooner? There might have been enough power for even one call for help. What was the stupid bitch thinking, leaving it on at all? Wasting the battery.

It was as Bree turned to ask exactly that, vomit and anger burning in her throat, that she realised Alice was still sitting in the same position, leaning against the rock. She hadn't moved.

'Alice?'

There was no response. The relaxed pose of Alice's limbs now looked floppy and puppet like. Her back was at an awkward angle, too, with her head lolling back. She didn't look peaceful. She looked vacant.

'Shit. Alice?'

Bree had thought Alice's eyes were closed but she could see now that they were a tiny bit open. Little white half-slits stared at the grey sky.

'Can you hear me?' Bree could barely hear her own voice over the pounding in her head.

There was no movement and no response. Bree felt light-headed. Like she wanted to sit down next to Alice, perfectly still, and disappear.

Alice's half-slitted eyes continued to stare until Bree couldn't stand it anymore. She stepped sideways so she could no longer see her face. The back of Alice's head looked a little strange and Bree leaned as close as she dared. There was no blood, but the skin of her skull looked mottled and purple where her blonde hair parted. She stepped back, her eyes on the ground.

She nearly missed the object wedged between Alice and the base of the rock. It was almost completely hidden by Alice's lower back. Only the end was visible, circular with a glint of metal. Bree stared at it for what felt like a long time. She didn't want to touch it, she didn't want to admit she recognised it, but already she knew she couldn't leave it.

At last, Bree made herself crouch and with her fingertips, she grasped hold and pulled out the industrial metal torch. She knew the name would be scratched into the side, but it still took her breath away to see it glinting in the light. *Beth*.

It's gone too far. Alice doesn't get to threaten you and just get away with it.

In a single reflex action, Bree pulled her arm back and threw, sending the torch spinning into the bush. It hit something with a thud and disappeared. Bree's hand tingled. She wiped it on her jeans. Spat into her palm, and wiped it again. Then she looked back at Alice. Still sitting, still silent.

Two doors swung open in Bree's mind and with a single shake of her head, she slammed one shut. The woolly feeling was gone now, and her head felt suddenly very clear. She needed to move.

Bree glanced down the path. It was empty. For now. She wasn't sure how long she'd been there. Had anyone else heard the phone ring? She listened. She couldn't hear any movement, but the others would be waking soon, if they weren't up already.

She did the bag first. That was easier. She checked once more that the phone was dead, then slipped it into a side pocket and grabbed the straps of the backpack. She carried it into the bush, far enough that she couldn't see the path, and propped it behind a tree. She stood and, for a terrible moment, could not remember which way the trail lay.

Frozen on the spot, Bree took deep breaths, making herself calm. 'Don't panic,' she whispered. She knew which way she needed to go. She sucked in a final big breath and made herself walk straight, in the direction she had come, through the long grass and the trees, faster and faster, until she could see Alice sitting against the rock.

She almost stopped short at the sight of the back of her head, the blonde hair lifting in the wind, the awful stillness. Bree's pulse was beating so fast she thought she might pass out. She forced herself to run the last few steps and, before she could change her mind, had hooked her hands under Alice's armpits and pulled.

She walked backwards, dragging Alice deeper into the bush. The wind whirled around her, scattering leaves and debris across the ground in her wake, as though she had never been through there. Bree pulled until her arms ached and her breath burned in her chest and until suddenly she was stumbling and falling.

Alice – the body – fell one way, flat on her back, her face to the sky. Bree landed heavily against a dead tree stump, her eyes hot with tears and fury. She wondered briefly if she was crying for Alice, but she knew that she wasn't. Not then, anyway. At that moment, she only had enough tears for herself, and her sister and what they'd somehow become.

As if her heart wasn't aching enough, it was only then that Bree registered a stinging sensation in her arm.

Chapter 32

S omething caught Falk's eye.

Far below, at the base of the falls, he saw the flash of a high-vis jacket as someone crept out of the tree line with a familiar gait. Carmen. She positioned herself at the base of the waterfall and Falk saw her head tilt upwards, looking for them. It was too dark to see her face, but after a moment she raised a single arm. *I see you.* Around her, officers were moving slowly into place, trying not to draw attention to themselves.

Lauren hadn't seemed to notice and he was glad. He wanted her attention as far away from the drop as possible. Through the roar of the water, Falk heard footsteps echoing on the wooden bridge. Lauren must have as well because she turned her head towards the sound. Sergeant King came into view, flanked by two other officers. He stayed back, but lifted his radio to his mouth and muttered something Falk couldn't catch from that distance.

'I don't want them to come any closer.' Lauren's face was

wet, but her eyes were dry and her expression was set in a way that made Falk nervous. He thought he'd seen that look before. It was the look of someone who had given up.

'That's okay,' Falk said. 'But they're not going to keep away all night. They're going to want to talk to you, and you should let them. If you come away from the edge we can try to sort this out.'

'Alice tried to tell me about the photos of Margot. Maybe if I'd listened, everything would be different.'

'Lauren –'

'What?' She cut him off. Looked at him. 'You think you can fix this?'

'We can try. I promise. Please. Just come back to the lodge and talk to us. If you won't do it for yourself then –' He wavered, unsure whether it was the right card to play. 'There's still your daughter. She needs you.'

He realised instantly it had been the wrong thing to say. Lauren's face tightened and she leaned forward, her knuckles bright white where she gripped the ledge.

'Rebecca doesn't need me. I can't help her. I've tried so hard, her whole life. And, I swear to God, I know I've made mistakes but I did the best I could.' Her head was down as she stared into the abyss. 'I've only made things worse. How could I do that to her? She's just a girl. Alice was right.' She leaned forward. 'It is my fault.'

Day 4: Sunday Morning

The first thing Lauren heard when she opened her eyes was the screaming outside the cabin.

She felt movement around her, heard someone standing up, then the trample of feet against the floorboards. A bang as the cabin door swung open. She was slow to sit up in her sleeping bag. Her head throbbed and her eyelids were heavy. Alice. The memory of the trail came to her immediately. She looked around. She was the only one in the room.

With a sense of dread, Lauren stood up and went to the doorway. She looked out and blinked. There was some sort of commotion in the clearing. She tried to work out what she was seeing. Not Alice. Bree.

Bree was slumped by the remains of last night's fire, clutching her right arm. Her face was pale.

'Elevate it!' Beth was shouting, trying to pull her sister's arm over her head.

Jill was flipping frantically through a thin leaflet. No-one was looking at Lauren.

'It says we need a splint,' Jill was saying. 'Find something to keep it still.'

'What? What kind of thing?'

'I don't know! How should I know? A stick or something! Anything.'

'We have to go,' Beth shouted, scooping up a handful of broken twigs. 'Jill? We have to get her to a doctor right now. Shit, hasn't anyone done a first aid course?'

'Yes, bloody Alice!' Jill finally turned to the cabin and saw Lauren in the doorway. 'Where is she? Wake her up. Tell her we've got a snakebite.'

Lauren had the surreal thought that Jill meant to go and wake her from the path, but instead the woman was pointing at the cabin. As if in a dream, Lauren lurched back inside and looked around. She was still the only one there. Four sleeping bags on the ground. She checked each one. All empty. No Alice. She hadn't come back.

There was movement in the doorway and Jill appeared.

Lauren shook her head. 'She's gone.'

Jill froze, then all at once grabbed her own backpack and sleeping bag from the floor and shook them out.

'Where's my jacket? It had the phone in it. *Shit.* That bitch has taken it.'

She threw her belongings down and turned, slamming the cabin door behind her.

'She's bloody gone and she's taken the phone.' Jill's voice was muffled outside. Lauren heard a cry of outrage that could have come from either one of the twins.

She pulled her boots on and stumbled outside. She knew

where the jacket was. She had seen Alice stuff it behind a log the night before. Lauren wished now she'd never got up in the night to go to the toilet. She wished she'd taken a minute to wake the others instead of chasing after Alice in the dark. She wished she had been able to stop her from leaving. She wished a lot of things were different.

Lauren could see the splash of colour behind the log. She reached down.

'The jacket's here.'

Jill snatched it from her and rummaged through the pockets. 'No. She's definitely taken it.'

Beth was standing over Bree, who was still slumped on the ground, her arm immobilised in a makeshift splint.

'All right. What are our options?' Jill was breathing heavily. 'We stay put. Or we split up, leave Bree here –'

'No!' the sisters said in unison.

'Okay. Okay, then we'll have to walk. We'll all have to help Bree, but which way –' Jill spun around.

'Keep going north,' Lauren said.

'Are you sure?'

'Yes. Stick to the plan. Keep as straight as we can, as fast as we can, and hope we hit the road. It's our best bet.'

Jill considered for a fraction of a beat. 'All right. But first we need to look for Alice. Just in case.'

'Are you kidding? In case what?' Beth was open-mouthed.

'In case she's gone to the toilet and twisted her bloody ankle, I don't know!'

'No! We have to go!'

'Then we'll be quick. The three of us. Leave Bree here.' A hesitation. 'And don't go too far.'

Lauren was already running through the long grass towards the trail.

'Alice had better hope someone else finds her,' she heard Beth say. 'If I get to her first, I'll bloody kill her.'

Lauren was breathless as she ran. She could still feel the weight of Alice as they'd fallen and the shock as the air was knocked out of her lungs. She could still feel the sting of the words.

At the memory of that, Lauren slowed a little. The trail looked different in the daylight and she nearly missed the spot. Nearly. She was past the large smooth rock almost before she realised it. She stopped, turning, understanding in an instant what she was seeing. Nothing. The rock stood alone. The path was empty.

Alice was gone.

Lauren felt dizzy as the blood rushed to her head. The trail was deserted in both directions. She looked around, wondering how far Alice had got. The bushland gave no clue.

She scanned the ground, but there was no sign of her bracelet. Could she have lost it at the cabin and not realised? There was nothing to see, but the air had an odd tangy scent and she had the sensation that the area had been disturbed. She supposed it had been, in a way, but as she looked around now, she could see little evidence of their fight. Her legs shook only a little as she turned and walked back.

Nearer the cabin, Lauren could hear the faint shouts of the others calling for Alice. She wondered if she should do the same, but when she opened her mouth, the name stuck on her lips.

Chapter 33

Lauren stared down at the water. She took a breath through clenched teeth and Falk seized the chance to take a fast step towards her. She was so focused, she didn't notice.

Falk could see they were both shaking with cold, and he was scared Lauren's frozen fingers could lose their grip, whether she – or he – was ready or not.

'I honestly didn't mean to kill her.' Lauren's voice was almost lost in the crash of water.

'I believe you,' Falk said. He remembered their first conversation. It seemed a long time ago, out there on the trail, with the night all around them. He could still picture her face, overwhelmed and unsure. *It wasn't any one thing that went wrong, it was a hundred little things.*

Now, she looked determined. 'I wanted to hurt her, though.'

'Lauren –'

'Not for what she did to me. That's my own fault. But I

know what Margot did to Rebecca; that she prodded and baited her. And maybe Margot was smart enough to hide it, and Alice shouted loudly enough to make the school look the other way. But I know what that girl did. She is exactly like her bloody mother.'

The words hung in the freezing mist. Lauren was still looking down.

'So much is my fault though.' Her voice was quiet. 'For being so weak. I can't blame Alice or Margot for that. And Rebecca will realise that one day, if she hasn't already. And she'll hate me for it.'

'She still needs you. And loves you.' Falk thought of his own father's face. His handwriting scrawled across his maps. *With Aaron.* 'Even if she doesn't always realise it.'

'But what if I can't make it right with her?'

'You can. Families can forgive.'

'I don't know. Not everything deserves to be forgiven.' Lauren was looking down again. 'Alice said I was weak.'

'She was wrong.'

'I think so too.' Her answer caught him by surprise. 'I'm different now. Now, I do what I need to do.'

Falk felt the hairs on his arms stand up as something shifted in the atmosphere. They had crossed an invisible threshold. He hadn't seen her move but suddenly she seemed much closer to the edge. Over the side, he could see Carmen looking up, poised. He made a decision. This had gone far enough.

He was already moving before the thought was fully formed. Two fast steps across the rocks, the surface as

407

slippery as glass under his soles, and his fingers outstretched. His hand closed around her jacket – his jacket – grabbing a handful of fabric, his grip clumsy with cold.

Lauren looked at him, her eyes calm, and with a single fluid action, she shrugged her shoulders, folded her slim torso forward and shed his jacket like a snakeskin. She slid from his grasp and with a movement marked by both decision and precision, she was gone.

The edge was empty, as though she had never been there.

Day 4: Sunday Morning

Jill could see her own fear reflected in the three faces staring back at her. Her heartbeat thumped and she could hear the others' rapid breathing. Overhead, the pocket of sky carved out by the trees was a dull grey. The wind shook the branches, sending a shower of water down on the group below. No-one flinched. Behind them, the rotten wood of the cabin groaned and settled as another gust blew through.

'We have to get out of here,' Jill said. 'Now.'

On her left, the twins nodded immediately, united for once by their panic. Bree was clutching her arm, Beth supporting her. Their eyes were wide and dark. On her right, Lauren shifted, the briefest hesitation, then nodded. She took a breath.

'What about –'

'What about what?' Jill had lost patience.

' . . . What about Alice?'

An awful hush. The only sound was the creak and rustle as the trees gazed down on their tight circle of four.

'Alice brought this on herself.'

A silence. Then Lauren pointed.

'North is that way.'

They walked and they didn't look back, leaving the trees to swallow up all that they left behind.

Chapter 34

Falk yelled Lauren's name but it was too late. He was talking to empty air. She was no longer there.

He scrambled across the rocks in time to see her plunge like a dead weight into the water. The splash as she hit was swallowed up by the roar of the falls. Falk counted to three – too fast – but she didn't surface. He dragged his jumper over his head and wrenched off his boots. He tried to suck in a deep breath, but his chest was tight as he took a step forward and jumped. All the way down, the only thing he could hear over the rush of water beneath him and the rush of air above him was the sound of Carmen shouting.

He slammed into the water feet first.

An eerie nothingness enveloped him and he felt suspended in a void. Then all at once the cold hit him with brutal force. He kicked upwards, fighting the urge to gasp until he broke the surface. His chest was burning as he sucked at the damp air, the cold of the water forcing the oxygen out of his lungs as fast as he could take it in.

The waterfall spray blinded him, stinging his face and eyes. He couldn't see Lauren. He couldn't see anything. He heard a faint noise over the deafening roar and twisted around, wiping his eyes. Carmen was on the bank. Next to her two officers were grabbing a rope. She was yelling at him and pointing to something.

Lauren.

The thundering curtain of water would pull her under, he knew instinctively. He could already feel the fingers of undertow snatching at his feet, threatening to drag him deep. He took a breath, trying to force air into his seized lungs, then swam in a mongrel mix of strokes towards her.

He was a reasonable swimmer, he had grown up by a river, but the pull and thrust of the water made it difficult to gain any traction. His clothes were weighing him down, dragging him backwards, and he was glad he'd had the presence of mind to pull off his boots.

Ahead, the figure bobbed towards the danger zone. She wasn't thrashing, she was barely even moving, as her face dipped into the black water for seconds on end.

'Lauren!' he yelled, but the noise was swallowed up. 'Over here!'

He caught her just metres from the pounding base of the falls and grabbed hold of her, his fingers frozen and clumsy.

'Leave me!' she screamed. Her lips were a ghoulish purple-blue and she fought now, kicking him away. He swept an arm across her, pressing her back to his chest, gripping tight. He could feel no heat at all from her body. He started kicking as hard as he could, forcing his heavy legs to move. He could hear Carmen calling to him from the bank. He tried to follow her voice but Lauren was pulling away harder, clawing at his arm.

'Let me go!' She was lashing out, dragging them both under water. Falk was blinded, his face plunging below the surface before he had a chance to draw breath. Lauren sent an arm flailing backwards, slamming into him and sending his head under again.

Everything was muffled, then he resurfaced, water in his mouth, half a breath, not enough, and he was under again, his grip loosening as the woman struggled against him. He held on, fighting against the animal instinct to let her go. He felt a shift in the water and another arm reach out, not Lauren's, not struggling. It hooked under his armpit and pulled. His face broke through the surface and something else looped under his arm, a rope, and suddenly he didn't have to fight to stay afloat. His head was above water and he gasped, sucking in air. He realised he was no longer holding Lauren and panicked.

'It's okay, we've got her,' a voice said in his ear. Carmen. He tried to turn, but couldn't. 'You've done the hard bit, we're nearly at the shore.'

'Thank you,' he tried to say, but could only gasp.

'Just focus on breathing,' she said as the rope tugged painfully under his arm. His back scraped across the rocks as he was hauled out by two officers. As he lay on the muddy bank he turned his head to see Lauren being dragged out. She was shaking, but she had stopped fighting, for now.

Falk's lungs ached and his head pounded, but he didn't care. He felt nothing but relief. He was shivering so hard his shoulderblades were knocking against the ground. A blanket was thrown on him, then another one. He felt a weight on his chest and opened his eyes.

'You saved her.' Carmen was leaning over him, her face in silhouette.

'You did too,' he tried to say, but his face was frozen and he struggled to form the words.

He lay back, trying to catch his breath. The bushland parted around the falls and for once, he could see no trees. Just Carmen leaning over him and the night sky above her. She was shivering hard and he pulled part of his blanket over her. She moved closer and all of a sudden her lips were on his, cold against cold, and he closed his eyes. Everything was numb except for the singular warm rush inside his chest.

Too soon it was over and he blinked. Carmen was looking at him, not embarrassed, not regretful, her face still close, but not as close.

'Don't get the wrong idea, I'm still getting married. And you're a bloody idiot, you shouldn't have jumped.' She smiled. 'But I'm happy you're okay.'

They lay quietly, breathing in unison until a ranger approached with another space blanket and she rolled away.

Falk stared at the sky. Out of sight, he could hear the treetops swaying, but he didn't turn to see. Instead, he watched the faint stars above, looking for the Southern Cross, like he had all those years ago with his dad. He couldn't see it, but it didn't matter. It was up there some-where, he knew.

His body was cold where Carmen had been, but a warmth in his core had begun to spread through him. As he lay there, watching the stars and listening to the rustle of the trees, he realised his hand didn't hurt at all anymore.

Chapter 35

Falk sat back to admire his handiwork on the wall. It wasn't perfect, but it was better. The early afternoon sun was streaming through the windows, illuminating his flat with a warm glow. In the distance, the Melbourne skyline was shining.

It had been two weeks since he and Carmen had left the ranges for the last time. Falk hoped it was the last time, at least. He felt he could go a long while before needing to walk among those trees again.

He had been home for three days when the anonymous brown envelope had arrived. Posted to the office for his attention, it contained a memory stick and nothing more. Falk had opened the contents and stared at the screen. He'd felt his blood quicken.

Get the contracts. Get the contracts.

He had stared and scrolled for more than an hour. Then he'd picked up the phone and dialled a number.

'Thank you,' he said.

On the other end of the line, he heard Beth McKenzie take a breath.

'Did you hear BaileyTennants has done the dirty on Bree?' she said. 'They're all distancing themselves, trying to wash their hands of her.'

'I had heard that.'

'I'm not working there anymore either.'

'No. I heard that too. What will you do now?'

'I don't know.'

'Maybe something with that computer science degree,' Falk said. 'You were wasted in that data room.'

He heard Beth hesitate. 'Do you think so?'

'Yes.'

It was an understatement. He scrolled through the files as they spoke. They were all there. Copies of the documents Alice had requested and sourced through the BaileyTennants archives. Some things she had already passed to them. Some she had not. The contracts stared back at him in black and white, and he felt a rush of relief and adrenaline. He could imagine Carmen's face when he told her. Falk scrolled back to the start of the files.

'How did you −?'

'I just never trusted Alice. She was always rude to me. And she and Bree worked too closely, it would have been easy for her to blame Bree if she was doing something wrong. So I made copies of her requests.'

'Thank you. Sincerely.'

He heard her sigh. 'What will happen now?'

'To Bree?'

'And Lauren.'

'I don't know,' Falk said truthfully.

An autopsy had confirmed Alice had died from a bleed on the brain, most likely from hitting her head on the rock near where her body was found. Both Lauren and Bree would face charges, but Falk privately hoped the final count wouldn't be too severe. Whichever way he looked at it, he couldn't help feeling sorry for them.

The Baileys were already embroiled in a very public investigation into indecent images allegedly circulated by Daniel's son Joel. The media had got wind of the scandal, publishing double-page analysis pieces complete with photos of Joel's leafy private school. He had been expelled, according to reports. Margot Russell's name had been kept out of it, for now at least.

Thanks to Beth, the Baileys now had more trouble coming their way. Falk couldn't muster any sympathy for them. The family had profited from others' misery for two generations. Jill included. Whether she'd felt she had a choice or not, when it came to the family business, she was very much a Bailey.

Since leaving the ranges, Falk had spent a lot of time thinking. About relationships and how little it took for one to turn sour. About holding grudges. About forgiveness.

He and Carmen had attempted to visit both Margot and Rebecca. Margot was refusing to see anyone, her father told them. Refusing to speak, refusing to come out of her room. He had looked terrified.

Rebecca had at least consented to leave the house and sit

silently across from them at a café table. Carmen ordered sandwiches for all of them without asking, and the girl watched while they ate.

'What happened on the waterfall?' she asked eventually. Falk gave her an edited version. As truthful as he could make it. Heavy on love, low on regret.

The girl looked at her untouched plate. 'My mum hasn't said much.'

'What has she said?'

'That she loves me and she's sorry.'

'That's the bit you should pay attention to,' Falk said.

Rebecca fiddled with her napkin. 'Was it my fault? Because I wouldn't eat?'

'No. I really think it ran a lot deeper than that.'

The girl looked unconvinced, but when she got up to leave, she took her sandwich wrapped in a napkin. Falk and Carmen watched her through the window. At the end of the street, she stopped by a bin. She held the sandwich over the lid for a long while, then with what looked like physical effort, put it in her bag and disappeared around a corner.

'It's a start, I suppose,' Falk said. He thought of the hundreds of little things that had added up to go so wrong. Maybe hundreds of little things could add up to go right.

After a few days thinking at home, Falk had then spent a few more acting. He'd gone to a furniture shop to buy a couple of things, then bought a couple more while he was there.

Now, he sat in his new armchair in the corner of his

flat as a patch of sunlight moved across the carpet. It was comfortable and had been a good decision. It made the place look different. Busier and fuller, but he thought he liked it. And from his new vantage point he could see his latest change clearly.

The two photographs of him with his father hung on the wall, framed and polished. It changed the feel of the room, but he thought he liked that as well. He had meant what he had said to Lauren at the waterfall. Families can forgive. But it wasn't enough to mean it, you had to live it.

Falk looked up now, checking the clock. It was a beautiful Friday afternoon. Carmen was getting married the next day in Sydney. He wished her well. They had never spoken about what had passed between them on the bank of the falls. He sensed for her it was an encounter that was best kept fleeting. He understood. His suit jacket and a wrapped wedding gift were waiting with his bag. Ready for his flight to Sydney.

It was nearly time to leave, but he thought he had just long enough for a quick call.

He heard the dial tone down the line and could imagine the phone ringing at the other end in Kiewarra. His hometown. A familiar voice answered.

'Greg Raco speaking.'

'It's Aaron. Are you busy?'

A laugh down the phone. 'No.'

'Still skiving off work?' Falk said. He pictured the police sergeant at his home. Not back in uniform just yet.

'It's called convalescence, thanks, mate. And it takes a while.'

'I know,' Falk said, turning over his own burned hand and examining the skin. He did know. He had been lucky.

They talked for a while. Things were a little better since the drought had broken. Falk asked after Raco's daughter. After the Hadler family. All doing okay. And everyone else?

Raco laughed. 'Mate, if you're that curious, maybe you should come and see for yourself.'

Maybe he should. Eventually, Falk glanced at the clock. He had to get moving. Catch his plane.

'Listen, are you bored with this convalescence of yours yet?'

'Very.'

'I'm thinking of going for a hike. One weekend. If you feel up to it. Something gentle.'

'Yeah. Definitely. That'd be really good,' Raco said. 'Where?'

Falk looked at his dad's maps spread out on the coffee table in the warmth of the afternoon light. The sun glancing off the picture frames on the wall.

'Anywhere you like. I know some good places.'

The careful pencil marks showing him the way. There was plenty to explore.

Acknowledgements

Once again I am lucky enough to have been surrounded by a wonderful group of people who have helped me in so many different ways.

A sincere thank you to my editors Cate Paterson at Pan Macmillan, Christine Kopprasch and Amy Einhorn at Flatiron Books, and Clare Smith at Little, Brown, for your faith and unwavering support. Your insight and advice has been invaluable and I am truly grateful for the many extraordinary opportunities you have created for my writing.

Thank you to Ross Gibb, Mathilda Imlah, Charlotte Ree and Brianne Collins at Pan Macmillan, and to all the talented designers, marketing and sales teams who have worked so hard to bring this book to life.

I would be lost without the help of my incredible agents Clare Forster at Curtis Brown Australia, Alice Lutyens and Kate Cooper at Curtis Brown UK, Daniel Lazar at Writers House and Jerry Kalajian at the Intellectual Property Group.

Thank you to Mike Taylor, senior reptile keeper at Healesville Sanctuary, Senior Sergeant Clint Wilson from Victoria Police, and Grampians Gariwerd National Park visitors and community team leader Tammy Schoo, for kindly sharing their knowledge and expertise of native wildlife, search and rescue procedures and camping and hiking techniques. Any mistakes or artistic liberties are my own.

I am indebted to the many dedicated booksellers who have championed my books with such enthusiasm and, of course, to all the readers who have embraced the stories.

Thank you to the Elwood mums and their beautiful babies for your warmth and friendship. You have been a beacon of light through it all.

As always, love and thanks to my wonderful family who have supported me at every step: Mike and Helen Harper, Ellie Harper, Michael Harper, Susan Davenport and Ivy Harper, Peter and Annette Strachan.

Above all, my deep gratitude to my remarkable husband Peter Strachan – the help you have given me spans years and would fill pages – and to our daughter Charlotte Strachan, our love, who has made us so much more.